ONLY BREATH & SHADOW

ANDREW TWEEDDALE

To

Eoin & Amanda

and

Kim & Gareth

Thank you for your support

***

First published in the UK in 2026

Text copyright © 2026 Tweeddale Consultancy Ltd

Edited by Robin Seavill

Front cover design Andrew Tweeddale and Canva

Back cover and spine design Clint England

ISBN: 978-1-7-396122-4-5

PREFACE

Only Breath & Shadow was originally planned to be the second in the Castle Drogo series, however, it had a troubled gestation period. I struggled with the story and hoped that having time away from the character of Christian Drewe would help me to envisage him more clearly. When I finished writing my second novel, *A Remembrance of Death*, I started preparing a timeline, commencing with the death of Sir Julius Drewe in 1931 and then the major events occurring in Austria for the next eight years. This brought me into contact with the real-life characters of Gil and Eleanor Kraus and Paul O'Montis. I sketched out a rough story line in which I developed ideas and scenes. The characters were created very quickly, and I started preparing detailed character sheets for each protagonist. I also had about twenty pages of material, which I had deleted from *Of All Faiths & None* and *A Remembrance of Death* that involved Christian Drewe. Some of it was used, some of it is still in a file that is better left unread.

My novels blend fact and fiction. The mission of Gil and Eleanor Kraus to save fifty children is one of factual events in the book. I was aware of Sir Nicholas Winton, the English stockbroker who helped six hundred and sixty-nine children escape from Czechoslovakia; however, when I started writing *Only Breath & Shadow*, I knew nothing about Gil and Eleanor Kraus or Bob Schless. They were Jewish Americans who came to Vienna to save fifty Jewish children. I felt I could not omit their story from the book and therefore weaved what they did into my own piece of fiction. I also knew nothing about the cabaret artist Paul O'Montis (born Paul Wendel), whose tragic story, moving from stardom in Berlin to his eventual incarceration in Sachsenhausen concentration camp, serves as a core thread in the narrative.

One of the main challenges that I faced was writing from the unique perspective of a blind protagonist. I read a few books containing visually impaired characters, and searched Youtube for explanations about games that blind people played, or navigating a room, or discerning one note of currency from another in a wallet. This led me to narrate a significant part of the story without the sense of sight. Christian experiences Vienna with the "crystalline notes" of church bells and the "warm yeast" of bakeries to the "choking reek of diesel" from Nazi tanks entirely through sound, smell, and touch.

There was also a moral theme that I wanted to include, relating to the indifference of the world to the plight of refugees. At a time when hundreds of thousands of people faced persecution, some of the wealthiest countries in the world met in 1938 at the Évian Conference and largely refused to lift refugee quotas, leaving thousands of Jews stateless, trapped and ultimately to die in the atrocities that followed. It is an historical fact that Hitler saw the world's indifference to the plight of the Jews as a victory. While the world turned a blind eye, it was left to individuals to make a difference. The moral message is encapsulated in the irony that Christian, who is physically blind, "sees" the humanity of the persecuted while the world around him does not. He lives in a world where blind eyes see better than blind hearts. *Only Breath & Shadow* is a story about an era that should not be forgotten. It contains scenes that some readers may find disturbing but, this is not a bad thing. There is much that is happening in the world today which has similarities to the past.

Once again, this book would not have been written without the unerring support of my wife, Keren, who acts as editor, beta reader, and someone who I can talk to about the developments in characters and plot. This novel, as well as the other two I have written, would not have been completed but for her.

And all our knowledge is ourselves to know.
Alexander Pope

Contents

THE LOST!

1

26 JULY 1934

As Christian dreamt on, he heard her voice. She was close to him, fastening her St Christopher around his neck and whispering, "I'll find you." He swallowed as his recollections blurred together. He felt he would soon wake up; but not just now, he needed a few more moments with her. They were together and she took his outstretched hand, and they danced. Gliding across the floor, with his fingers barely touching her waist, they became a single *us*, moving in time; moving to a rhythm that was theirs forever. And then they ran through the moonlit streets, until breathlessly they stopped, turned, stared into each other's eyes and kissed. It was all too brief, as he tumbled down into darkness and pain and the sound of her screaming. Christian struggled to wake up, as the hereafter hurt too much.

There were mornings when the dream did not cease, the fear did not wake him, and he remembered the Somme. She was there, a lost soul calling out upon a troubled ocean. He knew that, except in his dreams, she had been taken from him. On those mornings when his nightmares continued, he could sense her in the darkness, where the heat, smoke and the weight of the earth were burying her alive. He tried to reach out and touch her, but she could not feel him. He shouted, but she could not hear him. He knew she was alone and petrified, and he could do nothing but dream on until the screaming stopped. Those mornings, after he awoke, he would think about taking his service revolver from a shoebox in his wardrobe and joining her.

As he lay in bed, he knew that the pain was still too close to fade, despite there being more than five thousand yesterdays. He sat up, checked himself as he had been taught and tried to picture his room. He moved his legs over the side of the bed, stood up, and slowly walked barefoot to the bathroom, one foot carefully in front of the other. He knew there should be nothing to trip him, but he could not forget what had been drummed into him. He stretched out his hand as he came to the door and felt for the door frame. Three steps forward, exactly four feet, and he stood in front of the sink. Turn left, one step. He would have left the toilet seat down, but, as always, he checked. He sat down, emptied his bladder, reached for the chain, and pulled it. He stood up, returned to the sink, washed his hands, and carried out his daily ritual of brushing his teeth and shaving. He did the same every morning, standing in front of a mirror, as if it were a relic to be worshipped.

He lifted the glass of his watch and felt for the position of the hands on the face. His housekeeper would arrive shortly, although there was enough time for a shower. When the door to his apartment opened, he was sitting at the dining room table, hair still damp. He said, "*Guten Morgen*, Frau Huber," as he did almost every morning, and she returned the greeting, calling him "Herr Christian". The monotony of consistency provided him with security. It had been the same for over a decade, since he returned to Vienna to live. He would spend the next hour eating his breakfast and Frau Huber would read the newspapers and his correspondence.

"*The Times*," said Frau Huber, reading slowly from the newspaper in English, "writes that the assassination of Chancellor Dollfuss makes the name of Nazi stink in the nostrils of the world." She made a dismissive sound, folded the paper and placed it on the table. It was a sound she made every time she said the word, 'Nazi'. "And you have two letters, one from America and one from England."

"The one from America first," said Christian. "It will be from Tomas." He heard her pick up a knife, cut open the paper, and unfold the thin sheets. She read the date and remarked that it had taken less than four weeks for the letter to arrive and that it was a miracle how quickly things happen nowadays.

"Herr Tomas writes," began Frau Huber, "that they arrived in New York two weeks ago, and that Herr O'Montis has been a success in the theatres on the Upper West Side of Manhattan, but away from Manhattan, things have been mixed. He writes that New York is lively, but that most of the people are a little too bourgeois and seem only interested in money and being middle class." She paused as she read ahead. "Herr Tomas says that you would think that no one in New York has ever seen a Viennese cabaret or a man with a monocle in black tie and tights. They plan to go to Philadelphia next, and then Washington and Chicago before returning to New York. Herr Tomas says that he is worried that outside of New York, the Americans may not enjoy the show but Herr O'Montis is certain it will be a success." Christian knew Frau Huber was paraphrasing. Tomas would never write 'Herr O'Montis'; it would always be 'Paul', his beloved Paul; however, she was old-fashioned.

"There is a *p.s.*," said Frau Huber, "Herr Tomas says that Frau del Rio has decided to stay in New York and Herr O'Montis is looking for a new female singer."

"And the letter from England, who is it from?" Frau Huber looked at the envelope and told Christian it was from his mother. Christian took a deep breath. He knew what the letter would say because his mother had been struggling since the death of her husband two and a half years earlier, and the castle where she lived was costing a fortune in upkeep. She would ask when he was coming home to England, but he could not imagine ever returning. There was nothing left there for him.

2

28 July 1934

Christian shook away the remnants of his dream, and, for some inexplicable reason, his first thought was about the funeral of Chancellor Dollfuss. It had been the main subject of conversation in the Viennese coffeehouses for the last few days. Everyone was expecting trouble. Dollfuss would have a state funeral with his corpse in a metal coffin on a gun carriage with six plumed, black horses. The entourage would walk behind the coffin and be armed with pistols. Frau Huber insisted on going, as a sign of respect for Austria's murdered leader. Christian was uncertain whether to attend. Dollfuss was a fascist, although not a Nazi. He had opposed Hitler on the issue of the union of Germany and Austria, the *Anschluss* as it was called, and had been assassinated by a group of Austrian Nazis, who had shot him and left him to bleed to death without a doctor or a priest.

After breakfast, Frau Huber, as she always did, read the newspapers.

"Killing him like that was indecent," she said, believing that without confession, Dollfuss' soul would be suspended in purgatory. She proceeded to tell Christian how Mussolini had sent troops to stop Germany from invading Austria.

"Did he?" said Christian, surprised that Mussolini opposed Hitler.

"One of the newspapers also says that the American president sent a telegram to Hitler, expressing his horror at the events," continued Frau Huber, "and Britain's *Daily Mirror* is now calling Dollfuss 'one small in body but great in heart.'"

"The *Daily Mirror* wrote that?" queried Christian. "They were criticising him only two weeks ago."

"And there's another letter from Herr Tomas," Frau Huber said, as she opened it and started reading. "Herr Tomas writes that they have gone to Philadelphia, but the show was cancelled after the first night because it was too controversial." Frau Huber took a breath, and Christian could hear a hint of disapproval in her voice as she continued reading. "Herr O'Montis has made the decision to go straight to Chicago, and then back to New York before returning to Europe, where, Herr O'Montis says, the natives know how to enjoy themselves." Tomas ended the letter by saying that he was looking forward to coming home to Vienna.

Christian wondered why, of all places, Tomas and Paul had decided to take Paul's cabaret show to America. The Americans had their own style of cabaret shows, which was so different from anything in Berlin or Vienna. In America, the shows were structured. They were not risqué but a sanitised version of a Berlin cabaret. Paul's shows were anything but structured, where skits would turn into songs, and despite toning down the show for an American audience, Paul still insisted on an array of pretty boys, with lipstick and mascara, kissing each other as he sang his hit song, 'What Are Your Feelings, Moritz?'.

"I'll be going out today," said Christian, as he got up from the table.

"Anywhere special?"

"Just the park," he replied.

"And will you be meeting anyone?" asked Frau Huber.

Christian picked up his braille book, which he had left on the corner of the table.

"Yes," he said, "Sherlock Holmes."

Although there was much about Vienna that Christian enjoyed, it was also a city with frustrations. The Inner Stadt, where Christian lived, was isolated from the poverty that the rest of Vienna was experiencing. In its squares, people drank coffee and gorged on pastries, to the sound of barrel organs. Ladies and gentlemen still took horse-drawn carriages, which ambled along the streets with the metal of the horses' hooves clipping on the hard flint cobblestone. It was a scandal not to wear a hat or bonnet, and Austrian gentlemen, who had served in the war, still groomed proud moustaches. It was a city that longed for its past. However, on the perimeter of the Inner Stadt or in the new districts that were growing up around the city, things were different.

It was a city where poverty was prevalent and where people blamed each other for the hardships of their lives. Christian heard the arguments and condemnation in bars and clubs, where most people lived a hand-to-mouth existence in a country crippled by reparations. Broken pavements were never repaired and were a hazard for him and the tram, train and bus companies could be relied upon for their ineptitude. Censorship was widespread and nothing of consequence had been performed in the theatres for decades, except in the little backstreet cabarets, the *forty-niners* as they were known, where the shows scandalised and shocked the middle classes. The government voiced their disapproved of the nightclubs, brothels, and the little cabaret theatres and it was becoming all too common for *artistes* to be attacked with the police turning a blind eye. Communists and fascists would denounce each other or the Jews, the gays, or the upper classes, and Christian was quietly becoming more concerned for his friends, who stood on the edges of society.

Christian, however, had no hesitation in stepping out into a cacophony of noise from his apartment in the city centre. Each sound and smell was a signpost or a warning. When he had returned to Vienna after the war, Christian would walk each day through the city with Tomas. Tomas would describe the buildings around them and every postbox, storm drain, bench or lamp post. Tomas would describe each junction as Christian counted his steps, as he had been taught in the rehabilitation hospital for wounded soldiers. As he walked, Christian would note the smells of the city; the diesel from the traffic, camphor from a pharmacy or the smell of warm yeast from the bakery would be a marker that he etched into his memory. Coffee, flowers, or the aroma of hot, sweet savouries provided a clue to where he was. Every corner and every junction of the city had unique smells and sounds, and, in that first year in Vienna, Christian tried to learn them all. If he ever got lost, he would stop, stand as still as a statue and listen to the world around him.

The Stadtpark was more than a kilometre from his apartment, past St. Stephen's Cathedral and Mozart's house. It was a place of winding paths and secret gardens, where ladies with small dogs would take a morning walk and men on bicycles would exercise. At the park's southern end was the magnificent Kursalon, which had been built as a spa pavilion but was now used for concerts and in its east wing was the Yohan restaurant and café. It was a green oasis, away from the city's growing pollution, and Christian found a bench and opened his book.

A woman's voice interrupted him.

"Good morning, Herr Drewe." The voice was warm, but he did not recognise it. "It's Frau Friedmann," the woman continued, "Otto Friedmann's wife." Christian closed his book.

"Good morning," he replied and started to stand.

"Please don't get up. I didn't want to disturb you; however, I told Otto that sometimes I see you here, and he said I should pass on his compliments." Frau Friedmann felt a tug on her sleeve, and her son Aaron whispered something.

"Shush, Aaron," she responded.

"I was injured in the war," replied Christian, who had overheard the child's question.

"Does it hurt?" Aaron said, without a moment's hesitation. His mother immediately squeezed his arm, and his next question was choked back.

"Not anymore," replied Christian. He knew that the young boy was referring to the burns to one side of his face. He lifted his hand and touched the scarring then turned that side of his face away from them. "Please thank Herr Friedmann. I appreciated all his help in finding me that villa near St Gilgen."

"Did Otto tell you I grew up a few kilometres from there?" said Frau Friedmann, "and my mother still has her house there."

"He did," said Christian. He wondered how long it had taken Frau Friedmann to decide to come over and talk to him. He could hear in her voice a slight reticence, as if she was struggling with what to say.

"It's such a pretty place with its little beach and lovely church."

"It is," replied Christian. Frau Friedmann felt another tug on her sleeve.

"Yes, we'll go now, Aaron," she said. "I'm afraid with four young children, Herr Drewe, you're pulled from pillar to post."

Christian lifted his hat ever so slightly, and as he was about to bid Frau Friedmann and Aaron goodbye, he asked where her other children were.

"With Otto," said Frau Friedmann. "Every Saturday, he takes them to ballet lessons at the Academy of Music and Dramatic Art. Otto thinks they dance like angels, but he's a father, and fathers have blind spots when it comes to their daughters."

"I know one of the dancers there," replied Christian. "What are your daughter's names?"

"Hanna, Frieda and Rosa," said Frau Friedmann.

***

The Yohan restaurant boasted delicious classics, such as Wiener schnitzel of suckling calf and a selection of cheeses that would put most French restaurants to shame. Christian was taken to a table and was asked by the waiter whether he would have his usual. He listened as the restaurant filled with people, many of whom had been to the funeral of Dollfuss earlier, and were talking about the political situation. "They're hanging the culprits in the streets, already," said one person. "Hitler's now denying he had any involvement in it," said another with derision. Christian heard that a new Austrian chancellor had been named, cut from the same cloth as Dollfuss, and was looking to Mussolini for support.

Half the country seemed to want unification with Germany, and the rest opposed it. Christian listened to the endless chatter as the sun beat down on the veranda and everyone who spoke seemed less tolerant, some saying that the country had gone to the dogs because of the Jews. There was a prurience when they spoke about the old Weimar Republic and a few people said that its lack of morality had led Austria into the gutter. Occasionally, he might overhear someone say that disabled people should not be allowed out in public and that in Germany, the laws permitted the forced sterilisation of those people who were considered unfit, such as people with epilepsy, schizophrenics and those who were deaf.

As Christian sat quietly eating his lunch he continued to catch snippets of conversations. When his main course was finished, he called for the bill, deciding against dessert. What he found most concerning was the intolerance, which everyone seemed to have. It had started in the far-right press, the constant dehumanising of Jews and minorities and now out in the restaurants he was hearing the same words repeated. He got up and started tapping his way towards the door with his white stick. Like a biblical sea, the crowds parted as he came towards them, and he made his way out of the park, hearing the church bells of the city chime two.

He decided to go to one of the numerous coffeehouses, where a talk on the decline of the Viennese theatre was to be given. He stopped as he got to the square outside of St Stephen's Cathedral and heard music. He started thinking about the day he met Rose Braithwaite, twenty years ago, and wondered whether things would have been different if he had had the courage to tell her how he felt. However, he could not change the past. A single violinist played, and he listened intently. The music was passionate, dark and threatening. Most people walked past, ignoring the virtuoso, although an occasional person would drop a few coins which would rattle in a metal tin. A few children stopped and were pulled away by busy parents, saying they had no time just to stand around. The playing was faultless. Suddenly, the music sweetened with longing and passion and then concluded. Christian clapped his hands, took out his wallet and made his way towards the violinist and felt for a ten schilling note, which he had folded in a specific way.

"Thank you," said the violinist, as Christian handed him the money.

"Your playing was beautiful," said Christian. "Which orchestra are you with?"

"I used to play with the Munich Philharmonic, but for a Jew, it's no longer possible and so I've come to Vienna looking for work."

3

— · —

25 AUGUST 1934

With a familiar feeling of an unrelenting agony, Christian awoke. He had dreamt about a day twenty years earlier when he had gone to St Thomas' Hospital to visit his younger brother, Basil. He had not expected to see Rose Braithwaite there and she had teased him because he had forgotten her name. He remembered looking into her eyes, but they were now the eyes that he dared not meet in dreams, accusing him of deserting her when she needed him the most. When he got up, he was still tired and went to the bathroom. He checked his watch as he got dressed. Frau Huber would be arriving soon.

Another letter from Tomas arrived that morning saying that they were about to set sail for England. Tomas said that the last few shows went as well as could be expected, but the Americans did not understand what Paul was trying to do. Christian smiled to himself. On stage, Paul was a performer. If the Americans did not like Paul's show, then Paul would make it more outrageous. Tomas would no doubt have told Paul that he should dress more conservatively, take out the satire from the show, and give the audience what they want. Tomas would say that the Americans liked the songs and the dancing and would want to say they had seen a Viennese cabaret, so long as it looked like a Broadway show.

"Finally," said Frau Huber, "Herr Tomas writes that the new singer, Claire Astor, was well received on the last show and that she is coming to Vienna with Herr O'Montis and the orchestra, as Herr O'Montis said he would introduce her to his record company who might be able to help her make a record."

"Did he?" said Christian, more to himself than Frau Huber. Paul hadn't made a record for a long time and his record company, Deutsche Grammophon, had dropped him a year ago after the Nazis had arrested him. It was after a performance at La Scala in Berlin in October 1933. Paul had headlined the festival and Joseph Goebbels, who had recently become Hitler's Minister for Public Enlightenment and Propaganda, had attended. Goebbels wanted all art forms to be regulated in accordance with the moral views of National Socialism. What Paul did on stage was the antithesis of this. Goebbels marked out Paul as a particular degenerate, and Paul was arrested and convicted, but he was released on appeal and fled to Vienna. Tomas had sponsored and produced Paul's new cabaret show in Vienna and a tour of Amsterdam, America, London and Paris.

"I'm going out this morning," said Christian, after Frau Huber had finished reading the letter, "to the Vienna State Academy."

"In the morning?"

"I'm meeting one of the ballerinas there," answered Christian.

"Is she pretty?"

"I believe so," said Christian.

"Why don't you invite her here for lunch and I will cook *Schweinsbraten*," suggested Frau Huber, "and I can tell you if she's pretty enough."

"She's a friend," said Christian, "and she's Jewish, so you can forget making a pork stew." He got up and went into the hallway.

"You'll never have a family if you don't find a wife," said Frau Huber, shaking her head, as Christian left his apartment.

***

The Vienna State Academy of Music and Dramatic Art taught almost every form of dance from ballet to jazz and modern. On Saturday mornings, they gave ballet lessons for children too young to be enrolled in the academy, and scores of mothers and an occasional father would bring their children with the hope that the next Anna Pavlova may be discovered. Otto Friedmann was one such father. In most things, Otto was perceptive, reserved and prudent; however, when it came to his three daughters, he had a blind spot. What the ballet teacher saw as a deficiency of coordination, Otto saw as spontaneity. What the ballet teacher thought was a lack of timing, Otto thought was the ability to improvise. In short, his three daughters could do little wrong, especially the youngest, Rosa, and Otto genuinely believed that when the veil of mediocrity fell from the ballet teacher's eyes, she would see what he saw.

Christian was met by Rachel Kraus in the entrance hall of the Vienna State Academy. They had been introduced six years earlier on an evening at the Yohan restaurant and café. She was one of the rising stars of the ballet company and he was there with Tomas, who knew a few of the dancers. Her English was faultless and she had a love of literature, and although their social circles did not regularly cross, they found that they enjoyed each other's company when they did meet.

"It's lovely to see you again," said Rachel Kraus, kissing Christian on the cheek, "but why here?"

"I thought we could lunch, and you seem to have been away for months."

"I've been touring," responded Rachel. "But that doesn't explain why you asked me to meet you here."

"There are three young girls here who want to be ballerinas, and I thought I could introduce you to them after they have finished their lesson. I hope you don't mind, but their father was very kind to me. You may know him, Otto Friedmann?"

"I don't recall the name," said Rachel.

"He's a lawyer at Karl Vogel Rechtsanwälte."

"My uncle may know him," said Rachel. "However, more importantly, where are you taking me for lunch?"

"The Three Hussars," said Christian nonchalantly.

"How did you manage to get a table *there*?" she asked. "If I tried and, if I could afford it, I would be put on a waiting list for a table sometime next year."

"I know the owner," said Christian.

"My little brother will be jealous. He's been wanting to take his girlfriend there for months and is still saving up for it."

"Would you like me to arrange something?"

"No!" said Rachel emphatically. "He's spoilt enough as it is by my parents."

Only one man sat outside the dance studio with sixteen mothers. As they approached, Otto stood up.

"Herr Drewe," he said, with a note of surprise, "my wife said she had met you last month, but I didn't expect to see you here."

Christian extended his hand. "Herr Friedmann, I hope you don't mind, but I wanted to introduce your daughters to a friend of mine, Fräulein Rachel Kraus, one of the academy's dancers." When the introductions were concluded, Rachel said she would look in on the lesson.

"They don't like it when they are disturbed," warned Otto, who had learnt this from bitter experience.

"They'll make an exception," said Rachel, who smiled back at Otto reassuringly.

***

The entrance to The Three Hussars was octagonal, with arches leading into two dining rooms. The walls around the lobby dripped with gold mosaic, as if Klimt had rained down his paintbrush, and next to each arch was a brass figure of an angel holding a crown of lights. Walking into The Three Hussars was almost a religious experience; however, eating there was better. As Rachel cut into her veal steak, she said, "They truly were quite terrible."

"All of them?" asked Christian.

"Without exception," replied Rachel. "The smallest one was a particular show-off." She dipped the piece of meat into the piccata sauce and put it into her mouth. "However, each can now say that they have danced with one of the ballerinas at the Vienna State Academy." She looked at Christian as he slowly ate a salade niçoise, moving his fork delicately around the plate and impaling pieces of egg, potato, olives and tomatoes. "May I ask," she continued, after swallowing the meat, "what Herr Friedmann did for you?"

"When I decided to buy a villa last year, he came with me and drove me from one town to the next. He listened to what I wanted, ensured that a gardener and a cook were appointed, and helped negotiate a favourable price. It was nice to do something for him, and even if, as you say, they were quite terrible, they will feel special today. And what about you?"

"At the moment, life is good," said Rachel. She reached over to a roll on her side plate, tore a piece off and said, "With bread all sorrows are less."

"You made that sound like there's a *but* somewhere."

"I may be worrying about something and nothing," said Rachel. She leant a little closer to Christian and whispered, "My father says that troubles are to me as rust is to iron." She paused. "But I look at Germany, and it frightens me when I think it's only a matter of time before the Nazis take power here."

"Will they?" asked Christian. "The new chancellor seems as determined to keep Austria's independence as Dollfuss was."

"You may not have noticed, but they killed Dollfuss," Rachel responded.

4

15 SEPTEMBER 1934

Christian sat in his dining room, listening to the bustling city four storeys below. He had finished breakfast, and Frau Huber had read a letter from his mother, which complained about how she had not seen anyone, especially her youngest son Basil and his family. It had been nearly three years since Christian had last been to England, when he had gone for his father's funeral. Basil and his wife, Celia, had tried to give the impression of being a happy family, but they could not hide the tension and Christian felt that their relationship had become as cold as the stone walls of the castle in which his mother lived. He often wondered why his father had built the castle after his elder brother's death in the war. He could not imagine a more reserved, austere place; it was so English. It was ironic, he thought, that the last great castle built in England was for a shopkeeper. Napoleon would have so approved.

Christian heard the front door open.

"Is it safe to come in?" shouted Tomas as he wandered into the dining room. "I hoped I'd find you here."

"It's nine o'clock in the morning," said Christian. "Where else would I be?"

"Do you think Frau Huber could be an absolute darling and prepare me some eggs? I've been up all night and I'm famished." He smiled, pushed back his dark wavy hair, opened his blue velvet jacket, and flopped into a dining chair opposite Christian. "I feel myself wasting away as we speak."

"I'm doing it now, Herr Tomas," shouted Frau Huber from the kitchen.

"You really ought to marry her," said Tomas, "if only for my benefit."

"Don't you start," said Christian firmly.

A moment later, Frau Huber came in with lightly scrambled eggs.

"Herr Christian already has a girlfriend," Frau Huber said, placing the plate on the table.

"I... It's..." stammered Christian.

"A dancer," said Frau Huber. "I told Herr Christian to invite her for a meal so I could see if she was good enough for him, but he refused."

Frau Huber went back into the kitchen.

"Who was she?" asked Tomas.

"Rachel," said Christian. "She did me a favour and we lunched together."

***

Christian sat in a small nightclub next to Tomas, as Paul performed a set of new songs and sketches. Paul started with a skit, marching around the stage, wearing a brown shirt, swastika armband and a small moustache and complaining about the weather. There was then a sketch about Chancellor Schuschnigg sitting in a confessional box with a pistol, shooting workers as they walked towards him to confess their sins. The crowd was noisy, and Paul sang three of his most popular songs. Afterwards, he introduced Claire Astor, who sang a Cole Porter song. It was her accent that Christian noticed, so different to the guttural Germanic tones he heard every day. Christian listened intently, as Tomas described how she looked and what she was wearing and concluded that, "some people might think of her as quite a dish... if you like that kind of thing."

"Where did Paul meet her?" whispered Christian.

"In New York," said Tomas. "Paul and I saw her in a show in a club where we were taken one evening, and her voice caught Paul's attention. A few days later, Paul met her again, and she agreed to tour with us. Paul told me that he had never met anyone who wanted to leave a place so badly."

"Why?" asked Christian.

"Because she agreed to Paul's offer before he had even told her what she would be paid."

"So, what is she being paid?" asked Christian.

"Don't ask. It's so little, even I'm embarrassed by it."

"You won't have a problem if Paul asks her to join us for dinner this evening?"

"None," said Tomas. "Although, she's not the usual type of girl you find singing in clubs. She intelligent and speaks her mind."

***

"Let me introduce you to Herr Drewe," said Paul to Claire, as they stood outside of the club under a dim, flickering streetlamp. "He's an English gentleman, and a dear friend of Tomas'." He turned to

Christian, as Tomas waved at a taxi. "And I have the pleasure of introducing Miss Claire Astor." Christian bowed his head slightly. She looked at him with his large fedora hat, silk dinner suit, dark glasses and a patch that covered his scars. Paul had said he had been burnt and blinded in the war, and she stared, trying to see the extent of his injuries under the flickering streetlight, and then felt just a little ghoulish like an undertaker measuring a corpse.

Christian said how much he enjoyed her singing, as a taxi pulled up.

"Café Central," he said to the driver.

"You are a gentleman of habit," said Paul.

"Would you prefer to go elsewhere?" asked Christian.

"I never object to the Café Central," responded Paul.

A magnificent marble staircase was in front of her, as Claire walked into the Café Central, and above was a Venetian-style glass ceiling. Christian led them through the restaurant with Tomas beside him, who whispered that the poet Jürgen Becker was sitting in the corner. Tomas, Paul and Becker had been close acquaintances until six months ago when they had fallen out, and now Becker spent most evenings here and had become almost a fixture. He was going bald, dressed in a dark suit, tie, and a stained white shirt with a wing collar. People left him alone, as he was always tight after ten-thirty, encircled by an aroma of brandy and cigars. He would occasionally scribble in a little journal he kept in his pocket, but he had published nothing of consequence for nearly twenty years.

"His failing is that which he sees in others!" said Tomas in a whisper, quoting a line from Becker's most famous poem. As if he had heard Tomas mocking him, Becker looked up, waved his hand jovially at them, and mouthed something that none of the group heard, but which Tomas and Paul both knew was *Arschfickers*. They ignored him and went to their usual table near the window. As they sat down a cigarette girl immediately approached them.

"Do you smoke?" asked Christian, turning towards Claire.

"Occasionally," she said, and Christian ordered cigarettes for the table and gave a few coins to the girl. Tomas lit Claire's and was about to light Christian's, but Claire stopped him and said she would do it, as she was sitting next to him. She turned to Christian, and he heard a match being struck on the side of the matchbox. As it ignited, he could smell sulphur and a slight warmth as the match approached his face. He winced involuntarily and then steadied himself as he breathed in. The tobacco crackled slightly as it burned. Her face was close to his.

"Thank you," he said.

"My pleasure," she responded. Christian could sense her face was still close to his.

"I wouldn't look too closely if I were you. It's not pretty?"

Claire blushed slightly. "No," she said, "it's not. I was told that you were injured in the war."

"It's not something I talk about," he answered, and turned his head as he heard a champagne cork popping. The waiters knew them so well that they no longer had to ask what they would be drinking; it was always a bottle of '29 Krug and a white Burgundy with supper. Paul often said that if he was ever seen drinking Liebfraumilch, he should be put up against a wall and shot. Tomas always laughed at that, although Christian knew that in less glamorous circles, Paul would be more than happy to drink whatever he was offered.

Christian could hear the cigarette girl still standing behind him. Her soft slippers scuffed the floor slightly as she tried to find a comfortable stance, where her legs would not ache. She would have been there all night, thought Christian, and now is hoping we will drink and smoke too much. He felt across the table for the ashtray, stubbed out his cigarette, and turned to the girl. He asked for two packets of cigarettes and a box of matches, gave her a large tip and wished her a good night.

"Thank you, sir," she said gratefully, putting the money in her purse before heading for the kitchen.

Claire sat back in her chair, watched the girl walk away, and saw that she bent down by the door of the kitchen and rubbed the back of her calf. She looked at Christian, who was listening to Paul and Tomas. He had slightly winced when she brought the match towards his face to light the cigarette. She could only guess at the extent of the burns behind the patch he wore. He would have once been handsome, she thought, and as she stared at him, Christian turned.

"How did you meet Paul?" he asked. However, Paul interjected when he heard his name being mentioned.

"I was in a perfectly divine little theatre off-Broadway. The Americans would say it was off-off-off Broadway." His face lit up, and he laughed in a high-pitched tone. He had a roundish shaped head, a dimple on his chin, a small nose, thin lips, piercing brown eyes, and dark, angular eyebrows. Claire thought that there was something about his features that made him look like an otter and that behind the joviality, there might be a darker side. His voice trilled along in the same tone with which he often sang. "Claire was in a play and had to sing at the end, and I thought what a perfect songbird."

Paul turned back to Tomas, and the two continued talking while Claire stubbed out her cigarette.

"So, what made you leave America and come with Paul to Europe?" asked Christian.

"It's a long story for another day," said Claire. She smiled and then looked at Paul, her eyes narrowing, as if trying to ascertain whether she had made a mistake in coming to Vienna. He acted like a famous star, but as they toured, he was clearly past his prime. It was true that every-one knew his name in music hall circles, and Deutsche Grammophon had released several of his songs when he was in Germany. However, that was some time ago, and Vienna was not Berlin.

She had now been touring with Paul for nearly a month, and life was so different to her time in New York. She found that her German was not nearly as proficient as she thought. She had asked one of Paul's 'pretty boys' about rooms in Vienna and been given a recommenda-tion. She had taken it because she could not afford a hotel, although it was an absolute flea pit. She thought about changing it but had to work every evening and, despite being exhausted, was expected to join Paul and his guests.

Claire sat quietly as Christian told them about what had happened during their time away. He had views on the Nazi uprising, Dollfuss' assassination and the hangings in the street. However, as the evening wore on, it was the concern that Christian had for his friends and other people that Claire noticed. Christian had called the cigarette girl over and bought the cigarettes for the table. He had thanked her, tipped her generously and wished her a goodnight. Neither Paul nor Tomas would have noticed the cigarette girl and would not have thanked her. Also, Christian asked questions and seemed more interested in Claire's answers than his own questions, and he moved the conversation to things that might interest her. He suggested galleries she might visit, the most beautiful parks for afternoon walks, and cafés where they served the best ices with whipped cream.

"Is it all right if I call you Christian?" she said when they left at a quarter to two.

"All my friends do," he replied, "except for Tomas, who calls me Kit."

"Kit Drewe," she said, sizing up the name as a possibility. "No, Christian is right for you."

5

— · —

24 SEPTEMBER 1934

Claire glanced over at her alarm clock on the bedside table and groaned when she saw it was nearly ten. The room she had rented was in the Wieden district of the city, but at the southern end, and each day the windows of the building would rattle as goods trains came into the nearby railway station. It was an old, musty house where the dilapidated rooms were partially furnished with frayed, patched-together sofas and chairs, which the landlady, Frau Eder, referred to as antique pieces. Claire got out of bed and looked at a photograph of her parents on the mantelpiece over the small fire. They were both dead, her mother having been killed in a car accident when she was sixteen, and her father having committed suicide during the Depression. They had left her with nothing except debts and feelings of guilt.

Claire thought about what she would do. She was twenty-seven, in a foreign country without a cent. Her belongings could be packed in two large suitcases. She had spent the last ten days regretting her decision in choosing these rooms, but everything else seemed so expensive. She decided to take a walk in the park just before lunchtime and hoped she might catch the eye of a young gentleman or soldier. She looked at herself in the mirror and realised she was beginning to look more like her mother. There were glimpses of her in her smile and the way she held herself. Yes, she thought, she would find a gentleman of means, and then she caught the reflection of her father's eyes judging her.

***

Despite it being near the end of the month, it was a warm day, and Christian had asked Frau Huber to pack a picnic to take to the Stadtpark. He spread out his picnic rug on the grass, took out his book, and lay down. Within a quarter of an hour, he had fallen asleep in the autumn sun and only woke when someone spoke his name.

"Mr Drewe... Christian," said a woman's voice, with a soft American accent. Christian paused and felt for his glasses. They were in place, and he tried to sit up. "When you had said that you liked the Stadtpark, I did not expect to find you sleeping here," she teased.

"Miss Astor, Claire," said Christian, embarrassed to have been caught napping, "forgive me if I don't get up, but at my age... I might appear a little ungainly."

"At your age?" said Claire, enjoying the fact that he was embarrassed. "How old are you? No older than forty-five, I'd guess?"

"I turned forty-two this year," replied Christian, who was trying desperately to think of something humorous to say.

"Oh," said Claire, but she knew he was not upset as he was smiling.

"I would ask you to join me, but I didn't think of bringing a chair."

"I don't mind sitting on the ground, and at least you won't see how ungainly I am when I plop down beside you."

"If it would make you feel better, I'll turn away," he laughed.

She dropped as elegantly as possible, trying to keep her skirts from rising above her knees. She giggled as she fought with the material.

"What's so funny?" asked Christian.

"Nothing," said Claire, "except we may both have blushed if you had seen my landing."

"Your landing?"

"How I plonked myself down next to you." She raised her knees and curled them under her skirts like a cat on a pillow. "It was such a nice day. I thought I would stroll through the park."

"And how did you find this little corner?" asked Christian.

"Just luck."

"I'm afraid I have brought only a picnic, but if you don't mind sharing?"

"I would love that," said Claire, enthusiastically. "I'm sure it will be the best meal I've eaten since the last time I saw you."

"I can't promise anything," said Christian, hoping that Frau Huber had not prepared too much sauerkraut. "And are you still singing at the cabaret with Paul?"

"I am," said Claire, "but I must find somewhere else to work."

"Don't you like it there?"

"I do," she said emphatically. She moved her head closer to Christian's ear, as if she were about to tell him the most shocking secret, and added, "But Paul doesn't pay me very much."

"Doesn't he?" Christian replied, pretending to be surprised.

"Hardly anything," she added in the conspiratorial whisper both had adopted. "And I had no idea how expensive everything would be here in Vienna."

"Do you know what I would do?"

Claire shook her head and added, "No," when Christian didn't immediately respond.

"I would tell him that if he doesn't pay you three times what he is paying you now, you will be on the first boat back to New York."

"But he won't…"

"And tell him you've been offered a job at the Fledermaus. Paul never goes there, and they are always looking for new singers."

"But I haven't!"

"And say it with confidence, Miss Astor."

Claire thought about it momentarily and agreed she would do that.

"Is there anything else I can help you with?" asked Christian.

"Nothing," said Claire, "unless you can find me new rooms. The one I rented is an absolute dump." She giggled again.

"Why don't you just leave?"

"Because I can't afford to."

"Now, may I ask a favour?" said Christian.

Claire hesitated a moment before saying, "Yes."

"May I feel your face? It's the only way I can know what a person looks like."

Claire shuffled on the ground so that she could sit next to him. Then, she took his right hand and placed it on her forehead.

"Close your eyes," he said.

He moved his fingers across her forehead and back to the centre. He then slowly let his index finger down her short, straight nose, stopping for a moment at the tip. His finger and thumb slid down her two nostrils so that they were on either side of her mouth, and then he brought them together over her top lip. She opened her lips slightly. It was almost instinctive, as if she felt she was about to be kissed. She could feel him just inches away from her face, breathing slowly, and a scent of cedarwood from his cologne. His thumb and finger traced their way back along her top lip, then ran down her cheeks. She took a breath. His middle finger stroked her neck, underneath her chin. His fingers felt strong. His right hand moved back up her neck to the lobes of her ears. He touched her gently behind the ear. She swallowed. She suddenly felt his other hand caress the opposite side of her face – his fingers circled the lobes of her ears, and then he moved them slowly inward across her closed eyes and then up the sides of her nose, until his fingers came together like a monk in prayer.

"Thank you," he said. She opened her eyes and looked directly at his sunglasses, which reflected her image.

"And what do you think I look like?"

"I think you are as beautiful as your voice," said Christian.

"I didn't expect you to be Prince Charming," she responded.

"I suppose I have to be charming," said Christian, "to hide the fact that I look like a monster."

"It's not…" began Claire, but she knew it was true, and he would have known if she had lied. She did not know what to say next.

"Are you hungry?" he asked, changing the subject quickly to fill the void of silence.

"Famished," said Claire, relieved.

"I will set out the picnic," Christian felt to his left, where he had placed the hamper. "My housekeeper," he continued, "Frau Huber, always makes enough food to feed an army. There will be smoked salmon, a few slices of terrine, a chicken leg, breads, olives, a pile of sauerkraut and strudel."

"Just for you?" said Claire, thinking that this was more than she had eaten for the whole week.

"I give the strudel to the ducks," responded Christian, "and I throw away the sauerkraut, but you can never tell my housekeeper that; she would skin me alive."

6

25 MAY 1935

At eight a.m., the wooden gates of Linz Prison creaked open, and Ernst Schmidt was escorted onto an empty street on the city's outskirts. He held a cardboard box containing some clothes, toiletries, and a bible, which he read most evenings. He was thirty-one, over six feet tall, and had straight brown hair, which he oiled and combed backwards. He wore a suit, and anyone passing would have assumed he was a lawyer visiting his client in prison rather than someone who had just been released. He was blessed with the looks of a film star who might be cast as a gangster, as he had eight small scars across his face, which he had received in a car crash when he was in his early twenties. He, however, allowed rumours to circulate that they had been inflicted when duelling in his student days. There was something about him which made one wary. It may have been the flintiness of his blue eyes or the detached way he studied people. He looked at his watch as a car turned the corner at the bottom of the road and drove towards him

As the car pulled up, Schmidt saw that his wife was driving, and his three daughters were sitting in the back. His expression did not change as he waited for her to get out of the vehicle.

"I told you not to bring them here," he said quietly to his wife as she gave him the car keys.

"I could not find anyone to look after them at such short notice," Gretchen Schmidt said. Schmidt had spent nine months in prison of an eighteen-month sentence for his role in the uprising against Chancellor Dollfuss. His early release came after Hitler made a concession to the new Austrian chancellor saying that Germany had no intention of mixing in Austria's internal affairs. Schmidt walked around the car. He opened the boot and placed his belongings inside before getting into the vehicle. He told his daughters that he was sorry he had been away for so long but that his business abroad had taken longer than expected.

Linz was a tired, austere city with medieval-styled buildings, which fifty years ago teemed with merchants from around the world. Schmidt drove through the quiet streets, passing the old tobacco factory that had once employed so many people and which the authorities had finally decided to knock down.

"Nothing ever changes," Schmidt said to his wife, "and nothing will change until the Nazis gain power and we get rid of every Jew."

"Why?" asked his youngest daughter.

"They don't have our values," said Schmidt. "They just take from our community and give nothing back and their men... Well, they prey on young girls."

"They don't need to hear about that," whispered Gretchen to her husband. "They're too young."

"They need to know the truth," replied Schmidt.

He parked the car on the driveway and then hugged each of his daughters as they got out of the car.

"I'll be in my study," he said to his wife. "I have things to do."

Schmidt had joined the Austrian Nazi Party, just after he received a doctorate in law. In the following year he started his own law practice and married Gretchen, who he had met at university. A few years later, in early the 1930s, he instituted a terror campaign in Linz against the Jews, which was funded by the German Nazi Party. Schmidt arranged for explosives and tear gas to be set off in public places in Linz and focused attacks on Jewish-owned businesses. People were injured and two bystanders killed. The government banned the Austrian Nazi Party, who went into hiding until the uprising against Dollfuss.

Although not involved in the assassination of Dollfuss, Schmidt commanded men and took control of the radio station in Linz without a shot being fired. The new government under Chancellor Schuschnigg was quick to act and, with Mussolini's assistance, Italian troops arrived at the border to aid Austria and prevent a German invasion. Hitler hesitated, reluctant to start a war with one of his allies, and the coup d'état failed. Schmidt was arrested and imprisoned.

In his study, Schmidt found a pile of unopened correspondence. One letter was from the Law Society in Vienna and advised him that his licence to practise as a lawyer had been revoked because of his criminal record and stated that if he wished to appeal the decision, he should attend a hearing at the Law Society in Vienna at the start of the following month and notify the Law Society. Schmidt tore up the letter after he read it, hardly believing that they could take away his livelihood as well as his liberty.

7

6 June 1935

The train from Linz to Vienna did the hundred-mile journey in less than three hours. However, culturally, Linz and Vienna were worlds apart. Linz was in upper Austria, with its rich history that was tied to Bavaria and Germany. Vienna was in lower Austria and was a broad church, with many Austrians, Czechs, and Hungarians living side by side. In Linz there were less than seven hundred Jews living in a population of three quarters of a million people. In Vienna there were more than 176,000 Jews, making up around nine per cent of the city.

Schmidt took a taxi from the train station but the traffic to the Inner Stadt was congested. The Law Society was on the second floor in an office just off Stephansplatz and Schmidt entered the building and dashed up the two flights of stairs. He rapped loudly on the locked wooden door with its brass nameplate and waited a few moments to be let in by a receptionist, who informed him he was late and that his hearing had started ten minutes earlier. He was out of breath and wanted a glass of water but was told that he needed to immediately attend the hearing before a sentence was passed in his absence.

Schmidt had the impression he was entering a meeting where a decision had already been made. The small room with two windows was filled with articled clerks, secretaries and three examining magistrates who sat behind a table on a podium at the far end. When the usher advised the tribunal that Herr Ernst Schmidt was in attendance there was a silence, and everyone watched as Schmidt took a seat in front of the magistrates and began to set out his papers.

"Herr Schmidt," said the chairman of the examining magistrates, "we did not think that you would be attending."

Schmidt looked up from his papers towards the three magistrates.

"Well, I'm here," said Schmidt.

The chairman of the examining magistrates spoke quickly to his wingmen and then looked at Schmidt.

"It is most unusual, Herr Schmidt, not to advise us of your attendance prior to the hearing date. However, we shall proceed. I am Herr Otto Friedmann and my colleagues for this tribunal are Herr Dietrich and Herr Müller." Otto Friedmann pulled his chair up to the table and opened a bundle of documents that lay in front of him. "Right then," said Otto, leafing through the papers. "You are a lawyer and principal of the firm E. Schmidt Rechtsanwälte."

"I am," replied Schmidt.

Otto looked down from the podium at Schmidt and his bushy eyebrows furrowed over his eyes.

"The charges against you, for which you were convicted, were incitement to riot and criminal damage."

"They were," said Schmidt, who paused and asked for a glass of water. Otto shook his hand at the court usher, indicating that she should get Schmidt a carafe and a glass.

"And these are imprisonable offences," said Otto, "which carry more than five years' imprisonment. There is therefore a *prima facie* case made out that your licence to practise law should be revoked."

"The offences," said Schmidt, "although technically imprisonable for more than five years, would not in the circumstances ever attract that level of punishment. The objects that were damaged were the doors to the radio station in Linz and the only people *allegedly* put in fear or hurt by my actions were a group of Jews who were outside the radio station."

Whether from embarrassment or impatience, Otto shifted to and fro in his chair. The examining magistrate to his left, whom he'd been talking to before, leant over again, and whispered something in his ear. Otto nodded his head and whispered something to the other magistrate before saying to Schmidt, "So, you are arguing *de minimis* and that the sentence is disproportionate to the offence itself."

"Precisely," said Schmidt, who thought that at least one of the examining magistrates had understood his case and might support him.

"And do you have a statement in mitigation for us?"

Schmidt stood up slowly and looked at each of the examining magistrates in turn. He focused on the one to the left of Otto and smiled before he started reading from his prepared notes, saying that nothing he had done had been dishonest or likely to bring the Law Society or the law into disrepute. He spoke for twenty minutes, highlighting that all his accounts were in order and that his practice had not once been reprimanded by the Law Society.

"In conclusion," said Schmidt, after taking a sip of water, "the offences that are alleged against me must be mitigated by what I was seeking to achieve by my acts. I sought nothing more than a society in which honesty and decency are paramount and where decent Austrian men and women can know that their children are safe on the streets."

"Really?" said Otto.

"I have not finished," said Schmidt, rapping the table with his fist. The loud knock caused the heads of the other two examining magistrates to look up. "I sought nothing but that *we* as Austrians follow and align ourselves with Germany. I sought nothing but that the law should follow that of Germany and that all judges and lawyers should swear the following oath, as they do in Germany: 'I swear loyalty to the Führer of the German Reich and people, Adolf Hitler, obedience to the law, and conscientious fulfilment of the duties of my office, so help me God.'"

"But we are not in Germany," said Otto, "and I am proud to say that we do not have to swear allegiance to Adolf Hitler for it would be a sad day for the law if that were so." Otto then banged his gavel on the table and silence immediately fell. "The evidence is overwhelming, Herr Schmidt, innocent people were injured. These were people in the wrong place at the wrong time. They were Jewish Austrians and the only reason that they were targeted by you, and your group of thugs, was because of their faith. As a person of the Jewish faith, I find that these actions are heinous and that your early release from prison was not because of the seriousness or otherwise of the offence but because of political machinations. That you come before this tribunal today and claim that these acts are *de minimis* does not speak well to either your character or honesty. My colleagues and I are in agreement on this matter, and this tribunal confirms its previous order that you should be stripped of your licence to practise law and debarred from practising law for the remainder of your life. I would add that if I could impose a harsher sentence I would, and believe that you are not a fit person to hold any public office. However, I am constrained only to pass a sentence relevant to your practice as a lawyer." Otto banged his gavel once more. "Your appeal is dismissed. Do you have anything else to say, Herr Schmidt?"

Schmidt stared at Otto and collected his papers and walked to the back of the room. He stopped at the door and looked back at the tribunal as they started putting their papers away and shouted,

"Austria is a Christian country, and I advocate for nothing but the will of God. I will remember you, Otto Friedmann, and what you have said today!"

8

27 June 1935

With his main source of income gone, Schmidt needed work and he took almost any job he could get, going into town each day. However, manual labour only paid thirty schillings a week. On days without work, he would sit in the main square. He preferred being alone there rather than going home to his wife and daughters, who would only ask him questions about why he was not working. He didn't even try to get work in any of the Jewish factories, they knew exactly who he was. His mortgage was being subsidised by his father; however, that could not go on forever as his father would be retiring soon and Schmidt started to wonder how long it would be before he had to start selling things – his house, his car, paintings or his wife's jewellery.

Towards the end of June, he received a letter from Himmler requesting that he attend a meeting in Munich to discuss how Hitler could support the Nazi Party in Austria. One hundred schillings was transferred to his account to cover the expenses, and he drove his family to Munich on the last weekend of the month, explaining to Gretchen that he might be offered work.

"And we can treat the children as well," Schmidt added, and promised to make time to play with them.

Gretchen and the children went to the Chinese Pagoda in the park while Schmidt went to a beer cellar for his meeting. Himmler was there when Schmidt arrived and they ordered lunch. They talked about what was happening in Germany, compulsory male military service and the expansion of the laws against homosexuals.

"Now," said Himmler, wiping his mouth as he chewed, "is not the time to bring Austria into the German Reich, but you must be ready when the time comes. Our Führer has decided to look first towards the Saar region and then the Rhineland before seeking the *Anschluss* with Austria." Himmler leant closer to Schmidt so they would not be overheard in the large beerhall. "Do not," he said, "be swayed by the words you hear but only by our Führer's actions. He may say he has no intention of joining Austria with Germany but look to see what he does. He will bring every German under our banner."

"And the money?" asked Schmidt.

Himmler handed over an envelope stuffed with a thousand schillings. "Use it to support those faithful to the party," he added. "Our time is coming and next month be here on the last Saturday. There will be more money and new instructions. *Sieg Heil!*"

"Heil Hitler," Schmidt responded, with a pride he had not felt since before his arrest. He left the beerhall and went straight to the park, and true to his word, he spent the afternoon with his three girls playing hide and seek.

9

— • —

16 September 1935

It was Schmidt's third trip to Munich and he went alone. He still did not have a full-time job, as all the office and factory owners were struggling to make ends meet. Every schilling that the State earned was going on reparations. The only people who seemed to have money were a small group of Jews and people began asking how they became so rich. There were whispers and then rumours saying that the Jews had got rich by stabbing Germany and Austria in the back. Hindenburg, the former president of Germany, had even said that the German Army had been betrayed, claiming that the army had not lost the Great War on the battlefield but had been undermined by the Jews and socialists who fomented strikes and labour unrest and who forced on Germany and Austria the humiliating terms of the Armistice of 1918.

Schmidt sat in the beer cellar in Munich reading a newspaper and waiting for Himmler to arrive.

"And how are things in Linz?" said Himmler, who had walked up to the table unnoticed.

"Linz does not change," said Schmidt, as Himmler sat down. "There are less Jews there than a year ago and everyone I speak to is in favour of joining with Germany. The problem in Austria is not

Linz but Vienna, it's a cesspit... a shithole, where Jews can rob decent hard-working Austrians."

"And what do you suggest?" asked Himmler.

Schmidt tapped his fingertip on the article he had been reading. "The same laws in Austria as you have here," he said. "We must have laws that prevent Jews from having any rights in society and the law in Austria that prohibits a Nazi from holding an official position needs to be rescinded."

"Our Führer says the same thing," said Himmler.

"And we need more articles in the newspapers to show how the Jews have betrayed our country. We need to persuade our young Austrians that their country is not just a forgotten remnant of the past. We need an Austria that our children can be proud of, one that can dominate the rest of Europe as part of a united Germany. We also need to know..." Schmidt emphasized the point by again tapping his forefinger on the newspaper article, "that we are not alone, that Germans in Hungary and in Czecho-Slovakia want what we want."

"Trust the Führer," said Himmler, as he passed over an envelope full of money, "and what you want will happen soon."

"I know," said Schmidt.

"And what can we do for you?"

"All I want to do is help," said Schmidt.

"And would a position in Linz's police force be something that would be of interest to you?" asked Himmler, as he wiped the corner of his eye with his middle finger.

"Of course," said Schmidt.

"It might take a few months to finalise, but things are happening. Expect a change when you get back to Linz. Your name is being mentioned."

"What I could do from there would be felt across Austria. I could clear the streets of Jews, homosexuals and the other filth that pollutes us."

***

Schmidt was usually a man of cool emotions, but he returned home from Munich with presents for everyone. There was a smile on his lips and despite his wife's caution about a bird in the hand, his good mood could not be quelled. He played a game of questions and forfeits with his children that afternoon, in which he would ask them a question and if they did not tell the truth, there would be a forfeit. It was game he was good at.

He booked a table for the whole family at Linz's finest restaurant that evening. Although Gretchen disapproved of any wanton waste of money, she had not been out to eat in a fine restaurant for nearly a year and the pork knuckle that she had braised for most of the day was transferred unceremoniously into the bin. She took her husband's arm as they walked into the courtyard of the restaurant with their three girls.

"Herr Ober," said Schmidt, loudly as he entered the restaurant.

"Herr Schmidt, Fräu Schmidt," said the waiter as he took their coats, "it has been too long." The waiter looked at the children and made some appreciative sounds and then puffing out his chest and pulling down his black waistcoat, so that the white cotton of the bottom of his shirt was partially hidden, he walked them to their table.

During a meal that lasted a little over two hours and consisted of a dish of pork, which was not nearly as good as the one lying at the bottom of the Schmidts' bin, Schmidt was greeted repeatedly by bankers, lawyers and the upper classes of Linz. Gretchen smiled on each occasion when someone came over with a platitude or a greeting of friendship. As she looked at her husband with the small scars on his face and his hair combed back, relaxing in the company of the upper classes of Linz, she realised that they feared him. They knew what he had done when Dollfuss was assassinated, and they knew what he could do. They may not like him, thought Gretchen, they might even despise him, but they were afraid of him, and they were right to be afraid. For the first time in a long time, as she looked at her children eating three large plates of apple strudel, she had no worries about money or about their future.

10

12 OCTOBER 1935

If life was not a bed of roses, neither was it a garland of thorns. The Fledermaus theatre may not have been Carnegie Hall, but it was bigger than the little cabaret shows that Paul played, and Claire had second billing after the famous tenor, Richard Tauber. As she left the stage that evening, the pianist stood up and kissed her hand. The applause continued so long that she was forced to return for an encore.

Claire found herself backstage after the show, where plenty more hand-kissing and self-congratulatory chat occurred. As usual, and led by the dashing Richard Tauber, they headed for the bar around the corner, where Richard ordered the first round of drinks. The bar was noisy, too noisy for Richard, who leant over to Claire suggesting they go on to the Café Central.

"Why? It's such a dull place."

"Because I can't hear myself think in here. Come if you want; it's your choice."

There was no question of Claire staying, evenings out with Richard Tauber were always fun; however, the Café Central would not have been her first choice. It was a Saturday night; Paul and Tomas would be there, and she had not spoken to either of them for months. A year ago, she had asked Paul for a raise, and he had given it to her, albeit under protest, and Tomas had arranged a shared house for her in a more fashionable area of the Wieden district at the same price she was paying. However, a month later she had received a call from the manager of the Fledermaus who had heard her sing and offered her a regular spot on their new revue with Richard Tauber. She dropped Paul like a hot potato.

The Café Central had not changed one iota. She stifled a giggle when she saw Jürgen Becker sitting at the same table where he had sat when she had first visited. He was still drunk in a stained white shirt. She then looked across the restaurant and saw Paul, Tomas and Christian at the table by the window. She swallowed, as she thought that Paul was always capable of making a scene.

"Are you all right?" asked Richard, as they sauntered through the bar and restaurant.

"Fine," said Claire. "Just some people I haven't seen for a while." Richard looked across the restaurant.

"It's Paul O'Montis, isn't it?" he said, staring across the smoke-filled room. "You can never be certain when he's not wearing *those* tights and has trousers on."

"Yes, it's Paul."

"And Tomas Skeres," Richard added, "but who is the other person?"

"Christian Drewe," answered Claire. "He's a friend of Tomas'. He's blind."

"Could you introduce me?" asked Richard, and they wandered over.

Tomas overflowed with charm, calling Claire a little canary and asking her and Richard to join them. Paul stood up, kissed Claire on both cheeks and then hugged Richard Tauber, as if he were a long-lost brother. Quickly, Paul and Richard became animated, and their voices rose until they broke into a song, and, for a reason that Claire did not know, Tomas joined in. She sat down next to Christian as the three men sang, with the waiters and the diners looking on.

"I hadn't realised," said Claire to Christian, "that they knew each other this well."

"They met in Berlin in 1931," said Christian, "Richard left when the Nazis came to power, but Paul stayed on." Christian waved for a waiter and ordered a glass of champagne for Claire. "It's been a while since we bumped into each other. How are you?"

Claire looked at him. He had hardly changed in the year. He wore a beautifully cut dinner suit edged with silk, a white shirt and a black tie. He still had the brass-rimmed dark glasses and a black fedora hat with a grey grosgrain band.

"You are always so elegantly dressed," she said, "even when you sleep in the park."

"Thank you," laughed Christian, "although that was not an answer to my question."

"Life is treating me rather well at the moment," she said, leaning closer to Christian in the noisy restaurant so that she did not have to shout. "While Richard steals the plaudits at the Fledermaus, I have been mentioned in one or two reviews. I was sorry to leave Paul, and Tomas was a darling for helping me with new digs."

"You know," said Christian, "you don't need an invitation to come and see us. We're always here on a Saturday night and at some club or another on Thursdays and Fridays."

"I have a much quieter lifestyle," replied Claire hesitantly. It was not entirely true. However, the places where Richard Tauber took her were very different to the clubs that Paul, Tomas and Christian frequented. Richard liked the opera and was invited into the drawing rooms of minor royalty, places where Paul could never step.

The song finished, and the restaurant broke into polite applause. Claire stood up and introduced Richard to Christian.

"I wanted to meet you," said Richard, "to thank you for helping to produce the show."

"It's my pleasure," said Christian, "and I'm pleased it's a success."

"With regret," said Richard, "at the end of the year, I will have to leave the Fledermaus, as I have agreed to sing with the Vienna State Opera and then tour."

"I suppose I knew this day would come," said Christian.

"And, of course, you discovered the talented and charming Miss Astor."

"Hardly," said Christian, "Paul discovered her in America."

"However, it was you, I hear, who insisted she be put on the bill at the Fledermaus."

"I may have suggested it," said Christian, who picked up his glass of champagne and took a sip.

"Anyway," said Richard, "I wanted to thank you personally, and I didn't want you to hear that I was leaving in the press."

As Richard walked back to his group, Claire hesitated. "Why didn't you tell me?" she asked. "I had no idea that you had sponsored me."

"It was a pleasure," said Christian. "Paul, Tomas and I all knew that you could do better than singing in those little cabaret clubs, and we just gave you a nudge in the right direction."

***

What troubled Claire the next morning was the news that Richard Tauber would leave the show at the end of the year. Without a star like Richard, they could not fill the eight-hundred-seat theatre night after night. She would need another job, but she did not want to return to the chorus line, and singing in places like the Kabarett Simpl or other small cabaret shows would mean less money. She thought about packing up her bags and moving on; but where? She would just be starting again, somewhere new. If she were ever going to succeed, she thought, she needed to stop running every time things became difficult. She looked at the photograph of her parents on the bookshelf in her bedroom, who smiled back, as if they agreed with her.

Claire put on a dressing gown and went to the kitchen and made a pot of coffee. She poured a cup and drank it black with two sugars. One of the girls who she shared the house with put her head around the door.

"I thought I heard someone up," she said.

"Sit down, Angela," said Claire. "I have a problem, and I would like some advice. I know something which is not yet public knowledge and affects me."

"Which is?" said Angela.

"I can't tell you," said Claire, "but if I needed to find another job quickly, what would you suggest I do?"

"A musical revue," suggested Angela.

"Do you know of any shows that are looking?" asked Claire.

"No... but... something will come along sooner or later."

"Anything else?" asked Claire.

"Perhaps," said Angela, "you could try films. You speak English, French and German, and you're really pretty. You'd be great doing that and would have no trouble getting a part somewhere."

11

24 JANUARY 1936

Tomas sat in Christian's dining room and, after reading the evening papers to him, said he was concerned that Austria might align itself with Germany, which would mean that he and Paul would have to leave the country. Christian shook his head and said it was unlikely to happen soon and anyway before too long Hitler would be exposed, and the middle-classes would remove him as surely as you cut out a cancer.

"Chancellor Schuschnigg and his vice-chancellor," continued Christian, "gave an undisguised snub to Germany at the national rally in Vienna a few days ago. Schuschnigg said that authority should never mean tyranny, and that Austria would remain independent and free."

"The problem," said Tomas, "is that you don't understand Austrians. We pretend to be liberal, but most of us want someone to blame for the poverty we're living in."

"But joining with Germany, is that the answer?" said Christian.

"No, of course not," replied Tomas. "But everyone here envies Germany's economy and we all want to have a bit of their wealth."

"So, you think Austria and Germany will unify?"

"Yes," said Tomas, "and however much I fear it, I think it's inevitable."

***

Claire paid little attention to politics. It was the closing of the show at the Fledermaus three weeks earlier that pre-occupied her thoughts. Her attempts to find a role in a film had been disastrous. At twenty-eight years of age, she was neither a starlet nor a matriarch, although one director thought her the perfect age for the casting couch. An expletive and a slap to the side of his face was her response before she stormed out. However, she needed to pay her rent and therefore contacted the manager at the Kabarett Simpl, who she knew, and was given an hour spot three times a week. It was a step-down, but a necessary one until something better came along.

Vienna was becoming seedier. Perhaps it had always been seedy, thought Claire, but when she first came to the city it was exciting and new, and she hadn't noticed. The men seemed older, and the dancing girls and boys seemed younger. She often left straight after her performance, not wanting to hang around and be propositioned or touched. After a year with Richard Tauber, her act was so polished that she could go on stage with little or no rehearsal and sing a few American tunes by Cole Porter, Jerome Kern or Irving Berlin. She would wear a sequinned dress and long gloves, giving the appearance of being aloof and seductive, and would stare at unknown faces pretending that here was just a little taste of Hollywood. The Kabarett Simpl was a small theatre, where people would sit at round tables listening and watching political sketches. At ten p.m. the music would start and at midnight the dancers would take to the stage. The drinks were expensive and champagne and cocktails outrageously so. It was always dark there, with a clientele made up of people who did not want to be recognised.

It started filling up at nine p.m. and was always packed by midnight, when half-dressed dancers would come on and the band would play tunes with more vigour and urgency. After Claire finished singing that evening, and the lights were raised before the next act, she saw Paul sauntering in with his arm around a young man.

The Kabarett Simpl had never been one of Paul's haunts. The shows they put on were not outrageous. They catered for Austrian businessmen putting on mild political satire, American jazz, and half-naked dancers in corsets, tassels or feathers. It was titillation and Paul's appearance was unusual, as no one would know him there.

She went to the bar after she had got changed and ordered a glass of white wine. She could see Paul and his companion in a small corner, talking closely, Paul's mouth by the young man's ear, Paul's hand on his thigh. She decided to go over and speak to him but as she took a step towards him, Paul's hand lifted, and he gently turned the young man's face towards his and kissed him. She stopped and went back to the bar. It was better, she thought, to disappear. She gulped down her drink, got her coat and left the club, feeling despondent because this was the best job she had managed to get.

Four hours later Paul staggered out from the club into the freezing morning and wrapped his coat tightly around him. A half-finished bottle of Austrian fizz poked out of his pocket. His breath billowed up into the icy air. The young man was a step behind him.

"Shall we get a room?" Paul asked. "I know a little hotel around the corner."

"I bet you do," replied the young man. "But you haven't told me how much you'll give me? You know, I haven't done this before; not what you want, anyway."

"Don't make me laugh," said Paul, looking at the thin young man. "Anyway, I can't give you anything tonight, but I'll give you a present when I see you next."

"I don't do it on tick."

"You know I'm good for it," said Paul, pleading.

"I know your boyfriend's good for it," answered the young man.

"I can give you a cheque. I'll make it out for cash."

"I don't think so. I heard that your cheques bounce more than a tennis ball." Paul looked at him. He wasn't going to beg anymore.

"Fuck off then!" said Paul.

"At least give me the money for a taxi home," whined the young man. Paul opened his wallet, took out a note and threw it at him, turning on his heels.

He didn't see the young man pick up the note, as he wandered back towards the main square where there were cabs, or hear what he shouted after him. The market women were already setting up their stalls of vegetables and fruit. Many of them had newspapers stuffed under their coats to ward off the cold. An occasional woman would nod as he walked by, one even called him by his name. Some woman shouted that he should get himself a market stall, "as he's always up at the same hour as me." Others laughed that he better have his fun now, "because it wouldn't last long when the Nazis got into power." He ignored them. He would be forty soon, in his prime, he thought. As he walked across the square he saw a cab. He was uncertain where he would go. Tomas would be asleep, and it would be a mistake to wake him at this time. There would be too many questions about who he had been with and then raised voices. He looked at his watch and decided it was too late to go to another club, and anyway, he hadn't much money on him after spending so much on some awful fizz. He got into the cab and gave his address.

"Good evening, Herr O'Montis," said the cab driver, "on your own tonight?"

"Just drive," said Paul, but the cab driver prattled on about what Chancellor Schuschnigg had said at the rally the previous day and that, like it or not, nothing that Schuschnigg said would deter Hitler.

Paul closed his eyes as the cab driver continued to talk; as the profundity of the world was revealed to him in the idle chat of a taxi driver, the laughter of the market women and the desperation of a young man needing cash.

***

Schmidt put down the newspaper and smiled. They had printed his article in the newspaper precisely as he had prepared it. It mentioned no names, but everyone would know who it was referring to. It referred to a group of people who were decadent and skirted the edges of a degenerate bourgeois life. They were the people who frequented the brothels, the clubs, dives, and the small cabarets. They mixed with people who catered for perversion and pain. They were those who saw work as something to be shunned and flicked the pages of the books of the Marquis de Sade for their dull amusements and thoughtless pleasures. Theirs were unnatural delights; theirs were subtle pleasures, which decent, hard-working Austrians would turn away from in disgust.

Gretchen looked at him as she brought in the breakfast plates and asked why he was smiling.

"Because we're getting our country back," Schmidt said.

"But Chancellor Schuschnigg says..." Gretchen began.

"Schuschnigg's a parasite," said Schmidt, interrupting her. "He'll be gone soon."

"Oh," said Gretchen, as she placed orange juice and hot toast on the table. "May I bring in the children?"

"Yes."

Schmidt stood up, adjusted his uniform and watched as his three daughters entered the dining room.

"Your father has something important to tell you," Gretchen said.

"It is a good day for you and for Austria," Schmidt began. "I have been promoted to *Chefinspektor* – a senior inspector in the police force, which will mean more money, and I promise you, my little angels, that from today your lives will be better and our streets safer. I will make sure that every degenerate and pervert is imprisoned."

12

16 NOVEMBER 1936

Tomas had said that Claire was singing at the Kabarett Simpl and that they should go. It was known to be a little raucous after midnight when the prices of the champagne went up and the girls wore less. The midnight shows attracted older businessmen with deep pockets. It was one of the more established places on the edges of the Inner Stadt, amid a score of new clubs selling American cocktails, mineral water, Veuve Clicquot or some cheaper German fizz. Many of the places that had recently opened had French or Moroccan names, and there were plenty of hotels nearby renting rooms by the hour.

It was just before nine-thirty when Christian, Paul and Tomas arrived. Christian could hear the champagne corks popping and a few girls squealing and guessed that at least one old gent would wake up tomorrow to find that he had given his bank account a good thrashing. After ten minutes, Paul complained that the satirical revue was lacking in satire and said he was going to Leopoldstadt to listen to a street singer who had some new ballads. Tomas became irritable as soon as he had gone, complaining that Paul was always going to one show or another.

"He says," said Tomas, "that he needs to listen to the newest popular songs if his shows are to stay relevant."

"Isn't it true?" replied Christian.

"Yes," said Tomas, "but you know Paul. By two o'clock in the morning he'll have an entourage with him."

"Why don't you go with him?"

"He doesn't want me there. He's forty and wants a last fling."

"Don't you mind?"

"I mind every time he comes to my apartment smelling of booze and cheap aftershave."

"Say something to him."

"I have, a hundred times. Paul says he's sorry and says it means nothing, but two weeks later he's doing the same thing again."

Around them sat the businessmen and middle classes who sought to escape the seriousness and anxiety of their lives, whether it was work or marriage. They went there for diversion, some to laugh and forget their worries, others to watch a pretty girl dance the fandango to the explosion of music or sway to a sensual samba. It was, for everyone, a place away from the ordinary humdrum, where for a few schillings you could be made to feel special and see a pretty girl smile. However, Christian's world was composed of other senses. There was no swaying or smiles of young girls. There were no satin-draped red lights or flickering swirling images on the wall, just the heat of a crowd in a small room constantly chatting. Above the talking, the band continued to play and then he heard her voice. She had not been introduced but just started singing and Christian moved a finger to his lips and said to Tomas,

"It's Claire."

Tomas stopped speaking and turned to the stage. "Yes," he said, as he watched her in front of the band in a sequinned cocktail dress staring blankly at the small dancefloor as she sang. "She looks out of it."

"What do you mean?"

"As if she's half asleep," said Tomas.

"Drunk?"

"No," replied Tomas, and as he continued to look Claire crumpled to her knees.

***

Claire awoke alone under a silk sheet. She was in her underwear; she looked around for her dress but could not see it. She wrapped herself in the sheet, left the room and with the quiet and careful steps of one who felt they should not be there, she wandered down the hallway and into the living room. She noted very little in the darkness, except for the sumptuous rug beneath her feet and the baby grand piano by the window. She looked out onto the quiet streets below as the sun came up. She could make out the am Hof church from the window, but whose apartment this was she did not know. All she knew was that her mouth was dry, and her head throbbed.

She left the living room and went into the kitchen, where she took a glass from the shelf and filled it with water. She drank it quickly, poured herself another and then pulling a chair from underneath the kitchen table she sat down. She remembered little about the previous evening and from a kaleidoscope of dreams, she tried rearranging her memories. She had dinner with friends and was at the club at half past nine. She had been talking to the new pianist about her father. It was seven years ago that he had committed suicide, and the pianist had asked what had happened. She remembered the words tumbling out. She told him about how she had gone to his study, knocked on the door, entered and found her father dead in his chair. He had put the barrel of a pistol in his mouth and blown his brains across the room.

"I'm sorry," the pianist had said. "Do you know why?"

"Money," said Claire. "Love. I don't know."

"This will help you forget," said the pianist, taking a velvet pouch from his jacket and pulling out a small pipe. "It dulls the pain of the present and the past."

However, it had not; instead, it had brought the souls of the dead fleeing from their graves, to invade her dreams. She remembered being on the stage, singing, and feeling that her parents were there, watching her in the audience. She could not look at them and stared at the floor and then started crying. She vaguely recalled seeing Tomas fussing about, and then Christian had spoken to her, full of anxiety. So similar and so different to her father. The same warm, rich tone that was full of honesty and concern, which as a child had made her feel safe.

"Do you want coffee?"

She started, turned and saw Christian standing by the door in his dressing gown and dark glasses.

"No," she said. "Sorry if I woke you. Is this your apartment?"

"It is," he replied. "How are you?"

"Dreadful. How did I get here?" Christian took a step into the room.

"You collapsed," he said. "The doctor said it was a cocktail of alcohol and drugs. Tomas thought it would be better if we brought you here rather than calling an ambulance and then having the police and the press turn up."

"Thank you."

"Do you want to talk about it?" said Christian sitting down opposite Claire.

"It's a long story."

"I have nowhere else to be."

***

Frau Huber made breakfast, but she did not smile. Any young lady who was that attractive would cause problems for Herr Christian, she thought. She knew the type with their long dark hair, blue eyes and red lipstick, who could stare across a room and make men fall in love with them. She had seen enough Greta Garbo films to know that kind of woman, Anna Karenina or Mata Hari, women not to be trusted. She was also too thin, which for Frau Huber was never a good sign, and she played with her breakfast and drank far too much black coffee. If the list was not long enough, Frau Huber also noted she was American, and while Americans were acceptable in small doses, she thought that Herr Christian needed an Austrian Fräulein who would produce lots of children. Frau Huber therefore thought it best if Fräulein Astor did not stay longer than was necessary and sought to interrogate her on a few matters.

Why haven't you got a husband?... What do you do?... Do you like children?... Are you a Catholic or a Protestant?

Claire replied that she loved children but not until she had found the right man. Christian listened quietly and nodded, thinking Frau Huber could not object to that answer. When Frau Huber asked about Claire's religion, Claire replied she was an agnostic.

"Not Catholic or Protestant?" Frau Huber asked again.

"I believe in a God, but I simply don't know which faith he favours."

It was a clever answer, thought Christian, although Frau Huber did not think that cleverness was the most attractive quality in a woman.

"And don't you like my breakfast?" said Frau Huber, looking at the half-empty plate.

"It's lovely," said Claire. "It's just that I'm not hungry."

"Frau Huber makes the most marvellous stew and dumplings," said Christian.

"Does she? I must try them one evening."

13

— · —

23 NOVEMBER 1936

Frau Huber stood with her arms crossed in the kitchen, peering through the half-opened dining room door. Christian did not need to be sighted to know that as he and Claire ate, they were being observed and, as he swallowed each mouthful of stew, he made the appropriate noises of satisfaction for his audience. However, there is also a universal truth that even the lightest dumplings are, by their very nature, a little stodgy and, by the time you finish your second dumpling, the constitution of an ox is required. It does not help when your guest surreptitiously places the occasional quarter of a dumpling onto your plate as she refills your water glass.

"Finished," said Claire, and then added, "that was delicious."

"Have you?" said Christian, who despite eating non-stop still a had a potato, a piece of meat and, surprisingly, half a dumpling on his plate. "Should I ask Frau Huber to serve you seconds?"

"You dare," whispered Claire. "I'm about to pop."

"You're not going to manage strudel then, are you?"

"Is there more?" She leant closer to Christian and quietly said, "If I ate like this every day I would need to buy a new wardrobe every month."

Christian swallowed the final piece of dumpling and called for Frau Huber, thanked her, and said that he and Claire had decided to go to the Christmas market at the Schönbrunn Palace and they would come back later for a plate of strudel and that she ought to get herself home.

"Do you mind," he asked Claire, as he heard Frau Huber in the kitchen washing the dishes, "taking a walk around the Christmas market?"

***

As they stepped out of the taxi, the aroma of mulled wine was unmistakable with a hint of cloves, cinnamon, nutmeg, ginger and anise. Mixed into the heady aroma was the smell of roasting chestnuts and sweet desserts. It was the smell of Christmas. They slowly ambled towards the palace through the crowds and Christian could hear the tinkling of glass baubles surrounding him.

"Shall we get something to drink?" he suggested, "and then you can tell me everything there is to see."

Wrapped up in coats, scarves, and hats, or to be precise, a large brown fedora and a silver fox fur pillbox hat, a style once favoured by a hundred tsarinas, they appeared as any other well-to-do couple. She was animated, pointing out the candle makers, glass blowers, wood carvers, metal workers, potters, needleworkers, and an assortment of other artists and artisans. He was attentive, asking questions. Their only difference from a hundred other couples was his white cane and dark glasses. She enthusiastically described what she saw, and he listened with an attentive nod and a ready laugh. She told him that she was having an audition for a new musical, and he asked about it, saying he was sure she would get the part. However, he could sense that she did not want to talk about this.

"Is anything the matter?"

"Nothing," she said. "Paul is touring the Netherlands over Christmas and the New Year and asked me to join him. I said yes, although I have reservations. There is nothing worse than having Christmas out of a suitcase."

"You don't have to go," said Christian.

"I'm currently a singer without a job and I need to pay rent. I appreciate what Paul is doing for me. He didn't have to help me."

As they stood at a stall that served apples dipped into a sickly-smelling, red mixture of candy, Christian heard his name being called and turned his head.

"Is that you, Rachel?" shouted Christian, but he already knew the answer.

"Who?" said Claire.

"Rachel Kraus. I'll introduce you," said Christian, as Rachel approached, breathing hard in the cold evening.

As Christian made the introduction, the two women stood appraising each other. To the casual observer, they seemed as if they could be sisters with Claire being a year or two older. They were the same height and build. The three of them made their way out of the crowds to a little café on the edge of the market. They made small talk as they sipped from large mugs of hot chocolate, covered with whipped cream and topped with cinnamon. The noise of the market captured Christian's attention as families walked by with shrieking children, who wanted to play around the Christmas tree. He thought of his brother's children and smiled. Christmas carols were being sung somewhere nearby, and those who had had a third glass of mulled wine would join in, unaware that every note they sang was out of tune. He found himself humming along to *Stille Nacht, Heilige Nacht* and then *O Tannenbaum.*

The following week was a mixture of telephone calls and taxis, hot chocolate and strudel. At times, he wondered why these two women even asked him along, as once they started talking, he was surplus to requirements. While they looked like each other their interests were very different. Rachel loved the arts and talked about ballet and literature. Claire loved musical theatre, jazz and what she called dime-store novels. Claire spoke of growing up with her two older sisters. Rachel told her about her great-grandfather and how he had come from Germany and started a bakery in Leopoldstadt over seventy-five years ago, and how some of her family had gone to England and others to America. Rachel also talked about her younger brother, Jakob, who was studying literature at the university and who wanted to be a teacher despite her father wanting him to be a baker and take over his business. After a week, the owner of the café at the Christmas market would address them by name, Herr Christian, Fräulein Claire and Fräulein Rachel. They spoke in English, and then, two weeks before Christmas, Claire went on tour with Paul, and the afternoons and evenings at the Christmas market ended.

14

7 December 1936

Across the Danube and away from the hubbub of Vienna, Donaustadt was a developing suburb, and Rachel's father had built a villa there fifteen years earlier after he opened his second bakery. It was just forty minutes into Leopoldstadt on the bus and even quicker for Jakob Kraus who had a bike and didn't mind breaking a sweat. For Abe Kraus, who had a car, it took no time at all.

"You can't expect Jakob to help, he's a boy," said Rachel's mother, as she sat in the kitchen.

"You've spoilt him," said Rachel, pulling open the cutlery drawer with a little more vigour than she intended.

"He's in his final year," responded Rachel's mother, "it's important that he studies." However, from the sound of the gramophone, it was clear that Jakob's mind was elsewhere.

"He'll eat his meal and then go back into town for the night," said Rachel.

"He's young."

"He's irresponsible."

"I've noticed you complain about everything your brother does, Rachel. You won't find a husband by being like that."

Rachel choked back a reply. Her mother always came back to that topic, a husband, especially now she would not be touring with the ballet company. In previous years she had always toured with the Vienna State Ballet Company but this year they were going to Munich and Berlin and there was no place for a Jewish dancer. Everyone in the troupe had wrung their hands but, "What could be done?" said the director of the ballet company. Rachel had thought of joining a smaller dance company and had even gone to Stella Kadmon's show at the little cabaret theatre Der liebe Augustin, but she could not imagine herself gyrating every night to Latin rhythms in little more than patchwork of tassels. More importantly, she could not imagine what her father would say if he ever found out.

However, was the idea of finding a husband so absurd? Rachel knew many men, but her parents would never countenance anyone for a husband but a Jewish man. Most of the men she knew in Leopold-stadt were conservative and would expect her to stay at home and raise children once she had married. However, the idea of giving up her independence did not fill her with joy, and she knew that if she carried on dancing there would always be the whispers and the tutting of old women at the markets and around the synagogue. Her husband would be accused of not being able to provide for his wife. Her children, if she had any, would be pitied for not having a mother to bring them up. But then how long did she have left as a dancer? Four maybe five years at best and then what would she do?

"You're daydreaming," said her mother.

"Sorry," said Rachel. However, she struggled to focus on preparing the meal. She had rarely been without work for the last five years and now she had nothing to do until the ballet company's tour of Germany was over. The last two weeks she had met Claire most evenings at the Christmas market, but Claire was now away for a month. Rachel liked her, as she seemed so hopeful about her future. "My next big break will come along sooner or later," Claire had said to Rachel. "Christian says these things are like buses, you wait forever for one and then two come along at the same time." Rachel admired her resilience, singing in little cabaret clubs, night after night.

"And what do you wear?" asked Rachel. "I once went into Der liebe Augustin to see Stella Kadmon's show, and I came out five minutes later with my cheeks blushing as red as a London bus."

"I usually wear a gold sequinned dress," said Claire, "and long gloves. It's more a Marlene Dietrich look than Mata Hari."

Rachel dropped four eggs into the boiling water and then continued to chop the chicken livers. She hadn't yet asked Claire about her relationship with Christian. She had assumed, when she first met them, that they were together as they were arm in arm. However, nothing she said in the following weeks suggested that he was any more than a friend. She didn't kiss him goodnight or flirt with him. He, as always, played the part of the perfect gentlemen, making sure she had everything she could want and was attentive, respectful and kind. He would sit next to both, listening without the need to speak or be the centre of attention. However, it was the way he listened to her; the way he hung on her every syllable. If Rachel did not know how Claire thought about Christian, she was certain how he felt; and with that realisation came a small pang of jealousy.

"You know I have no patience for cooking," Rachel mumbled to her mother, as the chicken livers stuck to the pan.

"I know," said her mother, "but it hurts when I stand for too long, and the doctor says I should stay off my feet. But what do doctors know?"

Rachel looked at the clock on the wall. Her father would be home any minute and would expect his meal on the table.

"You know, Papa is doing well and perhaps we could afford a cook to help us?" suggested Rachel.

"Papa might be doing well," said Rachel's mother, "but you know what he will say. Why do I need a cook when I have a wife and a daughter at home all day?"

"But..."

"That's just the way it goes, Rachel."

"We could afford it at a pinch. I know Papa has been renovating our old apartment in Leopoldstadt for Jakob, but can't he find a little something to make our lives easier?"

"Your father will just say, find yourself a rich husband."

"And then he'll say," Rachel added, "with money in my pocket, I am wise and handsome, and I sing well too."

15

25 December 1936

Every city possesses its own character, but for those who navigate the world without sight, these differences become fundamental to existence itself. This truth struck Christian with unexpected force when he returned to Austria after the war. In the darkness of his existence, he had assumed Vienna would be much like London, one city of shadows resembling another. He couldn't have been more wrong.

The church bells alone had revealed his mistake. Where London's bells had boomed with deep, resonant authority, Vienna's rang out in bright, crystalline notes, more glockenspiel than bass. The air itself also told a different story. The scents rising from the city's cafés, bakeries and shops possessed a richness, a vibrancy that his time in England had never prepared him for. As his cane tapped its steady rhythm along the pavements, navigating the market-lined streets, new and distinct aromas were everywhere: cinnamon's sweet warmth, the earthy tang of tanned leather, chocolate melting in copper pots. They were smells so vivid they blurred the line between scent and taste. But gradually, the foreign became familiar. The extraordinary differences that had once caught his attention settled into the rhythm of daily life, transforming from novelties into the unremarkable texture of home.

Christian was quiet and uncomfortable sitting on the calf leather seats of the Rolls Royce, as it made its way out of the Inner Stadt to the city's outskirts. It had been sent by his mother to take him to a villa she had rented for the Christmas holidays. Everything had a strange familiarity. The smell of saddle soap on the leather reminded him of his life in England, long past. The chauffeur, George Poley, who drove, had been with his family since they were boys. They had fought together in the Great War, and it had been George who had been there on the Somme and pulled him out of no-man's-land. These were memories that Christian had spent twenty years trying to forget. However, the silence was awkward, like a discarded lover.

"How is her ladyship, George?" Christian called out over the noise of the vehicle.

"Her Ladyship is perfectly well," said George, as if any other response would be unheard of.

"And is she enjoying Vienna?"

"She is looking forward to seeing you, Sir." Christian paused for the briefest of moments before responding.

"George, you don't have to call me sir when we're alone."

"Yes, Sir," replied George.

Christian smiled to himself. It did not matter that George had saved his life and that the debt Christian owed him could never be repaid, George, like his father before him, would never be able to call him by his first name. It would blur the distinction in their relationship and make his position impossible.

"I was sorry to hear about the death of your father," Christian said.

"Thank you, Sir," responded George without the slightest hint of emotion.

"I have fond memories of him."

The car soon arrived at the villa which had three-metre iron gates and walls to surround it as a symbol of wealth and status. George got out of the vehicle and pushed open the rusting heavy gates which grated loudly. Christian could hear George making a disapproving noise, as if the lack of maintenance to the property was something that he took personally. George got back into the car and drove up to the front door and, as soon as he had applied the handbrake, got out again to open the door for Christian.

"I wonder if I might trouble you to help me to the front door?" asked Christian, however, George knew it was not a question and was already putting his hand underneath Christian's elbow to assist him.

"The pleasure is mine, Sir," said George, as they got to the front door.

"George, I know I have said it before but thank you."

"There really is no need, Sir."

Lady Frances had not visited Vienna for nearly twenty-five years and had some trepidation in coming. She feared that she would not be able to forgive the Austrians for the death of her eldest son Adrian in the war and the injuries caused to Christian. The war had broken her family. However, she had not seen Christian for over five years, and therefore she made the effort to go. When Christian was brought into the living room, they exchanged greetings and wished each other a Merry Christmas

"Will I ever convince you to come home to England?" asked Lady Frances

"I doubt it," said Christian. There was a musky smell that permeated the property as he sat in the living room, the villa having stood empty for many months before Lady Frances' arrival.

Lady Frances appraised her son. His charcoal suit was immaculately pressed, as was his shirt, and his shoes were polished. Someone was looking after him, and for that she felt a breath of happiness.

"You're looking well, I will concede that."

"I am well," said Christian.

"But are you happy?" asked Lady Frances. "I was happy with your father when we were all together at Wadhurst Hall before the war." She paused. "You know, I never wanted to leave there, not even for the glitz of London. I remember people coming down to visit and thinking I was terribly dull."

"I'm afraid that I have booked us a score of things to do in the next month," said Christian. "I hope you can manage some recitals, museums and a few evenings dining out."

"As long," said Lady Frances, "as we have time together and you tell me everything that has happened to you."

"And you tell me about yourself and Basil, Celia, Robert and the twins."

"I'll tell you over lunch."

Lady Frances cooks had prepared the same Christmas lunch that she would have eaten in England. Smoked salmon was followed by roast goose, with a stuffing of pork and pistachio nuts, and the oblig-atory Christmas pudding with cream. Except for the goose, nothing resembled an Austrian Christmas dinner. Christian had brought a box of cream-filled pastry rolls that had been prepared by Frau Huber. Lady Frances had courteously thanked him when she was given them and sent them directly to the kitchen for the servants to eat.

"So, how is Basil and his family?" asked Christian.

"Where to start?" said Lady Frances. "The twins are seven and look like their mother with her auburn-coloured hair, which is fine for Catherine but will result in Howard being bullied at school. Catherine is just like her mother, headstrong and determined, and Howard is a mixture of both. He's as clever as Basil but doesn't like working too hard. Catherine can twist Basil around her little finger."

"And Basil?"

"He expected he would become a King's Counsel, and he hasn't, and that I think has knocked some of the wind out of his sails. That reminds me," said Lady Frances, "that there was something I needed to talk to you about. I have been advised by my lawyers that to avoid death duties it would be prudent to make a gift of some of the monies I have to you and Basil."

"It's really not necessary," said Christian.

"It's my decision," said Lady Frances. "Your bank account will be credited with one hundred thousand pounds on the last day of this year."

"Thank you, Mother, but I don't need it."

"Now, what were we talking about? Oh yes, Basil. The children adore him, and there's a bond between him and Robert that seems to have grown over the years."

"And what's Robert doing now?"

"He's at Edinburgh University doing an engineering course. We don't see him often, which is a shame, because he is such a nice young man, and he can fix anything."

"And Celia?"

"She's still working at Dr Barnardo's. I sometimes lose patience with her as she spends so much of her time with orphaned children and seems to forget her own and her husband. She is always in an aeroplane and, when she's not abroad, she's at meetings. Basil had to employ more help to look after the twins. I thought I would have a quiet word the last time I saw her..."

"You didn't?" said Christian, slightly horrified at how that would have turned out.

"It was just a quiet word, woman to woman," said Lady Frances. "However, when she told me what some of these children went through and the conditions they had to live in, you do have to admire what she's doing."

"So, you said nothing?"

"Almost nothing," said Lady Frances, and shrugged her shoulders, "and at least she's doing something worthwhile and not gadding around like so many young women today. If I thought that were the case, I'd have given her a piece of my mind."

16

—·—

12 JANUARY 1937

They went to the Vienna Opera House on the evening before Lady Frances was to return to England. Tomas secured a box for four of them and Christian invited Claire, who had returned from the Netherlands. Tomas played the part of host and escort to Lady Frances, making amusing observations about Austrian and Germanic operas. As they entered the foyer, he pointed out the frescos, including those of the Magic Flute on the veranda.

"Do you and Christian come for the season?" asked Lady Frances.

"Goodness, no!" said Tomas, astounded by such a question. "We're a terribly low-brow pair, I'm afraid." Tomas paused and then added quietly, "They perform Wagner and Strauss incessantly here, which seems like an everlasting trip into Valhalla; although you can't say that too loudly now, as the fascists seem to like that bombastic din."

"Did you know," said Lady Frances, who leant closer to Tomas, "that in England we have a Public Order Act which makes it illegal to wear political uniforms and has stopped political marches? The government took one look at that odious little aristocrat Oswald Mosley and his black shirts and said, 'Not in our country.'"

"I have always said," replied Tomas, "that the English are such a sensible nation. You see fascists and you stop them going out of doors."

"And tell me about the young lady that Christian is with."

"Claire Astor," said Tomas, "is a singer of chansons."

"A singer?" Lady Frances frowned, turned her head and looked down the staircase where Christian and Claire were following. "She's attractive, I'll give her that. Most of the men are looking to see who she's with."

"She's just returned from singing with a friend of mine, Paul O'Montis, and is still looking for her big break."

"But what is she like?"

"Forthright and independent," said Tomas, "although, she rarely talks about her past. I was told her mother died in a car accident when she was a child, and her father killed himself during the Depression. She was left with no money and has worked ever since." Lady Frances cast another glance towards Claire, this time a less disapproving one.

The opera went on for two and a half hours with a story about the relationship of a blacksmith and a landowner's daughter, and the devil and a pair of golden shoes. There were moments when Christian felt he would fall asleep and other moments where Rimsky-Korsakov's score soared, although, when he left the opera house, there was not one tune he could recall.

"I've taken the liberty of booking a table for supper," said Tomas, as Lady Frances approached the Rolls-Royce that was waiting for them, "but I'm afraid it will be pork or Wiener schnitzel, although it's the best in Vienna."

"I think I shall like that," said Lady Frances, "and it will give me time to get to know Claire."

Claire smiled. "I would like that as well, and," she added, noting a choker around Lady Frances's neck, "your ladyship's necklace is beautiful."

Lady Frances' hand went up to the strings of pearls, with gold, diamonds and a sapphire in the centre. "A gift from my late husband."

The Figlmüller restaurant had opened thirty years ago and was thought by many Viennese to be the place to eat schnitzel. It was unpretentious with its wooden window frames and stone frontage. Inside, it resembled a bierkeller, built of brick with buttressed arches and large chandeliers. The tables were wooden and bare, and the chairs were unpadded and utilitarian. Waiters in black bow ties and waist-coats hurried between tables, taking plates covered with thin, crisp schnitzels and side dishes of potato or green salad. It was noisy, even by Austrian standards.

Lady Frances was not what Claire had expected. She did not have that reserved, stuffiness which the English aristocracy was known for, nor was she condescending. When she had spoken to her chauffeur outside the opera house, she appeared interested in what he had to say, and she did not put on any airs or graces with the waiters. She tried her best to speak German when asking for something and laughed at herself when the limits of her knowledge overtook her. However, Claire also had the impression that in another setting, her manners and her etiquette would be flawless, as if she had grown up around royalty.

"Tomas tells me you're a singer," said Lady Frances.

"Yes, your ladyship."

"Please, don't call me your ladyship. I am Frances to my friends and Lady Frances to acquaintances, and, as I hope we shall be friends, please call me Frances."

"Of course," said Claire.

"Do tell me, how did you end up here, singing with Paul O'Montis? That must be a story."

"He saw me in a show in New York," said Claire.

"But why come here?" asked Lady Frances.

"Well... I guess I was running away," Claire said quietly. "After my dad died and we lost the house, I came to New York thinking I could start over, maybe even make a name for myself. But the truth is, I was scraping by. Cities like Vienna, Paris, London sounded glamorous, and I think that is what I wanted. My sisters were off living their own lives in different states, starting families. And me? I didn't have much reason to stay. So, when the opportunity came, I jumped at it."

"Any regrets?"

"Plenty," Claire said, with a small shrug. "But what's the point in complaining? For a while, I thought things were really starting to take off. I was singing with Richard Tauber and for me it felt like a big break. But now I'm right back where I started, doing the same old routine. But sitting around feeling sorry for myself ain't goin' to change anything. Nobody ever got anywhere that way."

"I envy your gift," said Lady Frances. "I was never musical and my singing voice... well let's not speak of that." The two women laughed, and Lady Frances added, "How long have you known Christian?"

"Just a couple of years."

"And are you close friends?"

Christ! thought Christian, as he listened to his mother manipulating the conversation, thank God she's going back tomorrow, she's worse than Frau Huber. But he knew he would miss her and that her heart was in the right place.

"I'd like to think so," Claire said, a discreet smile playing at the corner of her mouth. "He's been good to me, real good. Always there when I need someone."

She glanced over at Christian and noticed that he was blushing.

17

1 April 1937

Schmidt parked his new Steyr 125S cabriolet in front of the police station. It was an exclusive two-tone blue and cream edition, with the headlamps set on top of the front wheel arches. It was a car that turned heads, and, as a *Chefinspektor,* he wanted people to know who he was. As he entered the police station, he said good morning to the two officers at the front desk, walked along the corridor and up the stairs to his office on the first floor. His secretary had a coffee waiting for him as he sat down, and he immediately went through his correspondence before turning his attention to the reports and charge sheets that had been issued the night before.

"Is Sergeant Brun here?" he called out to his secretary. Schmidt could hear her phoning down to the officer's room before confirming that he was in. "Tell him to come up."

A few minutes later, Sergeant Brun lumbered up the stairs and into Schmidt's office. He was out of breath when he arrived and started to sweat.

"You issued a report," said Schmidt, "about someone painting the word 'Jude' on a shop window."

"It was Manny Adler's, the tailor behind the synagogue. He came in and complained. He said it was a group of kids and that he would be able to recognise them if he saw them again."

"Ignore it," said Schmidt. "And, if he complains again, make him wash off every bit of graffiti from the street market."

Sergeant Brun shrugged. He wasn't going to argue with Schmidt, although Manny Adler had never done anyone any harm.

"However, that's not the reason I wanted to speak to you. There was an article in the newspapers this morning." Schmidt took out a copy of the newspaper from his briefcase and put it in front of Sergeant Brun. "It's about Italy's Minister of Foreign Affairs, Count Ciano."

Sergeant Brun peered at the paper. He hadn't read the article and had no idea why Schmidt was showing it to him. His stomach rumbled as he thought about his coffee, which was downstairs getting cold, and his potato and bacon fry-up.

"Italy says that the joining of Austria and Germany is inevitable," continued Schmidt, oblivious to the mystified look on his sergeant's face, "and that Britain and France will do nothing about it. When the *Anschluss* happens," said Schmidt slowly, as if he were explaining it to a child, "and we become part of the Greater German Reich, then German laws will apply here and we will finally be required to rid ourselves of the communists, the asocials, the Jews, and the homosexuals."

"Yes, sir," said Sergeant Brun, baffled as to why he needed to be told this.

"There's a Jew that is of interest to me called Otto Friedmann. He's sits as a magistrate for the Law Society and works at Karl Vogel Rechtsanwälte. I want a file opened on him and I want to know what he's doing."

18

— · —

2 APRIL 1937

The picturesque town of St Gilgen lies on the Wolfgangsee, a large lake near Salzburg. It was named after St Giles, the patron saint of the physically disabled, who absolved the emperor Charlemagne of an unspeakable sin that could not be confessed. When Christian bought his villa, he recounted the story of St Giles to Tomas, who asked what sin could be so unspeakable. Christian said that no one knew except God, but in Charlemagne's court they whispered that the emperor had slept with his sister, Gisela, who gave birth to Roland, the knight who sought the Holy Grail. Tomas laughed and said that if St Giles could arrange for any sin to be forgiven, it would be the perfect place for him and Paul.

The town of St Gilgen is surrounded by the mountains and foothills of the Alps, which run down to the lake's edge. In early April, if the winter season persists, it is possible to ski, but that year, the beautiful green valley saw multitudes of flowers blooming, and the air was full of scent.

"What made you choose this place?" Claire asked, shouting over the noise of the car engine. It seemed to her that the valley and the small town far below were picture postcard perfect, but she had no idea why a blind man chose one place over another.

"It has everything I need," said Christian. "I'm far enough out of the town not to be disturbed but close enough to walk in along the Pilgrim's Path. The grounds of the villa go down to the water's edge, and you feel as if you're in another world. Just wait until we get there."

Claire continued to drive down the mountain road with St Gilgen below her.

"Had you been to St Gilgen when you lived here before the war?"

"No," said Christian. "Just over five years ago, I spoke to Tomas about finding somewhere for the summer and he told me about the many beautiful towns in this area. I had just received an inheritance and discussed the idea of buying a villa with my lawyer, Herr Friedmann, who knew the area well. We came to Hallstatt, Bad Ischl and here. I told him I wanted a villa on the lake where I could swim, and he found me the one I bought. It's a few hundred yards up a little dirt road next to the railway station."

"But why here?"

"Because people still live here all year. Normally, I don't come in winter, although Tomas borrows it when he wants to get away from everything. I hope that one day my brother and his children will spend a summer with me here. There are restaurants nearby, and a little beach on the lake that many families go to."

"Can I ask something else?" said Claire, as she turned off the main road and drove down a narrow, unmade lane.

"Of course," said Christian.

"When you go swimming in the lake, how do you know where you are?"

"I have a small area of the lake roped off," replied Christian, "so that whenever I touch the rope, I know I can follow it back to the shore, like Ariadne's thread."

Claire slowed the car as she went up an unmade path and then she turned into an opening and stopped the car in front of a beautiful stone villa with wooden bay windows and balconies of dark wood. They climbed the six steps to the front door and Christian pushed it open and shouted to Frau Huber that they had arrived. The villa was spotless, the shutters were open, and the rooms were aired. In the main living room, a fire had been lit for them. It smelt of oiled wood and books. Frau Huber was in the kitchen commanding a cook and a maid as to how things should be done. The maid took their cases to their rooms, and drinks were served in the living room. The evening sun was on the horizon, and Christian suggested that they sit in the bay window with its lead mullions so Claire could watch the sunset behind the lake. She wrapped her legs under a blanket as the evening air was cold.

"Thanks for bringing me," she said, gazing out of the window at a reflection of the yellow and orange sky on the lake. A few sailing boats tied to buoys sat motionless, and the undulating mountains in the distance were as black as coal.

"It reminds me of a place I went to with my parents when I was very young," she said, her mind somewhere else.

"You went to the mountains?"

"No," said Claire. "It was the ocean, but it's that feeling of peace you get when you're next to water. That's what I mean." she shook her head slightly, as if there were memories she did not want to disturb and then changed the subject. "Did I tell you that Paul's latest record will be his goodbye song?"

"Tomas didn't say anything about Paul giving up singing," replied Christian.

"No, Paul's not giving up; he couldn't, he lives for the spotlight. It's his goodbye record to Vienna."

"When will Paul leave?" Christian knew that sooner or later this day would come. He had thought he would have been more shocked by the news, but it felt like hearing about an aging relative who passes away after they have been ill for some time.

"I don't really know... but soon, I think. I told Paul I'm done running all over Europe like a refugee. I guess I'll have to find something more permanent, though maybe going back home to America is the only real option left."

"Something will turn up," said Christian, confidently. "Something always does. And Tomas? Did Paul say anything about him?"

"Nothing," answered Claire. "Hasn't Tomas spoken to you?" She paused a moment and looked a Christian who had lowered his head. "I assume he'll go with Paul," she added. "However badly Paul behaves, he does love Tomas, and I don't think either could survive without the other."

***

The next morning, after breakfast, they walked to town. Christian wore an Aran jumper and tweed jacket, which marked him out as a foreigner. Claire also wore a knitted jumper and a thick wool skirt. They ambled along a gravel path with a wooden fence at the edge of the lake, Christian's white cane flicking from side to side in front of them. A gentle breeze blew ripples on the otherwise still waters. The long branches of overhanging trees dropped down to the lake's edge, creating at times a covered walkway. Claire put her arm in his for the ten-minute walk to the village, and, as they entered the main street, she could see the domed church of St Gilgen, where Mozart's grandparents had been married. They found a coffee shop and sat there for most of the morning, talking about Tomas and Paul and what she would do.

"I remember when Tomas first met Paul," said Christian. "It was in Berlin in November 1931. I recall the date because my father had died that month, and I had to go back to England."

"I'm sorry," said Claire.

"Paul was very much the rage in Berlin at the time, and his records and shows were popular. Tomas had gone there thinking to open a gallery, and they met. A trip that was supposed to last a few weeks turned into a few months. Tomas then spent half his time in Berlin and half his time in Vienna, and Paul would come to Vienna whenever he was not performing. Everything was going well until the Nazis came to power."

"He rarely talks about what happened," said Claire.

"Berlin was changing. People were becoming tired of the cabaret singers openly mocking everything. I think it was in October 1933 that Paul appeared at the La Scala Festival in Germany, where Goebbels saw him. It wasn't the songs; it was the political satire and the mocking of Hitler that they would not permit. Can you picture Paul with a small black moustache, a swastika armband on his dinner suit jacket, and a pair of tights on, openly putting his hand in his underpants, looking down quizzically and shouting 'one ball?' Goebbels issued a warrant for his arrest a few days later and Paul landed in prison. He appealed the sentence and fled. Tomas has been trying to reinvigorate Paul's career ever since."

"He still does that skit in his shows on occasion," laughed Claire.

"He will always do it," said Christian. "It's Paul's way of sticking two fingers up at Hitler and fascism."

"Do you know where he got the idea for it?" asked Claire.

"From a street singer."

***

It was another evening where Claire confided in Christian, who listened without judging. She told him about how she struggled after her father died, working at two jobs to make ends meet. She told him how she resented her father for killing himself and how she felt betrayed by the person she trusted the most. She had hoped that Vienna would be a fresh start, and that she would be able to forget and forgive but the memories and the pain still lingered.

"After my mother died," Claire said, "I took care of him for five years. My older sisters were married, off living their own lives in other states. When my father lost his business during the Depression, I was the one who found work at a department store. I'd come home every night, cook, clean, try to keep things together. We were barely scraping by."

Christian could hear in her voice just the slightest tone of bitterness. She paused and looked out onto the lake.

"Then one day I came home, and he'd shot himself. I was twenty-two. No note, no explanation."

"I can't imagine how much that must have hurt you," said Christian.

"When the closest people can do that to you," said Claire, "you become a little more wary of everyone." She turned in her seat and reached across the coffee table for her glass of wine. She took a gulp. "I suppose that why I'm still alone. D'you know, I meet hundreds of men in the clubs where I sing and they're all the same. The rich ones think that a few schillings entitles them to whatever they want. As if I'm supposed to be grateful. And the younger ones, well they're just boys really, hang around the stage door night after night, whistling, shouting that they'll die of a broken heart if I don't smile at them."

She shook her head and laughed bitterly.

"They haven't the faintest idea," she continued. "But you... you're not like them. I feel at ease when I'm with you. Like we understand each other. You listen as if I'm the only one in the room."

She leant over and kissed him lightly on the cheek, then pulled back, almost shyly.

"Sorry," she murmured. "I was just remembering that evening you showed me the Klimt painting you have and those beautiful pictures you'd done yourself." She sniffed and brushed a hand under her nose. "I don't know why I'm sitting here going on about my life... when you've been through far worse."

As they spoke over dinner, Christian considered saying how he felt about her, but he sensed it was the wrong time and did not want to come across as one of those men she had to deal with at her club.

"Sometimes, you remind me of my father," she said, as she sipped at a glass of wine. "In a good way, I mean," she added, putting down her glass.

"In what way?" asked Christian.

"You're dependable, honest and kind. My father was like that for most of my life until my mother died and then he lost his way. I sometimes blame myself for not seeing it or sensing the pain he was suffering."

Claire took another mouthful of stew.

"I was just thinking how wonderful these dumplings were," she said loudly enough for Frau Huber to hear in the next room.

"Just the right tone," said Christian in a whisper and they both laughed.

"Could you ask her to cook something less stodgy?" muttered Claire conspiratorially.

"I've walked across no-man's-land," said Christian, "and I'd do it again, but I won't under any circumstances come between Frau Huber and her dumplings. No one is that brave or stupid."

She giggled.

"I'll ask," he whispered.

Frau Huber knocked on the door, entered and inquired whether they had finished. Christian said that they had and that they would take coffee and dessert in the living room beside the fire.

"And please don't stay up for us," he added, "we'll do the dishes."

It was just those last four words that Christian said that brought a hundred memories of Claire's home in America flooding back. It was what her father would say after dinner every evening when she was growing up. Her father, her two sisters, and Claire would go to the kitchen to do the dishes. It was just a small household chore that her father insisted that they do because when you do the dishes, there are no secrets, as one plate is scraped, washed and then passed to another person who dries it, while another person puts it away. All the stories of a family are told when you do the dishes. Every boyfriend you've ever kissed is discussed, as is every heartbreak. Every hope and dream is laid before the family. For a moment she wanted to kiss him, but he was so reserved, and she felt he might be embarrassed.

19

—·—

4 APRIL 1937

Claire lightly knocked on Christian's door. There was no answer, and she knocked again a little harder. Again, there was no answer, and she pushed the door ajar and looked in. Frau Huber was sitting on the side of the bed, in her dressing gown with a lamp on the bedside table. It was the first time she had seen Christian without his glasses and his one eyeless socket looked, in the shadows of the flickering lamp, like a pock-marked crater on the moon. Frau Huber turned her head and looked towards the door and shook her head firmly, indicating she ought not to come in.

Claire waited apprehensively outside until Frau Huber came out a few minutes later.

"He's sleeping now," Frau Huber said.

"I heard screaming," Claire responded, pulling her dressing gown around her.

"He sometimes has nightmares. He's had them for as long as I've known him."

"What about?"

"The war," said Frau Huber. "My son used to have the same type of dream when he came back from the front. It's the thing that they won't talk about, not to anyone who hasn't been there." For a moment, in the gaslit shadows, Claire thought Frau Huber's face softened, and then she said bluntly, "Go back to bed, Fräulein Astor, Herr Christian will be fine in the morning."

Claire went back to her room, but sleep didn't come easily. She revisited the whole weekend. For once, she thought, I let my guard down. I told him things I hadn't spoken about in years; my past, the parts I usually keep hidden away, even the quiet hopes I barely admit to myself. He had listened to her, interested in what she had to say. He always did, she thought, but when I wanted him to express his feelings in return, to talk about himself, about what he feels, he said almost nothing. It wasn't coldness... just distance. He remained careful, ordered, regimented like the life he leads, as if he was hiding something.

She knew instinctively that he felt something for her; but her eyelids weighed heavy in the early hours. He listened like it mattered, she thought, like what she was saying was important to him. That meant something... must mean something. But she had heard the stories about the men who came back from the Great War and never really came back at all. Who built walls so high around themselves, not even love could find its way in. When she pictured his face with the scars and missing eye, she knew that part of him was still stuck in 1916, somewhere in no-man's-land on the Somme. He was there among the relentless shelling, the bullets, blood, lice and rats and, as she fell asleep, Claire wondered whether she would ever be strong enough to rescue him from there... if anyone could.

***

Christian lay on his bed and lit a cigarette. He rarely smoked this early, but he was exhausted as if he had not slept at all. He could hear Claire as she came out of the bathroom, the flush of the cistern, and the bang of the bathroom door. Her bare feet pattered on the wooden floor, as she scampered back to her room. Frau Huber marched everywhere, and Tomas walked without a care in the world. He guessed that there would be the smell of talcum if he entered the bathroom, and things would be moved. Apart from Tomas, he hated having guests, as this required him to change his routine. He had to be careful when walking around the villa in case a chair had been moved or a cabinet door left open. But, he thought, she could be an exception. He liked too many things about her; he liked her vulnerability blanketed in warmth and her thoughtful observations. He liked the way she accepted him.

He wondered what he would say at breakfast. He remembered Frau Huber being with him and heard her talking to someone outside his door. He still, on occasion, dreamt about Rose, despite twenty years having passed since her death. He wondered how it could still hurt so much, and, if it was love, how he could explain that to another woman. Would any woman want him when he shared his bed with the ghost of a long-dead love or when he often hoped he would not wake?

"I'm sorry if I woke you," he said, as he walked into the dining room, one foot carefully in front of the other.

"Frau Huber said you were having a nightmare. I understand... I do."

Christian heard concern in her voice.

"Yes, a nightmare," he responded as he sat down, but said nothing more for a moment. He did not know how to talk about it, where to start or what to say. A stiff upper lip was what was expected and for a second, he wished he was alone, without the feelings of embarrassment.

"Would you like to tell me about them?" asked Claire, almost in a whisper.

"Not now, perhaps one day," he said, and hoped she would not continue the conversation.

"I understand," Claire replied. However, her voice was full of uncertainty and she turned away from him. He reached across the table, felt for the fruit bowl, took an apple and bit into it.

"Please don't pity me," he said and swallowed the piece of apple. He knew that pity was not something to build a relationship upon.

***

"Don't fuss," said Christian, as Frau Huber stood in front of him and did up one of the buttons on his jacket."

"It's no fuss," said Frau Huber, but she knew he wanted her to stop, and she dropped her arms. "Dinner will be something a little lighter, maybe some freshwater prawns and a little potato salad." She looked at Claire. "Something not so stodgy, that is the word, isn't it, *ja*?"

Claire's face reddened. Christian, however, seemed oblivious.

"Where are you walking to?" asked Frau Huber, as Christian picked up his cane.

"I thought we'd walk along the Pilgrim's Way to St Wolfgang and then lunch there before taking the boat back."

Frau Huber looked at Claire's shoes and smiled. Why do pretty women never wear sensible shoes, she thought.

The Pilgrim's Way is flat as it winds its way around the lake. However, after three kilometres, as you get to the monastery at Falkenstein, the road suddenly goes up. There is a man-made path, and, as you meander around the lake, there are beautiful vistas. Alpine plants grow on the hillsides and there are many wayside shrines where one can seek a blessing from a forgotten saint. They stopped at the Fürberg hotel, which had been an inn since 1708 and was known in the area for its coffee and pastries. Claire sat rubbing her foot under the table as Christian told her they had gone about a quarter of the way. The owner was telling them about the hotel, which sits on the edge of the lake in a small area of forest. In summer, the hidden bays are full of people who swim out into the refreshing waters. Boys, whose commonsense has yet to catch up with their years, dive into the lake from cliff edges. It is a place to relax where the years of the past melt away in the golden, vaporous atmosphere of heady evenings. It is a place where everyone becomes a child again, where the calm of the universe runs through every visitor like a spiritual breath.

Two mugs of steaming hot chocolate and a selection of pastries, for which they were justly famous, were placed in front of Christian and Claire.

"Here," said Claire, "feels like a different world."

Christian heard the heavy wooden door of the hotel squeak open, and a family entered. There were the voices of children: one, two, three, four, who ran directly towards a table in the corner and sat down. They knew the hotel as they discussed what they would have. One said hot chocolate with whipped cream and a pastry, although others preferred the apple strudel. The parents sat down after them, and within a minute the owner was over next to them, greeting them like long-missed relatives and taking their order.

"Would you excuse me?" said Christian. "I know the people who have just come in," and he stood up and walked with his stick towards their voices.

A few minutes later the family were standing in front of Claire being introduced. Claire noted the man's broad smile and deep brown eyes that wrinkled in delight as he introduced himself. He reminded her of an uncle who was known to enjoy a practical joke. His wife was a little sterner, a little more formal. The couple were very different from each other. She had long blond hair that had been tied up, while his was now grey and thinning. She had an elegant face with a straight nose, while he looked a little like a vaudeville comedian, who could make any child laugh.

"Otto and Anna," said Otto Friedmann.

"And our four children, Aaron, Hanna, Frieda, and Rosa," added Anna.

"I invited them to join us, if you don't mind," said Christian, as the four children scraped chairs across the floor.

"We decided to come for a few days," said Christian, "as the weather was so pleasant."

"We did the same," said Otto, "as it's the Easter holidays."

When the proprietor arrived with the hot chocolates, pastries and strudel, Otto Friedmann introduced Christian to the proprietor, saying that he owned the villa just outside St Gilgen.

"I've not had the villa long," said Christian, "only a few years."

"Well, if you are friends of Herr Otto and Frau Anna," said the proprietor, "you're welcome." He looked at Claire. "And your wife's name?"

"Fräulein Claire Astor," said Christian, "but she's not my wife, just a friend."

They talked for an hour and a half until it was nearly lunchtime, and then they decided to have lunch together. After lunch, and a few glasses of wine, they found a piano in a corner and Christian played while Claire and the children sang. By the time they left, it was nearly four, and Claire suggested that they should wander back rather than go a step further on.

"To be honest," she said to Christian, "my feet are a little sore. I think I have a blister."

"Do you want Papa to look at it?" asked Rosa. "He went to medical school before he became a lawyer."

"I did a year at medical school," said Otto.

"It's just a blister," said Claire, "I think I'll live." However, Anna was already looking in her handbag for a plaster.

***

"They were adorable," said Claire, as she cut a prawn in half. "And the little one Rosa was so cute, you just wanted to pick her up and hug her. How old is she?"

"Seven, I think," said Christian. "I only met the children once before, three years ago. You were fabulous, singing all those songs with them."

"They wouldn't let me stop," said Claire. "Once you told them I was a singer."

"How many hours were we there?" asked Christian.

"Four or five. I think they were the nicest family I've ever met. When we were about to leave, Anna gave me her telephone number and said that when I next go shopping in Vienna, I had to call her."

20

7 MAY 1937

Frau Huber closed the newspaper, folded it with deep creases, and placed it firmly on the tabletop, saying, "That will show him that Austria cannot be pushed around." She stood up and let out a deep breath. Christian and Tomas were unsure whether she would add something further but she turned and went back to the kitchen, taking the breakfast plates with her, which were unceremoniously clattered into the sink. Tomas looked at Christian.

"So, Chancellor Schuschnigg is flexing his muscles. I didn't think he would have the backbone to raid the Nazi Party headquarters," said Tomas, "and then publish the documents."

"And what about you and Paul?" asked Christian. "Are you still planning to leave Vienna for Prague?"

"Yes, I don't think this makes a difference, but there is less urgency now. Other people we know are moving. Anton Kuh plans to move there this month."

"But why Prague?" asked Christian.

"They speak German there, so Paul can still perform."

"And what will you do with your studio?"

"I'll find someone to run it," said Tomas.

"And your apartment?"

"You are full of questions this morning," said Tomas.

"I'm sorry but you can't expect me not to have a dozen questions when my oldest friend tells me he is moving to a different country."

"What I have decided to do is rent my apartment as I'll need some money in Prague. I hope to be able to come to Vienna every month for a few days, if possible, and I was also hoping I could stay here, if that's not inconvenient?" Tomas stopped talking as Frau Huber came in and cleared the remainder of the breakfast dishes. She stood at the door with a tray full of plates, cruets, cups and saucers.

"There will always be a bed for you here, Herr Tomas," said Frau Huber, "unless Herr Christian gets married, but that's not likely if he doesn't ask someone."

Tomas stood up to go and said, "I'll see you this evening, around nine at the Yohan café."

***

Christian hadn't seen Claire for a month since St Gilgen and while much of the intermediate period was taken up with Tomas' forthcoming move to Prague, he felt remiss that he had not managed to meet up with her. However, on returning to Vienna he had spoken to an acquaintance who was putting on an American musical and mentioned that Claire might be perfect for the leading role. He had heard that she had got the part and that she was now practising night and day for the show's opening. He decided to telephone his mother, something he had not done for months, and picked up the receiver and told the operator he wanted to make a long-distance call.

"Good evening, Christian," said Lady Frances, once they had been connected.

"Hello, Mother."

"Is everything all right?" she asked. "It's just that you don't often call out of the blue."

"Everything's fine. It's just that I wanted some advice."

"You haven't wanted my advice since you were a child."

"You're not making this easy, Mother," said Christian.

"Making what easy, Christian? You haven't told me what you want."

"It's about Claire. You remember her, we went to the opera together when you were here at Christmas."

"I remember her well," said Lady Frances. "A beautiful and intelligent young lady."

"I've been wanting to ask her out."

"I thought that you had already done that."

"As friends," said Christian, "however, that's all."

"My darling," said Lady Frances, "that's everything. That's where you start and end."

"I'm not sure you understand me," said Christian. "What I mean is that we are fine as friends, but... well, you know."

"Christian, you're not listening. None of that is important. It may be important to you and how you feel about yourself, but if she likes you, it may not matter to her."

"But..."

"There are no *buts*, Christian. If you walk into a room believing in yourself, then others will also believe in you."

"But..."

"Be yourself, Christian, and the rest will follow, and I don't want to hear any more buts. So, goodnight and think about what I have told you. And by the way... I expect a telephone call a little more often than once every other month."

"But…" However, all that Christian could hear on the other end of the line was the dialling tone. He lifted the cover of his watch, felt the position of the hands and realised that he would be late for his evening with Tomas and Paul.

***

It was no good crying over spilt milk, or at least that is what Claire's father used to say to her. He hadn't called her, and she did not know why. She wondered whether she had inadvertently done something to upset him. Perhaps it was just his reserve, British men were impossible, she thought. However, she was certain that they had got on and even Frau Huber seemed more cordial to her, serving up a lighter dinner on the last night. They had sat drinking rich red Burgundies before an open fire that spat, smoked and crackled as the damp cedarwood dried. They had played whist and cribbage with braille playing cards. He seemed to retain so much in his brain, remembering numbers and scores. They had talked about politics, the arts and literature, and it surprised her how much he knew.

However, he came with baggage and not just the physical disabilities. There were the nightmares and that reserve that he had built around him, which created an impossible wall to surmount. She did not mind that his life was ordered or that he had a routine and liked everything in its exact place; she could cope with that. It was the emotional barrier, and his refusal to discuss it. Spending time with him, she had seen that whenever he felt unsure of himself, he would put his hand to the St Christopher that he wore around his neck. When she thought about him, she could hear her father's voice warning, "If you buy a dog with three legs, don't complain that it doesn't run fast."

She looked over at the wall clock and realised she had to get her skates on if she was to be at the theatre on time for another preview. She could not be late, as she had been cast in the leading role as Mimi Glossop in a new production of *Gay Divorce*. The leading man, who played Guy Holden, had what the newspapers called *Eleganz*. She wasn't sure whether it was her imagination, but when they kissed at the end of the musical, it seemed to last longer and longer the more times they practised.

After having some minor success on the stage in Germany, Reinhold Böhm decided to audition for the role of Guy Holden. His English was not particularly good, but, as the script had been translated into German, all he had to do was learn the English words to the songs. He was tall, had an easy-going attitude, and had a rich tenor voice; he could dance well, being thin and muscular. As the lead man, Reinhold was earning more money in Vienna than he had done in his life, and enjoyed the social scene that Vienna offered. He was popular with the chorus line and kept secret the fact that he had a wife and a toddler in a little village near Bremen.

Reinhold was not the type of man you brought home to your parents. Most fathers wished they had been like him when they were younger, and most mothers remembered someone like him who had broken their hearts. He wasn't the type of person that Claire would normally gravitate towards, but he was fun, charming and carefree, and Claire thought she needed that after having to deal with Christian's reserve and lack of emotion. After the preview, a group of twenty of them went to the Yohan café and took a table inside.

Tomas noticed them as they walked into the café. Reinhold had his arm around one girl from the chorus line and his other around Claire's waist. Claire held a cigarette, drawing gently on it as she wandered across the floor. She blew out the smoke, which coiled and twisted in the air like a wraith, and then she looked at Reinhold as they stood before their table. She pulled him close to her and kissed him passionately. The group shouted their approval, and then Claire looked at the girl from the chorus line and shook her head.

Reinhold ordered champagne. They were loud and in good spirits as they finished one bottle after another. Tomas knew no one at the table except for the producer of the show, who was looking pleased with himself. They had just received a review of a preview from earlier that week, and the musical had been given five stars and both Claire and Reinhold had been singled out for their faultless performances.

"I think we should move on," said Tomas, "perhaps to the Café Central?"

However, Paul was already tight and responded, "No, it's going to get livelier here, and the Café Central has become so dull. The last time I went there they didn't have a table."

"I'm thinking about going home soon," said Christian.

"Isn't that Claire?" said Paul. "Let's go over!"

"I'd prefer not to," said Tomas. Christian heard something in Tomas's tone of voice. It was said more as a command than a suggestion. Paul was about to ignore him and get up, but he stopped himself when he saw Claire kissing Reinhold.

"They do look a little preoccupied," Paul said, laughing.

Christian could hear the group chanting and asking for a song from the show, and Reinhold and Claire stood up. Reinhold's rich tenor seemed perfectly suited to singing a bluesy-jazzy song.

"Like the beat beat beat of the tom-tom
When the jungle shadows fall
Like the tick tick tock of the stately clock
As it stands against the wall
Like the drip drip drip of the raindrops

When the summer shower is through

So a voice within me keeps repeating you, you, you"

Claire joined in, and the two voices complemented each other. The Yohan café became silent as they continued singing, people realising that they were hearing something intimate, like two people sharing a secret.

"Night and day, you are the one

Only you beneath the moon and under the sun

Whether near to me, or far

It's no matter darling where you are

I think of you

Night and day..."

Christian started clapping before the song had ended, and then the café broke into thunderous applause. As it quietened, he said, with a thrill of excitement, "We must join them." Suddenly, there was another cheer, and he asked, "What's happening?"

"He kissed her again," said a waiter who was passing.

THE
FATEFUL
YEAR

—·—

21

19 February 1938

The newspapers love a scandal, and the revelation that Reinhold Böhm was married, and that the American actress and singer, Claire Astor, was the co-respondent in divorce proceedings, made headlines. The press took the high ground, claiming that the adulterous couple had brought shame to the institution of marriage, and published a photograph of Frau Böhm clasping her two-year-old child while standing at the door of her small cottage. They traded in hyperbole, focusing on the decadent lifestyle of the adulterous couple, the lavish parties, the wasteful indulgencies, the extravagant jewellery, the fast life; and the rot that was the Weimar Republic.

It came as a surprise to Claire that Reinhold was married. The first she knew about it was when a journalist stood on the threshold of their apartment, asking for a quote. She confronted him when he had returned from an afternoon at his club. Reinhold shrugged and said, "What difference does it make?" and poured himself a glass of schnapps. She had packed her bags and left before he poured the second.

In the week following the exposé of the affair, it was impossible to obtain a ticket to see *Gay Divorce*. People packed the theatre to see the couple acting as Mimi and Guy, falling in love with one another, even if the applause at the end of the show was muted. Then, one evening, as Mimi said that she expected to see Guy in her room at midnight, someone shouted, "Not if his wife's there." The audience erupted with laughter, and a week later the show closed.

Claire was philosophical about it, saying that another part would come along soon, but four months on she had found no other work but singing in bars. Her money was quickly running out. Her friends said that everything would be forgotten in a few more months, that this was Europe, where affairs were common and forgiven. As she sat one morning looking at the chipped paint on her toenails, there was a knock on the door.

Anna Friedmann looked at Claire in her silk dressing gown, with no make-up on and said, "It's eleven-thirty, Claire. Get dressed, put on your face, and I'll return in half an hour. We're going out."

Claire could hear the bells of St Ulrich strike twelve, as Anna helped her into a cab.

"Where are we going?" Claire asked.

"It's a surprise."

The taxi took them to the edge of the city centre and then onto the ring road, passing the Hofburg Palace, the Burggarten and the opera house.

"Are we going shopping?" asked Claire, as they headed into the heart of the city.

"No, we're not going shopping," said Anna, who sat admiring how Claire had transformed herself from looking like the morning's leftovers into a glamourous actress in less than half an hour. The taxi turned left, right, left and then right again, finally stopping in front of Vienna's finest restaurant, The Three Hussars.

"I thought we would have lunch," said Anna, as she handed a few coins to the taxi driver. The door to the restaurant opened, and the owner greeted them in person, telling them they were in the library.

The library was lined with bookshelves and large mirrors, lit with gaslights and decorated in warm colours. It was a room to be comfortable in, with armchairs upholstered in green velvet, starched wine linen on the tables, and perfectly cut crystal glasses. However, it was all the people standing in the room that surprised Claire; there was Rachel Kraus and her younger brother Jakob, Tomas and Paul, Otto and his children, Christian, as well as twenty other friends.

"Happy birthday," Anna said, and it was repeated by everyone.

The waiters in their striped waistcoats came in quickly and brought a selection of *hors d'oeuvres*. Titbits such as chicken in jelly, foie gras, tomato mousse, vegetable terrine, and smoked salmon were offered on blinis or dark rye bread. Corks popped as chilled Laurent Perrier was opened, and for those who did not drink, or were too young to do so, there was freshly squeezed orange and pressed apple juice.

"Whose idea was this?" asked Claire. Anna looked over towards Christian.

"His," she answered.

"How is he?" asked Claire.

"Go and find out," said Anna.

"I think I hurt him."

"Worse things have happened to him in his life."

"I'm not sure what to say to him."

"You'll think of something."

Christian had planned the party for a month after he had heard that Claire's fortunes had changed. It had been four months since her name had been plastered across the papers, and *Gay Divorce* closed. Christian had heard rumours that Claire had not yet found a new part.

It coincided with a growing disenchantment, with Austria's economy stumbling along, and people feeling poorer and tightening their belts. The theatres were emptying, and shops and restaurants had fewer customers. The Viennese wanted someone to blame, and fingers were pointed at the Jews, the communists, the Roma, the Sinti, as well as the British, French and Americans, who had imposed such severe reparations after the Great War.

Claire crossed the room and stood beside Christian. She laid a hand on his shoulder and leant in, pressing a gentle kiss to his cheek.

"I'm told I have you to thank for this," she murmured. "Thank you."

"My pleasure," said Christian. "We've missed having you around." Claire felt there was a touch of reproval in his voice, even if there was a grain of truth in what he said. She had ignored her friends and enjoyed the whirlwind romance with Reinhold, the parties and the lifestyle and then she had hidden away like a scolded child when everything had come crashing down. "Anyway," continued Christian, "have a glass of champagne as it's a tradition of mine to drink champagne on someone's birthday."

She took a glass from a waiter.

"Have you spoken to Paul and Tomas?"

"Not yet," said Claire.

"They came from Prague last night just to wish you a happy birthday," said Christian.

"How are they?"

"They're both well, although talking to Paul, you would think this party had been arranged in his honour. He doesn't change."

After lunch, they took a dozen taxis for the short drive to the Kursalon in the Stadtpark. One of the smaller rooms had been hired and a small orchestra was already waiting to play waltzes by Johann, Josef and Eduard Strauss. When the orchestra took a break, Paul persuaded the pianist to play his most famous tune, and he sang. Afterwards, he called for Claire to join him, but she smiled, shook her head and said, "Another day, darling."

At the end of the afternoon, as she looked at thirty of her friends laughing and dancing, she wondered what she would do next with her life. As the orchestra began to pack up, the Friedmann family came over with a present, a handbag in two-tone plum and cream. Tomas gave her an exquisite silk scarf, which looked as if it had fallen out of a painting by Gustav Klimt and Christian gave her a choker of pearls, like those worn by his mother when she had come to Austria two years ago.

Claire was about to leave; her coat was on, and behind her, two waiters had their arms filled with presents, when she saw Frau Huber standing by the door.

"I didn't want to disturb your party," said Frau Huber, as Claire walked over to her, "but I did want to give you a little memento."

"You would have been more than welcome to have joined us," said Claire.

"I wouldn't have known what to wear to somewhere like this," said Frau Huber, looking around the sumptuous hall. "I thought you might find this practical."

"May I open it?" said Claire. Frau Huber nodded, and Claire began to tear off the paper, revealing an Austrian cookbook.

"I have taken the liberty of inscribing it," said Frau Huber, "and adding a recipe or two of my own at the back."

Claire opened the book to the front page and read the few words in Frau Huber's neat handwriting,

"Thank you, Agnes," said Claire and her hand instinctively went to her face and she wiped a tear from her eye.

22

—·—

9 MARCH 1938

Everyone in Leopoldstadt had heard the news from Buchenwald concentration camp, and Rachel was telling her brother Jakob that he had to be more careful. The rumours were that there had been a public execution in Buchenwald of someone, simply for being a Jew. It had been early in the morning on the previous day, and the prisoners were herded into a small area, in tight ranks, shoulder to shoulder, block next to block. The SS were also on parade, standing in a horseshoe formation around the roll call square. In the centre of the square was a set of gallows and machine guns were trained down on the prisoners from the towers of the prison camp. A solitary prisoner of Buchenwald walked between two lines of SS men with an impassive look. His steps were short, regular, almost puppet-like, as if he were being carried by a set of strings. The prisoners whispered to each other that they must have injected him with something, for this was not the man they knew. The judge in a black robe pronounced the sentence, broke a white stick and threw it behind him. The prisoner's chains were then removed, and he was led to the gallows.

"It's important that we speak out against this," said Jakob. "We must make a stand, or it will be too late."

"It's important we stay alive," Rachel responded. "That's the only thing which *is* important."

***

Frau Huber put down the newspaper and, with a shake of her head, left Tomas and Christian in the dining room. She had referred to Chancellor Schuschnigg as a *Dummkopf* three times, after she had read that he had called for a national vote to resolve the *Anschluss* question once and for all. When she left the dining room, Tomas had seen how red her face was, that she was biting her bottom lip, and thought better than to mention it.

"What do you make of that?" he asked.

"I think Chancellor Schuschnigg is playing his last card," said Christian. "What else can he do? There were Nazi demonstrations last week calling for the joining of Austria and Germany and Hitler has threatened to invade. Schuschnigg is between a rock and a hard place."

"I suppose he is," said Tomas.

"And are you going back to Czecho-Slovakia today?"

"Yes," said Tomas, "where else can I go? And you? Are you staying in Vienna?"

"For now," said Christian. "Hitler doesn't want trouble with England, and I'm still hoping that everyone will wake up and see him for what he is."

"I'll telephone you when I can," said Tomas, "but it's not always easy to get an international line, although I did yesterday and spoke to Paul. He told me he has been performing in a club near the Jewish quarter. I said he was crazy, but being on stage for Paul is the same as breathing. He's doing that skit where he puts on a little black moustache, goose-steps across the stage while everyone boos, and then looks down into his underwear and shouts, 'just one?'"

The downstairs buzzer was pressed and Frau Huber answered it. She called to Tomas that his taxi had arrived.

"Come back soon, Herr Tomas," she said.

Tomas picked up his case and went into the hall, stopping at the door. He kissed Frau Huber on the cheek.

"Look after him," Tomas whispered, "and keep him safe."

"Haven't I always?" she whispered back.

"Of course," he responded, "but it's more important now than ever."

23

— · —

10 March 1938

Leopoldstadt was the main hub of Vienna's Jewish quarter which had been allotted to the Jews in 1622. It bordered the Inner Stadt, the old city, and was where the Leopoldstädter Temple could be found, perhaps the most beautiful and certainly the largest Jewish temple in Vienna, built in 1858, with the intent of bringing a community together. It was one of forty Jewish temples in that part of the city, which housed a thriving Jewish population of one hundred and eighty-five thousand people. It became the focal point of the demonstrations which started on the 10th of March, with hundreds of Nazis coming into Vienna from other cities and towns. Schmidt had been working for this moment for over three years, and he left his wife and children that morning, saying proudly that Austria would rise beside Germany.

A line of eight coaches awaited Schmidt to take demonstrators from Linz to Vienna, and he saw hundreds of people milling around, all wearing red swastika armbands. Many of them had the previous night filled the prisons of Linz; they were thugs, wife beaters, petty criminals and drunks. As they boarded the coaches Schmidt stood with his arm raised in a Nazi salute. Schmidt had reservations about releasing so much dross onto the streets, but the cause was everything.

A few hours later he watched as they marched through the streets of Vienna just before noon, shouting *ein Volk, ein Reich* – one people, one kingdom. As they had been instructed, many of them made their way into Leopoldstadt, throwing stones at Jewish shops. The police were spread thinly, however, the sympathies of many police officers were with the Nazis, and some stood by watching majestically.

Schmidt had been instructed by the German High Command that he was under no circumstances to be involved in any riots or to do anything that may lead to his arrest. He had also been ordered to be in Linz on the evening of the 12th of March. He was one of the men who had been chosen to be part of the welcoming group to meet the Führer.

***

Christian picked up the telephone and first dialled Anna and Otto at their home, but the phone kept on ringing. He then called the law offices of Karl Vogel and spoke briefly to Otto, who reassured him that both Anna and the children were safe and had gone to their lakeside house at St Wolfgang. He telephoned the number he had for Rachel, but the line was dead and then he called Claire and suggested she move to his apartment until the demonstrations were over.

"Things aren't that bad here," said Claire. "There's just a lot of hot air, and from what I can tell most people are watching a few Nazis rather than marching with them. There were even some boos as the Nazis walked past."

"I couldn't get hold of Rachel and I heard that they were destroying Jewish shops."

"She'll be safe. She and her family live a long way out of the city," said Claire, "and the only trouble was in Leopoldstadt. Have you spoken to Otto?"

"I managed to get hold of him and he told me that Anna and the children had gone to the lakes. I know you don't live in Leopoldstadt, but I would feel better if you came here for a few days."

"If there is any violence near where I live then I promise to hide away with you."

The demonstrations carried on the next day, slightly larger with many more police officers giving Nazi salutes. Again, Jewish shops were damaged in Leopoldstadt, and those who came out and sought to defend their property were beaten. The word *Jude* was daubed in paint across shopfronts and temples throughout the Jewish district.

By the early evening of the 11th of March, Christian was desperate to know what had happened. He had listened to the wireless through-out the day, even eating his meals on his lap. He had tried to phone Rachel a dozen times, with no response. Every time he dialled he felt a little more nervous. He could feel that something was happening. The street sounds were different, as if the city was holding its breath. There would be a silence, broken by the regular chiming of church bells, ringing like a glockenspiel and then shouting in the distance. His legs itched to get up, but his head told him that this was not the time to go blindly around the city. He felt inadequate, less than a mere spectator, as there was nothing he could do.

In the evening, Chancellor Schuschnigg addressed the Austrians on the radio, saying, "The president of the Republic of Austria has asked me to communicate to the Austrian people that we will not put up any resistance to violence."

He spoke about Hitler's ultimatum to appoint a new chancellor and a government following the recommendations of the German

Reich. He regretted that the Austrian government had lost control of the situation and concluded his resignation speech by saying, "I take my leave at this hour with a German word and heartfelt wish: God save Austria!"

Christian realised that with those few words the First Austrian Republic, which had existed since 1918, had ended. The darkness of Nazism was closing over Austria, and there was no way of holding it back. At least, he thought, Paul and Tomas were safe in Prague. Across the city, Rachel Kraus sat huddled with her family listening to the radio. When her mother finally turned it off, Rachel wept bitterly, fearing what was coming.

24

12 MARCH 1938

Despite the resignation of Schuschnigg, Hitler invaded and that morning Arthur Seyss-Inquart was appointed as the new chancellor and a swastika flew over the Austrian Parliament.

"There's nothing but propaganda on the damned wireless," grumbled Christian, as Frau Huber opened the front door. "Don't take off your coat, we're going out," he shouted.

"*Guten Morgen*, Herr Christian," said Frau Huber, "but what about your breakfast?"

"*Guten Morgen*, Frau Huber, we shall be having breakfast out," said Christian. "I need to know what's going on."

Frau Huber rebuttoned her coat and, with a shake of her head, said, "I have had breakfast."

"Have another," said Christian, "I need you to be my eyes for today. We'll go first to the Café Imperial for breakfast," said Christian, "and from there we can plan our day." Frau Huber could tell that he was trying to hurry.

"Why there," said Frau Huber, "when my eggs will be better?"

"Because the purpose of the visit," answered Christian, "is not to eat breakfast but to listen to the gossip."

"If you say so, Herr Christian."

Despite her seeming indifference to eating a second breakfast, Frau Huber quickly finished the eggs benedict and followed that with a pastry and two cups of the café's famous Wiener Melange – half a cup of brewed coffee with half a cup of steamed cream, topped with milk foam. Christian ate slowly, listening to the gossip from artists, musicians and politicians who had come to the café for the same purpose; to find out what was happening.

He heard that the Nazi High Command had sent both Himmler and Heydrich to Vienna and some people whispered that German troops had crossed the border. A diplomat from the American consulate also said that Hitler himself was on his way. People were asking whether, after the *Anschluss*, Austria would remain independent but under German control.

"Of course," said one man, who spoke with a sense of authority, "Hitler would not dare to make Austria part of the German Reich, it would be a breach of the Treaty of Versailles. Britain and France would never stand for it." He was contradicted immediately by another person who said that France and Britain would not care, and that Hitler had already breached the treaty when he marched 22,000 troops into the Rhineland two years ago.

"But what difference does it make?" said another.

"It will make every difference," replied the second man. "If Austria becomes part of the German Reich, it will no longer be its own country. Everything that makes Austria unique will be wiped away in a second, its laws, its customs... everything will go."

Christian and Frau Huber moved on to the Café Landtmann and then the Café Central. Christian heard confirmation that the German 8th Army had crossed the border and that the border post between Austria and Germany had been removed. Thousands of people were said to be lining the way, as tanks and armoured cars rolled into Austria to the sound of the cheering crowds. But most things were just speculation. Some people thought that Hitler would be arriving in Vienna that evening. Others said that he would not come for a few more days or at all. Some people said that the new Austrian chancellor was forming a new cabinet, others said he would be gone by the end of the week, but, as lunchtime arrived, everybody started talking about one thing – the crowd of Nazis marching towards Leopoldstadt.

***

Ein volk, ein Reich; ein Volk, ein Reich, the crowd chanted endlessly as it moved towards the Jewish quarter. Frau Huber said that most people were dressed in normal clothes, some with Nazi armbands and flags, and the Nazi salute was being given by thousands of people. She saw that a few carried stones, but most of them were in a good mood, celebrating a new hope. But soon the laughter and the smiles faded as they came to a row of shops. The crowd entered one store and dragged out a Jewish man of sixty, forcing him to paint the word *Jude* on his shopfront window. In the distance, out of sight, she heard glass shattering.

"Let's come away, Herr Christian," said Frau Huber, putting her hand on Christian's shoulder. "There's going to be trouble here."

Christian stood still, listening. The mood was changing slowly, the voices were getting louder, and the tone was becoming threatening. The violence against a small minority was getting worse. The Jews were being blamed for every perceived ill that the Austrians had endured and were enduring. Christian remembered similar things happening in Vienna just before the Great War started. He had got into a fight at the time when he saw some young men throwing stones at a

Jewish woman. He had received a bloody nose when he intervened, but the lady had managed to get away. Now, the same thing was happening, and he stood powerless, unable to help anyone. He felt emasculated by his blindness and realised that a darkness was again falling over Austria.

***

Hitler's motorcade moved over the iron bridge in Linz, which spans the Danube. Hitler stood in an open-topped car at the front of the cavalcade, as hundreds of thousands of people lined the streets. Soldiers stood to attention as the cars went past. The bridge had been decorated with green foliage and large swastikas on each footing. Hitler was in uniform with a peaked cap and a long trench coat. He looked from side to side as the vehicles crossed the bridge, as confident and as sure of himself as Caesar crossing the Rubicon, but this wasn't an invasion; it was a victory parade.

Schmidt watched as the cars rolled forward and into Linz. Most of the buildings had been adorned with Nazi insignia. Every child had a flag, most with swastikas, and a quarter of a million people ran after the motorcade. Near the City Hall, Hitler was welcomed by Chancellor Seyss-Inquart, who had come that morning from Vienna, as well as the Mayor of Linz and other officials. Schmidt stood in that line, every button on his uniform polished and his shoes shining like glass. The Mayor of Linz proclaimed that Article 88 of the Treaty of Versailles, which set out the boundaries between Austria and Germany, was now gone.

As Hitler spoke to the crowds at Linz, everyone stood with their arms raised in the Nazi salute. Schmidt had never seen the Führer as emotional as he was, so full of joy, his voice almost breaking when he spoke.

"When you are called on to give a confession of faith," shouted Hitler to the multitudes before him, "I hope the day may not be far distant – I hope I can be proud of my home province. I hope you will show the whole world that German unity can never be dissolved.

"Just as you are ready to do your share," Hitler continued, "Germany also is determined to stand by you. The German soldiers who have marched in are fighters for the entire nation, for the unity of the Reich, for the might and greatness and glory of Germany now and forever. *Sieg Heil!*"

The crowd surged forward as Hitler finished. Schmidt watched them, overjoyed and ecstatic. They started singing *Deutschland Über Alles*, and then the Nazi hymn, the Horst Wessel song. Tears were running down his cheeks as Schmidt sang as loudly as he could, and he looked out into the crowd with the hope of seeing his own children.

In the afternoon, Hitler entered the City Hall, and the crowds stood outside cheering. Hitler was forced to appear on the balcony time and time again to respond to the thunderous noise. He promised them new bridges, new infrastructure, new buildings that a Reich could be proud of.

"And this is Major Ernst Schmidt," said the Mayor of Linz, as Hitler started to prepare to leave Linz for Vienna.

"*Mein Führer*," said Schmidt.

"More than anyone here," said the mayor, "Major Schmidt has been the one who has helped prepare for this day both here and in Vienna."

Heinreich Himmler, Chief of the SS, leant over to Hitler and whispered something in his ear. Hitler stopped in front of Schmidt and thanked him for being a true son of the Reich. Schmidt smiled, bowed and then looked at Himmler. He hadn't seen him in years, since those meetings they had in Munich in 1935.

"I need a word," said Himmler quietly to Schmidt.

"Anything," replied Schmidt, and the two walked to one side of the hall.

"I have a list for you," said Himmler, "of the names of people that the Reich is interested in detaining. They are people who we believe would undermine the Reich and pose a threat. He took out the list from the inside pocket of his jacket and handed it to Schmidt. "You'll know some of the names."

Schmidt opened the list and looked down it. There were the names of artists, journalists, lawyers, priests, cabaret performers and authors such as Felix Salten, Anton Kuh, Egon Friedell, Fritz Grünbaum and Paul O'Montis.

Hitler left the City Hall soon afterwards, walking past a troupe of his soldiers, Hitler Youth and children. He stopped twice, speaking to the children, and then departed in the direction of Vienna to chants of *Sieg Heil, Sieg Heil*. The motorcade was followed by a marching band through a sea of waving banners, each with a swastika. The words, *Ein Volk; Ein Reich; Ein Führer* had been affixed to the town hall in letters six feet tall. Hitler raised his arm in a Nazi salute to the crowds. They cheered as he stood in the car in his military uniform, having discarded his coat in the glorious afternoon sun.

25

15 MARCH 1938

Flags were on every public building and private dwelling in the Inner City, except those owned by Jews. All morning, crowds gathered in front of the Hofburg Palace to see Hitler declare that Austria had become a state of the German Reich. They stood shoulder to shoulder, so that not one blade of grass could be seen on the palace lawns. They laughed with the German soldiers, and some cried with joy. As Hitler stood on the balcony, the Viennese, so often relaxed and friendly, stood to attention, arms raised in a Nazi salute.

From his apartment, Christian could hear the crowd of two hundred thousand people cheering as Hitler declared that the *Anschluss* was their liberation.

"The oldest eastern province of the German people shall be," shouted Hitler from the balcony, "from this point on, the newest bastion of the German Reich. This is my greatest accomplishment." The crowds cheered, shouting *Sieg Heil* repeatedly. "As leader and chancellor of the German nation and Reich, I announce to German history, the entry of my homeland into the German Reich." Christian could barely make out the words through the triumphant screams of the crowd. "Austria is liberated," he heard Hitler scream. However, what the Austrians were being liberated from and why so many tanks and machine guns were needed, Christian did not know.

The telephone rang and Frau Huber picked up the receiver, greeted the caller in English and told Christian his brother was on the line. She put her hand over the mouthpiece and added that Basil ought to practise his German, as it had got considerably worse over the last few years.

"Why has he never brought his family to Vienna?" she added. "It's six years since he was here."

Christian took the phone and put his hand over the mouthpiece and then quietly said, "They're busy. He is a lawyer, and she travels around the world."

"It's wrong that he makes her work," said Frau Huber. "A woman's place is at home with her husband and children."

"We're living in the 1930s, not the 1830s," Christian responded, and then placed the receiver to his ear and took his other hand off the mouthpiece. "Basil, it's been months since you called."

"Christian," replied Basil, "the telephone works both ways. Not only can I call you, but you can call me."

"I do, but you and Celia are never in."

"I thought we ought to talk."

"I assume this is about what is happening here," said Christian.

"Yes," said Basil. "We're concerned."

"There's nothing to be concerned about," said Christian, "Hitler doesn't want trouble with the British."

"Perhaps," said Basil. It was said in an understated way, almost as a question, which, to any English person who heard, meant that he thought the previous statement unquestionably wrong.

"At the moment, things are very much the same except that there are Germans in uniform on every street corner. I want to believe that the Austrian people will wake up and see the Nazis for what they are, a group of thugs and bullies."

"Mother called me yesterday. She thinks you should come home."

"This is my home," said Christian emphatically, "and it has been for more than fifteen years."

"She thinks that Hitler won't stop with Austria."

"That may be true," said Christian.

"How bad was the unrest in Vienna?" asked Basil.

"There was some trouble in the Jewish area but not generally across the city. If the cheering crowds are anything to go by, I would guess that most of Austria supports joining with Germany."

"And you? How have you been keeping?"

"I'm well. Things have changed now that Tomas has gone but I still go out with friends and acquaintances."

"And Mother said to make sure I asked you about Claire, although I don't think you've ever mentioned her to me."

"She's a friend," said Christian, "an American." Christian paused, as he considered how best to explain to Basil who she was. "We were... are... good friends, however, I don't think there will be anything more. She just broke up with someone... and it was messy."

"Ah," replied Basil. "So, Mother's next question of whether there's any chance of wedding bells soon is a 'no'."

"Yes, and tell Mother to mind her own business," Christian responded.

"Don't shoot me," said Basil, who heard the terseness in his brother's voice, "I'm only the messenger."

"And how are things between you and Celia?" asked Christian.

"You know better than to ask," said Basil. "Things are very much the same, although she has a new job that takes up even more of her time. It's something about foster homes for refugees."

26

— · —

2 APRIL 1938

The nightmares returned, darker and more brutal. He remembered the flamethrower and the pain of the burning liquid that stuck to his face. He dreamt about being dragged across the Somme by George Poley, who was barely old enough to have been there, and did so without concern for himself. He recalled Rose's voice, coaxing him to cling on to life, but the words faded, and he heard the hatred in Hitler's voice. He heard the crowds shouting *Seig Heil*, and he dreamt about the dead men that he had led on the battlefield. He could picture their faces, young men, some just boys, who followed him as he led the charge on the first day of the Battle of the Somme.

In the weeks following the *Anschluss*, Vienna changed. The antisemitism had always been there, but now it bubbled to the surface, as if the stigma of being a racist had been expunged. Groups of Jews were forced to scrub the pavements to remove pro-independence slogans. Shop owners were made to paint *Jude* on the windows of their shops. Policemen prevented non-Jews from entering Jewish shops. Things quickly got worse. Jews were chased, spat upon and beaten in the streets and some desolate souls, who could take the hurt no more, committed suicide. There was a sense of foreboding, and people started to make plans to flee.

"You can't call them isolated incidents," said Otto to Christian. His bushy eyebrows furrowed as he thought about the things he had seen on the streets. "How many isolated incidents must there be before something becomes systemic; a dozen, a hundred, more?"

"What I was trying to say," said Christian, "was that things could be worse."

"Things can always be worse," said Otto. "Every Jew knows that."

"So, what are you going to do?"

"I have relatives in America," said Otto, "I'll try and take my family there."

"What does Anna think?"

"She'll suggest that we stay at St Wolfgang where she grew up."

"What's wrong with that?" asked Christian.

"Everything!" said Otto. "When Austria becomes subject to German law, I won't be able to work as a lawyer, because my right to practise before the Austrian bar will be revoked. My citizenship will be revoked, and my children will have to register as Jews before they will be allowed to attend the local school. It's why I asked you to come in to see me."

"I don't follow?"

"In the next few months, I am likely to be prevented from practising law at this firm. I have already discussed it with Herr Vogel, the principal of this law firm, and it has been decided that I will not take on any new cases and just work on those matters that I have."

"I see," said Christian. "And are you asking me if I want to move my work to wherever you're going next?"

"No, no, quite the opposite," said Otto. "I've worked here for twenty years, and Herr Vogel is one of the best lawyers I have had the privilege of working with. He is treating me remarkably well, given the circumstances. I know other Jewish lawyers who have already been dismissed from their firms. I wanted to reassure you that when I do leave it will have nothing to do with Herr Vogel or this firm, and that you should carry on instructing this firm whenever you have a legal issue."

***

"Good evening," the *maître d'* called, and Christian responded with the same greeting. They were seated at their usual table, and Claire picked up the menu and studied it. The Hotel Astoria was very much unchanged since their last visit, except for the swastika flag that fluttered at the front of the building. The staff were the same, and the menu was unchanged. The clientele was also the same, although there were a few German officers in uniform dining in the restaurant and sitting in the bar area. Claire thought about having the salade niçoise, which was always good, and the steak. Christian felt for his glass of wine.

"And let's toast your success," he said, lifting his glass. "It's not every day that you land a new role in a musical."

She raised her glass as well and touched the edge to his.

"It's only a stand-in role," said Claire. "The lead actress has decided to go back to England, and the show is only going to run for another three months, until the summer."

"It's still a great accomplishment," said Christian.

"Did you have anything to do with it?" Claire asked. She looked at him intently, watching the chandelier's light flicker across the dark lenses of his glasses. "Because every time I need a hand, somehow, you're always there, like you know I need you."

Christian gave the faintest shrug, a small, careful smile on his lips. "Me? I had nothing to do with this."

Claire didn't press him.

"Even so," she said, her voice barely above a whisper, "you make me feel like I matter. You listen. You see me for who I am, and who I'm still trying to become." She paused, the moment stretching between them. "And yet... there's still a barrier between us. We don't talk about it, but it's there all the same."

She let the words settle in the space between them, not expecting an answer, only needing to say them.

"I'm sorry," said Christian, "the fault lies with me."

Claire looked at him. He had been unusually silent for most of the evening, struggling with small talk, as though his mind was elsewhere. She guessed he was thinking about Tomas and Paul, neither of whom could return to Vienna now.

"Tomas will be fine," she said.

"Sorry?" Christian said, startled from his thoughts.

"Tomas," she repeated. "He's more resilient than you give him credit for. I remember the first time I saw him; I thought a feather might knock him over. Velvet jacket, cigarette holder, calling everyone *darling* or *dearest*." She shrugged. "But underneath all that pretence he's tougher than he looks."

Christian didn't respond to that. Instead, after a pause, he asked, "Would you like to dance?"

She looked over towards the dance floor. There were only one or two couples there and, sensing his need to change the subject, she said, "Why not?"

She led him to the dance floor, and he gently held one hand and placed the other lightly on her waist. They moved together as the orchestra began a slow waltz.

"I still can't quite believe I'm dancing with someone who's blind," she said, her head drifting close to his shoulder.

"The dancing part's easy enough," he said, stepping two beats to the left and guiding her with him. "It's the not bumping into people that remains a bit of a challenge."

Claire laughed, genuinely, but inside she felt there was a distance between them. She couldn't shake the feeling that they were moving through something much more complicated than a dance. It wasn't that he was blind, although if he were sighted that would have made things easier. It wasn't the scarring to his face. There was no *us*, not really. Just two people trying not to stumble, trying not to say too much, trying to find their way through an unseen room, step by uncertain step.

"Do you mind if I cut in?" asked a German officer.

"Actually, I do," said Christian. "Actually, I would mind a lot."

27

JULY 1938

The first transport of Jews and political prisoners to the Dachau concentration camp left Vienna on the 1st of April 1938. Many tried to buy their freedom and go abroad, and many did not return. On the 10th of April 1938, nearly ninety-nine per cent of all Austrians who were permitted to vote supported the annexation of Austria into Germany, only twelve thousand people voted against it. The fabric of Austrian society changed; schools became segregated, and Jews had to make declarations to the police about what assets they owned. Jews lost their jobs in every walk of society and soup kitchens were set up to feed them. The desperate and the destitute besieged the Jewish welfare offices and emergency aid flooded into Austria. The Nuremberg Laws of 1935, which defined who was a Jew, became law in Austria in May 1938 and, from that date, two hundred thousand Jews in Austria became stateless.

Jews were divided into three groups. The first were the confessional Jews, those who had been born and grew up in the Jewish faith and adhered to it. The second were those born to Jewish parents, but who had converted to other faiths. The third class, who were proclaimed to be Jews by the Nuremberg Laws, were people, even Christians by observance, who had a single Jewish grandparent. This last group were known as *Mischling*, referring to the mixture of bloods, and in many respects were worse off than other Jews because there were no religious groups or foreign countries that would help them leave Germany or Austria.

Jews sought to escape Austria in those weeks following the *Anschluss*, although the elderly and the infirm refused to be chased out of their country where countless generations of their family had lived before them. The borders of many countries were quickly closed, and those who sought to cross the border could be shot as spies. In the pretty town of Évian-les-Bains, on the French-Swiss border, a conference took place in July 1938 to try and resolve the refugee crisis. Over one hundred and fifty thousand Jews had already fled Germany and tens of thousands of Jews were trying to leave Austria. Despite President Roosevelt initiating the conference, America was not prepared to lift any border restrictions to allow more than a small quota of refugees in, and, of the thirty-two countries that attended the conference, it was only the Dominican Republic and Costa Rica that were prepared to take more refugees. The representative for the Jews in Palestine, Golda Meir, was not allowed to speak but could only observe.

As the newspapers were read to him by Frau Huber, Christian's mood darkened as he thought the world had stopped caring for those people who needed help the most, and that a world without empathy was a brutal place. Christian thought that if every country that attended the Évian conference took just thirty thousand refugees, there would not be one Jewish refugee left in Germany and Austria. The Nazis saw the world's indifference to this crisis as a propaganda victory and Hitler wrote in the newspapers that if other countries would be prepared to take the Jews, he would help them leave.

Although the governments of many countries were not prepared to act, certain individuals and organisations began to consider what actions they could take. One organisation was the Brith Sholom in Philadelphia, which started discussing how fifty Jewish children could be brought to America. Three of its members, Gil and Eleanor Kraus and Bob Schless, met with the American authorities about how this could be achieved.

***

Frau Huber busied herself with a dozen tasks as she prepared for the summer move to St Gilgen. The larder was emptied, the newspapers were stopped, covers were put over the furniture and the mail redirected. Christian tried to spend as much time as possible away from the apartment on the days before the move, as he had been told that he was simply getting underfoot. He lunched out, strolled in the parks and went to talks at the coffeehouses and the university. In the evenings he went to concerts and would, at least once a week, drop into the theatre where Claire was singing. As he sat eating breakfast on the day that he was leaving for St Gilgen, Frau Huber was grumbling about how much work was still to be done.

"You have not said," continued Frau Huber, "whether Fräulein Astor will be joining us?"

"Her show is due to finish in a few weeks," said Christian, "and she said she'll join us then. Was there any post today?"

"Just one letter from Herr Tomas. Sorry, it slipped my mind. I'll get it now."

When Christian left the dining room, it was not Claire that he was thinking about but Tomas. The Germans in the Sudetenland of

Czecho-Slovakia were demanding that they be allowed to join with Germany, and although Prague was not within the Sudetenland, it meant that Germany was encircling the city. Tomas' letter was short, with no return address or telephone number. It said that Paul and he were well and that they were going to move to a new apartment soon. It ended by saying, "You get the feeling that everyone is watching you and I hate going out. You would hardly recognise me; my hair is now grey and I wear the most boring bourgeois clothes just to fit in. Paul tells me I am beginning to look like an insurance salesman! I will write again when I can."

28

AUGUST 1938

To many people old enough to remember a time before the Great War, it appeared that their lives were lived in periods of either war or peace. Christian remembered both a time in uniform and a time without, and each part of his life was very different. As Germany expanded its reach across Europe, first in the Rhineland, then in Austria and now with its sights upon the Sudetenland, he thought that, like a rolling wheel, a time of war was fast approaching. He considered it strange how so many young people thought of war in glorious terms, of honour, of duty, of faith and love. He did not. He had seen dead soldiers on the battlefield. He also knew that to think of war and peace as two separate things was to misunderstand the link between them – wars began in times of peace, and peace did not start simply because bullets were no longer fired.

Christian began to fear that they were now closer to war than they were to peace. He had hoped that the Austrians would see Hitler for what he was, but the opposite had happened. They saw Hitler as a saviour. They believed Hitler's declarations that Germany was a peaceful country with no hostile intentions. However, Christian recognized that Hitler was marshalling his country along a dusty thoroughfare that would inevitably lead to war and death and the country that he once called home sought only to appease this warmonger. It was a country as blind as a fool's heart.

***

The Wolfgangsee was chilly, even at the height of summer. It was not so cold as to make you shiver, but cold enough that those unused to the waters would step tentatively into them, one slow step after another, pausing to allow themselves to become accustomed to the coolness upon their skin. The children, of course, threw themselves headlong in, screaming and screeching, splashing and diving, and would swim so far out into the lake that concern would swell up in their parents' hearts until their shouts to return to the lakeside were grudgingly acceded to.

These were days of picnics and singing, of lying in the grass and feeling the sun upon your skin. The children ran wildly, excitedly, hid in the thickets, and with sticks in hand, would decapitate the heads of raggedy thistles. As the long, glorious summer continued unabated, the grass slowly turned yellow and then brown. Every day, Christian, Claire, Otto, Anna and the children went to the lake, oblivious to the outside world. Each day they swam, and in the early evening, with a bottle of Riesling bobbing in the cold water, Christian would lie upon a picnic rug, the tips of his fingers touching Claire's hand.

It was, in many respects, an idyllic time, and for the first moments since his childhood, Christian felt part of a family. The children tried to ignore the scarring of his face. They were guarded to begin with but over time they began to ask him questions about a world without shape or colour. They played blind man's buff to see what it was like to be sightless, tumbling over in the grass again, and again, and again.

Claire was quieter than usual. She was uncertain why she had come and what she wanted. Anna and Otto were the opposite, laughing at everything, even those things which were not particularly funny. However, as the last days of August arrived, the days became shorter, and there was a slight chill in the evening air. Christian wondered when they would return to Vienna, although no one had spoken about it. It was in those moments when the outside world scratched at his life that he put his hand to the St Christopher around his neck and prayed to the universe to let everything remain unchanged.

Frau Huber prepared baskets of food for supper and had the gardener bring them down to the lakeside when the edges of darkness began to eat away at the day. Claire opened each basket as if it were a Christmas present, unwrapping cheeses, chicken, olives, salads and pickles. The children were by then famished and would gnaw on drumsticks until there was nothing but bone. Freshly made lemonade was poured into jugs and drunk too quickly. Smoked salmon sandwiches with cucumber and a squeeze of lemon were for the adults. Across the waters, Christian could hear young men calling to their girlfriends on the lakeshore as they sailed their boats into St Gilgen. A brass orchestra would soon start playing in the village square, but he knew that Anna and Otto would not go. Even here, Christian thought, Hitler's words were taking hold.

"Anna and I need to return to Vienna for a day or two next week," said Otto, as if he were reading Christian's mind.

"Why?" said Christian. Otto looked at his four children, who were now eating the cakes and cream rolls from one of the baskets. They sat apart from the adults, whispering and laughing with cream smudged around their lips.

"We need to find out what is happening with our visas for America. So far, I've heard nothing, and we also need to disclose our assets here to the authorities."

"I thought you had to do that by June?"

"We did," said Otto, "but there was a delay in the transfer of the property to Anna after her mother's death and therefore an issue about the amount of inheritance tax."

"Is that a problem?" asked Christian.

"It shouldn't be," said Otto, "however, you never know with these things. We wanted to ask you and Claire a favour, and I quite understand if you refuse."

"What is it?" asked Christian.

"Could we leave the children with you for two days? They are generally not a problem, although Aaron can be boisterous. It will be easier than taking them around Vienna from one bureaucratic office to the next."

"If Claire is agreeable, then yes."

"Anna asked Claire this afternoon," said Otto, "and she said she would be happy to help."

"Then," said Christian, "it will be our pleasure to have them."

Otto leant over and squeezed Christian's shoulder, then went to talk to Anna.

Four children, thought Christian, there would be nothing to it. Hanna and Frieda, the two oldest girls, who were fifteen and thirteen respectively, could almost look after themselves. Aaron was ten and Rosa was eight but, thought Christian, Frau Huber and Claire would manage to look after them. They could play in the garden and then sing songs in the evening, like they had done a few years ago at the restaurant along the Pilgrim's Way.

"Claire," Christian called out across the green lawns that rolled down to the lakeside, "it seems we have four children to look after."

"How hard can it be?" she shouted back.

***

There was a moment when Christian had to accept that he was more like his younger brother than he cared to admit. He liked things just-so, but then, his condition dictated a regimented lifestyle or at least that was how he justified it to himself. He would, when required, accommodate Tomas whenever he came back to Vienna. Four children, however, were a different kettle of fish. It was the noise, as they each ate a bowl of muesli and then eggs, followed by the toast and preserves. And, he thought, why did they need to bring their toys to breakfast?

"Can't you keep control of them?" he asked Claire, who took a deep breath before answering.

"Don't be such a fuddy-duddy."

"I may be many things," said Christian peevishly, "but one thing I am not is a fuddy-duddy."

"You've done nothing this morning except complain. First, it was because the children had drunk all the orange juice, then you made a big thing about the eggs, and now it's the noise!"

"I had to wait until Frau Huber made more eggs, and by that time, the coffee was cold, and all they did was constantly shout at each other."

"I know," said Claire. "But you have no idea how tired I am. At two o'clock this morning, the two eldest girls came into my room and got into bed with me. They said they had a nightmare, and when I woke after a terrible night's sleep, there were all four of them there."

"What do you propose?" asked Christian.

"Do something with them," Claire said, "I just need a little more sleep."

"What do you expect me to do with four children aged eight to fifteen?"

"I don't know," she said. "Teach them something."

There was something about Frau Huber and her tone of voice that instilled in a child the feeling that there were lines that should not be crossed. When she said that they would be going into the library and would need to sit quietly, they complied. When she shushed them after a few minutes, they stayed shushed, and when she came with hot chocolate and cream rolls an hour later, they all with one voice thanked her and her departing words of "No crumbs" were complied with to the letter.

"I thought," said Christian, as they sipped at their hot chocolate, "that as you will be going to America, you might like to learn a few words of English."

"Is English different to American?" asked Aaron.

"They're very similar," answered Christian. "A bit like Spanish and Ladino."

"What's Ladino?" asked Hanna.

"It's very similar to Spanish with some Hebrew," said Christian.

"Couldn't we learn that?" asked Frieda.

"But I don't know either Ladino or Spanish," answered Christian.

"Why did you mention it then?" asked Rosa, who looked dejected at the idea that she was going to have a school lesson.

"A poem," said Christian. "We're going to learn a poem," and at once, before there was room for objection, he recited the whole of *The Owl and the Pussy-Cat*. However, he soon realised that the problem with a nonsense poem is that when translated, it makes less sense and loses its rhythm. It took him the best part of ten minutes to explain to the two youngest children that there is no land where the Bong Trees grow and no such thing as a Bong Tree anyway, and even more time to explain that a runcible spoon was not a completely made-up object. Frieda and Hanna, who had already had six years of English lessons at school, were bored and could not understand why they were trying to learn a poem that made no sense at all. After nearly two hours, the two youngest children managed to recite the first four lines of the poem, and Christian decided that he should take all his small victories and went to find Frau Huber, hoping that more hot chocolate and pastries would keep them quiet.

"Poems," she said, shaking her head, as she basted two chickens. "Weren't you ever a child?"

"What do you mean?" asked Christian.

"Have you forgotten what it was like to be young?"

"What do you suggest?"

"Take them out on the lake in a boat."

"But I can't sail."

"Rent a boat and a captain who can sail it for you. Just by the beach there is Müller's, and a three-hour sail around the lake this afternoon will keep them quiet and bring you back here for dinner."

"What will we need?" said Christian.

"Some snacks," said Frau Huber. "I've made them already and, of course, their bathing suits."

The boat was just over thirty feet with a mainsail and a jib. Initially, Christian was a little tentative getting on board as the slight swell of the lapping water made his footing unsure. However, Claire held his arm, and her grip was surprisingly strong. The captain suggested that they sail up the shoreline, where the children could swim and then across the lake and back to St Gilgen.

After his initial apprehension, caused by the swell of the water, Christian began to enjoy the experience as the wind took hold of the sails, and the boat skimmed across the surface. By the time they were making their way back, he was helping with the sails when they needed to tack, and only once nearly lost his head when Aaron almost forgot to tell him to duck. On the final leg of the journey, Hanna and Frieda started reciting *The Owl and the Pussy-Cat*, and when they disembarked at nearly six o'clock, Christian found himself hoping that they could do the same the following day.

29

1 September 1938

It had been a dreary day, and the settling evening was overcast. The clouds had rolled in over the mountains in the morning, bringing with them the threat of a storm, and they were advised not to take a boat out on the lake. The Friedmann children had played in the garden, with Rosa and Aaron not wanting to go far away from Claire. In order to lift the gloom, Frau Huber had made a beef stew with dumplings for their dinner and the children were sitting eating it when Christian heard a car on the gravel driveway. Claire peered out of the window as the car pulled up, and together they went to the front door.

"Something's wrong," Claire said, as she watched Otto and Anna slam the car doors shut and rush towards them. Christian could hear them on the gravel path scattering small stones as they hurried in the evening light.

"We need to go back," said Anna. "Every Jew in Austria is required to move into Leopoldstadt. We must go."

Claire looked at Otto, who seemed unable to speak, and then she looked at Anna, who wiped a tear from her cheek.

"Come in, come in!" said Christian. "The children are having dinner."

"They must hurry," said Anna. "We've got to go."

Claire had never seen Anna and Otto like this. Anna was always organised and in control. She was the family's bedrock, but, as Claire looked at her, she could tell that she was ready to fall to pieces. Without her strength, Otto seemed adrift and did not know what to do. Claire opened her arms and took hold of Anna.

"It's all right," she whispered. "It will be all right."

Christian stood silently trying to think of what he should say. They had hidden themselves away in St Gilgen for over a month and now the realities of life had caught up with them. As he heard the muffled sobs of Anna, he said, "What can I do?" However, Otto did not reply. But what could he do? Christian thought. Although he had asked sincerely, he knew there was a nothing a blind man could do. There was nothing anyone could do, and those who did stand up and denounce the Nazis were immediately arrested and imprisoned. He felt inadequate. "I'm so sorry," he added. However, the words were lost in the evening breeze.

"There were soup kitchens everywhere," Otto finally said, "and so many people were homeless and starving. One of my neighbours was queuing for food. He had been beaten. He had refused to scrub the streets, and the Nazis had beaten him up."

"And we must go to the police station to have a J stamped into our passports, like we're criminals," said Anna, who had stopped crying, "and take Jewish names, Israel and Sara. They told us that the names Anna and Otto were not of Jewish origin."

"They can't!" said Christian. "And your visas for America. Have you got those?"

"No," said Otto. "They've not been rejected, but so many people are applying for a visa that it could take forever."

Christian could hear the slight, chronic fever of bewilderment in his voice. He wanted to put his arm around Otto's shoulder and hug him, like Claire had done with Anna. It would have been what his older brother Adrian would have done, but the years of reserve encircled and prevented him.

"British Palestine may be possible," continued Otto, "but I doubt it. There's nothing to do but wait and hope and pray."

"Even if we get our visas from America," said Anna, "we now must give the Nazis almost everything we own; our home, jewellery, money, everything of value that we've saved all our lives for, as a condition of leaving. They tell us that we will be given credit to buy German goods when we are in America, but you don't know what to believe."

"I'm so sorry," said Christian once again. He felt that those meagre words were so inadequate. He had heard the bitterness in Anna's voice and the helplessness in Otto's.

"There's nothing to do," said Anna, who took a handkerchief from her handbag and wiped her eyes. "I'd better look in on the children and see if they have finished. People told us that they will send you to Dachau for even a minor infraction, and they're opening more concentration camps; we heard that they've even opened a camp here in Austria at Mauthausen near Linz."

Anna put her head around the dining room door to see four children quietly eating bowls of stew. When she came in, they ran to her.

"Have you had a nice time?" Anna asked them, as they wrapped their arms around her.

"Have you been crying, Mama?" asked Frieda.

"Only tears of joy to see you," said Anna, who hugged and kissed each child lovingly, "but we have to go."

"Back to St Wolfgang?" asked Hanna.

"No, Vienna," said Anna, and looked at her eldest daughter. "There's one more thing I must tell you. Our home... we'll be sharing it with two other families."

"Why?" asked Hanna.

"It's just we have so much room and there are so many people. But you'll like them, I promise."

"I don't want to live with other people," said Rosa.

"It's not our choice, darling," said Anna.

30

—·—

4 SEPTEMBER 1938

The Kraus family were evicted from their villa, as a German officer laid claim to it, and they moved into their flat in the Leopoldstadt area, that Abe Kraus had renovated for his son. There were only two bedrooms and Jakob slept in the living room on a camp bed, rather than sharing the bedroom with his sister, as he had once done when he was a small boy. He had passed his university finals in June but was not allowed to graduate, as new laws prohibited all Jews from enrolling at universities or continuing their studies. He started working at one of his father's bakeries but had no interest in baking challah or bagels. He loved books and as soon as the bakery was locked up in the afternoon, he would go home, shower and change and then go out to a talk on literature at a coffeehouse in the Leopoldstadt area.

That afternoon, Jakob had point-blank refused to take Rachel to the Rösthaus café. She pretended indifference, saying that the literary cafés of Vienna had long since gone, and that a few old men and boys, talking banally about dime-store novels, could not be described as a literary café. She knew she was being sullen, however, his refusal irritated her as the writer, Felix Salten, would be there, and she wanted to hear him speak. He was one of the few Jewish names from the literary café group still living in Vienna and Felix Salten could pack the room. He used to speak with other authors such as Kafka, Thomas Mann and Robert Musil, and they would discuss political essays until their voices became raised, and their tongues sharpened.

The Rösthaus café was next to the old coffee roastery and smelt of roasted coffee beans, which Jakob described as being like burnt popcorn. When Jakob arrived, Felix Salten was sitting at the front of the coffeehouse, speaking to a few other eminent writers who had attended. He looked distinguished with his wavy dark hair and clipped moustache and was introduced as one of Vienna's leading literary lights for the last quarter of a century. He blushed slightly as a list of his books and plays was read out and then stood up, put his hand in front of his mouth and coughed before speaking.

"I see many who are not here," said Felix Salten. He moved his head left and right, looking across the café. He was referring not only to Anton Kuh, who had escaped to America, but also to Alfred Polgar and Franz Werfel, who had both fled abroad, and Egon Friedell, who had committed suicide when the Nazis came to arrest him. The room was packed, and Jakob, as well as many other young men who had come to hear him speak, stood at the back. Non-Jews did not attend as they would be classified as Jewish sympathisers if they came to a meeting in Leopoldstadt.

It was the books that the Nazis had banned which were of interest to Jakob. There were hundreds of them which were being burned, including those that supported communism, such as Lenin, Marx, Hemingway and Engels, or writers critical of the regime, such as Thomas Mann, Virginia Woolf and Remarque. Karl Kraus, Kafka, Freud and Felix Salten were also on the list of banned authors because they were Jewish. However, Jakob could not understand why the Nazis had banned the books of HG Wells and when Felix Salten asked if there were any questions, Jakob's hand rose quicker than anyone else's.

"You're home early. How was it?" shouted Rachel, as Jakob slammed the door of their apartment shut.

"The same as always," he answered. "Noisy with everyone wanting to talk about who's been arrested."

"I told you!" said Rachel.

"What are you preparing for dinner?"

"Vegetable soup with matzo balls."

"Again!" said Jakob.

Jakob put his book on the kitchen table and washed his hands in the kitchen sink.

"I asked Salten why HG Wells' books had been banned."

"What did he say?" asked Rachel.

"He said that it was not his novels that were thought of as being ideologically unacceptable to the Nazis but his non-fiction books such as *First and Last Things* where he advocated socialism. Salten seems to know everything. He also said he would be leaving for Zürich next month"

"He's going?"

"He fears he will be arrested if he stays," said Jakob. "It's why we left early. Someone said there was a group of SS officers near the Rösthaus."

"I thought he would have fled already," said Rachel. "After all, you don't have to be a genius to work out what his allegorical stories are about."

"Not everyone reads them that way!" said Jakob. "Salten told an anecdote this afternoon about how he had sold the film rights of his book, *Bambi*, to an American, who had no idea what it was about. He explained to the American that it was not a children's book but was about the persecution of the Jews in Europe, saying that 'Man' represented those who chased and hunted the Jews. The American was apparently shocked when he heard this and told Salten that if the book were ever made into a film, it would need to be changed, and Salten replied, 'If you want to change the story, why did you buy the film rights?'" Jakob laughed and Rachel smiled, despite herself.

"Go get Mama and Papa. I'm just about to serve dinner."

"Are they sleeping?" asked Jakob.

"Yes, Papa was tired when he came home. I asked him whether he wanted to leave, but he said it was still his home, why should he leave, and where would he go?"

"He has a point," said Jakob. "I said the same today at the meeting; that the time had come when we should refuse to be pushed further by the Nazis and should start fighting back."

"You didn't say that!" said Rachel. "Are you so stupid to blurt that out at a public meeting?"

"I was just saying what people were thinking. You have said the same."

"But never in public," said Rachel. "Now get Mama and Papa!"

She had just started spooning the soup into bowls when she heard boots clattering on the stairs outside their apartment. She held her breath and prayed, but then there was a loud bang on the door and a shout of, "*Polizei, aufmachen!*"

31

—·—

18 September 1938

As Schmidt set down his newspaper, he looked at his wife across the table and said, "Even the communists are saying that no one wishes to help those Jews trying to get to Switzerland or Czecho-Slovakia. They are comparing them to a man who is drowning, and that people see him from both banks of the river and would be ready to help him, so long as he doesn't reach their side." He smirked, the left side of his mouth curving ever so slightly upwards, and then added, "That's quite funny, I might use that in my speech this evening."

Gretchen smiled as well as their housemaid cleared away the breakfast plates, and the children sat quietly waiting to be told they could leave the table.

"Don't you think that's quite funny?" asked Schmidt, still looking at his wife.

"Of course, dear," said Gretchen. "Will you be wanting dinner when you get in?"

"No," said Schmidt, "I'll be late. Eichmann will be at my talk this evening."

"Eichmann," said Gretchen. "Wasn't there a second-hand Hoover salesman called Eichmann in Linz?"

"The same," said Schmidt, "however, he's now in charge of the Office of Jewish Emigration."

"Eichmann… but he was so dull," said Gretchen. "Everybody thought so."

"Never say that again," said Schmidt, "at least not in public. He may only be a lieutenant, but he has the ear of Hitler's inner circle. He's seen as being effective since he moved every Jew in Austria to Vienna and won't let them leave unless they hand over everything they own."

"But where will they go?"

"Who cares," said Schmidt. "The truth is no one wants them. Britain, France and America wag their fingers at us, but they are no different. They take a few Jews at a time. The Arabs in Palestine have also said, 'no more'. I never thought I would agree with a stinking Arab."

He turned in his chair to look at his three young daughters. Everything that he had wanted, everything that Hitler had promised was coming to pass. He wanted to say to his girls that he was a true son of the Reich and that they must be daughters of the Reich as well. That he would never stop until only decent, upright Austrians lived on Austrian soil and that they could hold their heads high as they took back their country. But as he looked at them with their hair in ribbons, with white ironed blouses under navy dresses, he knew that they did not care about things like politics, and so he laughed and told them that they had better get to school or he would be in trouble with the principal.

32

—·—

1 OCTOBER 1938

Christian had spoken to Tomas that morning on the telephone.

"Here in Prague," Tomas had said, "Chamberlain's Munich Agreement is seen as a betrayal. Representatives of Czecho-Slovakia were not permitted to take part in any of the negotiations. How can they do that? And then they agree to give up the border region between Czecho-Slovakia and Germany, which is Czecho-Slovakia's only line of defence against Germany." Tomas had paused as he tried to control his rising outrage. "We've been hamstrung! The British have hung us out to dry."

By the afternoon, as Christian sat in front of the radio listening to the news about the Munich Agreement and the fate of Czecho-Slovakia, he could do nothing but agree with Tomas's assessment. The Czecho-Slovakians had been hung out to dry. The newscaster said that Neville Chamberlain had returned to London with the desire for a European peace, and that Germany respected that. That when Chamberlain had disembarked the plane from Munich on the 30th of September, he had waved a piece of paper and claimed that the Czecho-Slovakian problem had now been resolved and that it was a prelude to a larger settlement where the whole of Europe might find peace. Chamberlain had proudly said that he and Herr Hitler had agreed that England and Germany should never go to war again, and that there should be peace for our time.

The newscaster read out that German troops had crossed the border and occupied the Sudetenland, without firing a shot. Christian groaned. What were Britain, France and America doing, he thought. In 1914, everyone was so keen to start a war, and he could not see the sense in it. Now, everyone wanted to appease Hitler and ignore the brutality he was inflicting on so many innocent people. The newscaster concluded his report by quoting Mr Chamberlain when he said that the Czecho-Slovakian crisis was, "A quarrel in a faraway country, between people of whom we know nothing."

"They're throwing them to the lions," said Christian, as he stood up and turned off the wireless.

"What else could they do?" asked Frau Huber, who also stood listening.

"Threaten war," said Christian.

"I've never heard you say that before," said Frau Huber.

"There's no stopping Hitler. When you see a rabid dog, you shoot it, you don't pat it on the head and hope it won't bite you. I don't know what game Chamberlain is playing, but if he thinks the result will be anything but war, then he's delusional. And Tomas..." Christian paused as he considered how all of this would affect Tomas. It was only a matter of time before Hitler took Prague. Paul would have to flee, but where was there to go? Poland had closed its borders, and Romania was now a fascist state. He remembered that his mother had warned, months ago, that Hitler would not stop at Austria.

33

6 NOVEMBER 1938

J akob Kraus went to the quarry feeling nothing but anger and hatred. The old man who had been in the bunk above him had died in the night. Christof Knoll, the Kapo, ordered Jakob to drag the corpse out and afterwards get to his unit for the day's work. Jakob lifted the corpse in his arms and walked out of the barracks, muttering that the only good German was a dead German. He rushed back from the infirmary to join the headcount, and then his unit marched out of the gates, all the prisoners in leg irons. Jakob looked back at the camp, an old munitions factory in the Great War, and wondered how his country had let itself become enslaved.

Jakob had been convicted of inciting violence against the government. He pleaded guilty on the advice of his lawyer and asked for clemency. The Gestapo had made several similar arrests, mainly young Jewish men. Schmidt's view was that these Jews, who had been fomenting unrest, were anarchists and, if released, would be a threat to the security of the state. In his opinion, their sentences were not nearly severe enough and that they needed to be made an example of, so that no other Jew would ever threaten the party.

It was a cold morning, but within minutes of swinging a sledge-hammer, Jakob was sweating. His shaved head itched, and he stopped momentarily to wipe his forehead. An SS guard shouted at him, and he continued breaking stones, as he had done for the last two months, dressed in his blue-and-white striped jacket and trousers and a cap of the same material. The clogs he wore still hurt his feet, although he was relieved to have had his leg irons removed.

"You're a filthy swine. What are you?"

It was the coldness of the tone of voice that Jakob noticed. He did not turn, but answered, "A filthy swine, sir."

"I didn't hear you."

"A filthy swine, sir!" Jakob bellowed.

"Oh, I like you," whispered the voice in Jakob's ear, "you've got balls. Now we're going to play a game."

"Yes, sir!" replied Jakob.

"Turn around." Jakob slowly turned, expecting to be slapped in the face by an SS guard, but instead he stood looking up at a Gestapo officer. Jakob's hands started trembling, and he put them behind his back. The officer had many small scars across his face and was a good three inches taller than Jakob.

"The game we shall play is called hide and seek. Do you know it?"

"Yes, sir!" shouted Jakob, after pausing for a second.

"I will count to one hundred, and you need to hide, and I will try and find you. If you get back to Dachau without me finding you," said the officer, "then you win and nothing will happen to you, but if I find you, you lose. Do you understand?"

"Yes, sir!" bellowed Jakob.

"It's a game I play with my three daughters."

"Yes, sir!" shouted Jakob.

"Now run," said Schmidt, and he started counting, "One, two, three, four, five..."

34

9 NOVEMBER 1938

Rachel Kraus heard the news on the wireless. The story was not sensational; it was about the third secretary at the German Consulate in Paris who had been shot by a seventeen-year-old Jew, Herschel Grynszpan. However, this third secretary was from an aristocratic German family and Hitler, personally, sent his best doctors to Paris, but the gun shots proved fatal and within forty-eight hours the man was dead. It was the excuse Hitler needed to purge the Jews from the Greater German Reich.

***

In the 1850s, following years of poverty and hardship, Rachel's great-grandfather left Germany to come to Vienna. The other member of his family went to England and the United States and, over the many years that followed, they lost contact. Rachel's great-grandfather started a bakery in Leopoldstadt. After he died, it passed to Rachel's grandfather and then to her father, Abe Kraus, who loved bread, its smell, taste and texture. They were well off, in comparison to most people, and as neither Abe Kraus nor his wife were spendthrifts, they managed to save enough money for a second bakery and a house in the suburbs. In remembrance of his father, Abe Kraus would often repeat what his father used to say when breaking bread: with bread all sorrows are less.

Rachel had two uncles who also lived in Vienna and after the *Anschluss*, one sold everything and went to British Palestine. The other brother, however, refused to leave. He, like Abe, took the view that Austria was his home, where his business was, and where his children and four grandchildren lived. Abe would shrug whenever anyone asked whether he planned to leave Austria and then remark, "Until my boy Jakob is home, the only way I will ever leave Vienna will be in a box."

The doorbell of their small apartment trilled, and Rachel shouted out from the kitchen that she would get it. They were not expecting anyone, and she opened the door to find a postman with a telegram. She knew it was bad news, took a deep breath and looked at him squarely, as if the act might somehow prevent him from giving her the news. However, he looked back at her, with a sadness in his eyes. He had seen that expression on at least twenty other faces in the last two months, and said, "This is for your father, Fräulein Kraus. I'm so very sorry." She held the telegram as the postman turned and went back down the stairwell. Her mother shouted for her to come in and shut the door, but she stood staring out into the hallway of the tenement block, and then she opened the telegram and slowly read it.

"Killed while trying to escape" were the words used. She did not know how she would tell her parents.

35

—·—

10 NOVEMBER 1938

Anna Friedmann picked up the telephone to hear a voice cry, "God help us, Anna! The synagogue is in flames!" Anna listened and then tried to calm her friend, as she was told that although fire engines had arrived, they were only spraying the other buildings. Choking back sobs, Anna's friend hung up the telephone with the words, "What are we going to do?"

"Otto!" Anna shouted. "Bolt the door!" Otto ran in from the other room where the children were, and they decided to turn off every light. In pitch darkness, Otto and Anna crawled back to the front room like thieves, looking out of their windows as the night sky started turning red with the flames of burning buildings across Leopoldstadt. They stared incredulously, saying little as one fire after another started, until they fell asleep in each other's arms with dried tears on Anna's cheek.

"It's a pogrom," said Anna, the next morning, when she telephoned Claire. "We heard glass breaking in the street and went to see what was happening. Our neighbour, Herr Akerman, was standing at his window watching what was going on. Nothing happened for a while, and then we heard screaming, followed by more breaking glass. Herr Akerman was dragged out of his house, beaten by the soldiers and left in the courtyard. Frau Akerman ran out and wrapped her arms around him, wailing as if he were dead. Otto wanted to go out and help, but I told him not to, and then an ambulance arrived and took the body away."

Claire sat silently on the other end of the line, not knowing what to say.

"I heard this morning," continued Anna, "that they had killed him. He was a tailor and never hurt anyone in his life and they killed him."

Otto stayed with the children for most of the day, trying to keep them occupied with puzzles and games, while Anna refused to set foot in the street. When evening came, Otto went out to get bread and milk. Buildings were still smouldering, and he saw soldiers rounding up Jews and arresting them. He hid, half thinking that he should give up this fool's errand and go home and that it was unlikely there would be bread or milk for sale. He waited until he thought things had quietened and turned onto the next street. He could see across the road a member of the Hitler Youth kicking an old man, who lay on the ground trying to protect himself. Otto stared, mouth open and then shouted and ran at the thug, bellowing as loud as he could. The youth turned and ran, looking back to see whether Otto was following him, but Otto was only interested in getting the old man to his feet and back to the man's apartment.

He spent half an hour with the old man, washing grazes, putting ice on the bruising on his face and bandaging his stomach. There were no broken bones, Otto thought, but possibly cracked ribs.

"You'll need to go to the hospital," said Otto. "Have you any family?"

"A sister," he said.

"I have to go," said Otto, "my wife will be worried, but I will be back tomorrow."

The old man tried to stand up but was unable. "Thank you," he said, "but I've reached the end of my journey."

"You'll be fine," said Otto.

"None of us will be fine," said the old man. "That boy wanted to kill me. I was no older than he was when I fled the pogroms in Russia. I did not think I would ever see a life worse than the past I endured at that time."

***

Abe Kraus's bakery on the ground floor of the tenement block was being destroyed. The windows had been smashed and men with axes were breaking every machine, shelf, light and cabinet. On the floor above, the rooms of a Jewish doctor were being ransacked as well as the apartments of a dentist and journalist. In her flat, on the floor above, Rachel had locked and bolted the doors and drawn the blinds to the window.

"They are sure to come up," cried Rachel's mother, shaking with fear as Abe tried to quieten her.

"What should we do?" said Rachel, trembling as she spoke.

"They'll be looking for money and valuables," said Abe. "We need to give them half of what we've got and hide the rest."

"Just give them everything," screamed Rachel's mother.

"But we'll need some money, Mama, if we're to go," said Rachel. Abe and his daughter looked at each other, and Abe knew that unless they fled Vienna, he might lose a daughter in addition to a son.

The noise below quietened, and they sat in the living room all evening until nearly midnight, when they heard people coming up the stairs. They held their breath. For a moment, Rachel hoped that they would go back down. For a moment there was not a sound until a fist thumped on the door. Abe stood up and went to the door. The thumping continued and he unbolted and opened it. In front of him stood two uniformed SS men and a man in civilian clothing. Rachel could not hear what her father said but a second later they barged past him and came into the living room.

Everything was in its place. There were two silver frames on the coffee table and a crystal vase. A small clock ticked loudly from the mantelpiece. Pictures hung on the walls. They took the silverware and then started rifling through drawers before going to the bedrooms. They found Rachel's jewellery box and tipped its contents into a black bag. They demanded that Abe remove his watch and that Rachel's mother take off her wedding ring. When they thought that they had everything, they ordered Abe to put on his coat, but Rachel's mother became hysterical, and Abe tried to placate her.

"Get your coat now!"

Abe pleaded that he had done nothing wrong and that he was just a baker. The two SS soldiers again ordered him to get his coat and once again Abe pleaded with them. Rachel stood up.

"Call the director of the Vienna State Ballet Company," she said, "he'll vouch for us."

The SS officers ignored her and took hold of Abe's arm.

"I have his number," said Rachel. She paused. "Also call Herr Christian Drewe. He'll vouch for us."

"Who is Herr Drewe?" asked the civilian.

"He is a close personal friend of the British ambassador."

The civilian looked at Rachel and then waved for the SS officers to stop. They left, taking the valuables but leaving Abe. Rachel bolted the door behind them. She then heard thumping on the door of David

Rattner, her neighbour, and a few minutes later she heard banging as furniture was upended.

Two young men from their tenement building were arrested and taken to the concentration camp at Dachau. People said that they would be released soon but, as each day went by, it did not happen. Abe and Rachel talked about where they should go. They had relatives that they knew in England, but it was common knowledge that the British were only letting a few refugees in and that the issuing of visas could take many, many months.

"What can a Jew do but wait?" said Abe.

"That's all we ever do," said Rachel. "Jakob was right, we must act."

"And now Jakob's dead," said Abe.

Rachel broke down in tears. She wanted to get hold of her dead brother and shake him for being so stupid. She wanted to hear him laugh when he told one of his stupid jokes. She wanted to see him smile when he walked through the door or dance with his girlfriend, like he did at her nephew's Bar Mitzvah. She stopped crying but felt completely numb and exhausted.

"I'll make something to eat," she said.

"You don't have to," said Abe. "I can make us something."

"I'll do it," said Rachel. "I need to be doing something."

Six weeks after the pogroms of November, they packed their bags and Rachel's mother sewed money into the linings of their winter coats. Their passports had been invalidated, and they needed new documents to leave. After going to the Jewish emigration centre, they went to the Jewish Emigration Office at the Palais Rothschild to obtain their exit visas and pay the leaving tax, which involved them transferring to the Austrian State all that they owned, their apartment and Abe's business. However, as they waited for their travel documents, an issue arose as to whether their visas to Morocco were forgeries.

Rachel pleaded that the documents had been genuinely issued, but the SS remained adamant that proof was required to show they were not forged. Abe, his wife, and Rachel left the Jewish Emigration Office, and went to find the man from whom Rachel had purchased the visas; however, he had already left Vienna.

Dejected and desperate they returned to their apartment in Leopoldstadt, but that evening they were evicted. With no other place to go, Abe, his wife and Rachel went to stay with Abe's younger brother. They all shared a spare bedroom, not much bigger than a dozen square feet. The next evening Rachel went to the soup kitchen, speaking to no one, and brought back soup for her parents and her uncle and aunt. They slept on mattresses on the floor, fully clothed and covered with thin blankets. Months went by where they hid and slowly starved.

STRANGE GHOSTS

—•—

36

— · —

24 FEBRUARY 1939

In the bitterly cold darkness before dawn, Christian awoke to the incessant ringing of his front doorbell. Repeatedly the bell was pressed, so it sounded like an approaching fire engine. He went to the telephone by the door, picked up the earpiece to find out who it was, and then pushed the button to allow Claire in. He lifted the glass on his watch and felt the hands; it was a few minutes after six a.m., and, as he opened the door, he heard the lift rattle and grate as it brought Claire up the four flights.

"I've brought them," she said anxiously as she opened the lift cage.

"Who?"

"Otto and Anna's children," she said.

"Why, what's happened?" asked Christian.

"They've been arrested!"

At the sound of Claire's raised voice, the youngest girl, Rosa, began to sniffle and Christian could hear the other two girls trying to soothe her.

"Get them inside!" he said, stepping back to allow her and the children in. He heard one of the apartment doors below open, probably Fräulein Schneider, he thought. He started closing the door when Fräulein Schneider called out whether everything was all right.

"Everything's fine," he replied, "sorry to have disturbed you."

"We need to get these children to bed," Claire said, looking at the children. "They've been up all night. Can I take them to your guest bedroom?" And, as she spoke, she looked at the boy Aaron, who stood bewildered. He had cried the most during the night and was now almost too tired to take another step. The two eldest girls continued making a fuss over Rosa. Claire worried that if they could not stop Rosa from crying, they would all break down.

Once the children had been stripped to their underclothes and tucked into bed, Claire sat with them while they went to sleep. The eldest one, Hanna, was the last to sleep, pushing herself to stay awake, making sure that each of her younger siblings was safe. Forty minutes later Claire went to the kitchen where Christian had brewed a pot of coffee and was pouring a cup.

"Black," he said, as placed a cup and saucer before her. In the silence, except for the ticking of the grandfather clock in the hall, Claire began to speak about what had happened to Anna and Otto.

"When was the last time you spoke with them?"

"In November," said Christian, "just after the riots. They said they were frightened and planned to stay at home as much as possible. I telephoned a few times each week until their line was disconnected in December."

"They were sharing their house with two other Jewish families in the district," said Claire, "and were allocated two rooms."

"I know," said Christian. "Otto told me and said that it wasn't safe on the streets of Leopoldstadt and that I shouldn't go there."

"About ten days ago, the Americans approved their visas." Claire sipped at her coffee and then told him that Anna and Otto had started the process of compiling the paperwork to obtain their passports. "And then Anna contacted me to ask if I could come with them to the Jewish community centre, the *Kultusgemeinde*, as they might need some help with translations of documents sent by the American consulate." Claire took another sip of coffee and continued. "All their paperwork seemed in order, their tax returns, affidavits of their assets, military reports and transit permissions. Then we went to the Jewish Emigration Office, which is run by the SS. Otto thought there would be no problem and that in a week they would be travelling to Berlin to pick up the American visas and then to Hamburg to catch a ship to America. They needed to go quickly because the police documents are only valid for a few weeks. On the first day, they stood in one line after another and had to sleep there so as not to lose their place in the queue." She finished the last of her coffee and then rested her chin in her hands.

"God, I'm tired and those poor children are exhausted. I went home in the evenings and came back each day. They waited there for three days, the children as well. However, a problem arose when Otto asked for a certificate of harmlessness."

"What's that?" asked Christian, leaning across the table and gentle squeezing her hand.

"It shows that all your obligations have been discharged," said Claire, "and that you have no debts. However, there was an issue."

"What issue?"

"Something about interest on inheritance tax. It had to do with Anna's mother's house."

Claire breathed out heavily and buried her head in her hands.

"So where are they now?"

Claire took a deep breath and with her voice shaking said, "Dachau. Otto was sent to Dachau and Anna to Lichtenburg."

Christian stood up and moved to the window, lost for words. The grandfather clock in the hall chimed eight. Normally, he would have telephoned Sir Walford Selby, but, following the *Anschluss*, Sir Walford had been transferred to Lisbon as ambassador to Portugal. As a mark of protest, the British had not replaced him, and many staff at the consulate in Vienna had been reassigned. He knew no one there and suddenly thought about his father, who would have woken prime ministers and Satan himself if he thought it would do any good.

"There's nothing I can do," he said, "except call Karl Vogel in an hour."

Claire looked at him as he stood by the wall, his hand touching the dado rail for stability and reassurance.

"That's the lawyer that Otto worked for," said Claire. "Will he really help us?"

"I believe so," said Christian.

Claire said nothing.

***

Frau Huber listened quietly as Christian explained that there were four Jewish children sleeping in his spare room, and that they needed to go out quickly to see a lawyer. He told her that they were unlikely to wake up, as they had only been asleep for a few short hours, but that if they did awake, she should give them breakfast.

"We need to go," said Claire. "I want to be back before they wake up."

They walked through the market towards the law office of Karl Vogel. A year ago, there would have been fresh fruits, vegetables, artisanal cheeses, meats, spices, oils and baked goods. There would have been an unmistakable smell of loamy vegetables and the perfume of orchard apples; the fatty aroma of meat and the sour odour of cheeses and yoghurts; warm cinnamon and nutmeg and the heady scent of dried rosemary. However, there was now very little fresh fruit or meat, so each market trader vied with the others for every passer-by.

"It's so different," said Christian, "to the Vienna I knew when I first came here in 1913." His head moved slightly, as he listened to the conversations of people haggling at market stalls. "I was just a young man, and Tomas would drag me to places like this where he thought you could see the real Viennese. I did a painting of a street cleaner just near here."

Claire knew exactly which painting it was as it hung with a dozen others in his second guestroom where the four children slept. She looked at him. He did this whenever his mind was somewhere else. He would talk about something inconsequential and not about the real problem, and while she could rationally understand why, it irritated her.

"What are we going to do about the children?" she asked.

"I don't know."

"Shall we at least talk about it?"

"What's the point until we've spoken to Karl Vogel?" said Christian. He spoke in a measured tone, with his clipped accent. "There's no point wasting time on what-ifs."

"There's every point," said Claire. "If we talk about it, we may think of something that Karl Vogel wouldn't."

"Go on then," said Christian, "what ideas do you have?"

Claire looked at him as they walked into Stephansplatz. She could think of nothing, but it annoyed her that he wasn't even going to try and think of something. She wanted to talk about it. Four children had been given into her care, and she had no idea what she would do.

"My father used to tell me," Christian said, "that the best way of finding a solution to a problem was to think about something different."

"That is the stupidest thing, I think, I've ever heard."

"He was the sixth richest man in Britain," said Christian.

Claire laughed. "Really?"

"Yes," said Christian, "that was until the war started. The Germans sank a lot of his ships, so he had to hire some. He nearly went bankrupt and mortgaged just about everything he owned. People like Sir Walford Selby knew what he had done, which is why I can always contact him."

"Will you speak to Sir Walford Selby?" asked Claire

"I will, unless Karl Vogel cautions against it," said Christian, "although I doubt there is much he can do. However, he may still have contacts and might be able to pull some strings."

***

Karl Vogel sat in the boardroom of his law firm, where Otto had worked for over twenty years. He was in his sixties and appeared like an unkempt professor, overweight, with white hair and slightly flustered. However, his appearance belied the fact that Karl Vogel was extremely astute.

Christian and Claire explained everything that had happened. How Otto and Anna had gone to get travel documents and passports and how at the last moment everything had come crashing down. Claire explained that it was about inheritance. After an hour of talking, where Karl Vogel listened intently, he said, "You won't like what I have to say. We must not seek to challenge Otto and Anna's sentence."

"Why not?" asked Claire. She sat upright in her chair and looked at Karl incredulously, as if he had been stripped of all sanity.

"I'll explain," said Karl, looking down at some notes he had made. "If we apply to the court for Otto and Anna's release, it will fail. A few years ago, one of the prisoners was beaten to death in Dachau, and the Munich public prosecutor indicted the camp commandant. Hitler, however, stopped the prosecution and issued an edict stating that Dachau and all other concentration camps, including Lichtenburg, were no longer subject to German law as it applied to German citizens. The camps are run solely by the SS administrators, and they may punish as they deem fit. That is the source of the problem."

"But we are not challenging the camps' authority but only the decision to send Otto and Anna there," said Christian.

"Two things would happen, Herr Drewe, if we did that. The spotlight would fall on Otto and Anna, and their incarceration would continue so long as the legal challenge was before the courts, which could be months if not years. The German courts are in no hurry to hear cases involving Jews."

"But it's better than doing nothing," said Claire. She shook her head as she spoke and, in her view, she was clear that they had come to see the wrong lawyer. She could feel the annoyance rising in her.

Karl looked at Claire. "I understand your scepticism but, in my opinion, Otto and Anna were arrested because of a failure to declare their assets and they are required to pay interest on the undeclared sum. If we pay the outstanding interest, we can then get the claim struck out. Otto should then be released and Anna as well. It's likely to take a few months or more, but the authorities will not wish to keep them."

"More than a few months," said Claire. "They won't last that long."

"You're saying that there is a chance that Otto and Anna could be free in April or May," said Christian.

"There's a chance, yes," said Karl. "However, my concerns are for Otto. Dachau has a severe disciplinary and penal code."

"What can we do?" asked Christian.

Karl locked his fingers together, placed his elbows on the table and rested his chin on his fingers.

"There are three things I would recommend. First, we pay Otto's debt. Second, you speak to Sir Walford Selby and ask him to contact Eichmann's office at the Central Agency for Jewish Emigration. If he can convince Eichmann that this could turn into a political issue, Eichmann might order their release. It's a long shot but one I think we must take."

"And the third?" asked Claire.

"We get Otto and Anna's permission to allow their children to leave the country."

"Why do we need to do that, if they are going to be released shortly?" asked Claire.

"Because if something happens to Otto and Anna," said Karl, "then getting the children out of the country would become much more difficult."

***

Hanna Friedmann had the same strawberry blond hair as her mother and a sensitive oval face. Her eyes were cornflower blue, the same colour as the headscarf in Vermeer's painting of *Girl with a Pearl Earring*. Her father said that her smile was like an angel, but she had not smiled for days, and a look of concern lay heavy around her eyes.

She worried about her parents and what was happening to them or that she would be arrested and, if she was arrested, the things that might be done to her that she knew little about. She worried about her siblings and how she would look after them. She was the eldest Friedmann child, and would be sixteen in June, and, like every young Jewish girl in Vienna, she worried that her childhood was being stolen from her, one day at a time.

Claire and Hanna went in a taxi as far as the outskirts of Leopold-stadt, where they were dropped off and where their papers were checked. They were asked by an SS officer where they had come from and Claire said that they had been to the Jewish Emigration Office at the Palais Rothschild regarding Fräulein Friedmann's passport, and that they would be returning there later in the day. She smiled at the guards and she and Hanna walked into the Leopoldstadt area. A wolf whistle followed her that made her skin crawl.

"I'm sorry that I had to bring you here, Hanna," said Claire, as they arrived at the Friedmann house, where two rooms had been allocated to Otto and Anna. "But we need to get all your parents' papers and anything else of value."

"We hid them in here," said Hanna.

The room that they entered was dark, with shutters over the windows. There were four beds where the children had slept. Claire immediately noticed the smell of unwashed clothes as she walked in. Hanna pulled back a threadbare rug, lifted a floorboard, and then gingerly put her hand beneath the adjoining floorboard and took out a metal cake tin. She handed it to Claire, who opened it up. There were documents from the registry office, an affidavit from a relative in America saying that he was prepared to support the visa application of the Friedmanns, income tax forms, notices that their emigration contribution had been paid, and a detailed list of goods that they intended to take with them. There was also a small velvet jewellery bag with Anna's engagement and wedding ring and an emerald necklace.

"Is there anything you want to take with you for your sisters and brother?" asked Claire. "Toys, clothes, anything?"

"Some clothes I suppose and a few toys," said Hanna, looking around the dark room.

"Is there anything of value still here, as we may not be able to come back again?"

Hanna shook her head and tears started falling down her cheeks as she looked around the room, knowing that everything that her family owned could now be put into a metal cake tin and a few small suitcases.

***

Claire carried one suitcase and Hanna another, and they left the Leopoldstadt area within an hour of arriving.

"Hanna," said Claire, as she raised her arm trying to hail a taxi, "I want to tell you what we're doing so you can explain it to your brother and sisters. Your mama and papa asked me to look after you and I think that the best place for you to stay is in Herr Drewe's apartment, for as long as necessary. Herr Drewe has agreed to this." Claire looked at Hanna who nodded her head. "However, Jews are not allowed there and if someone were to find you there, you could be taken to an orphanage, and Herr Drewe would be in trouble with the police."

Hanna again nodded her head and mumbled something that Claire did not hear.

"It's important that you understand this because neither you, Frieda, Rosa or Aaron will be able to go out and play, and you can't shout or make too much noise. You must tell them this."

"I understand," said Hanna.

"You also need to know what we are doing to help your parents." Claire took hold of Hanna's shoulders and looked squarely at her. "First," she said, "you need to know that I will do everything I can to help them. Herr Drewe is paying the outstanding debt and therefore there is no reason for your parents to be detained. Also, I am going to become your legal guardian so that I can keep you and your sisters and brother as safe as possible."

Hanna nodded again, although she did not really understand why all of this was necessary.

37

28 FEBRUARY 1939

The telephone rang, and Schmidt casually picked up the receiver and was told by the operator that Adolf Eichmann was on the line. Eichmann spoke quietly, slowly and deferentially with no trace of emotion. He asked Schmidt what he knew about a Jew named Otto Friedmann. There was a pause as Schmidt tried to recollect the name.

"Five days ago," said Eichmann, "he was arrested because of an outstanding debt, a small inheritance matter. However, when I reviewed his file, I noted that he was a person of interest to the Gestapo and that you had been asked to be notified about him."

"It was some years ago," said Schmidt, "a personal matter."

"It would not bother me normally," continued Eichmann, "whether a Jew goes to America or to Dachau, it is much the same to me, but this morning I had a telephone call from Sir Walford Selby."

"The ex-British minister," said Schmidt. "What did he want?"

"He has a friend called Christian Drewe."

"I've never heard of him," said Schmidt. He grabbed a pen and made a note of the name, holding the receiver on his hunched shoulder.

"It appears that Herr Drewe wants to be the champion of oppressed Jews. He claims that the Friedmanns are his personal friends and requested assistance from Sir Walford Selby to intervene on their behalf."

"I see," said Schmidt. "But what can Sir Walford Selby do?"

"Nothing, sir," said Eichmann, "except make trouble." Schmidt could hear Eichmann take a deep breath. "He said that this Jew had been given a visa to go to America. I asked him how this was a matter for the British. He blustered for a few minutes and then said it was disgraceful that we were stopping decent hardworking Jews from leaving the country and that he would be speaking to his friends in the State Department of America and in Berlin. I told him, that the Friedmanns had been detained because of an outstanding debt and that this was an internal matter and he should stop wasting my time."

"I see," said Schmidt.

"Selby replied that he thought I had my facts mixed up and that the debt and interest on the debt had been paid and that it was me who had made the mistake. 'It's your career, Obersturmführer Eichmann,' was his parting comment." Eichmann paused before continuing, "I do not take kindly to being threatened, especially by an English windbag like Selby."

"And has the debt been paid?" asked Schmidt.

"Apparently so and by Herr Christian Drewe. I therefore have no reason to continue to hold the Friedmanns but, as you have expressed an interest in Otto Friedmann, I thought I ought to defer to you."

Schmidt remembered the hearing before Otto Friedmann nearly four years ago, and how Otto had said that he was not a fit person to hold any public office.

"Leave them where they are for the time being," said Schmidt, "and I will see what I can find out about Herr Drewe."

38

— · —

2 MARCH 1939

Schmidt sat in a room with the poet Jürgen Becker. Becker had put on weight and was now bald, except for a few strands of hair he combed over his fat head. His shirt was stained with red wine, and there was a tear in the sleeve of his jacket, where a police dog had bitten him. The once-famous poet of the Weimar Republic had been accused of a lewd act with a young man in a public toilet. Although he denied it vigorously, Schmidt explained that it was an open-and-shut case and that under subsection 175 of the German Criminal Code, it did not matter that he had not touched the other man; it was enough that they were together in the same cubicle.

"A pink triangle," said Schmidt, "that's what you will wear so that everyone will know you're a pervert."

"It wasn't like that," said Becker, who sniffed and wiped his nose with the back of his hand.

"It was exactly like that," said Schmidt. "Such a shame that your poetry will never again be read in this country, that your books will be burned, and your name will be eradicated from the history of the Greater German Reich."

Becker sniffed again and could not stop the tears running down his fat cheeks. Schmidt looked at him in disgust.

"The Greater German Reich can, however, be merciful," Schmidt added, and poured a glass of water and pushed it in front of Becker.

"What must I do?" said Becker.

"Information," said Schmidt. "I want to know about Christian Drewe."

"Why him?" said Becker. "I don't know anything about him, although I can tell you about his friends Tomas Skeres and Paul O'Montis."

"Paul O'Montis is a friend of Christian Drewe," said Schmidt, taking out a pen from his jacket and a notebook, "and is Drewe a queer?"

"I don't know. O'Montis and Skeres have been together for years, but I don't know about Drewe. He is usually with a female... an American singer who was in a scandal a while ago. Claire Ascot."

"And who is Tomas Skeres?"

"Drewe and him are friends. They were students together under Klimt. Skeres owns a gallery in Vienna and his family manufacture ski and sportswear. Skeres has been bankrolling O'Montis for years since he came to Vienna."

"And what does Tomas Skeres look like?"

"He is quite effeminate, thin, tall, brown hair, glasses."

"You could be describing half of the queers in Austria," said Schmidt.

"I have a photograph of him," said Becker. "One from a few years ago. I'll give it to you. He and O'Montis fled abroad."

"And what about Drewe?"

"He's still in Vienna."

"And what does he look like?"

"Well, he's blind."

"Blind?"

"Yes, he's blind and one side of his face is scarred," said Becker. "He fought in the Great War on the Somme."

"So where are O'Montis and Skeres?"

"I don't know for certain," said Becker.

"You're not being helpful," said Schmidt, who pushed back his chair and started to get up from the table.

"They're in Prague. I'm sure of it," said Becker, "I don't know where in Prague. I heard that they moved about. However, O'Montis still puts on shows near the old Jewish quarter, but no one must know I told you."

***

Adolf Eichmann listened attentively to what Schmidt was saying on the telephone and replied, "Thank you, Sturmbannführer Schmidt, I will certainly pass on this information to the High Command." Paul O'Montis had been on Himmler's list and was someone who was of particular interest to Goebbels for mocking the Führer and Nazi High Command.

"And he is a friend of Christian Drewe," Schmidt added.

"And, if you don't mind me enquiring, what have you found out about Herr Drewe?"

"I have an address, and men watching his apartment. Herr Drewe is blind and I have little information about him except that he is visited by an American nightclub singer and has an Austrian housekeeper. I will personally speak with the housekeeper and persuade her to help us find Paul O'Montis and Tomas Skeres."

"And who is Tomas Skeres?"

"Another queer who runs around with O'Montis," said Schmidt. "He's the money that has been funding O'Montis and has an art gallery in Vienna that was recently closed for selling degenerate pieces."

"Is he Jewish?" asked Eichmann.

"No."

"Then fortunately he's not my problem," said Eichmann.

39

— · —

4 MARCH 1939

Frau Huber read the letter from the Ministry of Defence. Nearly twenty-one years after her son had returned from the Great War, they were posthumously awarding him with the Military Honour Medal 2nd Class for his actions during the battle at Czernowitz in Poland. Her son had never spoken to her about it, as if he were ashamed of what he had seen and done. Twenty-one months after his return from the Eastern Front, he died when he was hit by a train as he was crossing the tracks near Vienna station. No one suggested suicide, as the military refused to believe that soldiers who had survived trench warfare for four years would then, when the fighting had stopped, take their lives. However, Frau Huber saw the torment and the depression and knew he was as much a war casualty as if he had been shot in the trenches.

It was a strange coincidence of life that led Frau Huber to Christian. When he returned to Vienna in August 1922, she was working for the Skeres family on their estate in Vienna. Her husband had been the head gardener before the war, and her son had briefly worked there before his death. However, when her son died, it was clear that the family wanted a couple to come and live on the estate full-time, and Frau Huber was not prepared to give up her apartment. It had been Tomas who had suggested that she become the housekeeper to Christian.

"You'll like him," said Tomas, when Frau Huber expressed her doubts. "He's a bit like Matteo."

And there it was, a comparison with her son. Frau Huber felt obliged to meet this English gentleman who had been blinded in the war, and she saw in him many of the qualities of her son. It was the little things; they were dreamers, full of creativity and imagination, and they cared about other people. She also quickly realised he was as damaged as her son had been. As she prayed in church, the following Sunday after meeting Christian, she thought God had given her a second chance to save a lost soul.

Frau Huber wore her best clothes to the ceremony, those she wore on a Sunday to church. She stood slightly apart from everyone else in the ceremonial hall, with its domed roof, feeling more than a little self-conscious. A score of other people attended, some in tailored suits and others in fine gowns, many of them the cream of society. If she could have left, she would have done so, but this was for her son, Matteo.

"You must have been very proud of him," someone said from behind her. "It is Frau Huber, isn't it?" Frau Huber turned, looked up at the tall officer and nodded. "The battle of Czernowitz was one of the fiercest battles in the war. The Russians pushed our heroic soldiers back but could not break our lines. Your son's regiment held its position and stopped the Russian advance east of Dobronoutz, despite suffering terrible, terrible losses."

Frau Huber nodded again, only vaguely knowing the location of the places that had been mentioned.

"After a week of fighting, the Russians regrouped and attacked to the north of Dobronoutz. They broke our lines, and it looked like they would advance on our flank and, to avoid encirclement, your son's regiment marched about fifty miles in twenty-four hours, with hardly a rest, and then went into battle. There was a point when it appeared that his regiment would have to withdraw, but after his sergeant was killed, your son rallied the remaining soldiers and stopped the advance. But you must have heard this story a hundred times."

The officer narrowed his eyes, as if recollecting the battle.

"My son never talked about such things," said Frau Huber.

"The bravest soldiers never do," he said, and waved to an orderly carrying a tray of drinks, "just like our Führer, who served on the Western Front. A glass of champagne, Frau Huber?" He picked up a fluted glass and handed it to her. "And how has your life been since your son's tragic accident?"

Frau Huber was unused to people talking about her son and hearing about him brought on conflicting emotions, pride and grief. She looked at the officer who talked about her son, as if he knew him, however, he would have been too young to have fought in the war. His uniform was immaculate and on one lapel he wore the SS insignia, and the other had four embroidered silver pips, signifying his rank as Sturmbannführer or major in the SS. He was quite handsome, except for the small scars on his face but, she thought, he had an air of arrogance about him.

"I've been a housekeeper for an English gentleman in Vienna."

"That must have been difficult for you, having lost both a husband and a son."

"No," said Frau Huber, "he's a decent man and was blinded in the battle of the Somme."

"And remind me, what did your son do after he left the army?"

"He was a gardener."

"Oh yes, at the estate of Herr Skeres where you and your husband worked for many years. Do you know their son, Tomas?"

"Of course," said Frau Huber. "I've known him since he was a boy."

"And have you seen Tomas recently?"

"He moved abroad," said Frau Huber, hesitantly.

"Did he? Do you know where he's gone to?"

"No."

"I would have thought that as he was Herr Drewe's oldest friend, you would have an address for him."

As the officer continued to ask questions, Frau Huber began to feel that this was less like a conversation and more like an interrogation. She lowered her gaze and shook her head and murmured, "You didn't tell me your name."

"Sturmbannführer Ernst Schmidt." He nodded his head formally.

"I think," said Frau Huber, "that I should like to meet some other people here."

"How remiss of me. Let me make some introductions," said Schmidt. He put his hand on her arm and guided her slowly through the crowds. "However, before I leave you, I need to ask for your help."

"And what help is that?"

"I would like you to prepare a report on who Herr Drewe meets each day. Can you do that?"

"Why?"

"Because, Frau Huber, we have evidence that Herr Drewe is conspiring with enemies of the state."

"I can tell you now that that's nonsense and you won't need a report from me to confirm it."

A faint smile played on Schmidt's lips, and he said, "I'm sure it is." He looked at a couple in front of him. "And now let me introduce you to Herr and Frau König, who lost their son at Ypres."

***

Both Christian and Claire could tell something was wrong. It was all the little things she didn't do that morning. She did not say '*Guten Morgen*, Herr Christian and Fräulein Claire'. She did not tell the children to eat up everything on their plates. She did not remark to Aaron that he needed to chew his food, nor did she comment that Frieda's hair plait needed to be retied. She picked up the children's laundry and then made their beds, without saying, as she did every morning, "Don't children make their own beds nowadays?"

"Frau Huber," said Claire, putting her head around the kitchen door, "is everything all right?"

"Why do you ask?" said Frau Huber, standing over a pot of water that was beginning to boil for the washing.

"You seem distant," said Claire. "Is it about the ceremony yesterday? It must have been emotional, spending the day remembering your son."

"It was difficult," said Frau Huber.

Claire sensed the boundary in her voice and decided not to ask anything further about the ceremony. "We're going out to the lawyer's office in a minute. Christian's talking to the children now. Will you be all right with them?"

"Of course," Frau Huber. "There is a mountain of ironing to keep the girls occupied, and an oven that could do with a proper scour from a strong boy's arm."

"Why don't you just let them play?" asked Claire. "They've been through so much."

"A busy child is a happy child," said Frau Huber. "That's what my mother used to say to me," and she picked up a handful of clothes and placed them in the boiling pot. She turned and looked at Claire. "When you return, I shall need to speak to Herr Christian. It is quite important."

"Why don't you speak to him now?" said Claire as she glanced at her wristwatch.

"Because you're late, if you're going to get to the lawyers by nine o'clock, and what I have to say to Herr Christian will take time."

"I'll tell him," Claire said, as Christian came into the kitchen wearing his coat, hat and shoes.

***

It was their second meeting at the offices of Karl Vogel, and they were rushed into the boardroom. Karl Vogel closed the door and said that it was probably better if the meeting was conducted privately without an assistant or a secretary present. He summarised the events of the last week, saying that after Christian had paid the outstanding interest, he had filed a motion in the High Court for the dismissal of the claim, and he was now waiting for a court date.

"And, most importantly," Karl added, "Sir Walford Selby has called Eichmann and Eichmann will now know that there are no grounds for holding Otto and Anna."

"And what do we do now?" asked Claire.

"Nothing," said Otto. "Eichmann may, as I hope, arrange for the release of Otto or Anna, or he may do nothing. He may simply not care what happens to them or know that there is nothing that Sir Walford can do."

"And if he does nothing, what happens then?" asked Claire.

"We have the charges formally dismissed and then at the next review period in the camps we hope that Otto and Anna will be released."

"And that will take a couple of months," said Christian.

"At best," said Otto.

Claire sat listening, picking at a fingernail in frustration. Ten days had passed, and she was losing all patience. She looked across the table at Christian, who had hung his head. She couldn't tell whether he was equally frustrated or thinking about something.

So, let's discuss what we do with the children," said Christian, raising his head.

"We continue to keep them hidden until Otto and Anna are released," said Claire. "What else can we do?"

"Get them to safety," said Christian.

"What do you mean by that?" said Claire.

"We take them abroad," responded Christian.

Are you suggesting that we just book some flights to London or New York and that's it, off we go?"

"No, of course not. They would be immediately sent back here unless all their papers were in order. I'm just saying that we might want to start looking into how we do that. I'm just thinking about our options."

Karl scribbled a few brief notes in his pad. He looked up at Christian first and then Claire. He could tell they were both worried and he knew they wanted to be given hope. However, he also knew that false hope was far more dangerous than fear.

"There aren't that many choices," said Karl. "Taking in their children was an incredibly kind and brave act. However, it is important that they are not seen at your apartment. You, Herr Drewe, could be in trouble with the authorities if Jewish children were found in an Aryan building."

"I understood that the morning I opened the door and let them in," said Christian.

Claire looked at Christian and wanted to hug him.

"So, the options are:" said Karl. He raised a finger. "America." He raised a second finger, "Britain." He raised a third finger, "Anywhere else, including British Palestine." Karl looked at both Christian and Claire, as they tried to digest the consequences of what he was saying.

"If you can get the children to America, that, by far, is the best course. Otto and Anna have visas for America, and it follows that if the children can be taken there then they can be reunited with their parents when Otto and Anna are released." Karl paused. "However, it will be difficult because America have strict visa requirements and without their parents the children will have to have individual sponsorship."

"What does that require?" asked Christian.

"A lot of work," said Karl. "But we're jumping the gun. In order to take the children out of Austria and into any other country Fräulein Astor will need a letter of guardianship. That must be our priority because without it, Fräulein Astor has no custodial rights."

"And how do we get that?" said Claire.

"We write to Otto and Anna."

"And how long will that take?"

"Maybe six weeks," said Karl. "We need to send Otto and Anna the formal documents, and they need to sign and return them to me."

"Why six weeks, if all they need to do sign and return a document?" asked Christian.

"Because in the concentration camps," said Karl, "they will only be allowed to receive one or two letters per month."

"And then what?"

"Let's not jump too far ahead," said Karl. "I'll need to do some research on the entry requirements for Britain and America and anywhere else I can think of. Can Sir Walford Selby help us?"

"Only a little," replied Christian. "I spoke to him and had an interesting conversation; officially neither Britain nor America can do anything to help Otto and Anna. However, Sir Walford spoke to the American consulate in Berlin, and they promised to extend Otto's, Anna's, and the children's visas for another six months. Sir Walford also said that there were some American agencies trying to bring Jewish children to America. He mentioned one agency, the Brith Sholom, and a man call Gil Kraus who wants to bring fifty Jewish children to America and suggested that we contact him if he comes to Vienna."

"Are you suggesting that we hand over the children to them?" said Claire.

"I don't know what I'm suggesting," said Christian. "However, if we can get them out of Austria we should, and if we can get them to America then at least you can go with them."

***

Jewish children were treated no better than their parents. They were boycotted everywhere, from public parks and schools. The one Jewish school in Leopoldstadt had been closed at the end of the previous year, and any education which the children got was at home. As thousands of Jewish parents were sent to the concentration camps, the Jewish orphanages grew in number. Jewish children were prohibited from playing with non-Jewish children. Food was short, and there was a lack of fish, fresh fruit and vegetables. The children began to look malnourished and were often ill or had rotting teeth. Diseases spread quickly in the overcrowded Jewish district.

Christian and Claire walked the few short minutes from Karl Vogel's offices to Christian's apartment. Claire tucked her arm into his as they walked, and with his white cane he tapped his way along the kerbside, counting the storm drains as he went.

As they arrived at the front door, she looked across the road at a small café, with a few tables and chairs on the pavement. "It's strange," said Claire, "you see the same faces hour after hour sitting at that café."

Christian opened the door, and they went in and pressed for the lift to take them up the four flights of stairs.

"Frau Huber wanted a word," said Claire, as they got into the lift.

"About what?" asked Christian.

"I don't know," said Claire. "However, she seemed out of sorts this morning."

"I noticed," said Christian. "I just assumed it was everything that was going on."

"Perhaps."

They got out of the lift and Christian opened the front door, to find Frau Huber waiting for him.

"Can we speak?" she said. "Somewhere private."

"I'll go and look after the children," said Claire, who took off her coat and shoes and put them in the hall cupboard.

"What is it?" asked Christian, as they sat down at the kitchen table with the kitchen door shut behind them.

"Yesterday," said Frau Huber, "when I was receiving Matteo's medal a German officer asked about you."

"What did he say?"

"He mentioned Tomas first and then said you were conspiring with enemies of the state. He asked me to spy on you and report to him."

"He did!"

"And there's someone sitting across the road, watching the apartment," said Frau Huber. "What are we going to do, Herr Christian?"

"About what?"

"The children," whispered Frau Huber. "They can't stay here, not now."

"I can't throw them out," said Christian, "I won't. They're terrified. Terrified for their parents and terrified for themselves. You should know me better than to think that there is any chance that I would abandon them."

"Fräulein Schneider is bound to notice," said Frau Huber. "She has a nose for mischief."

40

8 MARCH 1939

You had to drive down a road lined with cypress trees to reach Dachau, and at the end was a stone building with a slate red roof and a gun tower. It opened as a work camp in the mid-1930s for political opponents of the Nazi regime but a few years later it was extended to homosexuals and ethnic minorities. In March 1938, following the *Anschluss*, thousands of Jews were imprisoned there, and, in November 1938, after the riots, eleven thousand more Jews arrived. The camp was surrounded by barbed wire, gun towers and canals, and in the centre were the whipping horses used to mete out corporal punishment.

Prisoners of Dachau were described as enemies of the state by the camp commandant. Brutal punishments were often inflicted for minor infractions of the rules. Solitary confinement was not unusual, with a diet of bread and water or no food at all, and weeks of hard labour. The loss of mail privileges was often imposed, especially on new arrivals. The treatment of the Jews and the homosexuals was the worst. The camp guards would subject the Jews to hours of antisemitic tirades. The homosexuals were often beaten daily, and those who stood out might be castrated.

Otto worked in the forests cutting down trees during his first week there. It was not unusual for prisoners to attempt to flee out of the woods. Most were shot as they ran, and only one or two got out of the forest. Day after day, week after week, the number of inmates increased as asocial or work-shy Austrians and Jews arrived. The conditions deteriorated quickly, and the death rate rose. Many inmates went mad during the first days of incarceration, as they could not stand the beatings from the SS guards. Anything of value that a prisoner had was stolen. Typhus became a major problem, and, for days on end, there might be no water or sanitary arrangements in place.

In that first week, Otto heard rumours that a group of Austrian Jews had been taken to a nearby quarry and executed. The guards said they were trying to escape. Soon, all the barracks were filled, and prisoners who did not have a bed slept on the floor. Otto had a bed but wondered how long he would maintain it as each week, new prisoners arrived and pushed out the weakest. The Kapo of his barracks was brutal, and Otto knew that if he was to survive Dachau, this was a man he must never offend.

Mornings had a profound gloom. It did not matter how well or badly Otto slept; he always felt exhausted and wanted to stay in bed. However, that was against the rules, so he got up, folded his blanket neatly, left it at the base of his bed and got in line for the daily roll call. There were the usual grumbling and the stench of shit from the men with dysentery. However, as the bolts were removed from the barrack room door and pushed open, everyone stopped speaking and shuffled out into the courtyard. It was very quiet, except for the Kapos and guards shouting for the men to get into lines. A cough could make you start, and you ignored the man who crumbled to his knees beside you unless he was your son or brother.

Lumbering was hard work. All the new internees were required to do it, and Otto and the other prisoners were shackled as they marched out of the gates towards the forest. It was a two-hour walk, and immediately you arrived, you would work. It was a life where you were made to feel less than human, where you were hungry and abused. It was a life where you were suspicious of everyone, and people who would call you friend would betray you for a scrap of bread.

He didn't talk to many people in those first few days until he found a rabbi who held discreet services for the Jews. Slowly, one by one, introductions were made to other Jews who might be friends of acquaintances or distant cousins. As the days turned into weeks, a brotherhood began to form, and a simple word, a prayer, or a look would make Otto forget about where he was and drag him back into a lost reality. He tried not to think about his children. Claire had them, and they were safe; that was what he wanted to believe. It was a belief that he refused to question. He tried not to think about his beautiful wife, the mother of his four children, who was at Lichtenburg.

***

The women of Lichtenburg were almost forgotten because it was too hard to think about what they would have to endure. On her first morning in the concentration camp, Anna was told to get up when the bell rang and to stand outside for roll call. It was still dark, and a pale grey light rose from the east. At least it wouldn't rain, she thought, as she looked up at the sky. She wore a scarf over her shaved head and noticed that some other women's hair had grown back. She thought that perhaps time was measured that way here.

Like every other day, Commandant Kögel had everyone stand to attention in formation and, with her whole staff behind her, she inspected the sixty incarcerated women, shouting abuse at anyone who she considered unkempt, lazy or whom she disliked. Her voice seemed to be sucked into the walls of the damp courtyard as she slowly paced down one line of ten women and then another. The female guards who walked behind her held the leads of Alsatian dogs, who bared their teeth at the prisoners. Kögel stopped in front of Anna, the newest prisoner, saying, "Welcome, *meine Damen*, don't think you're anything special here because you lived in a fine house in Vienna." Anna said nothing but looked straight ahead, her heart pounding. "The barracks Kapo will be watching out for you." She stared at Anna for a few seconds before moving on.

It felt like an age standing there, and Anna's calves had begun to hurt.

"What can you do, you useless whore?" said her Kapo as she stood behind Anna. Anna said nothing.

"You speak when I address you," said the Kapo, "and *only* when I address you."

"I can sew," said Anna.

"With a machine?"

"Yes, with a machine," said Anna. "My mother was a seamstress."

"We always need seamstresses," said the Kapo, "but for the next few days, you'll be clearing rocks."

It was backbreaking work, and after a week her hands were calloused and every nail chipped or broken. She was shown how to tie bandages around her hands to keep them warm and stop jagged edges from cutting too deeply. It was a pointless task. There were six in her group, a mixture of criminals, Jews and prostitutes. For meals, they received a thinnish soup, and the women would place the tin cups of soup in their hands until they were nearly cool before swallowing it. Anna thought about her children constantly. She had left them with an actress from a different country with a different culture, and she worried that they would be abandoned if Claire returned to America. At night, she lay awake thinking that they might be being mistreated or abused. After a week, she had not received a single letter and wondered whether she had been forgotten.

Lichtenburg was a medieval dark castle with towers, dungeons, courtyards and endless halls. It was damp and cold. Standing in the inner courtyard and looking up at the towering walls, Anna felt escape was impossible. The female guards were brutal and took pleasure in inflicting pain and humiliation. Lichtenburg was inspected every month, and a few days before the inspection occurred were the worst days for every prisoner. Hours of scrubbing and cleaning had to be carried out in addition to the day's work. Every infraction would be met with a severe punishment. The guards would shout and hit any prisoner who dared leave the corners of their bed untucked or the lockers not correctly presented.

The first inspection that Anna endured came after she had been there for ten days. The guard noted some mud on her boots, and she was dragged out to the courtyard where she was stripped naked and tied to a wooden post. Warder Mandel was called. Anna shook in the cold until Mandel started beating her with a dogwhip. Mandel only stopped when she was exhausted and could hit her no more. The next day, when the inspection took place, Commandant Kögel assured the inspector that there was never any hardship for any prisoner and that they were there only to be re-educated. Anna had been told to say nothing if she wanted to live.

At the end of the second week, she received a letter from her children with a postscript from Claire. The postscript said that all her children were safe and well and asked whether she could sign and return the enclosed form, which gave Claire guardianship over the children while she remained in the camp. However, there was no form enclosed and when she asked a guard what had happened to it, she was told that it had been confiscated.

"Can I see Commandant Kögel then?" asked Anna.

"Of course," said the guard. "But you won't get that form, just another beating like the last one."

41

—·—

10 MARCH 1939

Sergeant Brun shivered in the frosty morning and wondered what he had done wrong to warrant being assigned to a stake-out in Vienna from sunrise to sunset six days a week. At least he had not been given the night shift. Most of the time he would sit in his car, but when the little café across the road from Drewe's apartment opened he went there for coffee and meals. He would sit by the window peering out at an apartment where all the curtains were drawn and few people came and went, except for the housekeeper and the pretty American singer, who had been cited in a divorce case that he had read about in the papers.

It had taken him a day or two to discover who the other tenants of the apartments were. There was Fräulein Schneider on the first floor, a busybody who would prattle on endlessly about everyone and what they did. She had told him that Herr Drewe used to go out most nights to one of those cabaret clubs, coming back at all hours. His friends were dancers and artists, she had said. "You know the type," she added, wrinkling her nose in disgust. The second floor was occupied by a doctor and his wife, who lived a quiet life. They described Herr Drewe as being an educated man, who made charming vases and used to hold, on occasion, very fashionable parties. The third floor was owned by an Austrian duke who had gone to live in Paris after the Great War. Fräulein Schneider said that he used to own the whole building but converted it into four flats and then sold three. He rarely came to Vienna but would, when he came, spend an evening talking and drinking wine with Herr Drewe.

Sergeant Brun's assignment could not have been easier. To watch the apartment block, record the movements of everyone entering and exiting, and follow Herr Drewe when he went out. After a week of surveillance Sergeant Brun knew that most afternoons Drewe would go for a walk on his own, either to one of the parks or to an afternoon recital. He did not go out in the evenings, and, after ten days, Sergeant Brun was convinced that this was a waste of time. Nobody had visited the apartment, and his reports contained so little information that he often thought that Schmidt might think he was skiving off.

Claire and Frau Huber twitched back the curtains.

"Yes, the fat Nazi is there this morning," said Frau Huber. It was how they differentiated the two men who undertook all the surveillance... the fat Nazi and the thin one.

"What's he doing?" asked Christian.

"The same as always," said Frau Huber, "eating a pork chop and a plate of potatoes."

"For breakfast?" said Christian.

"You do know what you're going to say to him?" said Claire, as she watched Frau Huber put on her coat.

"I do," said Frau Huber. "I just give him this piece of paper and say, this is for the officer in charge and that I'm going shopping."

"Exactly," said Claire.

"And if he asks me anything?" said Frau Huber.

"Well, I'll be watching and if you're there for more than a minute I'll come out and wave you over to me."

Frau Huber took a breath and opened the sheet of paper with the details of what Christian had done that week and looked at Christian once again.

"You do live a very dull life, Herr Christian," she said, as she refolded the paper and put it in her pocket.

42

—·—

16 MARCH 1939

Christian hung on every word the radio broadcaster said, as news that Hitler had given the president of Czecho-Slovakia un ultimatum was read out. "Either German troops be permitted to enter Czecho-Slovakia unopposed, or any resistance would be broken by force of arms, using all means necessary, including laying waste to Prague." The broadcaster continued, saying that the president of Czecho-Slovakia had chosen survival for his countrymen over independence and that Germany had marched into the capital. A recording of Hitler was played; saying, "It is the greatest triumph of my life! I shall enter history as the greatest German of them all." There was almost no resistance to the German occupation, and the broadcast concluded by saying that Hitler was on his way to Prague Castle and would proclaim that Czecho-Slovakia was now the German protectorate of Bohemia and Moravia.

"This will be seen as the final move before the inevitability of war," said Christian, as Claire sat reading a book.

"So, what next?" asked Claire, looking up from the page she was reading.

"They'll take the country's gold reserves, its factories, and agricultural lands. Of course, it's a breach of the Munich Agreement but Chamberlain's unlikely to do anything."

Christian turned off the radio.

"What about Paul and Tomas?" said Claire.

"I don't know," answered Christian, "I haven't heard from Tomas for weeks. I don't know where he is or what he intends to do."

"And have you heard from Karl?"

"Nothing. He telephones me every so often to say that we must be patient. I told him I wanted to discuss it with him this afternoon."

***

Christian was always, she thought, appropriately dressed. He had a suit for every occasion and every place, whether to a lawyer's office, a gala or just tea in the afternoon. In the years that she had known him; he had not on a single occasion worn something unfitting. Even when she had stumbled across him asleep in the park, all those years ago, he had sat up without a crease in his jacket. It was therefore in marked difference that she looked at Karl Vogel, who had rolled up his sleeves and unbuttoned his waistcoat, with a pile of legal texts and files scattered on his desk in front of him.

"It's been over two weeks since Sir Walford Selby contacted Eichmann," said Karl, "so we can assume he has no intention of contacting the camps and arranging for the release of Anna and Otto." Karl ran a hand through his white hair. He looked tired, thought Claire. It was not just the bags under his eyes or the wrinkles around his mouth. When he had greeted them in his office, he had been slow to get out of his chair, as if he might have just been napping a few seconds earlier.

"So, what's our play?" asked Claire.

"Do you remember," said Karl, "that I said we had three options?"

"I do," said Claire.

"Well, I think I need to tell you what they involve." Karl picked up his notepad and opened it. "I spoke with the British and American consulates here and in Berlin and also the *Kultusgemeinde*."

"That's the Jewish community centre, isn't it?" said Claire.

"Yes. As you know, we need guardianship papers to take the children to another country and then we need each child to be sponsored if they are taken to America. Each child would have to be sponsored by an American family, who would guarantee that all living costs associated with that child would be paid."

"Can't I do that?" asked Christian. "I have the money."

"No," said Karl. "The Americans require details of an American bank account, payslips and details of all your wealth. A sponsor must also be an American and you can only sponsor a single child."

"And how do we go about getting those sponsors?" asked Claire.

"Telephone friends and family," said Karl. "However, it may take months to get the required documentation and then you have to have them certified by an American notary."

"I don't know anyone who could help. One of my sisters might, but I haven't spoken to her in years," said Claire.

"The second option is taking the children to Britain," said Karl, "and this is by far the easiest option. Again, you must be appointed as the children's guardian and you must give a guarantee to pay any costs associated with returning them to Austria after the war, which is fifty pounds sterling per child. However, as things stand, this is your best option.

"So, we keep them hidden until we receive the guardianship papers from Otto and Anna and then we take them to England," said Christian.

"And the third option," said Claire.

"I've discounted that," said Karl. "At the moment there is revolution in British Palestine, as the Arabs claim too many Jews are entering the country and the British look as if they will impose quotas."

"There is just one problem," said Claire. She stood up and went to the window. "I'm an American and I can't stay in England forever and I won't leave the children."

***

Fräulein Schneider had nailed a sign to the outside wall of Christian's apartment block, saying *Juden verboten*. It was not unusual; signs hung everywhere in Vienna forbidding Jews to enter restaurants, cafés, theatres, parks, castles, museums, and public institutions. There were even signs forbidding Jews from sitting on street benches or walking along some roads. Every building owned by an Aryan was required by law to have one, but as soon as Christian was told about the sign, it took all of Claire's persuasion to stop him from tearing it down and throwing it in the street.

Supplies of food also became limited, and Jews could only buy food after Aryans had been fed. Every Jewish store throughout the city had been sealed shut. The contents of every Jewish shop had been confiscated by the state, gold and jewellery were required to be handed in, property was seized and sold to pay off the fines that the Nazis imposed on the Jews for the November riots. It was common for Jews to have to sell everything to survive.

Christian entered his apartment muttering to himself, and Claire slammed shut the door. It was getting dark outside with a flurry of sleet falling from the sky.

"At least that fat Nazi outside will freeze," said Claire, as she pulled off her boots. However, Christian's mind was elsewhere, as he thought about how to get the guardianship papers from Otto and Anna. Sending two more letters, as Karl suggested, seemed such an uncertain action. Frau Huber came out of the kitchen and told them there were pots of tea and coffee in the living room.

"Thank you," said Claire.

"May I also have a quick word with you both?" said Frau Huber.

"What is it?" asked Christian

"It's the children," she said.

Christian let out a sigh. "What have they done?"

"Nothing. They have done nothing," said Frau Huber. "They sit around in their room all day barely saying a word to anyone. They have nothing, a few toys and books is all they have."

"I know," said Christian,

"I'll get some more things for them tomorrow," added Claire.

However, Frau Huber had not finished and was not prepared to be interrupted.

"I know that both of you are doing all you can for their parents but, as I have previously said, it's not healthy for a child to do nothing. We must find them something to do and help them."

"What do you suggest?"

"Talk to them about what you are doing for them and their parents," said Frau Huber.

"I can do that," said Claire.

"No," said Frau Huber. "This is Herr Christian's home, and he should be the one." Frau Huber took a deep breath. "Second, the children need to be doing something. They need lessons, perhaps English, history, current affairs and piano, and Fräulein Claire... well... I am certain there must be something you can teach them."

"Is that it?" asked Christian. However, Frau Huber had not finished. She had spent the afternoon in the kitchen making a short list and she was not going to be side-tracked until every item had been said.

"Third, they need normality and structure. They will need to make their beds and brush their teeth, morning and nights. I will teach them how to cook and sew."

"What you're saying," said Christian, "is that they need to feel that they're not hiding away but having a life."

Claire went into the living room and poured herself a cup of coffee. She agreed that the children needed to be occupied, and she thought about what she needed to do. She was a cabaret singer and not remotely equipped to educate four children. What could she teach them? Neither maths nor the sciences were her forte. She might, at a stretch, be able to teach them some American history and perhaps French. The domestic sciences were Frau Huber's domain. Music and singing, she concluded, were where her strengths lay.

Frau Huber implemented her ideas immediately, telling the children that they would need to assist in the preparation of their dinner that evening. She watched as four children dragged their feet into the kitchen. She gave them all tasks, peeling and chopping vegetables, stirring pans and adding a pinch of salt to the stew. An hour and a half later the table was laid, and a tureen of chicken stew and plates of potatoes and vegetables were placed in the centre of the table. Frau Huber ladled out six bowls and watched in complete surprise as Christian choked on his first mouthful.

"It was Rosa's fault," said Aaron, as the children sat watching Christian spit out a piece of chicken into a napkin. "She thought it needed more salt."

Claire's heart skipped a beat as Frau Huber coughed.

"I thought just one pinch of salt seemed so little," explained Rosa, "and I thought Mama put in much more."

Be quiet, Claire thought to herself, for God's sake, don't say another word! She looked at Christian who was gulping down a glass of water.

"And *exactly* how much salt did Rosa add?" asked Frau Huber to Aaron.

"Three tablespoons," said Aaron.

"Heaped," added Frieda.

"It's a little too much," said Rosa, who turned to look at Frau Huber standing at the door. "Sorry."

"Well, I think it's delicious," said Claire, who put a spoonful in her mouth.

"Really?" said Rosa.

"Really," replied Claire.

"Well, don't let me stop you from eating it all up," said Frau Huber, who turned on her heel and went back to the kitchen. Claire took another mouthful of stew.

"Pass the potatoes," Christian said. He shook his head in disbelief. Four children had entered the domain of Frau Huber's kitchen and decided not to follow her clear instructions. It was as foolish as leading a charge across the Somme.

"Will she be angry if we don't eat it all up?" asked Rosa.

"No," said Christian. "Just eat the potatoes and the vegetables and we can have cheese and bread later when Frau Huber goes home."

"Fräulein Astor," said Hanna. "Is anything wrong? You look a little pale."

"I'm fine," said Claire, who put her napkin to her mouth, got up from the table as quickly as she could, and ran to the bathroom.

43

— · —

19 MARCH 1939

After breakfast, the children took their bowls to the kitchen and washed them under the critical eye of Frau Huber, who singled out Rosa's bowl for an extra rinse. Beds were made, and dirty clothes were placed in the laundry basket. The living room was to remain spotless, and Frau Huber required that every book and toy be in its correct place. The question, "Who used the bathroom last?" would result in a child running back to clean it. At eleven-thirty each morning, the children would file into the kitchen for a lesson on making pastry for a chicken pie, dumplings or strudel. When Frau Huber's back was turned, Aaron might tease Rosa about adding additional salt, and Hanna and Frieda would laugh. Frau Huber managed to maintain a disapproving look, like an attendant at an art gallery who watches a child's sticky fingers getting too close to a picture; but, despite her frown, she had not felt this happy in years.

Christian realised quickly that he had limitations as a teacher, but he struggled on regardless. He found that often the lessons were too simple for Hanna and Frieda or too difficult for Aaron and Rosa. However, over the following days he found solutions. He might ask Hanna or Frieda to read from an English newspaper or *Time* magazine and then have them summarise the article in German. He would prepare lists of words in English that they did not know. He would discuss the Palestine Conference, the Czech cabinet's escape to London, and Gandhi's hunger strike in India. When the grandfather clock in the hallway chimed eleven, the children got up for a break before going to the kitchen half an hour later.

"There's a piano and singing lesson after lunch with Claire," called out Christian, as they filed out of the room, "and put your books on the bookshelf," he added, but he knew they had already done it.

Lunch was a success, and the chicken pie was delicious. Christian could hear a warm sense of pride in Frau Huber's voice as she coached her young protégés to explain the meal to Christian.

"I," said Rosa, "made the pastry all on my own with butter and flour and everything."

"Did you?" said Christian. "It's excellent."

"Although Frau Huber did help me," she added, and turned towards the kitchen and smiled.

***

Sergeant Max Brun sat in the café across the street from Christian's apartment as Frau Huber left to go shopping the next morning. He licked his pencil and studiously recorded the event in his notepad and, after returning his pencil to his jacket pocket, he dug his cold hands into his pockets. She ignored him as she came out. His instructions were not to follow her but to keep surveillance on the apartment.

Frau Huber's basket was full when she walked back. She had managed to buy a leg of lamb, for which any restaurant would have paid an exorbitant price. She had also found some salami, and although not suitable for the children, she knew it was a favourite of Christian's.

There was no fresh fruit anywhere, and she worried about the lack of basic supplies. It was getting harder with so little food in the shops and more mouths to feed. However, she smiled to herself when she thought about Claire, who only nibbled at her meals, except when it was an overly salty chicken stew.

"You seem to be in a good mood this morning, Fräu Huber," said Sergeant Brun, as she approached the café.

"I'm sorry," she said, coming to a stop. "What do you want?"

"Another report," said Sergeant Brun, who stood up and walked over to her. "We want to know what's been happening."

Frau Huber looked at him. He stood about five foot ten inches tall, and she guessed he weighed more than one hundred and thirty kilograms.

"You know what's been happening." she said. "You sit here nearly every day recording who comes in and who goes out of here. There's nothing more I can tell you."

Sergeant Brun looked down into the wicker basket that she gripped with both hands.

"You look like you've enough food to feed an army."

"Herr Drewe is having some friends over," said Frau Huber.

"The attractive American singer?" asked Max.

"Amongst others," said Frau Huber.

"Well, remember to write down who is there in your report," said Sergeant Brun.

When Frau Huber opened the front door, she called out for Christian and Claire and anxiously explained that she had made a terrible mistake and had told the fat Nazi that people were coming to dinner. "He asked about all the food I had," she said, "and I couldn't say it was for four Jewish children, and the first thing that came into my head was you were having friends over. And he wants me to write it all down in another report."

"Well, let's just invite some friends over then," said Claire.

"And what are we going to do with the four children?" said Frau Huber. "Lock them in that small room and hope no one sees them?"

"No, said Christian, "but we are going to have to do something."

***

Thomas Kendrick and George Berry, from the British consulate in Vienna, stood at the door of Christian's apartment with their respective wives and thanked him for a very pleasant evening.

"I have to say, old chap," said Kendrick, "that when George and I received that telephone call from Sir Walford this afternoon, I did not know what to make of it. However, I was more than happy to turn up and if your housekeeper acquires another leg of lamb, please do not hesitate to invite me for dinner. It was top notch."

Claire laughed.

"You may be questioned by the SS when you get outside," said Christian.

"Well, we'll tell them to bugger off, won't we, George?" said Kendrick.

"When Sir Walford told us what you were doing..." said George, who placed a finger to his lips. "Well, just to say, you only have to pick up the telephone and call us if we can be of any help."

"I may do that," said Christian, "once we have resolved the guardianship issue."

"Well, old chap, goodnight," said Kendrick, and George Berry and their wives also wished Claire and Christian a good evening.

Christian closed the door as the lift started moving downwards.

"Well, that couldn't have gone better," said Christian.

"You're right," said Claire. It had been the first time in a month that she had seen the children animated, as Frau Huber marshalled and commanded them to serve drinks and snacks. The two eldest girls ate with Christian, Claire and their guests, who made a fuss of Hanna for her looks and Frieda for her excellent English and her general knowledge. However, it was Rosa who received the plaudits for making caramelised pancakes with rum-soaked raisins, or *Kaiserschmarrn*, as Frau Huber called them.

"Fräulein Claire," said Aaron, after everything had been cleared away and every piece of furniture returned to exactly it's right position, "why didn't we have to hide from those people? Herr Drewe told us that we needed to hide whenever anyone was here."

"Because, Aaron," said Claire, "those people wanted to help you."

"But why?"

"Because they're good people."

"And are Austrians bad people?"

"No, some are good, and some are bad, but that's the same the world over. Most Austrians are just struggling and want someone to blame for the hardship they are enduring."

"But why are they blaming the Jews?"

"Because they're different, and what frightens people is the unknown."

44

—·—

23 MARCH 1939

A month had passed since Otto and Anna's arrest and each morning either the fat or thin Nazi would be sitting opposite the apartment block watching. Frau Huber remarked that you could tell they were Austrian and then explained that a German Gestapo officer would stand half hidden in a doorway and consider it a matter of pride that he was never seen. An Austrian was different and would want you to know they were there. Fräulein Schneider, who lived on the first floor, now regularly knocked on the door with the pretence of asking for a bowl of sugar or a cup of flour, her eyes scanning the hallway for any type of incriminating evidence.

"If they knew about the children," Christian said, "they would have broken in." However, he began to feel that he was a prisoner in his own home. The children sensed that everyone was on tenterhooks, and they once again became withdrawn. They did their lessons; they made their beds and cooked each day with Frau Huber. The only time that they seemed to relax was when Claire was there, but when she left to sing on the weekends, they suffered that feeling of abandonment even more keenly.

"They're still not following me," said Claire, after the children had gone to bed. "They sit there watching or following you when you go out. The fat one *waved* to me from the café, right as I looked out of the window this morning. Can you believe it? Cheeky bastard."

"I intend to go and see Karl Vogel tomorrow morning."

Claire let out a deep sigh. "What for? So he can tell us 'To have a little more patience'? I'm climbing the walls doing nothing."

45

6 APRIL 1939

Paul O'Montis looked older than his forty-two years as he walked through Prague holding a small suitcase. He tried to act nonchalantly but his eyes flicked left and right, his lips were slightly pursed and his shoulders tense. He wore a suit and a Homburg hat, hoping to blend in with the businessmen who hurried in the early morning towards their offices. He was tired and he knew that there were risks being out, as German patrols were on every other street corner. However, his performance during the previous night had got the small crowd to their feet and deep within him he felt a sense of elation. When he had left the little underground basement, everyone encouraged him to organise another show and so, what else could he do? It was his way of protesting against the occupation.

As he got close to his apartment he was stopped, and his papers were inspected. He knew that if they were scrutinised, they would be exposed as forgeries; however, most German soldiers only glanced at the documents and maintained an attitude of a friendly occupier, at least to everyone apart from the Jews. He smiled, told the two soldiers in fluent German that he was there to buy materials for his factory in Vienna and then, with a forced smile, walked on. He didn't look back after he walked away. Never look back, he had been told; it was a sure sign that you were hiding something. He wouldn't be stopped again and would be at his apartment in five minutes.

"You're back," said Tomas petulantly as he heard the door open.

"Who else would it be?" replied Paul, closing the door behind him and dropping his bag in the hallway.

"That's not what I meant," said Tomas, who came into the hallway. "Whenever you go out, I worry you won't return."

"You worry too much, Tomas."

"And you don't worry enough, Paul."

"It's not that I don't worry, it's just that there is nowhere left for us to go, and I refuse to live in one small room forever."

"There's plenty of room here," said Tomas.

"You know what I mean, darling," replied Paul, kissing him on the cheek. "Let's not fight, as I want to tell you about last night."

Paul recounted the evening that had taken place in the basement of an old factory near the Jewish quarter, where a few cabaret artists, including himself, had put on a show to a small group of twenty-five people whom they knew. There had been no advertising, and no one said anything, except to those they trusted. However, in the bars and cafés, people talked about what was happening somewhere in Prague. Jazz music and schlager would be played, they said, and Hitler and Goering would be mocked. It was an act of defiance. It was the first time a cabaret show had occurred since the occupation. Paul recounted each act that had taken to the stage; he was animated in a way he had not been for weeks.

"I'm planning to do another," said Paul, "in two weeks."

Tomas looked at him incredulously. He knew there was no point talking to him about it. He had tried to stop Paul from going last night, but Paul had been adamant. He accused Paul of having a death wish, but Paul responded that he had nothing more than a life wish.

"Why don't we go to Poland?" suggested Tomas.

"What's there for us?" answered Paul. He smiled as he thought about the hopelessness of their situation, but he was sympathetic to Tomas' feelings. He knew that Tomas wanted to have an escape route, but he was tired of running.

"If one day I do not come through the door in the morning, don't go looking for me; just get on the first train you can to Vienna. You're probably safer there."

"I wouldn't ever think of leaving you," said Tomas.

"You have to, darling," said Paul. "If one day I disappear, promise me you'll run."

"Why?"

"Because if I'm caught," said Paul, "I don't think I would be strong enough not to tell them everything."

46

7 APRIL 1939

Christian, Claire and Karl Vogel sat in Karl's office saying little. The sun was setting, and the office was cold. Frau Huber had remained with the children, although they needed no looking after. In the evenings they would have their dinner and then sit listening to the radio or the gramophone before going to their room and would not be seen again until breakfast. Christian lifted the glass on his wristwatch and felt the hands; they had been there for just over an hour and nothing had moved on.

"Can we just summarise?" asked Christian. "We still have received nothing from Anna and Otto and without the letters granting guardianship to Claire, we can't take the children out of the country."

"Correct," said Karl.

"And you've sent more letters and forms to them."

"Yes," said Karl.

"So, what the hell do we do?" Claire snapped. She got up from her seat, folded her arms and glared at Karl. "It's just a matter of time before the children are found, let's not kid ourselves. They live in an apartment where the curtains are perpetually closed, and they walk around trying not to make too much noise."

"We wait," said Karl, who rubbed his eyes. "The claim relating to inheritance will be dismissed in four weeks' time at a court hearing and Otto and Anna could be released shortly after that."

"Or not!" said Claire. "It might be months before they are released, and our only plan is to sit on our hands and *wait* for that to happen or until we receive the guardianship documents."

"Yes," said Karl, "and we just have to hope that the Nazis don't change the rules for Jews to leave the country, although they are changing their laws every week."

Claire choked back a bitter laugh as her face reddened. "Well, that's just great, isn't it? We're waiting for the next law to screw us a little harder. It's not much of a bloody plan, is it?"

***

In the port of New York, Eleanor Kraus waved her hand vigorously as the *Queen Mary* sailed out of New York to England. Her husband, Gil, was on board with a doctor, Bob Schless. She stood there, incredibly proud of the two of them. As she lowered her arm, she could not stop a tear from running down her cheek and whispered a prayer under her breath. According to their schedule, Gil and Bob would arrive in Germany in ten days' time and then meet with the American consulate. They would be told what they needed to do to organise the rescue of fifty Jewish children and bring them safely to America. Gil and Bob took with them fifty-four affidavits of sponsorship that Eleanor had prepared. She had told them that there were four more than necessary because you never know what may happen. Each bundle of documents had been copied and ordered, and a notary had sealed each one.

47

—·—

10 APRIL 1939

Claire had felt frustrated since that meeting with Karl and then she snapped at Hanna. The second it happened, she hated herself. If anyone deserved patience and consideration, it was that girl, who her brother and sisters looked to for support. But Claire had felt ineffective, and when Hanna asked her, "What are you doing to help my parents?" she felt her own inadequacies rise inside. She just snapped back, "All we can bloody well do."

Christian hadn't said a word but just put a hand on the shoulder of the crying girl and took her back to her room. Claire looked as Hanna walked away and thought, "Christ, what have I done?" Christian spent an hour with the children explaining what they were doing, gently, calmly and coolly. That night, Claire didn't stay. She went back to her own apartment hoping that a little distance might give her some perspective. But she tossed and turned throughout the night. There was no excuse. None. Tomorrow she'd apologise. There would be more tears, hers and Hanna's, but that was the price of hurting someone you loved.

In the morning, she decided to walk to Christian's apartment. She still needed time to think about what she would say. As she passed a small café on the street with an open door, she noticed an empty round table, just big enough for two people. It wasn't the kind of place that she would normally choose. It had a shabby exterior with peeling paint; nothing grand about it. There were no soft lighting or velvet chairs and no waiters in black waistcoats or foreign newspapers. But that was what she needed, the smallness, the quietness, a place to sit unnoticed that did not ask anything of her.

She sat down. The table rocked slightly under her arm, and she imagined Hanna sitting next to her. She was thirty-two and no longer an ingénue, and she knew it. Hanna was fifteen with all the innocence of youth. Claire now had the occasional grey hair, which when noticed was extracted with ruthless precision. Hanna's hair, by contrast, was beautifully blond. Claire wore fashionable clothes, tapered skirts and blouses that clung, just enough. Hanna wore loose fitting cotton skirts that flowed like water. Looking at her reflection in the window, Claire saw worry lines and fatigue in her eyes.

She thought about her years in Vienna and her life in the theatres, and the songs, and the spotlights. None of it had left a mark. There had been the parties, affairs, diamonds, dancing; but in a decade, she thought, who would remember her? Maybe now at least she was doing something that mattered.

A black coffee was placed in front of her. She sipped it. Strong, chocolatey, perfect. It reminded her of the coffee she had been given when she had brought the children to Christian's apartment and her thoughts wandered to Christian. His kindness. His humility. His decency. In another life, maybe something more could have grown between them. But life has a way of placing obstacles before you. Next month she might be on another continent with an ocean between them. And then there was his past, which weighed so heavily on him like his St Christopher. He lived in a world inhabited by ghosts. Until he faced them, really faced them, there was no room for her.

She left a few coins on the table, stood up and stepped out into the street.

As she walked towards his apartment, she continued to think about him. It was the little things he did. The way that he quietly pulled strings for her, never wanting to be acknowledged or thanked. If he could have let her in, it might have worked, however, he seemed incapable of it. Reinhold Böhm had never made her feel that way. He was too obsessed with himself to see her clearly. Reinhold wouldn't have hidden four Jewish children in his home; he wouldn't have even considered it. Reinhold wouldn't be sitting with them now helping to teach them English or stumbling through piano scales. He would have left them standing outside his door!

***

There was a heavy silence at the breakfast table. Frieda had finished and was urging Aaron and Rosa to stop playing with their food and eat something. Hanna sat quietly, her eyes still puffy from crying. Christian said nothing but looked concerned. Frau Huber kept glancing at them, trying to piece together what had happened. The front door creaked open and Claire stepped inside.

"The fat one is there again this morning," she said to Frau Huber, nodding towards the street.

Frau Huber ignored the comment. "What happened last night?" she asked. She took Claire gently but firmly by the arm and pulled her into the kitchen.

"I lost my temper," Claire said before she could even sit down. "I know we all talked about staying calm in front of the children, but I lost my temper and snapped."

"What did you say?"

"It was so stupid," Claire said, shaking her head, and then explained what had happened.

"*Dummkopf*," Frau Huber bluntly retorted, folding her arms across her chest. "Of all the stupid things you could have done."

"I know." Claire's voice dropped. "I know. I'd take it back in a heartbeat if I could."

"Well, why are you still standing here like a bag of flour?" said Frau Huber. "You'd better go see my little *Liebling*."

"I will," said Claire. "You don't know how bad I feel." Her voice faltered and tears welled up before she could stop them. She wiped her face with the back of her hand.

"*Dummkopf*." Frau Huber continued to gaze at Claire, but her look was softer.

Claire turned towards the doorway and there was Hanna, standing with her breakfast bowl, frozen in place.

Claire rushed to her without thinking and wrapped Hanna in a tearful hug.

"I am so sorry," Claire whispered. "I am so, so sorry." Her voice broke, the words spilling out through a stream of tears. She held Hanna tightly, hoping that all could be forgotten in a long embrace. Frau Huber gently took the bowl from Hanna and slipped out of the kitchen.

***

Claire was with the children. She needed a day alone with them to rebuild bridges and Christian put on a long mackintosh, his hat and a pair of sturdy brogues and decided to go to Leopoldstadt. He knew he would be followed but he did not care. What would they report? That he had gone into Leopoldstadt looking for a friend. It had been six months since he had spoken to Rachel. He had tried telephoning her after the November riots, but the number had been disconnected. No one knew where she was or even if she was still in Austria, but he felt he had to try and find her.

It was a wet day, and, walking carefully, it would take him fifty minutes to go the two and half kilometres to Leopoldstadt. Christian decided to take the tram for part of the journey and asked an elderly man to help him onto the number one line. As the tram rattled and banged along, he thought about the previous evening. He had tried to talk to the children, but they were guarded. He did not know whether it was their reserve or his, or whether it was his blindness and how he looked. Claire did not seem to have that problem. She was able to make them smile and cry. She could gather them all in her arms because she wore her heart on her sleeve and that vulnerability allowed them to get close to her. He, on the other hand, lived with regimented precision, it was how he survived.

He had not always been that way; before the war and before his blindness he had been carefree. He suddenly stopped daydreaming, having lost count of the stops. He listened to the sounds around him and then asked how much further to Leopoldstadt. He knew he should never daydream when out; however, his mind quickly went back to the question of whether he could shed the reserve he had clothed himself in. Was he content that Claire and he were only friends? Did he want more? Was he frightened of rejection? He knew the answers to these questions. Yet, he believed, there was hope. They often spoke in hushed, confiding tones, and there would be the low, rich vibrancy of her laughter when he amused her. He might hold her hand when they entered a restaurant; it was the lightest touch, both tender and sensual. Why could he not open his heart to her? He had once led men across the Somme but now he felt as if he were a walking corpse bereft of sight and with no place in his heart for love. Had the regimentation of his life become so ingrained in him, like a piece of knotted wood, that he would struggle to be a husband? His thoughts tumbled and circled around, like a ridiculous maypole dance.

He got off the tram and leant into the strong northerly wind. A police officer stood at the entrance to Leopoldstadt and requested his papers.

"And what business do you have there?" asked the police officer.

"I'm trying to find someone," said Christian, as he put his papers back in his pocket. "I'm going to the *Kultusgemeinde.*"

"You're more likely to be robbed blind if you go in there," said the police officer. "Those Jews, they'll steal anything, even your shoes." The policeman looked down at Christian's polished brogues, "especially those shoes." Christian walked slowly into the Leopoldstadt district. He could hear behind him the fat Nazi talking to the police officer and wondered whether he would be followed to the *Kultusgemeinde*, but he doubted that the fat Nazi would go in on his own.

It may have been the storm-wind blowing through the cold buildings of Leopoldstadt, or the smell of privation, or the whispers as he walked by, or the fear of the unknown, but Christian felt anxious. It may have been that there were no shops open, no trilling of bicycle bells, no birdsong, or the familiar smells that he was so used to in the old city. As he tapped his way along the pavement, he felt that he was being watched, as if he was walking through a nest of vipers. He did not know precisely where he was and soon would have to ask someone for directions to the *Kultusgemeinde.*

"May I help you?" said a voice in the darkness. It was the warm, resonant voice of a man, old and educated.

"I'm trying to find the *Kultusgemeinde*," replied Christian.

"You are fortunate," said the man. "It is not far away, and I am going in that direction. May I ask what brings you here?"

"I am looking for a friend. Her name is Rachel Kraus."

"I don't know her, but they may have a record of her."

They walked along the street another fifty yards and then stopped in front of an old building.

"We are here," said the man.

Christian reached into his pocket and pulled out a coin, saying that it was just a small thank you for his help.

"It's not necessary," said the man. "You may not remember, but we met many years ago. You gave me money when I was playing my violin in Stephansplatz."

"They were happier times."

***

Herr Engel, the director of the community centre, the *Kultusgemeinde*, listened with sympathy as Christian explained that Rachel Kraus was a friend whom he had known for many years, and that they had lost touch when every Jewish person was required to move to the Leopoldstadt district, and he wanted to get in touch with her.

"It is not our policy to hand out addresses, even if we have them," said Herr Engel, "and you have not told me why you want to get in touch with her."

"I want to help her," said Christian.

"How?" asked Herr Engel.

"I don't know," said Christian. "If I am being honest, I am also hoping that she may be able to help me."

"May I ask what help you require?"

"It's a sensitive matter," said Christian, quietly. "I need a document to be sent to a person in Dachau and a person in Lichtenburg and I need them returned. The documents have been previously posted, but I don't know if they have been received. How are such things arranged?"

Herr Engel sat back in his chair and thought for a moment, putting a pencil to his mouth.

"You might bribe someone to take it for you," he said, chewing on the end of the pencil.

"I suppose my question is, how do you find that someone?"

"It's normally a guard, but there are people who go in and out of those camps who may be sympathetic – electricians, plumbers, tradesmen of that type. I can make some enquiries, but I cannot promise anything and, if someone asks me, we never had this conversation."

48

15 April 1939

Schmidt sat in his office. His cap hung on the door, with his trench coat and leather gloves. After the *Anschluss* he had discarded the uniform of the Austrian police and now wore the uniform of a major, or Sturmbannführer, in the Gestapo. He picked up a dossier that had arrived that morning, with the heading Christian Drewe and began reading. The reports of the surveillance lay on the top of the file, meticulously prepared. Frau Huber would arrive every morning at precisely eight a.m., except Sundays which was her day off. Her routine was like clockwork; except for the time she left which could vary. Schmidt skimmed through the papers. Fräulein Astor stayed most evenings, except on the weekend when she sang in a cabaret club. Schmidt scratched his head. After three weeks of surveillance, they had nothing. Drewe had made one trip to Leopoldstadt and two visits to his lawyers. He had one party where four people from the British consulate had been invited. He had gone walking on four afternoons in the parks of the Inner Stadt and had attended a musical recital on two other occasions. There was nothing of substance in Frau Huber's reports or those of the neighbour on the first floor, who complained that Herr Drewe was often practising his scales on the piano.

Schmidt wondered whether the moment had arrived to call off the surveillance. Nothing suggested that Drewe was in contact with Paul O'Montis or Tomas Skeres or any other asocial or communist. He may have gone to Leopoldstadt and may have Jewish friends, but he could not arrest an Englishman for that. He knew he had to tread carefully. Hitler did not want any trouble with the British or the Americans at that time without good cause. He lit a cigarette and stared at the wall. Everything seemed too neat and ordered. He saw that Fräulein Astor sang in a cabaret club on Fridays and Saturdays, but Drewe never went there. In fact, he never went out in the evenings, although Fräulein Schneider said he used to go out almost every night. There was only one weekday when Fräulein Astor did not stay. He reopened the file and looked at the report for Monday the 10th of April. Frau Huber had left the apartment at seven p.m. and Fräulein Astor had left at nine p.m. and returned at nine-thirty a.m. the next morning. All the lights of the apartment were turned off at ten p.m. and then the bathroom light had been turned on at midnight. Schmidt stared at the page oblivious to everything around him until the cigarette started to burn the top of his index and middle fingers. He stubbed it out. "Why would a blind man turn on a bathroom light?"

Schmidt picked up the telephone and called down to Sergeant Brun.

"Someone's hiding in Drewe's apartment."

"Who?" asked Brun.

"I don't know but continue with the surveillance and contact the telephone exchange. I want every call that Herr Drewe makes record-ed."

***

Berlin was full of palaces, statues, museums and theatres and was one of the great cities of Europe. It was also a modern city and very little of old Berlin remained in the tide of a rapidly rising new metropolis. Being a Jew in the heart of Nazi Germany, Gil Kraus felt ill at ease despite his being seen only as an American and the new laws that applied to Jews were ignored when one was an American. He could stay in any hotel he chose, go wherever he wanted and eat in the finest restaurants of Berlin without fear of condemnation or arrest. However, it was the little things that Gil noticed when he arrived in Berlin; how on every street corner there was a soldier in military uniform and how a weight seemed to hang over the people. Everyone was guarded in Berlin and knew the consequences of speaking out against the Nazis.

The American consulate in Berlin had no ambassador, as he had been withdrawn in protest over the November pogroms, so Gil and Bob Schless met with the American consul, Raymond Geist instead. Their reception was cordial, although Raymond Geist could not commit to helping them.

"The main problem has been sponsors," said Raymond Geist. "We often find that small children who are next in line for a visa cannot take up the visa because they do not have sponsorship in America, and therefore, no place for them to go, no home waiting for them. However, you have sponsors for fifty children. That makes a difference."

"Is that the only problem?" asked Gil.

"No," said Raymond. "Also, the families owe confiscation fines, and without money to pay the fines, they are not permitted to leave the country. If you would like a list of the next twenty-five children to be issued visas in Vienna, I can prepare it within the hour. These will be people who had registered to leave between the second of March and the second of April 1938."

"We can pay the fines," said Gil. "But what do we do then?"

"You go to Vienna, and you speak to Herr Engel, the director of the *Kultusgemeinde*."

"Why Vienna?"

"Because they are overrun with people trying to leave."

"And how can Herr Engel help us?" asked Gil.

"He'll put you in touch with the families of the people on our list," said Raymond Geist. "It's important to ensure that you only take children on our list. We must verify that they applied to come to America, otherwise, they will be turned away when they arrive in the States."

"No exceptions?" said Gil.

"No exceptions."

***

Eleanor Kraus was more than a little surprised when she received a call from Gil saying that he and Bob Schless were in Vienna. She shifted from foot to foot, as her husband described their meeting with Raymond Geist, the consul in Berlin, wrestling with an inner turmoil to interrupt and ask him a dozen questions. She was told that they gone to Vienna because there were thousands of Jewish children there who needed to leave Austria and that they had been given an office at the Jewish community centre.

"It's chaotic but safe," said Gil, "and there's more work than we can manage, even with Hedy Neufeld helping us."

"Who's Hedy Neufeld?" asked Eleanor.

"She's a nurse who was appointed to help Bob. You'll like her. Bob does."

By the time Eleanor put down the receiver, she had agreed to take a ship to Hamburg on the 20th of April where Gil would meet her and take her back to Vienna.

49

17 April 1939

Christian put down the telephone receiver, put on his hat and coat and went out. His first stop was to his bank in Stephansplatz and then to the tram stop. He was unsure whether he was being followed as the noise of the city prevented him from being certain. When he got off the tram at Leopoldstadt, he had his papers ready and was asked where he was going and the purpose of his visit.

"I have an appointment at the *Kultusgemeinde*," Christian said, and was allowed to enter without any further details being given. Sergeant Brun, who had followed him, stopped at the checkpoint and spoke to the officer there. He had no intention of going into Leopoldstadt on his own as there had been rumours of police officers being attacked by young Jewish Bolsheviks and so he made a note in his diary that Christian had gone to the *Kultusgemeinde*.

Christian slowly tapped the pavement in front of him as he made his way to the community centre. The anxiety he had felt before had diminished although he still had the sense of being watched. He thought about what Herr Engel had said on the telephone, that he might be able to assist with the matter they had discussed although it would be expensive.

Herr Engel was waiting in his office on the second floor and Christian was shown in. He was not offered tea or coffee, as they had none.

"I'm sorry for being so reticent on the telephone," said Herr Engel, "but you never know who's listening."

"I quite understand," said Christian.

"At least once a week the Gestapo come here asking about who has visited and what they want. They asked about you the last time they were here."

"And what did you tell them?"

"That you came looking for a friend, Rachel Kraus, but that I did not know where she was."

"And you didn't mention that other matter?"

Herr Engel laughed and said, "No! I thought it better to omit that part of our conversation. Now, would you like to tell me who you want these documents sent to and why."

Christian explained who Otto and Anna Friedmann were and why they had been arrested. He told Herr Engel that their children were being cared for by a friend of Otto and Anna's, however, he decided not to give a name or say that the children were living in his apartment.

"A lawyer told me that in order for a child to be sent to England on the *Kindertransport*, a parent or guardian needs to approve the child going and therefore we need letters of guardianship," said Christian. "We have previously sent letters, but nothing has been returned. It's been nearly two months now, and we do not know whether they have received the letters or if they can send a reply." Christian reached inside his jacket and pulled out two envelopes. "I would like one of these to be passed to Otto Friedmann in Dachau and the other to Anna Friedmann in Lichtenburg, and I would like them collected and returned as soon as possible."

"You understand that there are no guarantees," said Herr Engel, "and that the bribes will be expensive?"

"Yes," said Christian, reaching into his inside pocket and taking out a thick envelope, "but I would like to try anyway. This I believe should cover the expenses."

Herr Engel took the envelopes and placed them in the top drawer of his desk.

"Unfortunately, I have been unable to find where Rachel Kraus is, as people move about or are relocated almost daily here. I did speak to someone who knew the family. I was told that they had moved into an apartment above one the bakeries owned by Abe Kraus but that was confiscated by the authorities when they applied for exit visas to leave. They are probably living abroad or with friends or family, but I'm not sure."

"Could you keep on looking?" said Christian. "I would like to help her and her brother Jakob if I can."

Herr Engel took a deep breath. "Then you haven't heard about Jakob Kraus?"

"No," said Christian.

"He was arrested and shot while trying to escape, so the Gestapo claims."

"Jakob? But he was just a boy!" Christian put his hand in front of his mouth and shook his head in disbelief.

"May his memory be a blessing," said Herr Engel, after a moment. "I say that too often now.

"Please find them," said Christian, "and I don't care how much it costs."

***

The next morning, Frau Huber had gone to the market to buy whatever she could find when the telephone rang. Christian answered it, hoping it might be Herr Engel with a lead on Rachel, and had not expected to hear Tomas' voice on the other end. Tomas blurted out that Paul had been arrested the night before. Christian could hear the fear and disbelief in his voice, as if he was still coming to terms with news he could not comprehend.

"Is there anything I can do?" asked Christian.

"No," said Tomas. "I'm going to come home when I can. It might take me a few weeks."

"Don't come here," said Christian.

"I don't know where else to go!" said Tomas.

"Think of your *perfect house*," said Christian. "Go there."

"I don't understand," said Tomas.

"Your *perfect house*," repeated Christian. "It's where I pray to my patron saint."

"Thank you," said Tomas, "I'll see you soon," and then put down the receiver and Christian then heard another click on the line. He had noticed it a day or two ago and as he put down the receiver, he hoped he had not said too much.

***

The following day Schmidt read the transcript of Christian's telephone conversations. Tomas Skeres was coming back to Austria. However, if it was not Tomas Skeres who was hiding in Christian's apartment who was there? O'Montis had been arrested and there was no one else he could think of. He decided to call Eichmann to discuss the development.

"Yes," said Eichmann, "I heard yesterday that O'Montis had been arrested. Both Goebbels and Himmler have been advised of your involvement in locating O'Montis."

"I'm thinking of discontinuing the surveillance of Christian Drewe," said Schmidt.

"It is a matter for you," said Eichmann, "but I wouldn't have done that. When I spoke to Goebbels, he was clear that he wanted Tomas Skeres arrested; so, if it were me, I would double the surveillance and follow that American woman wherever she goes. There's every chance they will lead you straight to him, now you know he's coming back to Austria." Eichmann paused for a moment. "And what about the housekeeper, is she still sending you reports?"

"Every week," said Schmidt, "although, they could be written by Drewe himself, they say so little."

50

20 April 1939

Hitler's birthday was a public holiday, and all unnecessary work was forbidden. The parades began at daybreak with tanks and armoured vehicles driving through the city. Crowds lined both sides of the Hotel Imperial, and Gil Kraus and Bob Schless stood on the balconies of their respective rooms. Vienna was thronged with enormous crowds, cheering incessantly as the troops marched past. Nazi banners hung from every public building and booming triumphal music blared from speakers. Many in the crowd were in traditional Austrian clothing; the women wore colourful, embroidered dirndls and headscarves, and the men lederhosen with feathers in their hats. Soldiers were everywhere, wearing their brown shirts and red swastika armbands. However, what frightened Gil more than anything were the children, dressed up in the Hitler Youth uniform, in raptures as the army went past.

However, despite feeling uneasy, Gil found he could not stop watching the parade. It was mesmerising, like being at the Colosseum or at a public execution when the masked executioner raises his axe. The crowds were jubilant, not through fear but because they felt their lives were improving. Gil looked down at the singing masses and realised that what the Nazis had given them was hope. After twenty years of reparations since the end of the Great War, the Austrian people felt that the yoke of oppression was being lifted. Gil continued to watch as lunchtime passed, and then his phone rang.

"Yes," said Gil, expecting it to be Bob.

"There's an English gentleman downstairs who would like to talk to you," said the operator.

"Who is he?"

"Herr Drewe."

"I don't know him," answered Gil. "Did he say what he wanted?"

The operator paused before responding and said quietly, "He said he would like to talk to you about some children."

Gil knocked on Bob's door on his way downstairs.

"Put your shoes on and come with me," Gil said, "we have company."

***

"I don't know why," said Christian, "but for some reason I went there with so much hope." He sat in his living room opposite Claire, with the window open and the sounds of laughter coming from the streets. "The meeting was friendly enough; we had coffee in the foyer and then decided to talk in Gil Kraus' room as it was more private. It was strange but as soon as we started talking, I knew they could not help us."

"Why did you feel that?"

"It was just a sense," said Christian, "intuition. We were sitting together and both of us wanted to achieve the same thing. You and I are trying to get our four children out of the country, and Gil and Bob Schless are trying to take fifty children to America."

"So, what was the problem?" asked Claire.

"The problem was that Gil told me that the only children he could help are the ones identified by the American consulate. I asked him why that was when our children have been granted visas, but he responded that those were the requirements of the American consulate. Bob Schless then said he was truly sorry and that we should keep in contact while they were in Vienna and that Gil's wife, Eleanor, was coming here shortly. I started to get up and apologised for wasting their time. Gil took hold of my hand, shook it firmly, and told me that it hadn't been a waste of time, and that anyone who is helping any Jewish child would never be wasting his time."

Christian took a sip from a glass of wine in front of him. He said nothing for a moment, deep in thought.

"I still don't know how I will be able to leave those children if we get them to England," said Claire.

"I've been thinking." Christian paused. "You would be entitled to remain in England if you were married to an Englishman."

"No Englishman has asked me."

"I'm asking."

Claire looked at him. "That probably was the most unromantic proposal a woman could ever have. Do you know, you're an idiot, Christian Drewe," said Claire, shaking her head in disbelief. "An absolute, first-class idiot. You ask me to marry you, but you won't tell me anything about how you feel. I can't live like that. I can't. I need to share my life with someone." She got up. "I'm going to bed." She stopped at the door and looked at him. She hoped he would get up and follow her, fight for her but he continued sitting.

***

Karl listened as Christian recounted his meeting with Gil and Bob, scribbling down brief notes of anything he thought might be important. After he had finished, Christian waited for Karl to say something.

"It seems to me that nothing has changed," Karl said after a moment, "and all we can do is wait. If we get the consent forms from Otto and Anna then we have options, but until then there is no point making plans when all we have are maybes and what-ifs."

"It's been nearly two months," said Claire. "How sure are you that the charges against Otto will be dismissed in two weeks' time?"

"I'm certain of it," said Karl, "but then it's up to the camps as to when they will be released. If Otto and Anna don't break any rules they may be released a few weeks later. They have a visa to leave the country and the money to pay the exit taxes. There is no reason for the Nazis to keep them locked up once the charges against them are formally dismissed."

"I hate this bloody waiting," said Claire. "We are watched morning, noon and night and those poor children are scared out of their wits. They miss their parents and know that if they are seen or heard they could be dragged from Christian's apartment by the Gestapo. It's no life for them. No life at all."

"I don't know what else to suggest," said Karl. "If you try and get them out of the country without all the paperwork in order, they will be sent back, and their lives will be far worse. But you know that."

51

22 April 1939

Christian picked up the telephone and placed it to his ear and then heard a click. He asked the operator to connect him with Herr Engel at the Jewish community centre and gave the number. He listened intently as he waited for a few moments but could not hear any further sound until Herr Engel's voice greeted him.

"I would have come personally," said Christian, "but I thought a quick call might be easier."

"I have some news," said Herr Engel, "which will be of particular interest to your American friend."

After putting down the receiver, Christian called Claire and asked the children to come into the living room.

"At last," said Christian, who stood next to Claire by the piano, "I think I have some good news." He waited for the children to sit down before he continued. "Your parents have managed to send us letters which should confirm that Claire can act as your guardian. It means that we can take you to England, where you will be safe."

"Will Mama and Papa be there?" asked Rosa.

"No," said Christian, "but they can go to America, and we can take you there."

"But what if we can't find them?" Rosa said. Christian could hear the fear in her voice. It surprised him. He had thought that the children would be elated to know that they no longer had to hide away.

"Why aren't we going to America?" asked Frieda.

"We can't go to America," said Claire. She moved to the sofa where the children were sitting and sat down with them. "Listen to me." She put her hand lightly on Rosa's face. "We won't be allowed into America because we don't have all the documents we need, otherwise we would be taking you there. If your mama and papa were here with us right now, I know exactly what they would say. They would tell you that you must be brave and that your safety is the most important thing to them." Claire paused and looked at each child in turn. "And they would say that you have to go now."

***

Herr Engel sat with Christian and Claire throughout much of the afternoon, telling them what they needed to do to leave Austria. He had said the same thing a thousand times in that fateful year.

"While the children will not need passports to go to England using the *Kindertransport*, they will need passports if they are going on to America. You will also need travel documents, so that the children can travel to the Hook of Holland where they can board a boat to Harwich. To get their passports and the travel permits, Fräulein Astor will need to take the children to the Jewish Emigration Office on Prinz-Eugen-Strasse, which is the emigration centre run by the SS."

"Do we need an appointment?" asked Claire.

"I can arrange one," said Herr Engel.

"And what do we need to take with us?"

"The letter of guardianship, passport photographs of each child, train tickets to the Hook and, of course, the leaving tax. There will be hundreds of other people there all trying to leave Austria, so you may have to wait. Take some water and something to eat for the children."

"Is that it?" said Christian.

"Just one more thing," said Herr Engel. "As soon as I contact the Jewish Emigration Office to arrange your appointment, the Gestapo will know what you are about to do. Don't be surprised if they knock on your door."

52

—·—

24 April 1939

Eichmann's department was only interested in one thing, getting rid of the Jews. Eichmann didn't care how fast or how many and, for him, the quicker the better. However, the German government had requirements that had to be complied with to the letter, and even Eichmann was not so sure of his position at the Central Agency for Jewish Emigration as to break the rules. For Jewish children leaving the country, numerous documents had to be completed, signed and then sealed and a tax had to be paid. Eichmann therefore had no objection to Gil and Bob's presence at the Hotel Imperial or to what they wanted to achieve – ironically both wanted the same thing.

Schmidt had got in late after the weekend and had not expected to receive a call from Eichmann's office and was surprised to be told that Herr Drewe had met with two Americans who were planning to take fifty Jewish children to America from Vienna, and that Fräulein Astor had been given an appointment with the Central Agency for Jewish Emigration to take the Friedmanns' four children out of Austria.

"And what do you know about the four Friedmann children?" asked Eichmann.

"Nothing," said Schmidt. "I had assumed that they were in an orphanage somewhere, although it is possible that Drewe is hiding them in his apartment.

"And has there been any development with Skeres?"

"Nothing," said Schmidt. "He's gone to ground and Drewe is probably the only person who knows where he is."

"So, if I may enquire, what do you plan to do?"

"Keep up the surveillance until I find him," said Schmidt. "I don't intend to let a degenerate like Skeres walk the streets."

***

Christian had not had that nightmare for more than a month, the one in which Rose Braithwaite was crushed under the rubble of a broken basement ceiling, as fires burnt above her and the smoke choked her. It was the dream where he scratched blindly through the masonry to reach her, and her pain was his pain. It was the dream where he cried out in desperation with all hope gone, because he knew how the dream would end. It was a death he had lived innumerable times, however, this time someone was there holding him.

His breathing became more regular as he felt her arms around him. He could not make out what she was saying but it was soothing, warm, almost prenatal. He was exhausted.

"You were screaming in your sleep," Claire whispered, "but you're safe now."

"Don't go," he murmured, still on the edges of sleep.

"I won't," she whispered, but he did not hear.

When he awoke, Claire was looking up at the ceiling of his bedroom at a decorative medallion which had carved leaves of oak and four fleurs-de-lis. The ceiling was painted olive green, and the oak leaves and fleurs-de-lis gold. In the middle of the medallion, a brass chandelier hung that once held a myriad of candles. The cornicing of the room was equally elaborate, and between two sash windows was a coat of arms with a lion and a griffin either side of a shield with a crown above it. It was a room that had been designed for an archduke and was excessively ornate; however, as Christian had never seen it, he did not think to change it.

He reached out to a small beside cabinet for his glasses and put them on. He felt exposed, embarrassed.

"I'm sorry. How long have you been here?"

"About an hour or two," Claire answered, not really knowing how long it was.

"Thank you for staying." Christian pulled himself up so that he was sitting in bed next to her.

"Do you know," said Claire, still looking at the ceiling, "that this is quite possibly the most sumptuous room I have ever known anyone to sleep in. It's like being in a palace."

"It makes no difference to me." He felt for his watch, raised the glass and touched the hands. "It's nearly seven. You should leave or Frau Huber will be scandalised."

"But we know nothing happened."

"That won't stop Frau Huber from marching us down to the church and insisting that I make an honest woman of you."

Claire got out of bed and retied her silk kimono. "What was your nightmare about?" she asked.

"It was about a nurse who saved me during the war, and when she needed me, I wasn't there."

"You can talk to me about it," Claire said, pausing at the door.

"I know," said Christian, "but I find it difficult and now is not the right time."

She looked at Christian and wrapped her arms around herself as she stood there, shielding herself from any feelings he might have for her and ensuring that none she had were let loose.

"There never will be a right time," she said, "unless you make it."

***

In Vienna, all through the night, columns of soldiers marched out of the city towards the Protectorate of Bohemia and Moravia, which a few short weeks before had been called Czecho-Slovakia. Tanks, armoured vehicles, motorbikes and personnel carriers rolled northwards, the metal tracks grinding down the cobbled stones of the streets. The chemical smell of gun oil and the choking reek of diesel filled the air. The noise of the troop movements could be heard across the city, in hotel rooms, in clubs, and in the bedrooms of the quiet multitude, who had not spoken out because they had not yet been threatened.

In her apartment, Frau Huber could hear the sound, like the noise of a busy railway station. Her neighbour said no one knew for sure where they were going. On Frau Huber's kitchen table was a copy of the *Vienna Chronicle* with extracts from Hitler's latest speech in Berlin. He promised not to abandon a Greater Germany that had been built out of the ruins of the last war; that he would preserve peace; and prevent the Jewish Bolsheviks from retaking power.

She had been told the previous evening when Christian and Claire planned to take the children to England. Her first instinct was to say it was too dangerous, but she knew it was the only sensible course of action. However, it felt as if she were losing another son. And then there were the children, her little *Lieblinge*, who could not stay hidden forever or be sent to a Jewish orphanage. She put on her coat and buttoned it up to the top. It was rainy and windy outside, and she was suffering from arthritic pains in her fingers and shoulder. She could afford to take a taxi to Christian's apartment, but she had walked every day and so, with her headscarf tied tightly, she closed her apartment door and went out into the storm. She was drenched when she arrived at Christian's apartment. She counted the things that she needed to do. She needed to contact the removal company and pack Christian's belongings in addition to her daily chores of shopping, cooking, laundry and looking after the children.

***

It was nearly a thousand miles, as the crow flies, between Vienna and Castle Drogo, and as she sat eating her breakfast, Lady Frances Drewe felt every mile. The papers had been full of Hitler's birthday celebrations. The Black Guard Band serenading Hitler in the old Chancellery. Little children in the massed crowds waiting to hand Hitler posies as he walked past, and the inevitable parading of his troops, including the infamous Death's Head corps. The pope had sent flowers, and Cardinal Innitzer had said that Austrian Catholics would become, "The truest sons of the Third Reich." She shook her head in disbelief at the actions of the Catholic church. However, when she read that the British consulate in Berlin had refused to hang out flags to celebrate Hitler's birthday, she managed a rueful smile.

"There's a telephone call, m'lady," said her housekeeper, hurrying into the breakfast room.

"Who's calling me at this time?" asked Frances, looking up from her newspaper.

"Mister Drewe, m'lady."

"Did Basil say what he wanted?"

"It's Mister Christian," said the housekeeper, excitedly.

Frances left the breakfast table and said she would take it in her study. In the adjacent room, she sat on a sofa, reached over to the coffee table and picked up the telephone receiver.

"Christian, it's always lovely to hear from you but you rarely call this early. I was breakfasting," said Frances.

"I didn't mean to disturb you," said Christian. "Do you want me to call back?"

"No, I'm here now. I was just surprised. You haven't telephoned me for months."

"I'm sorry."

There was silence for a moment, and then Frances said quite matter-of-factly, "Are you going to tell me why you called?"

"I think I may be coming back to England. I'll give you a call when I know for certain. I wondered whether you could tell Basil. I've tried calling him, but he's always at work and Celia's never at home."

"Yes," said Frances. "I cannot make head nor tail of how they live their lives. They seem to be like strangers that pass in the night."

"You mean ships, Mother."

"No, I mean what I said, Christian. And where are you going to stay? I can arrange a room at the Bristol Hotel in London. You used to like it there."

Christian hadn't been to the Bristol Hotel for years. He suddenly thought about Rose Braithwaite, and his hand went to the St Christopher he wore around his neck. The last time he had seen her face was at the Bristol Hotel, after a fight with her fiancé.

"Are you still there?" said Frances.

"Yes, I'm still here. However, I thought I would come and stay with you."

"I thought you hated this place!" said Frances.

"I don't want to explain over the telephone. There are a few things I need to arrange, and I'll contact you when I come. Is that all right?"

"Quite all right, Christian. Although I must say you are being mysterious."

"I'm sorry, but I can't tell you too much now. I also wanted to say that I do love you."

"Whatever made you say that?" asked Frances, embarrassed because she could not remember the last time Christian had said such a thing. "I really must go, goodbye." She hung up the phone and sat in the chesterfield for a minute. I know, she thought, and I love you too.

53

—·—

25 APRIL 1939

To Hanna, England seemed far away, a frightening place where they did not like Austrians or Germans, and she could only guess at what it would be like. She thought that England would be a wet and foggy little island, where arrogant people lauded it over the rest of the world. She had been told that England had unfairly treated Germany and Austria. Her teachers had said that after the war, the reparations were crippling and unreasonable and that Austria had been wronged. Her teachers had said that Germany wanted nothing more than an Anglo-German partnership, but Britain rejected it, despite Hitler's agreement to limit the size of the navy. Even her father had reservations about the English. He had told her that England, although not perfect, was a better place for Jews to live than many other countries but that stopping Jews from going to Palestine, the promised land, was not right.

It was, however, the two months of living in a guest room of Christian's apartment with her sisters and brother that taught her more about Englishness than anything else. It seemed to her that being English meant that you just got on with things and did not complain. That when you gave your word, it became your bond, and, as Christian was fond of saying, you play with a straight bat, which confused her and her siblings immeasurably. It also seemed to her that all English people took tea in the afternoon, and most importantly, if you had nothing important to say, you talked about the weather.

Hanna thought that Christian was a strange man, often reserved but at other times animated. He said things she did not understand. He would play the piano and sing, "Yes, we have no bananas," and think it terribly funny. He was full of contradictions; he liked quietness, a braille book and his own company but delighted in going out with Claire. He told them about Klimt and how he had been given a painting, which was hanging in the room where they slept. He said that when he was younger, he had painted all the other paintings in that room. She wasn't sure whether to believe him or whether he had made up the story. She liked some of his paintings, but not all, some made her feel sad when she looked at them, as if behind the bright colours there was a hardship that had to be endured.

And then there was Frau Huber. Hanna had been terrified of her when they moved in as were her brother and sisters. Frau Huber told everyone what was to be done and expected that her orders be followed to the letter. Even Christian did what he was told. Mama and Papa, she thought, would never have let themselves be bossed around by a servant, but Christian did not treat her like someone he employed. She did the laundry, the cooking, sewing, shopping and cleaning, and then would sit with him in the kitchen, drinking tea and chatting like an aunt and her nephew as they nibbled at a Victoria sponge.

It had been two months since Hanna and her siblings had seen their parents, and each day made them feel more insecure. Christian had told them, just after they arrived, that he hoped Otto and Anna would be released soon but, when they weren't, he said it would be when the claim against her father had been dismissed. She had been told that last week the claim had finally been dismissed but still her parents had not been released. Christian now said it could be at any time in the next three months, but she thought he was only saying that to make them feel better. However, she clung to that hope, believing that even a false hope was better than no hope at all.

***

Christian knew precisely what things in his apartment should be packed and shipped to his villa in St Gilgen. There was the silver-ware, paintings, the gramophone and a score of other things from Persian rugs to pieces of Louis XVI furniture, which Christian said were unique. He said he would take only his clothes and toiletries to England, as he would return as soon as the threat of war was gone.

"But why not leave them here in your apartment?" asked Frau Huber. "Aren't they as safe here as at your villa?"

"They will be looked after in St Gilgen and what is most precious can be hidden."

"Of course," she said and began packing his belongings. She started taking out box after box from the top shelf of his wardrobe. In one box were things he had brought from England, which had belonged to his brother Adrian, photographs and some medals from his university days when he rowed for Cambridge. There was a lighter, a major's cap, and a book of poetry by Tennyson. The boxes were covered in dust, having been stored away and long forgotten. In another box were things from when Christian had been a soldier, including his uniform, dog tags and, at the bottom of the box, his service pistol and a box of bullets. The children were in their room, and she decided it would be better if the revolver and bullets were not in the apartment; after all, what good would they be to a blind man? She took them into the

kitchen and placed them in her bag. She could keep them at her home
until she decided how to get rid of them safely.

54

28 APRIL 1939

When she kissed the children goodbye, it was the closest Frau Huber had come to crying since the day she had buried her son. She hugged each child, giving a few words of advice, and told them their parents would be with them soon. She whispered to Hanna that there was nothing to fear as Herr Christian would keep them safe, even if his life depended on it. She kissed Claire on both cheeks and told her that happiness does not come from a pretty face but a pure heart. She stood before Christian but found she could not say a word. He kissed her on both cheeks and whispered, "I know."

Frau Huber watched as they left in two taxis, the luggage having been taken to the station earlier, and waved her hand as the vehicles departed. They were followed by the fat Nazi.

Christian was lost in the taxi, as there was no way to calculate the distance the taxi had gone. There were no steps, or storm drains he could count, no smells except for old, stale tobacco in the cab and only the heavy rumble of road traffic. Hanna and Frieda sat quietly with him as they travelled the four kilometres to the train station. Occasionally, they would turn their heads and look through the rear windscreen to ensure the taxi with Claire and their sister and brother was still there. As the taxi slowed, Christian began asking questions:

where were the main doors to the station? What road were they on? Was there anything on the pavement between them and the station entrance?

As soon as they had got out of the taxi, Claire, Aaron, and Rosa were beside them. Claire and the children looked around, as if they were saying a last goodbye. Christian thought about hurrying them along as the train would be going shortly, but he decided a few more seconds wouldn't hurt.

"We need to take the train to Frankfurt and change there for a train to the Hook of Holland. It will leave from platform two," Christian said, and Hanna replied that she would look out for signs for that platform as they walked into the foyer of the station. Christian began to count as he took his first step into the station. Inside the building, he felt more confident with the sound of steam engines, whistles and the clatter of boards directing passengers to a dozen platforms, taking them across Europe.

They walked to the gate, and Christian took out the tickets and passed them to the porter. When the porter saw the J stamped on the children's travel documents, he told them brusquely that it would be the last carriage and that Jews could only travel in third class.

"Christian!" screamed Claire, as they took their first steps onto the platform. "Our bags!"

"What about our bags?" replied Christian, uncertain of what had frightened her.

"They're on the platform, and our things are being searched."

"Stop it!" shouted Christian as they approached an SS officer, rifling through their belongings. Rosa and Frieda began to cry as dresses and underwear were strewn across the platform.

"Don't raise your voice to me," replied the officer, as Christian demanded to be told what they were doing. "We are checking to ensure you are not removing contraband from the country."

"Of course we don't have contraband," said Christian. "What contraband would we have? There's nothing here."

Claire put her arms around the children and pulled them to her. The train to Frankfurt started moving out of the station, leaving them on the platform.

"Jewellery," said the officer.

"What jewellery are you talking about?" asked Christian. "And even if there was jewellery, Fräulein Astor is entitled to take it out of the country as an American citizen."

"I will be calling the American consulate," Claire said, "and making a formal complaint."

The officer looked at her and the four children she was hugging.

"We have no complaint about Fräulein Astor's jewellery, and she is free to go. It's the jewellery we found in one of Jew's bags." The officer removed a green velvet pouch from his pocket."

"That's Mama's," shouted Hanna.

The officer looked at her coldly, satisfied that the child had incriminated herself.

"You see," he said, "they don't even deny it. No Jew is allowed to own jewellery, and this ought to have been submitted to the authorities months ago. The children will need to come with us. You, Fräulein Astor, can go on your way."

"And me?" asked Christian.

"You," said the officer, "are lucky that you're not being sent to a concentration camp."

"What for?" said Christian.

"For harbouring four Jewish children in an Aryan building and for liaising with degenerates and homosexuals."

"They're children!" shouted Christian. "For God's sake, you can't take them."

"You'll find, Herr Drewe, I can," said the officer. "Just know, Herr Drewe, your card is marked, and my superiors have told me to make it clear to you that if there is one more violation of our laws then neither the British consulate nor your friend Sir Walford Selby would be able to stop us sending you to a camp."

55

_— • —_

29 APRIL 1939

Without furniture and the children, Christian's apartment felt austere and cold. Gone were the rugs, the paintings on the walls, the statues and figurines, the crystal, the cut glass and much of the beautifully handcrafted furniture. What was left was only the baby grand piano in the drawing room, which had been impossible to move, the beds and linen, the kitchen chairs and table, as well as pots, pans and utensils. While it was not empty, it felt like a poor relation to what had been there that morning.

"We must do something," Christian said, as he sat at the kitchen table with his head buried in his hands.

"It's nine in the evening," Claire said. "We're not going to find out anything more until the morning."

"We haven't found out anything, despite spending all afternoon in that police station. Did you speak to Karl?"

"I did," said Claire, "he said he'd do what he can and would come and see us on Monday."

"First thing tomorrow morning I'll go back to the police station, and I won't leave until I have some news about the children," said Christian. "They must be terrified."

"Of course they will be," said Claire, "but it won't do anyone any good if you're arrested. Don't do anything stupid."

***

Frau Huber was distracted as she walked back from the market. Again, she had not been able to buy any fresh meat or fruit and, at an exorbitant price, had managed only to purchase some bacon, a few kilos of carrots, a bag of flour, milk and a cabbage. She had dried beans in her larder and knew she had everything to fashion a stew with dumplings. The coffeehouses were full. It did not seem to matter what privations the city endured; the one thing that the Viennese would not give up was coffee, even when they had no pastries. It was not unusual to see soldiers on every street corner and in every coffee shop, with their brown shirts and red swastika armbands. However, as she walked along Tuchlauben, she felt she was being watched, and when someone started walking behind her, she quickened her pace.

She was out of breath when she arrived at Christian's apartment at the far end of Tuchlauben, put down her shopping basket and searched in her purse for the keys to the main door of the apartment block.

"May I help you?"

Frau Huber turned and stood looking at Schmidt. "I can manage," she said.

"I insist," replied Schmidt.

"It's not necessary."

"It's *no* trouble." Schmidt smiled, bent down and picked up the wicker basket. She opened the door and went into the hallway with its marble tiles. She didn't want to get into the small metal lift with him and thought about climbing the stairs, but she was tired, and her shoulder ached. Schmidt pressed the call button for the lift, and she heard the cogs grate as the metal cage moved downwards from the second floor. Schmidt opened the cage, walked in and waited as Frau Huber entered the lift. She pulled the cage doors shut, and they stood there for a second.

"Which floor?" Schmidt asked. Frau Huber looked up at him and thought why is he asking; he must know which floor the flat is on. However, he stood waiting for her to answer, expressionless, looking at her as if they were playing a staring game.

"The fourth floor," she finally answered, and he leant next to her and pressed the button. The lift grated and groaned before it started moving upwards.

"It's surprisingly heavy," said Schmidt.

"Is it?" Frau Huber said as she stared at the floor.

"And what are Herr Drewe and Fräulein Astor having for dinner tonight?" asked Schmidt, peering into the wicker basket.

"Stew," she said. The lift came to a juddering halt, and she took hold of the door and pulled it open. "Thank you," she added, and stretched out her arm to take the basket.

"It was no problem," Schmidt answered, keeping the shopping basket by his side. "As I said, it is quite heavy, Frau Huber."

"What do you want?" she said.

"I want to know about Tomas Skeres."

"I don't know anything."

"Don't take me for a fool, Frau Huber. Where is he hiding?"

"How should I know?"

"Well, let me be clear, Frau Huber, you have lied to us already. You made no mention of those Jewish children in your reports, and we could send you to a work camp just for that. Now, I know that Skeres has left Czecho-Slovakia and I want to know where he is."

"I can't help you."

"You're treading a thin line, Frau Huber, and you're a fool if you try to help these degenerates."

"I really can't help you," Frau Huber repeated.

"If you help," said Schmidt, "then the lives of those four Jewish children that Herr Drewe seems to care about will become easier. We have no problem with them going abroad. However, if you don't help me... well... I can guarantee that they will never leave Austria and will join their parents. Do you understand?"

Frau Huber stretched out her arm again to take the shopping, and this time, Schmidt gave her the basket. She backed out of the lift and shut the cage door.

"Yes, I understand," said Frau Huber, "but as I said, I can't help you."

"I think you will," said Schmidt, "when you've thought it over." Schmidt pressed the bottom button of the lift. Frau Huber started shaking as the lift went down and out of sight.

***

The Jewish orphanage for boys was on the outskirts of the Leopold-stadt area. The girls were sent to a villa, once owned by a Jewish doctor, on an adjacent street. There had been an outbreak of scarlet fever in the girls' home, and Hanna, Frieda and Rosa were told to avoid contact with the other children. Hanna had no intention of getting close to any other child. She didn't want to get to know them, and she did not want to stay there. She decided the best thing she could do was to keep Frieda and Rosa close to her until Claire came for them, however, Claire did not come on the first day or the second. Hanna was warned by one of the staff that if she heard gunshots or fighting in the night, she and her sisters should hide. On the third day, she began to feel the terror of abandonment, and on the fourth day, betrayal. Deep inside her she felt resentment for her parents, who had placed all the family's burdens on her shoulders.

Hanna began to think about what she would do to survive if the Gestapo came. She did not know whether she would fight or go quietly. She wanted to believe that she would struggle with every ounce of energy; she would bite, scratch and kick, but it would be hopeless and would lead to punishment and pain. She ate her dinner quietly, ignoring Rosa's complaints that she was still hungry. Her skin crawled as she thought about what might be done to her. She was the eldest child, sixteen in less than two months, and had no idea what was ahead; every path seemed terrifying and unclear. Her father had told her that, "whosoever saves a single life, saves an entire universe." However, was not her life a single life, and who would save her if not herself?

"When will Herr Drewe come for us?" asked Frieda. Hanna looked at her. Frieda never said much, and Hanna thought she must be feeling the same fears that she was feeling. However, while Hanna thought that they would be abandoned, Frieda had an unshakeable belief that those who professed to love them would save them.

"No one's coming, Frieda," said Hanna.

"Why are you saying that?" cried Rosa.

"Because we must learn to survive on our own, Rosa." Hanna shook her head as she watched her youngest sister burst into tears. "Stop sniffling, will you? Crying will do you no good."

"Hanna," said Frieda, "leave her alone!"

***

The concourse of the train station in Vienna had a row of shops and kiosks, including a florist, a tobacconist and a coffee shop. Walking past, you could smell the perfume of lilacs and roses, which blended into the earthy smell of tobacco. A few steps further, your senses were awakened by the chocolatey and caramelised aroma of dark roasted coffee beans. However, Eleanor Kraus did not notice this as she walked along the concourse; all she saw were the scores of brown shirts milling around, and she leant towards her husband, whose arm she was holding, and asked him once more whether they were safe.

"It doesn't matter, it just doesn't make any difference now," said Gil. Eleanor did not feel encouraged. She continued to look at her husband and saw that he had changed in the few short weeks he had been away. He was exhausted and completely absorbed in what he was doing.

She asked him how she could help and what she would need to do, and he replied, "Everything. There's so much to do and so little time. You'll see." He hurried to the stairs, almost pulling Eleanor with him, and halfway up, an announcement was made that the Führer would be making a speech. It commenced immediately on every speaker in the station. Hitler said he had received a message from the American president, who was an imperialist warmonger. Everyone in the station stood motionless, listening. When the speech stopped, they climbed the rest of the stairs, left the station and took a taxi, passing the Nazi headquarters, the opera house and along the Ringstrasse until they came to the Hotel Imperial.

"Our room is searched daily," said Gil as Eleanor unpacked her things. "There's no point hiding anything, they're very thorough. We think it's the chambermaid since usually things are much tidier when we get back than when we left."

"Every day!" said Eleanor.

"Yes," said Gil. "The hotel also gives a report to the Nazis about who we see and what we do, and taxi drivers will report to them about where we go. If we abide by their rules, it seems they are happy to let us get out as many Jewish children as possible. Also, don't write anything in a diary which you wouldn't want them to see."

"Can we get a drink anywhere?" asked Eleanor.

"We don't go to any of the local bars as they're full of SS soldiers, even the hotel bar, but the dining room here is nice and quiet, with very few people. I think you'll like it. Anyway, we'd better get back to the *Kultusgemeinde*. I left Bob there with Hedy Neufeld, the nurse who's helping us, and they'll be drowning in paperwork."

"What's the *Kultusgemeinde*?" asked Eleanor.

"It's a community centre," said Gil, "where they arrange all the documents to help Jews leave the country before they go to the authorities and have the formal documents issued."

56

30 APRIL 1939

The next morning, Gil, Eleanor and Bob left their hotel and walked the three kilometres into Leopoldstadt along the tree-lined streets. The sun was shining, and a gentle breeze blew along the boulevards. There were many other people out, with families and elderly couples making their way to church for mass. Eleanor stifled a yawn, as she looked around at the city.

"How did you sleep?" asked Bob.

"Terribly," said Eleanor. "The noise of troops and armoured cars going past seemed to go on all night."

"You get used to it," said Bob.

"I suppose you must do," responded Eleanor. "It didn't wake Gil either. How far is it to the community centre? We went in a cab yesterday."

"About forty minutes away," said Bob, who looked around him as he walked. "I wish I had come here in happier times."

The community centre was next to the Jewish temple, with its coloured domes. As they walked past, Eleanor stopped to stare at the bullet holes in its walls, and Bob told her that it had happened during the November pogrom. They entered the community centre and went up to the second floor, where Gil and Bob had been given an office. Dozens of families were already waiting outside.

Klara Rattner was only eight years old when she sat in the waiting room of the community centre. She was tired and her eyes were red, having listened to her parents argue about whether she should be sent to America the previous night. She was recovering from measles, and her mother said that a sick child couldn't make the journey. Her father disagreed and was adamant that his only child had to go and that it was too dangerous to wait longer in Vienna.

"We may die here," Klara heard her father say, "but she's not going to die. She's going to go and lead a life in America."

Klara and her parents sat for six hours that day, waiting for their interview with the Krauses. Her father checked and rechecked the documents that he had been told to bring, fearing that there might be an error in one that would invalidate their application. When they were called in, he could hardly speak except to say his name and Klara's mother answered most of the questions. Klara was tested to ensure she would not struggle with life in America. She had to count backwards and was tested in maths and reading. She was then asked about why she wanted to go to America. When she had finished, she put on a brave face for her parents, not wanting to make their anxiety any greater.

For all the children, the interview process was long and tedious: name, address, occupation of the father, ages of parents and children, school reports, and health records. Bob, who spoke fluent German, and Hedy carried out the interviews. Gil explained, as best as he could, that they might be allowed to take some of the children to America, but it had not been confirmed by the American consulate in Berlin, and he could not say which children would be chosen. The children were encouraged by Bob to speak. Would they like to go to America? Would they be prepared to leave their parents? Would they like to live in a house with lots of other children? There were smiles and tears, hands were shaken, and the next family would be called and asked the same questions and then the next. The interviews carried on all day and the day after, and then they would choose their fifty children. Klara Rattner was the last child chosen.

***

Despite it being her day off, Frau Huber arrived in the morning at Christian's apartment and related the details of her encounter with Schmidt word for word, as far as she could remember them.

"Yes! Yes!" she repeated. "It was the same officer I met a few weeks ago at the ceremony when I received Matteo's medal."

"Are you positive?" said Christian.

"Yes. He's not someone you forget with the scars on his face."

Christian sat in the kitchen.

"So, he said he would stop us taking the children out of Austria unless we tell him where Tomas is," said Christian.

"That's what he said. What are we going to do?"

"I don't know," said Christian. "I really don't know."

He heard the cogs of the lift start revolving, the cable whirring and then the lift banged and clattered as it started moving. He lifted the glass of his watch and placed his finger on the hands. It wouldn't be Claire, he thought to himself. She wouldn't be back for another hour or two at the earliest. The lift stopped on the first floor, and he let out a deep breath.

"Did he say anything at the ceremony?" asked Christian.

"It was nearly two months ago," said Frau Huber. "I don't remember him saying anything, except that he knew you and Tomas were friends."

Frau Huber retied the belt of her coat and left the apartment, looking at her watch as she waited for the lift. She would be late for church, she thought. She had never been late, not once in as many years as she could remember.

57

2 May 1939

That evening, Eleanor, Bob and Gil sat in The Three Hussars, celebrating that they had a list of fifty children, despite not yet receiving confirmation from the American consulate that they could take any of them to America. Like so many restaurants in Vienna, it was almost empty as there was hardly any meat, vegetables, or fruit to be bought in the market. They were in a good mood when the restaurant door opened. Eleanor glanced towards the door and then stared as a man walked into the dining room, dressed in a dove grey suit and grey fedora. She thought there was something tragic about him, and it was not just because he was blind. An elegant younger woman walked beside him, her arm tucked through his left elbow, and in his right hand he held a white stick, which flicked left and right like the tongue of a viper. Eleanor dropped her eyes, not wanting to stare, but looked up again as Gil whispered, "That's Christian Drewe. The Englishman who's hiding four Jewish children." When Christian stood at the table, Gil said, "Mr Drewe, I wasn't expecting you."

"Forgive me," said Christian, "but Herr Engel told me you had made a reservation here, and Miss Astor asked me to make an introduction."

"I hope we're not disturbing your dinner," said Claire. "It isn't my intention to keep you for long."

"I'll get you a chair," said Gil, standing up to take a chair from an adjacent table.

"We wanted to know," said Claire, "how things were progressing and whether there was any chance that our four children could be on your list. I know you told Christian that you couldn't take them, but I wanted to ask whether it might be possible, as things have changed."

Suddenly, Eleanor felt deflated. They had come out to celebrate that they had fifty children, and now they were going to have to tell two people that the children they were keeping safe could not go.

"I'm sorry," said Gil, "but we've filled our quota. What's the problem?"

"Four days ago," said Christian, "we were on our way to the Hook of Holland to take a boat to England. We had got the children their passports and had received their identity cards from the British consulate here in Vienna. However, we were stopped by the SS, and the children were taken from us and put in an orphanage."

"I'm sorry," said Gil. "Are you trying to get them back?"

"Yes," said Claire. "However, it's not that simple. We were told that we would not be able to take the children unless we were prepared to give up a friend, who the Gestapo are looking for. We hoped that you could reconsider taking them because we don't know what to do."

"Unfortunately," said Gil, "that's impossible. I would have taken them in an instant but the American consulate in Berlin will only allow us to take children on their list."

"Can't you telephone them and ask them to make an exception?"

"I'm sorry," said Gil, "but we have our fifty children, and I can't tell their parents that some children have been replaced."

Claire placed her hand on Christian's arm. "I see," she said.

"I am sorry."

"I suppose we might try and take them to England again," said Christian, "and hope that we're not caught."

"Or Palestine," suggested Gil.

"The border's closed," said Christian.

"Officially," said Gil, "but I was introduced to some people who are still smuggling Jews into Palestine. They send them with tourist visas and put them on a boat from Marseille. They enter legally but then get lost in the crowd and live with family or friends. It's illegal and costs money, but they're getting people to safety."

"I wasn't aware of that," said Christian.

"The irony is," said Claire, "the children have been granted visas for America, but without their parents going with them they require a sponsor for each child, and we have not been able to arrange that."

"Did you say they *have* visas?" said Eleanor.

"Yes," said Claire, "they were notified in February by the American consulate in Berlin that they had been granted and could be picked up. That was just before their parents were arrested."

"Gil," said Eleanor, putting her hand in front of her mouth as she thought about what she would say next, "I think I may have an idea." She then looked at Claire and Christian. "It's a crazy idea and I have no idea whether it will work and it depends on the consulate in Berlin approving all our documents."

58

·

3 MAY 1939

The door handle rattled and then opened. Hanna stared, her hands trembling, until she saw that it was Claire. Frieda and Rosa squealed in surprise and burst into laughter. She had brought clean clothes, bread, toothpaste, combs and chocolate. She hugged them and said it had been impossible to come sooner, as she needed permission from the administrator because she was not Jewish. She told them Christian was doing everything he could to arrange for them to be taken out and promised they would not be forgotten.

Claire spent four hours with them, and, as she got up to leave, the two youngest girls cried. She promised to return the following day and the day after and bring cold chicken if Frau Huber could find one in the market.

"How are you coping?" Claire said to Hanna as they stood at the door. "You've been quiet all afternoon."

"I worry," said Hanna, "for myself and them. When you hear a creak outside the door in the middle of the night, you don't know what is coming next. I haven't got the strength to protect them."

"We'll pray it never happens," said Claire.

"I would trade those prayers for a bolt on the door," replied Hanna.

Claire pulled Hanna close, hugged her and kissed her on the forehead. As the front door closed and Claire walked along the driveway, she started crying.

***

The boys' orphanage was devoid of a single noise as thirty pairs of eyes followed the figure of Sturmbannführer Schmidt and Sergeant Brun striding towards the administrator's office. The Gestapo never came to the orphanage, and whenever they were seen in the Jewish quarter, it was usually to drag someone away. Schmidt rapped on the door and entered before anyone answered. He demanded that Aaron Friedmann be brought down. The administrator said that he would call someone to get the child, but Schmidt told him to get off his fat Jewish arse and get the child himself.

A few minutes later, the administrator returned with Aaron and saw Schmidt sitting behind his desk.

"Close the door on your way out," said Schmidt to the administrator, and he looked at Aaron. "It's Aaron Friedmann, isn't it?"

"Yes, sir," said Aaron, his hands trembling slightly.

"There's nothing to be afraid of," said Schmidt, who paused for the merest of moments and then continued, "... if you tell the truth. We will not be here long because I only have two questions I want to ask."

"Yes, sir," said Aaron, whose shoulders relaxed.

Schmidt took out a photograph and gave it to Aaron.

"Do you know this man?" Aaron looked at the picture.

"No, sir."

"His name is Tomas Skeres. Did he ever visit Herr Drewe?"

"No, sir."

"Are you certain?"

"Yes, sir."

"So, you never saw him at Herr Drewe's apartment?"

"No, sir."

"Now," said Schmidt, "the second question is, did Herr Drewe ever mention where Tomas Skeres was living?"

"He didn't, sir."

"Don't lie to me, boy." Aaron swallowed. His hands started shaking again.

"Honestly, sir, he didn't." Aaron paused.

"Do you know what will happen if you lie to me?" said Schmidt, leaning forward so his head was close to Aaron's. Aaron shook his head. "I'll tell you. If you lie to me, I won't be able to protect you or your sisters. The pretty one, the eldest, who's nearly sixteen, will find herself in a concentration camp, not as a prisoner, you understand, but making our soldiers' lives a little pleasanter. Do you understand me?" Schmidt stared at Aaron, who nodded. "Now, if you lie to me again, boy, that will be your sister's fate. So let me ask you one more time, did Herr Drewe ever mention where Tomas Skeres was hiding?"

"No, sir." Aaron started breathing harder. He could feel his face reddening and, between breaths, said, "I don't know anything about him... it's the truth. Herr Drewe didn't talk about things like that in front of us."

As Sergeant Brun and Schmidt left the orphanage, Brun asked whether Schmidt believed the boy.

"Yes," said Schmidt, "he was telling the truth."

"And would you have sent his sister to the camps to be a whore?"

"Yes," said Schmidt, "and I still might if they don't tell me where Tomas Skeres is."

59

5 MAY 1939

Often in Vienna, on a cool, dewy morning, the winds tumble along the boulevards and the cherry and maple trees sway, sending a commotion of intoxicating blossom into the air. On such days, as the slow ache of winter fades, Frau Huber would throw open the windows of Christian's apartment but, now she only heard the constant thudding of troops and tanks heading north and the oily smell of diesel and in disgust, she firmly shut the windows she had just opened.

Claire sat in the kitchen sipping a black coffee. Christian sat down opposite her and, without saying anything, she poured him a cup. They said nothing for a few moments, both missing the commotion that a houseful of children caused. They missed having a family breakfast, the oaty smell of porridge and the acidic tang of cooked apple, biscuits, eggs, jam and warm pancakes with syrup. They missed the hushed laughter, the teasing, squabbles and apologies. They missed their new normality that had, for Christian, brushed away two decades of repetition and silence. He thought about his brother's children and envied Basil every moment with them.

"What do we need to do today?" asked Claire.

"You need to see the children," said Christian.

"And you?"

"I'm going to find Rachel Kraus," said Christian, "even if it means knocking on every door in Leopoldstadt."

"Just to let you know," said Claire, "there are two officers outside this morning. The fat Nazi and someone I haven't seen before."

***

There was a bitterness in their voices and in the way that doors were banged shut, as if no one trusted him. By lunchtime, Christian felt dejected and went to the *Kultusgemeinde*, hoping to find Gil and Eleanor, as it occurred to him that as they shared the same surname, they might be distantly related. When he arrived, he was told by Herr Engel that they had left for Berlin.

"I can't believe that no one knows where Rachel and her family are," Christian said.

"They probably do know, but they're frightened," replied Herr Engel, who picked up a pencil from his desk and put the end between his teeth. "You show up, nobody knows who you are, and nobody trusts you. To be honest, who can blame them? There are over a hundred and twenty thousand Jews in Vienna, and every single one of them worries that the Gestapo will be looking for them next. Who would want to talk to a *goy* like you? It would be seen as a betrayal."

"But I just want to help."

Herr Engel coughed and cleared his throat. "I have made some more enquiries, but our resources are stretched so thin that there is only a certain amount I can do. Even I do not know where half the Jews live. They move from day to day, and no one gives their name when they come to the soup kitchen." Herr Engel put the pencil back down on his desk and then, sitting up in his chair, he continued, "They are a family that does not want to be found, Herr Drewe." He looked at Christian with a tense and troubled thought, "And it's almost impossible to find them when they think their survival depends on staying hidden."

"Even from people who want to help them?"

"From everyone," said Herr Engel. "I know that you say you want to help her, but how can you?"

"There are backdoors into Palestine."

"I know," Herr Engel said, his eyes narrowing. "But those back-doors are expensive to open."

"I am prepared," said Christian, "to help my friends, whatever the cost."

"I'll look again," said Herr Engel, "but I promise nothing."

***

Gil and Eleanor arrived in Berlin, booked into their hotel and then took a walk along the beautiful, wide, elegant streets. Berlin was very different to Vienna. In the capital of Nazi Germany, the shops were filled with everything from clothes, fine watches, wines and food. The streets teamed with well-dressed people and soldiers in full military regalia. Everyone seemed self-satisfied. However, most of all, Eleanor noticed that there were no billboards or signs saying, *Juden verboten*. In Berlin, the Nazi party had achieved its aim of eradicating a city of nearly all Jewish people.

The following Monday they went to the American consulate to meet Raymond Geist, the consul. The meeting went better than ex-pected and Gil and Eleanor were told that they could use visas that had not been taken up and all the sponsorship documents that they had brought had been reviewed and approved. They were told to book passage on a ship for America, leaving on the 23rd of May and that the day before they should bring their fifty children to the consulate for a medical examination and for the visas to be issued.

Gil and Eleanor were laughing when they got off the sleeper train in Vienna.

"Is this really happening?" asked Eleanor.

"Yes," said Gil, "it's really happening, and we'll be on a boat back to America shortly with our fifty children."

"And we can also help Claire and Christian," said Eleanor.

"Let's not make any promises," said Gil, "until we're certain."

60

9 May 1939

Frau Huber ladled up a beetroot soup and said it was borscht, despite not having any meat or vegetables. It tasted terrible, but Christian said that they must have it again and Claire added that she would certainly have another ladleful. They ate in the kitchen as it was the only room with a table and Frau Huber ate with them. She winced as she swallowed every spoonful.

"It is not necessary, Fräulein Claire, to have seconds," said Frau Huber. "You do not need to spare my feelings, I'm not Rosa." And at the mention of her name, she burst into tears. In over fifteen years, Christian had not once heard Frau Huber cry, and he sat there for a moment unsure what to say or do. Claire stood up, came around the table and wrapped her arms around Frau Huber's shoulders. The telephone in the hall started ringing and Christian stood up, said he would answer it and was relieved to leave before he himself became emotional.

"Good evening," he said as he picked up the telephone, "Drewe speaking."

"Ah, Mister Drewe," said Eleanor, "I hoped you would be in. It's Eleanor Kraus; I think we have some good news."

"Good news?"

"About your children," Eleanor said, excitedly, "we may be able to help."

"Can we meet?" said Christian. "This is not something we should share on the telephone."

"We'll be having dinner at our hotel this evening," said Eleanor. "They told us they had beef. Can you be here in half an hour?"

"Of course, and may I bring Claire and someone else?" asked Christian.

"Please do," said Eleanor. "Hopefully, we can make a party of it."

When Christian went back into the kitchen the two women were still hugging but the tears has ceased. Christian stood in the doorway until they noticed him and then told them to put on their coats and hats and telephone for a taxi.

"We're going to the Hotel Imperial," he said. "They have beef."

Claire unlocked her arms from Frau Huber and looked at Christian. "They have steak?"

"I make no promises," said Christian, "but I have an invitation for dinner for all of us."

"I can't possibly go," said Frau Huber. "Whoever heard such nonsense. I am not dressed to go out to a fine restaurant. I'll go home."

"You will not," said Claire. "I have plenty of clothes that will fit you."

"Your clothes?" said Frau Huber. "I'll be mutton dressed as lamb."

"You'll be radiant," said Claire, "and you are coming whether you like it or not."

There were not many people who would start an argument with Frau Huber with the slightest expectation of winning it. Similarly, Frau Huber did not argue with someone with any contemplation that she would lose. However, on this occasion, Frau Huber noted the tone of Claire's voice and decided to be led by her, despite her misgivings.

Within fifteen minutes she was standing at the apartment door, in a long skirt, a cream blouse, a cardigan of the softest alpaca wool and a string of pearls around her neck that would not have looked out of place if worn by Lady Frances Drewe.

***

Gil, Eleanor and Bob had posted out fifty letters that afternoon, each letter being identical and saying:

Dear Sir:

It is my sincere pleasure to inform you that your child will be included in our action to the United States of North America.

Please appear with your child tomorrow morning, Wednesday May 10, 1939 at 9:00 a.m. at Building 1, Seitenstetteng 4 (temple building), bringing with you the documents listed below.

If you do not have all the documents listed below, you must bring the missing ones on Thursday, May 11 (of this year).

You will have to sign a declaration whose wording is reproduced in the following enclosure. In addition, the children will be photographed here.

I expect with all certainty your appearance tomorrow, because failing to do so would jeopardize the inclusion of your child.

Sincerely,

Gilbert J. Kraus

Documents to bring with you:

1. Birth certificate of the child

2. Child's certificate of residence

3. Child's registration form

4. Parents' marriage certificate

5. Guardianship decree, if applicable

6. Proof of statelessness, if applicable

7. Passport (if existent)

Having left the *Kultusgemeinde* they took a taxi back to their hotel and changed for dinner and met Christian, Claire and Frau Huber in the foyer. They started the evening quietly, talking about Gil and Eleanor's trip to Berlin and then Eleanor explained that there would be no issue with the visas being granted directly to the Friedmann children, so long as they could meet the requirements of the American consulate: a decree of guardianship from the parents, birth certificates, passports, four affidavits from sponsors, and the medical health checks for all four children.

"Our plan," continued Eleanor, "is to book passage on the SS *President Harding* leaving Hamburg for New York on the twenty-third of May."

"We have the letter of guardianship," said Claire, "we have passports for them, and the children are fit and healthy, but how are we going to get four affidavits from American sponsors with all their bank accounts and financial details by the twenty-second of May? I could prepare one, if Christian loaned me some money, but I don't see how we can get the others in time."

"We can help there," said Eleanor. "When Gil, Bob and I started this a few months ago we decided that we would complete fifty-four affidavits in case of emergencies. They were all approved by the American consulate two days ago, and so we have four left over. We can use them for your four children."

"The problem is," said Gil, "how will you get the children to Berlin to collect their visas and then onto the boat without the Gestapo stopping you?"

Frau Huber finished her second glass of Riesling, as she sat listening. She had not said a word all evening, but then interrupted, "The one thing you can be sure with any German or Austrian is that they have little imagination. If they think that you are going on a train to Berlin it would not occur to them that you might get on a train to Munich."

"What are you suggesting?" asked Claire.

"Nothing," said Frau Huber. "It's just that if some of the cleverest people I know cannot think of how to get four children to Berlin unnoticed, there is little hope for the world."

Gil let out a deep breath and reached across the table and took a slice of bread and tore a piece off it.

"With bread all sorrows are less," he said as he put it in his mouth.

"What did you just say?" said Christian.

"With bread all sorrows are less. It's something my grandfather used to say."

"May I ask," said Christian, "where your family originally came from?"

"Germany," said Gil, "Why do you ask?"

"I have a friend," said Christian, "who has the same surname as you and uses the same expression."

"It a common enough surname," said Gil.

"But her great-grandparents also came from Germany," said Claire. "it's a bit of a coincidence."

"Can we meet her?" asked Gil.

"I don't know where she is," said Christian. "I've been looking for her for months, but you may be able to help me. No one in Leopold-stadt will talk to me, but they may talk to you."

61

— · —

10 MAY 1939

When Gil, Eleanor and Bob arrived there were fifty children and their parents standing outside the Jewish temple. They went in and sat on wooden benches.

"First things first," said Bob, clapping his hands to gain everyone's attention. "We need the temporary guardianship papers because without them we cannot take your children on board the ship."

There was silence as papers and pens were passed around by Eleanor and Gil.

"And there is another document to sign, which states that I am to become the children's guardian and curator." Bob paused to see if there were any comments, but no one said anything. "We will then," continued Bob, "take four passport sized photographs of each child. We need one for the German authorities, one for you to keep, one for the American consulate and one for our records."

Eleanor looked on, impressed as the parents quietly signed the papers, not crying or making a fuss that their children were being taken away by a stranger to a different continent. Perhaps, she thought, it was because everyone feared for the lives of their children. Perhaps it was the second-sightedness of a people who had suffered persecution since the days of Moses. But, as had happened on the *Titanic* over quarter of a century before, when the lifeboats were being filled, parents were now willingly giving up their children and asking Gil, Bob and her to bring them to a safer shore. They did so politely, thanking them all for their efforts. There were no outbursts and the tears that were shed were not seen.

As the children and parents started getting up to go, Eleanor suddenly had an idea and asked everyone to wait for just a second.

"Perhaps," she said, hesitantly, "one of you could help us?" The parents looked at her, wondering what help they could possibly give. "We are looking for someone in Vienna who we may be related to," she said, "Abe Kraus and his daughter Rachel."

"We know Rachel Kraus," said Klara Rattner, looking up at her parents. David Rattner walked over to Eleanor.

"They were our neighbours for a while," he said quietly, "but their apartment was confiscated when they tried to leave. I heard that they had moved to Abe's brother's apartment, but I haven't seen them for many weeks, but I will look for you."

"If they are there," said Eleanor, "could you tell Herr Engel? We know a friend of Rachel's who would like to help her."

62

11 MAY 1939

The Central Office for Jewish Emigration was set-up in the Palais Rothschild, which had been confiscated from the Rothschild family after the *Anschluss*. It was here that every Jew had to fill out the required documents before they could obtain their passports and get their travel papers. The SS also required that everyone who wanted to leave Vienna go there for an interview and to pay the leaving tax that every Jew was subject to because of the November riots.

Eleanor, Gil, and Bob met all fifty children and their parents outside the Palais Rothschild. A young Jewish man assisted them with their appointment and facilitated the obtaining of the passports for the children. He told Gil to pretend not to know a word of German and only speak in English and that he would translate everything. Gil did not ask why but agreed to follow his lead.

The Palais Rothschild had been stripped bare by the Nazis and contained only a few wooden benches and tables where the SS sat. The children and their parents had to stand as Jews were not allowed to sit in the presence of German soldiers and officers. The senior SS officer looked at the group and enquired why they were all there. It was explained to him that three Americans had come to take fifty Jewish children back to the United States. The SS officer rolled his eyes and said that if their papers were in order they would be issued with travel documents and passports after the leaving tax for each child was paid.

Gil was called over and asked numerous questions but stared blankly at the SS officer, while everything was translated. He was asked to produce the boat tickets that had been purchased that would allow for the children to leave the country. He did so; however, the SS officer quickly became bored as everything was taking so long to translate and therefore waved Gil away and called the children and their parents over. Each child was interviewed. Each child was given their travel documents and a passport. As Gil, Bob and Eleanor left the Palais Rothschild in the afternoon with the children and their parents, Eleanor saw Claire going in.

"What I require," said Claire, as she handed over her documents, photographs, passports, and five tickets from the Hook of Holland to Harwich, "are travel documents for me and four children."

A junior officer looked at Claire.

"Why aren't the children here?" he asked.

"They're at an orphanage," said Claire. "They already have passports and have paid the leaving tax and, therefore, all I need are the travel papers, which is why I have not brought them."

"This is most irregular," said the junior officer.

"I telephoned before I came," said Claire, "and I was expressly told that the children need not attend just for travel documents, as I am their guardian." The junior officer shrugged and then took the documents to the senior SS officer.

"Are we to be plagued by interfering Americans?" the SS officer said to himself, as he examined the Claire's documents. He then ordered the junior officer to make a check against the names of the children.

Claire stood watching as the bureaucratic wheels turned, her stomach knotted. The Nazis kept meticulous records of everything they did. It was something in their nature, she thought, that made them want to record for posterity every act that was carried out. It was as if they did not even consider that what they were doing was abhorrent. After twenty minutes the junior officer came back and whispered something to the SS officer.

"And you said you are taking them to England, Fräulein Astor," the SS officer said.

"Yes, I have tickets for them."

"The documents are all in order," said the SS officer, and directed her to where the travel documents would be issued. As he watched Claire leave, he said to his subordinate, "Call Sturmbannführer Schmidt in Linz and tell him that the American woman, Fräulein Astor, has just been given travel documents to take the Friedmann children to England."

***

The trial against Paul O'Montis was a staged affair, where the verdict and sentence had been decided before he set foot in the dock. The indictment referred to his birth name, Paul Wendel. The case was called before Judge Friederich Hofstetter. The prosecutor, a large man with whiskers and flabby jowls, opened the case.

"If it please you, Mister Chairman, the defendant, Paul Wendel, is a Jew who hid this fact by changing his name to Paul O'Montis. He is a degenerate cabaret artist and singer, who was arrested in 1933 for political statements he made at a cabaret performance. As the investigation went on, sexual encounters with young men were also examined, which led to the defendant being sentenced to one year and nine months in prison for violations of paragraph 175 of the German

Penal Code, which provides that," the prosecutor looked down at the statute book in front of him and read, "'An unnatural sex act committed between persons of male sex or by humans with animals is punishable by imprisonment and the loss of civil rights might also be imposed.'" The prosecutor looked up, turned slightly and pointed towards the dock, where Paul sat, his faced bruised and his hands cuffed.

"After being sentenced the defendant launched an appeal and while on release fled to Austria. A warrant for the defendant's arrest was issued. On the sixteenth of April 1939, the defendant was arrested in Prague. Not only did he have forged papers, but he was living in an area where Jewish people are forbidden to live." The prosecutor paused, so that the gravity of the act would be fully recognised by the judge. "Between 1933 and April 1939 the defendant continued to perform and has included degenerate material that has sought to undermine the German Reich. The defendant has not sought to contest the charges that have been brought against him, and the prosecution's case is that he should serve the remainder of his sentence and thereafter be transferred to a concentration camp on the thirtieth of May 1940, for an indefinite period."

Judge Hofstetter asked the defendant to stand. In the five weeks that Paul had been held incarcerated, he had become unrecognisable. His head was shaved, he had lost weight and had bruising around his eye, where once he wore a monocle. As Judge Hofstetter passed sentence, Paul stood dispassionately and when asked whether he had anything to say, placed his index finger under his nose, looked down towards his groin and said, "Just one!" He began to laugh in a high-pitched tone. Judge Hofstetter banged his gavel and demanded silence and that Paul be taken from his court.

"You are an undesirable," the judge shouted, as Paul was dragged away.

"And one day they will come for you," screamed Paul in reply, as he was pulled from the courtroom.

***

That evening a note was pushed under Christian's door from Herr Engel. Claire read it and told Christian that it said that Rachel and her family were still in Vienna. There was a telephone number of a person who might be able to pass on a message and that Christian should call the number from a pay phone at precisely seven p.m. After she finished reading the note Claire asked whether she should make the call, but Christian said he would go and put on his shoes and in his shirt sleeves and without his hat he went as quickly as he could towards the subway station at Herrengasse, where he knew there was a phone kiosk. He dialled the number, breathing quickly, and listened as the telephone rang and rang. He waited a minute with no one picking up and just as he was about to put down the receiver the phone was answered. There was silence on the other end.

"May I speak to Rachel Kraus?"

"I'm afraid I don't know anyone called Rachel Kraus." However, the person answering did not hang up.

"I was given your telephone number by a friend," continued Christian.

There was a pause. "Go on."

"My name is Drewe, Christian Drewe. I would like to help Rachel..."

Christian was interrupted, "As I said, I don't know any Rachel Kraus."

"If you find out where she is, please tell her that I will be in the café where we first met at three p.m. tomorrow."

There was no goodbye or acknowledgement, just a click and then the sound of buzzing. Christian stood there for a moment, wondering whether Rachel would get his message.

63

12 MAY 1939

Claire combed up her hair and forced it under a brown fedora. She looked at herself in the mirror wearing a dove grey double-breasted men's suit, which was two sizes too large, and felt self-conscious. She put on a pair of flat shoes and then took a pair of dark glasses and put them on. She wrapped a scarf around her face, took a white cane and left the apartment knowing that as soon as she walked out the door she would be followed.

Frau Huber stood watching from the kitchen window, until Claire was out of sight, with the fat Nazi walking twenty paces behind her.

"You can go," Frau Huber said to Christian. "There's no one outside now."

Christian left his apartment and pressed the button for the lift. A few minutes later he was walking towards the Stadtpark, knowing that he needed to be back in less than two hours before Claire returned. He arrived at the Yohan restaurant and café just before three and asked for a seat on the patio, where there were a score of tables and flower boxes teeming with geraniums and begonias. The smell of chocolate and coffee effused around every table and jasmine-scented lawns stretched out to the park gates where large boards, tied to the railings, hung, stating, *Juden verboten*. It was where Christian had first met Rachel, a decade before, when "Nazi" was a word almost unknown in Vienna.

Christian ordered a cup of coffee and listened to the world around him. While the uninformed may not have noticed the small details, Christian could tell that the ambiance had changed. The conversations were not as loud or as animated. No one talked politics. Husbands now brought their wives for tea and found that after years of marriage, they had nothing to say. The waiters were not as ingratiating as once they were. They came to the tables, took the orders, but did not spend time discussing the opera or the theatre. They had encircled themselves with iron railings forbidding Jews to enter, but, for a moment, Christian wondered who in fact were the prisoners.

As the bells of the Annakirche struck the hour, Christian began to wonder whether Rachel had received his message, whether the signs on the railings would deter her, or whether she wanted to see him. The last time that they met was at Claire's birthday party over a year ago. He wondered whether she would think that his failure to contact her was because he had antisemitic feelings. He hoped that she knew him well enough to know that that would never be true. The next fifteen minutes seemed to last an eternity as he worried that she may not turn up but then she arrived and sat down at the table.

She was different to her normal confident self, with trepidation in her voice.

"I wasn't sure whether to come," she said. "You know I could be arrested for being here." Christian sensed a slight accusatory tone in her voice.

"Sorry," he responded, "but I did not know where else to suggest."

A waitress hurried over to the table, the leather soles of her shoes patting softly on the stone tiles.

"Tea," whispered Rachel to Christian.

"Tea and lemon," said Christian to the waitress, "and also another cup of coffee for me."

Rachel let out a deep breath after the waitress had gone.

"The reason I wanted to meet with you," said Christian, "is that I heard that your family is having trouble leaving Vienna and I would like to help."

"Why?" Rachel said.

"Because you're a friend and have always helped me when I needed it," replied Christian. He spoke as quietly and as reassuringly as he could. "I intend to take a train to Salzburg in a week's time. I would like you and your family to be on that train and then go on to Marseille. Does that give you enough time to organise the paperwork you will need?"

"For what?"

"For going on to Palestine," said Christian. "I can arrange tourist visas for you and your family to go there." Christian paused, as he remembered what Herr Engel had told him. "I was so sorry to hear about Jakob. You have my deepest sympathies."

"Thank you."

Christian could hear in her voice the emotion that was welling up. He could not see the tears as they began to fall unwanted; however, as he heard the waitress walking towards their table with a tray and the tea things on it, Rachel took a breath and composed herself. The waitress started placing the cups, teapot and a plate of lemon slices on their table and then quickly left.

"There is one thing," added Rachel, as she started pouring herself a cup of tea. "I'll need some money to pay the leaving tax. The Nazis took everything from us."

"I'll get it from the bank. Can you go to the *Kultusgemeinde* tomorrow at noon?" said Christian.

"Yes."

"We need to speak about a few things," said Christian. "Now, drink your tea. I will go inside and pay the waitress, and you should be gone by the time I come out."

64

13 MAY 1939

Eleanor Kraus was thirty-six when she arrived in Vienna, and the mother of two children. She did not mind getting older; it didn't bother her, as she was always busy, and now she felt as young and as adventurous as she did when she turned twenty. Her marriage had been a romance, and she had not hesitated to come to Vienna when her husband called, leaving her two children with her sister. She lived a comfortable life in Philadelphia, and she enjoyed it; but she was all too ready to throw away comfort for a few moments of excitement.

As Eleanor hunched forward on the edge of the table to look at the woman who was next to Christian Drewe, she had the sense of knowing someone whom she had never seen before. The woman was pale and thin, with a small cleft on her chin, like Gil, and dark brown eyes. She had high cheekbones, which were pronounced because of her emaciation. Eleanor watched as the woman looked around her cautiously, as if unsure as to where she was or why. It was then that Eleanor saw two more people who were following in their wake, much older, more worn down by life and grey-haired.

"Gil," said Eleanor, "they're here."

Gil started to get up, adjusting his tie as he did so.

"Go on, go and meet them," said Eleanor.

Gil walked around his desk and through the open door into the reception area. The introductions flowed easily, with Eleanor standing behind Gil and Rachel introducing her mother and her father.

"Hell," said Gil, as he shook Abe's hand, "I could be looking at my grandfather." He turned towards Eleanor. "Honey, you never met my grandfather, did you?" Eleanor shook her head. "He was a great guy."

It was the first time that Eleanor had seen her husband relax since she arrived in Vienna. He spoke about the things he remembered from his childhood, the afternoon games of baseball as his grandmother, his mother and aunts cooked lunch. Abe listened, but these were stories in which he played no part, and while he smiled, Gil's life bore no resemblance to his own or his father's life working every morning in a bakery in Vienna.

"You said that we needed to talk," whispered Rachel to Christian, as Gil was asking what Abe knew about his grandfather's life in Germany.

"Do you remember the three girls you met at the ballet school with their father Otto Friedmann?" asked Christian.

"Vaguely," said Rachel. "It was years ago."

"They and their brother were at the party I threw for Claire at The Three Hussars, with their mother Anna Friedmann."

"Oh yes, I remember them now," said Rachel.

"Anna and Otto were arrested and sent to concentration camps," continued Christian, "and Claire has been looking after their children. It's complicated but she wants to get them out of Austria."

"But how does that concern me?"

"It doesn't, although I am going to ask a favour of you."

Rachel looked at him. He had asked her favours before, and they always came sugar-coated. She had accompanied him to England for his father's funeral, and they had travelled first class and then she stayed in a suite in a hotel in London. She had been introduced to the Friedmann girls and was rewarded with a visit to The Three Hussars. However, this time she was unsure how sweet the reward would be.

"When you leave Austria with your parents," said Christian, "I would like you to meet me at the station and help me onto the train."

"Of course," said Rachel, still trying to work out what it was that Christian really wanted.

"And I would like you to wear a red beret."

"Why?" she asked bluntly.

"Because when Claire leaves my apartment that afternoon, she'll be wearing a red beret."

"I don't follow," said Rachel.

"From a distance, you and Claire look similar."

"We do," said Rachel slowly.

"It would help us if the authorities thought that Claire was with me when I boarded the train."

"So, you want me to pretend to be Claire."

"Not precisely," said Christian. "It's just that…" Christian paused. "Damn it, there's no easy way of saying this. I'm being followed by the Gestapo who want to know where one of my friends is. They have said that they would not let the children leave Austria until I give him up. So, if the authorities think that Claire is on the train with me, they won't be looking for her and the children elsewhere."

"Would it help if I also had four children in tow?"

"Yes, but…"

"If you can get me eight more tickets to Palestine then I will have four children with me and my aunt, uncle, cousin and his wife."

"So, eleven tickets and visas in total?"

"Yes," said Rachel.

"And if I can't get the visas?" asked Christian.

"Then you can't, and I'll be there on my own wearing a red beret."

"We'd better arrange a meeting with Herr Engel so that the paperwork can be completed. Also, if we need to speak, the best way to communicate is through Gil Kraus, and," added Christian quietly, "until the day you leave, it's probably better that we're not seen together."

65

—·—

16 May 1939

Schmidt sat in his office at the Gestapo headquarters in Linz, a cigarette held between his lips. It was a small office in a new concrete building with small square windows. Iron bars had been fitted on the ground-floor windows, which contained several holding cells. In the basement, where the screams could only just be heard, prisoners were interviewed and tortured. The Gestapo dealt with political opponents, religious and ideological dissenters, career criminals, the handicapped, homosexuals, and the Jews. They were not large in number, but they were feared.

The Gestapo's actions were not subject to any judicial scrutiny and Schmidt, who had had his licence to practise law revoked, relished the power that had been given to him. He could bring in people under protective custody, without the need for judicial proceedings. The rights and wrongs of it no longer mattered as Schmidt could, within limits, do what he wanted. He exercised his power without temperance and with impunity.

Schmidt picked up a new file, which he had received that morning, and leant back in his chair to read it. His eyes flicked across the reports. The first said that Christian Drewe had left his flat and had gone to a public pay phone to make a call. There was also a recorded telephone conversation with the *Kultusgemeinde* about a woman named Rachel Kraus, who had not been mentioned before and he underlined her name.

He opened another report and read that Fräulein Astor had been to the Palais Rothschild and had received travel documents for the 21st of May and that she would leave the Hook of Holland for England the following day. He shook his head and wondered whether that stupid American woman really believed that she could smuggle those children out of the country without him finding out. The train that they had booked would first go to Salzburg, where they would change for a fast train to Frankfurt. It would stop at Linz on its way westward to Salzburg. He could guarantee that Drewe would also be with them, he was certain of it. Schmidt sat back in his chair and looked at the wall. He didn't have to do anything; they were all coming to him.

***

Claire and Christian went into the busy market, turning left then right and left again. As they came out into a small square Claire waved for a taxi and they got in and she asked to go to the subway. Claire looked out of the cab window as the fat Nazi hurried into the square, wondering where they had gone. They took the underground train to the second district and came out by a used car showroom. As they wandered around the forecourt Claire stopped and glanced at a sportscar, a Horch Vienna with its soft roof, long bonnet and angled back; however, it was a two-seater and of no practical purpose. The salesperson sensed that Claire liked it and as he came over tried to push the sale.

"A reliable five-seater family car," said Christian, "is what we want. Preferably in good condition with acceptable mileage. A Volvo PV802 would be perfect."

"But, sir," said the salesperson, a little deflated. "You'll look like... how can I say this... like you're driving around in a taxi. We have a Mercedes 170V or 230 and although they're second-hand they're a much better vehicle than a Volvo."

The Volvo was not a car that Claire would have chosen to buy, given the choice. It was not pretty and had already got the nickname of the Volvo Sugga or sow. It looked like a score of other taxis in Vienna. It had almost no redeeming qualities except that it was forgettable and would go on and on if it were serviced regularly.

Claire completed the paperwork in her name and Christian had his bank transfer the money and they left the showroom with Claire driving. The salesperson watched them leave and wondered why such an elegant woman was with a blind man with a scarred face who made her drive a Volvo Sugga. He shook his head. She could do so much better, he thought.

"I got a message from Eleanor Kraus this morning," said Christian, as Claire headed back into the city. "It seems that one of their children has come down with something infectious and they will need one of the extra affidavits."

"But that won't leave enough for us," said Claire, throwing a sideways glance towards Christian.

"It's not a problem," said Christian. "When I was at the bank this morning, I arranged for a sum of money to be transferred to your account in New York. You'll have enough to look after the children and little bit more. It should be more than enough to allow you to sponsor one of the children."

"How much more?" asked Claire.

"I transferred seventy-five thousand dollars to your account."

As Claire pulled away from a crossroad, she stalled the car.

"Bloody hell!" she said. "That's more money than I can spend in a couple of lifetimes. I can't take it, Christian." She took the car out of gear and turned the ignition key. The engine rumbled back into life, and she pulled away, grating the gears as she did so.

"You're going to need it," said Christian. "We've never spoken about it but there's a chance Otto and Anna won't ever leave Austria."

"Don't say that. I don't... I can't believe that."

Claire arrived near Christian's apartment without any other incident and remembered that there was a hotel nearby where she could park the car.

"What do we do now?" she asked.

"Now we do nothing. Tomorrow, you need to practise driving."

***

Every prisoner had to work in Dachau, and every prisoner formed part of a labour group, supervised by a Kapo. The SS would give the Kapo his orders and the Kapo would then carry out those orders. If the orders were not adhered to, the Kapo would be replaced, which usually signalled his death as the other prisoners would take their revenge. The Kapo was given free rein as to how to achieve the result required. The SS did not care whether he beat a prisoner, and if someone died the Kapo's duty was only to report it, since the roll call had to be right. No Nazi ever asked or cared why a prisoner had died.

The work that the prisoners did was fundamental to their chances of survival. If you could get a job inside or work where there was a chance of eating something, your hopes of living another day increased. Agricultural work, or in a kitchen, or an abattoir raised your chances of survival as you could scavenge food. If, however, your labour group had to work in a quarry or gravel pit, there was no possibility of obtaining food. Similarly, if your labour group had been assigned to do manual work, then corporal punishment could be used to speed up the work; but hitting a skilled tradesman operating a machine was not seen as an appropriate punishment.

When Otto arrived at Dachau, his occupation as a lawyer was placed on his record card. There was little need for a lawyer in a concentration camp and for the first few weeks Otto was assigned to cutting trees, where the SS liked to inflict their cruelties on intellectuals. There was also a hierarchy where Germans or Germanic people were at the top rung. Jews and homosexuals were at the bottom; they were not merely regarded as inferior but as having no right to life. They were allocated the heaviest work and were often forbidden from working in one of the better work units. If the prisoners had no work, pointless tasks would be created where prisoners would have to move stones from one place to another and then, the next day, carry all the stones back to their original place.

It was after the third week that an accident occurred when a falling tree injured three people. Otto dropped his saw and ran to the victims. He was able to set a broken bone and bandage up one of the other prisoners. In the evening the Kapo asked whether he had had any medical training, and Otto told him he had studied medicine for a year before deciding to change to law. The following day he was sent to the hospital, one of the better jobs in the camp, and for the next two months Otto did not put a foot wrong. He worked hard, showed his Kapo he was diligent, and survived.

***

Schmidt sat at his desk listening as Sergeant Brun explained how he had managed to lose a blind man and an American woman in Vienna. Schmidt wasn't surprised; Brun was an idiot who thought more about his stomach than his work. He could demote him, but there was little point. Brun did what he was told, no matter how incompetently.

"Enough!" said Schmidt. "I know what Drewe and that American are planning." He picked up the telephone and asked the operator to put him through to Eichmann.

"Good morning, SS-Obersturmführer Eichmann," said Schmidt, "I thought I would give you an update of my search for Tomas Skeres."

"Have you found him, Sturmbannführer Schmidt?" asked Eichmann.

"Not yet," said Schmidt, "but I should have him soon. As you know, Drewe and the American woman will be taking the Friedmann children to England and I plan to arrest the children at Linz. Drewe will then tell me where Skeres is."

"He hasn't up to now," said Eichmann, with more than a hint of reservation.

"But he will when I threaten to send the oldest Friedmann girl to one of the camps."

"We'll see," said Eichmann. There was a pause before Eichmann continued, "Sturmbannführer Schmidt, I need not tell you that Herr Goebbels does not like being disappointed. If Skeres is not in custody soon then Herr Goebbels may begin to look for someone who can get the job done."

"I see, SS-Obersturmführer," said Schmidt.

Sergeant Brun watched as Schmidt's face lost its flushed colour very rapidly. Brun guessed that something had been said in the conversation that had scared Schmidt, but then Eichmann had that ability to scare most people, except for those who did not know him and idiots.

"Is there anything I can do?" asked Brun.

"The housekeeper, Frau Huber. Do you know where she lives?"

"Yes," said Brun.

"Good, we may need her."

66

20 May 1939

Christian sat in the kitchen with a bottle of whisky on the table. He picked it up and poured himself a glass and asked Claire if she wanted one. She said 'No'. She had never seen Christian drink whisky and did not think that now was the time for either of them to get tight.

"Would you like to know what happened?" Christian said, moving his hand to the scarring on his face.

"Only if you want to tell me."

"I think I do. It was the first day of the Somme. I was just a young lieutenant in the Royal West Kent regiment, having completed my officer training six months before. I was commanding a small platoon of about thirty men, many who knew more about fighting than I ever would. It was seven in the morning when we attacked, and I led my men across no-man's-land. I blew my whistle, climbed the ladder out of the trenches and walked in front of my platoon. We got through the first few rows of barbed wire before the bullets started hitting us. I suppose we were lucky that we had a few minutes before they started firing. In no-man's-land you were totally exposed, you couldn't lie on the ground and pretend to be dead, and you couldn't go back. The only thing was to go forward, and as we got nearer the enemy lines their accuracy improved."

Christian took a sip from the glass. He felt he wanted to gulp it down and pour himself another but if he stopped talking, he knew he might struggle to start again.

"It was a flamethrower that got me. One minute I was walking and then a flame came out of nowhere and caught me on the side of my face. I think I was looking to my side to see who was still with me. Everything after that is confused."

"And how did you get back?" asked Claire.

"Private George Poley saved me. You met him, my mother's chauffeur. I've never told anybody this, but when I met him again, I didn't know whether I wanted to hug him or kill him for what he had done."

"Why?"

"Because I wanted to die. The pain was unbearable. I fell into a crater and Poley was there seconds later, otherwise I would have died. He covered my burns with wet clothes and kept me alive for hours. My company sergeant found us in the afternoon and the two of them waited until dark to pull me back to my own lines. I don't remember much, as I was unconscious and full of morphine. They carried me to a town where there was a hospital, and thousands of dead and wounded men. It was two miles away from the front lines."

Christian took a breath. Many people knew the story of how George Poley had dragged Christian back to his lines and then carried him to the town of Albert. George was a local hero for what he had done; however, Christian had only ever told two people about what happened next – his brother Adrian, who had been killed in the war, and Tomas.

"Albert is a small town, with a large catholic basilica in the main square. I'm told that it's quite a beautiful church. There is a story that a miracle happened there, hundreds of years ago, when a shepherd hit the ground with his staff and heard a woman's voice saying that he'd hurt her. When he dug into the earth, he found an effigy of the Madonna and a church was built on that spot, and one has been there ever since. In the war that church was turned into a hospital."

Christian once more sipped his drink.

"The reason why I told you that," he continued, "is because a miracle happened to me there."

"A miracle?" said Claire.

"A sort of miracle," said Christian. "I was conscious there for short periods of time. The doctors were giving me as much morphine as they dared and then I heard a woman's voice. It was the voice of someone I had fallen in love with a few years before, but we had decided to... well... it's complicated. I was in the hospital for about two or three days, and I don't think she left my side for more than a minute or two. She was there when I went to sleep and when I woke up. I remember she told me that I had to stay alive and when I left to go back to England, she said she would find me again. I don't think I would have survived those few days if it wasn't for her and when I left, she kissed me and whispered that she loved me and put her St Christopher around my neck. I know it sounds like a dream, except that I still have the St Christopher and will never take it off until the day I die."

"Did she find you?" asked Claire.

"No, she died there. Some people said that the British deliberately put the nurses' accommodation next to an ammunition dump, and then painted a red cross on it, hoping the Germans would never fire towards it. Other people say that it was just a stray shell. However, one night the building was hit. The nurses had taken shelter in the basement as the town was being shelled, and the ammunition dump exploded and the whole building caved in. No one survived. There were six nurses inside, but no one could tell the remains of one from another."

Christian cupped the glass of whisky in his hands and continued. "Her name was Rose, Rose Braithwaite, and I have never felt more human or exposed than when I was with her. She could look at me, and I would feel that she could see my soul and know what I was thinking. When we danced it was as if we were a single person. We lived in completely different worlds, but I have never felt closer to anyone. I thought I had lost her when I joined the army, but we found each other on the Somme. It was as if God had given us a chance to be happy. I was blind and scarred and nearly dead, but I knew that if I were with her then I could endure the pain and the blindness. When my brother told me what had happened to her, it was the most painful thing I had suffered in my life."

"And you dream about her?"

"Sometime. In my nightmares I try and hold her as she dies but can never reach her. I hated myself for not being there when she needed me, but I don't dream about her as often now."

"Why is that?" asked Claire.

"Because I've been given another chance."

"For what?"

"For everything. I wake up with a purpose, to ensure those four children get to safety, but it's not just that."

"Then, what?"

"It's because you're with me. The only reason my life has a meaning is because of you and I know that without you I would be only breath and shadow. You make me whole, and the idea of living the rest of my life without you terrifies me, more than any nightmare I've ever had. Ask me anything," said Christian, who swallowed as his emotions welled up inside of him, "and I will tell you. I will tell you because I love you."

Claire came around the table and put her hands on either side of Christian's face turning it towards him. She kissed him, slowly, passionately. Her right hand moved upwards and she began running her fingers through his hair. She breathed heavily as he pulled her close to him, kissing her fiercely. She closed her eyes for what seemed like minutes and then their lips parted.

"You know, you've got lousy timing," she said, as she opened her eyes and looked at him.

"I know."

"Tomorrow I'll be heading to Berlin, and you'll be going in the other direction."

"I know, but we have tonight."

67

—·—

21 MAY 1939

Claire stepped out of the apartment in a pair of flat shoes and a red beret as the afternoon sun cast shadows over the baroque buildings. She glanced right and saw nothing. Left, a man stood by a stationary car watching her. Her pulse quickened.

She crossed the road nonchalantly and turned right and then bolted into an alleyway. Behind her she could hear someone shout and then the heavy fall of boots.

Twenty paces ahead she reached the side entrance of the Leo Grand Hotel. She pulled at the heavy door and ran in. She didn't wait. She sprinted along the corridor past startled guests, who stared at her. Her breath caught as she saw the bellboy at the front of the hotel, but she hurtled past him. She was out onto Petersplatz, and merged with the crowd, her heart pounding and her ears straining for the sound of any pursuit.

Her car was parked across the street. She dashed to it, fumbled with the keys, started the engine. As she pulled away, she glanced in the rear-view mirror. A Gestapo officer burst out of the hotel, scanning the street as a dozen cars passed him, and Claire held her breath.

She turned the corner, disappearing from view, and only then did she exhale, hands trembling on the wheel.

Sergeant Brun sat in the car opposite Christian's apartment, and, when he was told that Claire had managed to lose the officer following her, he hit the steering wheel.

"You bloody idiot," Brun said, knowing that Schmidt would hold him accountable. "We better not lose Drewe!"

Two hours later a taxi pulled up in front of Christian's apartment just before three in the afternoon. Christian stood nonchalantly next to the taxi as his luggage was loaded, and then slowly he got into the rear of the vehicle, telling the driver that he was going to the train station and wanted to be dropped off at the side entrance. The taxi pulled away, and Sergeant Brun followed closely behind, not wanting to lose him in the Vienna traffic.

Christian sat back in the seat. He said nothing more to the driver but thought about the last few hours. Frau Huber had told him that the man who had chased Claire had returned to the car.

"She got away," said Frau Huber, but Christian knew it was only the first of many small victories that they needed to win.

"And now we wait," said Christian.

"And now we wait," repeated Frau Huber.

Frau Huber made coffee for them. Every ten minutes she stood up and went to the window to make sure the Gestapo officers were there. She said very little, as she and Christian had said everything meaningful over the last few days and Frau Huber was never a woman to waste words. At three-thirty, Christian said to her it was time to go, and Frau Huber replied, "Give my love to the little *Lieblinge*."

She then kissed him on the cheek, as she had done with her son on the day he went to war, put on her coat and walked home.

The taxi pulled up outside the side entrance of the station, and Christian was given his bags by the driver.

"Would you like me to find you a porter, sir?" asked the driver.

"It's not necessary," said Christian. "I am meeting someone here," and as he finished his sentence, he heard someone calling his name. Rachel Kraus, dressed in a red beret, pushed a trolley out of the side entrance and put Christian's two bags onto it. Beside her were four children. They turned and went into the station.

Sergeant Brun watched and as soon as they were inside the station he drove around to the front, parked and ran in and down the steps onto the concourse. He could see Christian, four children and a woman in a red beret go past the ticket porter. Christian went to first class and the rest of them got into the last carriage, which had been set aside for Jews. The platform was heaving with families, many of them getting into the last carriage. When the ticket porter got back to the gate, Sergeant Brun was waiting for him.

"The blind man you just assisted," said Max, "where was his ticket for?"

"Salzburg," said the porter.

"Are you sure?"

"Yes, it's not the first time he's been on this train."

"And will you be on the train?"

"Yes," said the porter.

"Check on him before the train leaves and if anyone speaks to him, find out who they are."

***

Claire arrived at the orphanage, got out of the car and walked up the driveway and rang the bell. After talking briefly with the administrator, she signed the discharge papers for Aaron, as had been arranged, and then she drove around the corner to the house where the three girls were staying. Within thirty minutes all the children with sitting with her in the car.

"Where's Herr Drewe?" asked Frieda.

"He's on his way to Salzburg," said Claire.

"Why has he gone to Salzburg?" asked Rosa. "Isn't he coming with us?"

"He's being followed, sweetheart," said Claire, who leant over and stroked Rosa's face, "and if they're following him, they won't be following us."

"I don't understand," said Rosa.

"I'll explain as we drive," said Claire.

The engine rumbled before it started. Claire turned her windscreen wipers on, indicated and then moved slowly onto the main road in the afternoon drizzle. She would head north, first to Brno, then Prague and finally to Berlin. She would cross the Austrian border in under two hours and be in Berlin the next morning.

***

Rachel looked out onto the platform at the station clock. The train would not be leaving for another five minutes, and before it did, she wanted to thank Christian. She put her head into the carriage where her parents were sitting with her uncle, her cousin and his wife and their four children and said she would be back in a few minutes. She walked back down the side of the train and then boarded again near Christian's compartment. He was sitting with a braille book on his lap.

"I came to say goodbye," said Rachel. "My parents are on board as well as my aunt and uncle, my cousin and their children."

"You shouldn't be here." said Christian, surprised to hear her voice.

"I won't stay more than a minute," said Rachel.

"I suppose it is goodbye then, although goodbyes seem so permanent. Did you know, I left Vienna twenty-five years ago on a very similar train." He raised his hand to his chest and could feel the St Christopher hanging there. "You ought to be going back now and, if you haven't done it already, get rid of that beret. Throw it out of a window as soon as we leave the station or hide it."

A knock on the compartment door disturbed their conversation, and the porter entered, asking to see their tickets and papers. Rachel handed over her documents, a certificate from the Reich Ministry of Finance, one from the local police authorising her to leave Austria, her passport stamped with a J, and her ticket. Christian took out his train ticket and passport from the inside pocket of his jacket and held them out for the guard to take. The guard went through the papers meticulously, mumbling to himself.

"Is everything in order?" Christian asked after a few minutes.

"We do not allow Jewesses in first class!" said the guard. "She must get back to where she belongs!"

Rachel turned to go.

"She was just going," said Christian, "she only came as a matter of courtesy to ask how I was and whether I needed anything." He took off his hat and glasses and turned towards the guard. The crater of the socket was burnt black. His other eye looked up and towards the bridge of his nose; the pupil was grey and milky, but the iris was still a beautiful green.

"She's not allowed to be here. She knows that!"

As Rachel left the compartment, the porter looked at her. "Dirty Jewess," he hissed.

"Blind eyes see better than blind hearts," Christian muttered under his breath.

***

Klara Rattner held her mother's hand as they walked along the platform at Vienna's train station. She could see the Krauses and Bob Schless in front of her. She could see the other children's parents standing with their children for what moments they had left, and she could see SS officers standing around the station. Her father was talking nervously about nothing of consequence. He said that when she got to the sea, her journey would just be beginning. He said that America was a new country, a vast country where everyone with an ounce of determination could make their fortune. He insisted that she practise speaking English each day, as she would need to translate for them when they arrived in America. However, she could only think about that final hug and kiss from her parents and wondered when she would see them again.

Eleanor went from one parent to another, assuring them that each child would be loved. Bob told them he would keep them safe, but Gil found it difficult to offer any words of encouragement, as he knew that some of the parents might never see their children again. Eleanor reminded the parents that they could not wave when the train pulled out of the station. Jews were forbidden from giving the Nazi salute, and a misinterpreted wave could result in an arrest. It was a damp, drizzly night, and as Gil, Bob, and Eleanor rounded up the children to put them on the train, the parents stared at the faces of their offspring. Their mouths were smiling, but their eyes were red and strained. No one waved as one child after another boarded the train. Eleanor stood watching, thinking it was the most heartbreaking display of dignity and bravery she had ever witnessed.

The oldest child to board the train was fourteen-year-old Alfred Berg. He had been chosen to replace five-year-old Heinrich Steinberger, the youngest on the Krauses' list, who had become ill a few days before their departure. Bob's opinion was that it was unlikely that he would pass the American medical test, and, therefore, instead of risking a place and possibly that of the other forty-nine children if he were contagious, they would replace him. However, it meant that Eleanor could only give Claire three affidavits and supporting documents for her four children when they had met the previous day.

****

The train journey to Salzburg started slowly, with stops at St Pölten, Melk and Linz. Christian opened his book and placed his fingers on the page. It would take three hours to get to Salzburg, and he would stay there for a few nights meeting with Karl Vogel and hopefully also meeting with Tomas, if it were possible. He couldn't concentrate on the book, and his fingers had to continually retrace the raised dots as he thought about Claire and the children. It was the unknown and the unforeseen that worried him. Would she be stopped as she crossed into Bohemia and Moravia? Where would she sleep? Where would they eat? Would she try and drive the twelve hours to Berlin? Every time his fingers crossed the page, another question popped into his head. Why hadn't he gone with them? But he knew that answer; he was of interest to the Gestapo, and the best place he could be was travelling in a different direction.

He checked his watch again. How many times had he done so in the last hour – four or five times? His fingers returned to the page: "It was not that he felt any emotion akin to love for Irene Adler. All emotions, and that one particularly, were abhorrent to his cold, precise, but admirable balanced mind." How many times had his fingers traced and retraced those dots? As many times as he had checked his watch, perhaps more.

"I love you and I will find you and the children in New York," he had said to Claire as she left his apartment.

She had kissed him and said, "I know."

He reached for the St Christopher around his neck, wanting the reassurance it so often gave him; hHowever, he felt no better as he touched it. He knew that it was just superstition and undid the chain, holding the silver pendant. It was the first time he had taken it off for nearly a quarter of a century. He knew every little mark on it, including a slight dint on the edge, which had been made when he fell in the hospital. He put it back on but struggled to secure the safety clasp.

His mind then went to Otto and Anna. Christian tried not to think about what they were enduring. Karl still thought there was a good chance they would be free at the end of the month and he prayed that Karl would be right. Everything was ready for them to leave Austria. Karl had their passports, other documents, and sufficient money to buy them train and boat tickets and pay any fines. All they needed were new travel documents and to pay the leaving tax. They could be in America by the end of June or July. However, with the thought of them reuniting with their children, there came a momentary pang of jealousy. Sitting in the train carriage, he thought he could have done nothing more. He had helped everyone he could: Tomas, Rachel, Claire, Otto, Anna and the children.

The train started slowing down as it arrived in Linz. Christian knew little of the town, except that Hitler had been born near there and wanted it to become one of the great cities of the German Reich. He heard doors opening and a few people getting on or off the train and picked up his book again. He heard a noise, as if a scuffle had broken out, and then there was the sound of a whistle and silence. He expected the train to move. It didn't. His compartment door was then thrown open.

"You are to come with me, Herr Drewe."

"Who are you?"

"Oberleutnant Maier."

"And if I decide not to come?" said Christian with a little more bravado than he felt.

"Then, Herr Drewe, I shall have to drag you off."

"It seems," said Christian, "that I am at your disposal," and he stood up and added. "Would you mind getting my bags?"

As he climbed down from the train onto the platform, he heard people talking, asking what was happening and why the delay. "Where are they taking him?" he heard a woman say, and for a moment, he thought that she might foolishly intervene. Somebody whispered, "He might be one of the asocials." Another said a communist, and another laughed and said, "What! Dressed like that?"

"Which way?" asked Christian.

"This way," answered Maier, who put his hand on Christian's arm as he walked straight ahead. Christian was surprised by how gentle Maier's touch was. He didn't grip his arm or pull him. He just placed his hand behind Christian's elbow and gently applied pressure. When they arrived at the staff car, Maier opened the rear door.

"Get in," he said, placing Christian's hand on the door handle and then putting his hand on Christian's head so he knew how far to lower it.

"Christian," said Rachel, as he got into the car next to her. "I am sorry about coming to your compartment. I didn't know they would do this or arrest you."

"It wasn't you," said Christian. Maier turned to them from the front of the vehicle and told them not to say another word until they got to Gestapo headquarters. The car pulled away. A group of inquisitive locals stood staring, but as soon as the car moved off, they dispersed. It took only a few minutes to get to the Gestapo head-quarters from the train station, and Maier led them downstairs to an interview room. He left them alone for a few minutes.

"Were you hurt?" asked Christian.

"No," said Rachel. "I just need to apologise for being in a first-class compartment. They'll then let us go."

"And your parents and other family?"

"They weren't interested in them. I said I would catch up with them in Marseille."

"What happened when they arrested you?"

"A Gestapo officer came into our carriage with the ticket collector, who pointed to me and asked my name and for my documents. He then asked what I was doing in a first-class compartment, and I told him. He asked me what I had said to you, and I told him, and then he asked me whether I knew Tomas Skeres. I said I did."

The door of the interrogation room opened, and Maier and an-other Gestapo officer entered, followed by Schmidt. Schmidt looked at them and then said in English, "Welcome, Herr Drewe."

Christian listened to the voice without being able to place it.

"I don't think I have had the pleasure," he responded.

Schmidt laughed. "An interesting choice of words for a person under the protective custody of the Gestapo." Schmidt sat down, took out a packet of cigarettes and lit one. "Now Herr Drewe," he said in German, "I hope you don't mind waiting a little while as we deal with your friend."

"This has nothing to do with Miss Kraus."

"Let me be the judge of that," said Schmidt.

"At least can we sit?" asked Christian.

"A Jew doesn't sit with Aryans," said Schmidt. "She can stand, and you as well. Now, Herr Drewe, I am going to ask Fräulein Kraus a few questions, and if you say one word, things won't go so well for her."

Schmidt drew on his cigarette. "Fräulein Kraus, where is he?"

"Who?"

"Where is he?"

"Who?"

"Where is he?"

Rachel's voice began to rise. "I don't know who he is. You've got to tell me who he is?"

"Where is he?" Schmidt looked at her dispassionately.

"I don't know," cried Rachel. "I don't know. He's here, standing next to me."

"Where is he?" repeated Schmidt with infinite patience.

"I don't know who you want."

Schmidt shook his head slowly and then looked at Maier, who took a step forward and slapped Rachel across the cheek.

"Who do you want me to say?" cried Rachel. "My father, my uncle, my brother..." and then she stopped and looked at Christian and whispered, "Tomas."

"There you go," said Schmidt, "you did know who we were talking about. On the train you told Oberleutnant Maier that you knew Tomas Skeres?"

Rachel looked at him without saying a word, not knowing whether he had finished his question.

"I would suggest," continued Schmidt, "that you answer when I have asked you a question." He knocked a piece of ash into the ashtray in front of him and then looked up at Rachel, slowly inspecting her from her knees to her forehead.

"Yes, I know Tomas Skeres."

"We are going to play a little game now, Fräulein Kraus. It's called questions and forfeits. I will ask you a question and you must tell me the truth and if you lie there is a forfeit. Do you understand?"

Rachel nodded her head.

"Now, a rule of the game is that at the end of each answer you must call me Sturmbannführer, so that I know you have finished your answer and because," Schmidt shrugged his shoulders, "it's just polite. Now, how long have you known Tomas Skeres?"

"About eight years, Sturmbannführer," said Rachel, her eyes looking down at the stone floor. Schmidt smiled.

"And you know that he's a homosexual?"

"No," said Rachel. Schmidt waited a moment and then looked at Maier and nodded his head twice. Maier walked up to Rachel and slapped her twice across the face.

"The first slap," said Schmidt, "was because you lied to me. The second was because you did not call me Sturmbannführer. Next time it will be harder, and then harder. Now, let us try again. Did you know that Tomas Skeres was a homosexual?"

"No, Sturmbannführer."

Schmidt nodded towards Maier, who again slapped Rachel across the face, who cried out. Christian took a step forward.

"I wouldn't do that, Herr Drewe," warned Schmidt. Christian could hear the coldness in his voice, and he stood still.

"Now, if the dirty Jewess is going to carry on lying, she won't look so pretty at the end of our little chat, and that would be a shame. So, I'll ask you a third time. Did you know that Tomas Skeres was a homosexual?"

"I suspected it," said Rachel, "but I never knew for sure, Sturmbannführer."

Schmidt stared at her for a moment.

"Are you married, Fräulein Kraus?"

"No, Sturmbannführer."

"Are you a lesbian, Fräulein Kraus?"

"No, Sturmbannführer."

Schmidt opened her passport. "You're twenty-eight years old, Fräulein Kraus and you are not married, and you're not a lesbian. You must be a disappointment to your parents. I had been told that Jewish women breed like vermin."

Rachel sniffed. "Yes, Sturmbannführer."

"Yes, to what, Fräulein Kraus?"

"I don't understand, Sturmbannführer."

"Well, are you a disappointment to your parents, or do all Jewish women breed like vermin?"

"Yes, to the first part, and I don't know, Stürmbannführer."

"Oh, we are making progress," said Schmidt. "Now let's return to talking about Tomas Skeres. Where he is?"

"I don't know, *Stürmbannführer.*"

"Where he is?"

"I don't know, *Stürmbannführer.*"

"Where he is?"

"I really don't know. I haven't seen him in years. Honestly, that's the truth."

Schmidt nodded towards Maier, who took a step and raised his arm.

"Sorry, Stürmbannführer. I meant to say Stürmbannführer."

Schmidt shook his head and Maier stood still.

"Why has Herr Drewe come to Salzburg?"

"I don't know," said Rachel, "maybe, he is going to his villa near here, Sturmbannführer."

"And where precisely is that villa?"

"I don't know," said Rachel. "I don't know."

Schmidt nodded his head towards Maier. This time, the slap knocked her down. She got up slowly, tears flooding down her cheeks.

"Manners cost nothing, Fräulein Kraus. Now compose yourself. Have you ever visited Herr Drewe's villa?"

"No, Sturmbannführer."

"But you do know that he has a villa?"

"Yes, Sturmbannführer. He mentioned it to me years ago. It's near one of the lakes."

Schmidt stared at her, knowing that there was nothing more she could tell him. "Now, we must decide what to do with you. Usually, we send your kind to concentration camps, and there is a new camp near here. You may have heard of it, it's called Mauthausen. Our soldiers are still constructing it, and a pretty thing like you wouldn't have to do any manual work if you stayed pretty. I might even come and visit myself. Would you like that?"

"No, Sturmbannführer."

"And then after I've visited you," said Schmidt, and paused. "Well, I don't really care what happens to you after that."

"Stop it!" shouted Christian. "What kind of man hits and threatens a woman? I am a friend of Sir Walford Selby, and I demand to speak with your commanding officer."

Schmidt laughed. "You rattle around the name of Sir Walford Selby like an empty scabbard. Do you think anybody cares about that fat-arsed, opinionated prick? Even your government sent him to Portugal. You're in no place to demand anything, Herr Drewe. I'm the head of the Gestapo here in Linz." Schmidt turned and looked at Maier. "Oberleutnant, take her to Mauthausen and tell the camp commandant that she is not to be interfered with until after I have visited her."

"You won't take her!" shouted Christian.

Schmidt got up from the table, walked past Rachel and stood before Christian. Christian heard a metal clip pop and the sound of something being withdrawn from a sheath. His instinct was to lower his face or raise his hands, but he knew it would do no good. He could smell Schmidt's hair oil as he stood in front of him and the acrid smell of nicotine. He swallowed, waiting for what would happen next. The blow from the baton hit him on his left-hand cheek, and he crumpled to the ground.

"Stay still," he said to himself. It had been drummed into him that after a fall, he should not jump up. He should check himself, get his bearings, and make sure he was able to stand. However, he saw no point in being beaten like a dog lying on the floor and began to rise. When he got to his feet, he rearranged his glasses.

He could sense Schmidt was again in front of him. He could hear him breathing. Christian took a deep breath and brought his right hand up to wipe away the blood he felt on his cheek. Schmidt took a step closer. Christian knew he was in front of him as Schmidt began to lift his baton, and he clenched his fist and punched as hard as he could, catching Schmidt on the side of the face.

Schmidt took a step back, recoiling more in surprise than from the force of the glancing blow. He raised his baton and brought it down onto the side of Christian's face, hitting his shoulder. Christian grunted and doubled over before the next blow hit him on the back. He lifted his hand, trying to stave off the next stroke against his face, but caught the chain of his St Christopher, which jangled on the floor. As he was hit again, he fell.

Schmidt seemed to be shouting incoherently, as blood pounded in Christian's ears. His hand reached out onto the floor to steady himself for the next blow, and he felt the warm metal of the St Christopher on the stone floor. He grasped it as the next blow hit him on his back. He could hear Rachel screaming, and then she was kneeling before him.

"Christian," she screamed, "tell him you're sorry."

Christian reached out his hand holding the St Christopher. "Take it," he managed to say. "It will keep you safe." Maier started dragging her away, and Schmidt again hit Christian on the head, and he blacked out.

Fifteen minutes later, Christian regained consciousness. He was sitting in a chair with his hands handcuffed behind his back. He did not know whether it was the same room or whether he had been taken to a cell. He could feel a breeze coming from a window and assumed that he had been moved, and then he smelt that expensive hair oil.

"You're here," said Christian.

Schmidt remained silent for a second before saying, "We have a lot to talk about."

"I'm not saying anything," said Christian.

"They all say that at the beginning," said Schmidt.

Christian heard wood grating on the stone floor as Schmidt got off his chair, and then he took three or four steps closer. Schmidt placed the barrel of his pistol on Christian's face. The metal was cold, and then Schmidt drew the nozzle of the Luger up to Christian's temple.

"You'll beg me in the end to kill you," said Schmidt. "You're a cultured man; there is no need to suffer."

"Go fuck yourself," said Christian, with a bravado that he did not genuinely feel.

Schmidt stepped back, placing the Luger beside Christian's ear, and squeezed the trigger. The sound was excruciating, and Christian screamed. He could hardly hear anything and wanted to cover his ears with his hands. Please, no more, he thought.

However, Schmidt was walking towards the door, and then he turned and said, "I look forward to talking with you tomorrow, Herr Drewe, when I hope you'll be in a more cooperative mood. Also, you should know that I will be contacting the border crossing at Holland. Those children that you seem to care about will never leave this country. You have my word." Schmidt left the cell and locked the heavy iron door behind him.

As Rachel was escorted across the courtyard, she turned and looked back at the Gestapo building when she heard the shot.

"Keep moving," said Maier, as they reached a truck which would take her to Mauthausen. "If he's lucky, he's already dead."

***

Schmidt sat at his desk and thought about contacting all the German border posts into Holland, but that would mean Himmler and Goebbels hearing about his failure, and that was not a course of action that he was prepared to take. He thought about his options. It was Skeres that they wanted, and now he suspected that he was staying at

Drewe's villa on the lakes. However, it could be anywhere. Fräulein Astor would have known where it was, but she was out of reach. He picked up his telephone and asked his secretary to contact Sergeant Brun.

"When you speak to him," said Schmidt, "tell him to bring in Frau Huber tomorrow morning and tell him that I expect him to be here no later than midday."

68

22 MAY 1939

Claire drove until her driving became erratic. That previous afternoon, she had been stopped at the Bohemia and Moravia border and presented her papers and those of the children. The documentation was in order, all taxes paid, and the permits allowing the children to leave Austria had been duly stamped. When asked where she was going, she said Berlin and then on to the Hook of Holland and showed the border guards five tickets for the boat to Harwich, leaving on the 23rd of May. They checked the boot of the car and went to verify the documentation. Minutes later they came back and waved her across the checkpoint. She struggled not to put her foot too firmly on the accelerator as she drove away. A few miles further on she pulled over onto the side of the road and lit a cigarette. She felt as if she would vomit.

"Fräulein Claire," said Rosa, "how much further?"

"I don't know, sweetheart," she said.

"Why don't you know?"

Claire counted to ten, drew on the cigarette once more, and said, "I think it's about eight hours more until we get to Germany." Claire wound down the car window and threw the stub out.

"I need to go to the bathroom," said Rosa.

"We'll stop shortly," said Claire. "I need to fill the tank with gas, and you can go then."

Eight hours later Claire crossed the German border and headed for Dresden. Frieda, Aaron and Rosa were asleep in the back and Hanna sat with a map on her lap. Claire wanted to keep on going but her eyes felt heavy and she closed them for a moment. Hanna screamed as the car started drifting across the road. It was then she decided to stop before there was an accident, pulled into a lay-by and fell asleep. She had wanted to sleep for no more than half an hour, but it was not until the sun started coming up at five-thirty that she awoke. Hanna was asleep next to her. She started the car and began driving again and would have murdered for a cup of black coffee. She decided to continue until the children woke and then would stop at a café for breakfast and a wash.

There was little traffic on the road, and she had time to think. If everything was going to plan, Christian would be in Salzburg; however, she worried what would happen to him when the Gestapo realised that she and the children had not boarded the train. He had been adamant that they had nothing to charge him with. He said that if he were arrested, he would contact the British consulate and that Hitler did not want a diplomatic issue with Britain.

It was the first time that she had to care for the children on her own, without either Frau Huber or Christian. It was he who risked being arrested. She thought about what Frau Huber had said to her a few weeks ago: "Happiness does not come from a pretty face but a pure heart." When Frau Huber had said this, she thought she had been referring to her; however, she now thought it may be Christian she meant.

"Fräulein Claire," said Hanna, rubbing her eyes, "can we stop soon?"

"Of course, Hanna. We'll pull over shortly so that you can get a wash and have breakfast."

"I'm too tired to eat," said Rosa.

"Well, I'm going to have pancakes," said Frieda, "covered in syrup and apple sauce like Frau Huber makes them."

"I'll have pancakes as well," said Aaron, "but I'll have two."

"One thing to remember," said Claire, "only speak English when you're in the restaurant."

"Why?" asked Hanna.

"Because if they think you're Americans, they won't ask me any questions about why you're with me and if someone does ask, I'll say you're my children and that we're meeting my husband in Berlin."

They did not have pancakes for breakfast, just eggs and bread and some milk. The owner of the small café, next to a petrol station, was a fat, gregarious man and his wife, who cooked, was inquisitive about everyone who passed through. Claire explained that they were touring, and that her husband worked at the American consulate in Berlin. They asked where they had stayed the night, and Claire said Dresden. One question followed another, and Claire decided that they needed to finish eating and move on.

Claire arrived at the American consulate in Berlin at ten in the morning. Halleck Lovejoy Rose, the third secretary, collected them from the reception area, and Claire introduced each child to him.

"The process is relatively straightforward," said Halleck, "because the decision to grant the children's visas was made last February. We just need to see all their documents, including their passports, your guardianship papers, and the affidavits of support. Once we have approved the documents the children will need to have a short medical inspection."

"There's a problem," Claire said.

"What problem?" asked Halleck.

"I only have three affidavits of support."

"That is a problem," said Halleck. He was a tall man with a small moustache and a goatee beard. "We had better go to my office."

The children sat quietly in the office, as Halleck and Claire discussed how to resolve the issue of the lack of supporting documents. Claire explained who she was and how the children had been put under her guardianship.

"I had thought," said Claire, "that I could prepare an affidavit here for the fourth child."

"Miss Astor," replied Halleck, "the documents you need to support an application require sufficient evidence to show you can support a child. Normally, that would include payment slips, savings accounts, pensions. However, you have told me that you are no longer employed as a singer and have no proof with you of any savings or pension."

"But I do have a bank account in the United States," said Claire.

"But Miss Astor you have no evidence with you of what is in that account."

"Couldn't you just call them?" said Claire.

"And how much is in the account?" asked Halleck, thinking this was a waste of time.

"Seventy-five thousand dollars," said Claire. "Give or take a few cents."

Halleck sat back in his chair and looked at her.

"You're saying you have seventy-five thousand dollars back home. I don't have seventy-five thousand dollars in America, and I'd pretty much bet the house that the consul doesn't have that kind of money either."

"It was a gift," said Claire, "from someone who..." She paused not knowing how to describe her relationship with Christian.

"It was from Herr Drewe," said Hanna. "He wants to marry Fräulein Claire." Claire blushed.

"I see," said Halleck. He looked at Hanna. "And does Fräulein Claire want to marry Herr Drewe?"

"Oh yes," said Hanna, "she just doesn't know it."

"Come back at four," said Halleck to Claire. "I'll check with your bank when it opens and if the money is there, we can sign an affidavit and have it notarised here. I'll need your passport and a letter authorising the bank to provide me with a statement." Claire handed over the documents. "Now, we'll need to carry out a medical examination of each child and interview them."

Claire sat in the waiting room as one by one the children went off to have the examination and interview. She closed her eyes. Halleck coughed twice when he returned.

"Everything's in order," he said, with a smile. "As soon as I get confirmation of your savings, we can issue the last visa."

"I do have two questions," she added. "Is there anywhere we can stay before we leave tomorrow?"

"You can stay here," Halleck said, and handed Claire a piece of paper.

"Is it a hotel or boarding house?"

"It's my home, and my wife, Mrs Rose, is expecting you and the children. There are clean beds for all of you and a meal later."

"My other question," said Claire, "is can you use five tickets from the Hook of Holland to Harwich for tomorrow? We bought them so that the Gestapo would think we were going to England, but we have reservations on the SS *President Harding* leaving Hamburg tomorrow evening."

"I will have them taken to the British consulate," said Halleck. "Hopefully they can use them to get some children to England."

***

The train pulled into Berlin station at eight a.m. sharp. Many of the fifty children had been homesick and cried during the previous night. It had been an unpleasant journey as the train rocked and rattled over the eleven hours that it took to get to Berlin. The benches in the train were too hard for the children to sleep on, and the floor was dirty and covered in straw. However, there was no alternative, and the children were made as comfortable as possible in the straw. The authorities had provided nothing but a cattle truck for the fifty Jewish children. By two-thirty a.m. the children were exhausted and asleep, and Gil, Bob and Eleanor took it in turns to go back to their compartment for short naps.

Berlin was busy that morning and the children were bewildered, hardly knowing where they were going or why. It was a different city which scared them. They were taken to a building owned by a relief organisation and given food and were able to wash and clean up. They also got a few hours of sleep before they went to the American consulate. The children were sent in groups just before midday and through the afternoon. Tears once again flowed, and the consulate began the process of interviewing each child and carrying out a medical examination. It was the late afternoon when all but three of the children had completed their interviews. They would do that the next day and then take the train to Hamburg, where in the evening the SS *President Harding* would set sail for America.

***

During the night Oberleutnant Maier uncuffed Christian, took him to the bathroom and then to a cell. As Christian entered, he could smell stale urine and when he touched the walls they felt damp.

"There's a bed by the far wall," said Maier, "although I can't guarantee its cleanliness or comfort and there's a pot next to it."

"It'll be better than a chair," said Christian, although from the smell emanating from the mattress he began to doubt it.

"Why don't you just tell us where Skeres is?" said Maier. "He's a homosexual, so why protect him?"

"He's my friend."

"How can you have friends like that? Doesn't it disgust you?"

"No," answered Christian.

"The bible tells us that what he does is an abhorrent sin and it's forbidden by God," said Maier.

"God didn't write the bible, men did."

"You deny the holy scripture," said Maier. "You're as bad as he is."

"The truth is a pathless land," said Christian.

"I have no idea what that means," said Maier, "but here is a little piece of truth for you. If you lie to Sturmbannführer Schmidt he will know and if you try and hit him again, he will kill you."

Christian was woken by the sound of the locks being undone and the heavy iron door groaning on its hinges as it was opened. A metal bowl, half full of thin porridge, was left in front of him with a spoon. Christian took a mouthful. It was bland but not too unpleasant and he quickly finished it. He sat on the floor with his back against the wall for two hours. His thoughts went again to Rachel. Schmidt had said to take her to Mauthausen. He did not know much about any of the prison camps. The Nazis did not advertise what went on in them and everything he heard was rumours. However, those rumours troubled him, and he regretted ever asking her to meet him at the train station.

He had put her at risk for Claire's sake, and he swore to himself that whatever happened he would not betray another of his friends. He heard the locks being opened and he stood up and went with two guards to an interrogation room where they sat him on a chair in front of a rough wooden table and chained his hands to the top.

"Good morning, Herr Drewe," said Schmidt, who wandered in ten minutes later, "I trust you slept well. Where are Fräulein Astor and the Friedmann children?"

"I wouldn't know," said Christian. He forced a smile, as he knew that as every hour passed, she was getting closer to safety.

"Now, do you remember my game of questions and forfeits? As you and Fräulein Kraus seemed to enjoy it so much yesterday, I thought we would play it again. So, where are Fräulein Astor and the Friedmann children?"

"I wouldn't know," said Christian.

Schmidt took a deep breath and then Christian heard a swish in the air before a baton come down on his wrist. He yelled out.

"Have you forgotten the rules of the game, Herr Drewe, or did you learn nothing from yesterday?"

"I apparently learnt nothing, Sturmbannführer."

"You will tell me what I want to know, Herr Drewe. It is just a matter of time; you do understand that?"

"It is a matter of time, Sturmbannführer, and every minute that goes by Miss Astor and the children are further away."

Schmidt took out a cigarette and lit it. He looked at Christian, knowing that what he had just said was true.

"You know, I am going to have to hurt you. Really hurt you."

Christian said nothing, as his throat had gone dry.

"Yesterday Sergeant Brun reported to me that he saw you, Fräulein Astor and those four Jewish children at Vienna station and board the train to Salzburg. However, when the train arrived in Linz neither Fräulein Astor nor the four Friedmann children were on the train. All we found was a red beret in the corner of the third-class carriage, which seemed to be owned by no one. Can you explain that?"

"Yes, Sergeant Brun is mistaken, Sturmbannführer."

"About what part, Herr Drewe?"

Christian paused before answering and tried to get some saliva into his mouth.

"All of it, Sturmbannführer." Christian breathed in hard thinking that the baton would fall on his wrist again. Schmidt looked at him.

"I will only punish you, Herr Drewe, if you lie to me or are disrespectful. Now, Sergeant Brun said that a woman matching the appearance of Fräulein Astor left your apartment at around one-thirty p.m. and that she was wearing a red hat. Is that correct?"

"I couldn't say what colour her hat was..."

"What about the time, Herr Drewe?" Schmidt interrupted.

"That sounds about right," said Christian. "We had finished a light lunch and..."

"There's no need to elaborate, Herr Drewe, about what you had for lunch. Now, Sergeant Brun reports that a woman matching the same description met with you at the train station at about three-thirty and she had four children with her. Is that correct?"

"Yes, Sturmbannführer."

"Sergeant Brun also states that he saw you with a woman with a red hat and four children walking along the platform."

"Yes, Sturmbannführer."

"So, Fräulein Astor and the four Friedmann children got on the train?"

"No, Sturmbannführer."

Schmidt drew on his cigarette. He looked at Christian for a few moments. He was struggling to tell whether he was lying. Normally, someone would look away or not blink if they were lying, but a man without sight did neither. Schmidt therefore listened to Christian as he spoke, hoping to discern any change in Christian's vocal tone or any incongruent gestures to suggest he was lying.

"But they were at the station?"

"No, Sturmbannführer."

"So where are they?"

Christian hesitated and then said slowly, "They left Austria, Sturmbannführer." Schmidt drew on his cigarette and breathed out. Christian could smell the woody notes from the tobacco and the acrid smell of nicotine as the smoke filled up the interrogation room.

"How? On another train?"

"No."

"By car?" Schmidt interrupted.

"Yes, Sturmbannführer."

"And whose car, was it?"

"Miss Astor's, Sturmbannführer."

"And what was the registration number of the vehicle?"

"I don't know, Sturmbannführer."

"Make?"

"A Volvo, Sturmbannführer."

"Colour?"

"I think they only come in black, Sturmbannführer."

"And where is she?"

Christian lowered his head slightly.

"I have no idea, Sturmbannführer."

The baton thumped down on his wrist and Christian cried out with pain. He could feel sweat dripping on his brow and once again his throat felt parched.

"I think you have a very good idea, Herr Drewe," said Schmidt.

"May I have a glass of water?" asked Christian.

"No," said Schmidt. "Now, where is Fräulein Astor going?"

"She has a car, travel documents and boat tickets from the Hook of Holland," said Christian. "I suspect she's in Holland, Sturmbannführer."

"That's the first information you've volunteered about Fräulein Astor, Herr Drewe. Is she really going to Holland?"

"I told you, Sturmbannführer. She has left Austria, and I do not know where she is now."

Schmidt hesitated. He could not tell whether Christian was telling the truth or not and decided to change the subject.

"It's of no importance to me, Herr Drewe, but you will tell me. But let us talk about Tomas Skeres."

"I don't know where he is, Sturmbannführer." Christian spoke quickly. Schmidt took a deep breath before the baton came down on Christian's wrist, and Christian screamed, thinking that his wrist had been broken. His head slumped on the table, as he gulped in air. The pain seemed to be tangible, as if it were a colour in his sightlessness. He prayed that the pain would stop and then smelling salts were put under his nose and he jerked his head up.

"We'll take a break now," said Schmidt, "and reconvene this afternoon so a friend of yours can join us."

***

Frau Huber heard a knock on her apartment door and went to answer it with a feeling of trepidation. She opened the door to find Sergeant Brun.

"You," she said. "What have you come here for, to arrest me because I'm not at work?"

"Frau Huber," said Sergeant Brun, wheezing after he had climbed the three flights of steps to the apartment, "You are required to accompany me to Linz."

"Am I?" said Frau Huber.

"In relation to a matter concerning Herr Drewe."

"He's left the country," said Frau Huber, as she watched Sergeant Brun trying to catch his breath. "Yesterday he went to Salzburg and then was going on to England."

"We would still like to speak to you about him."

"There's nothing I can tell you."

"He's being held in Linz," said Sergeant Brun, "and you will come with me."

"In Linz. What has he been stopped for?"

"For aiding a fugitive who has committed an offence against morality."

Frau Huber looked at him and knew that this was not a request. The Gestapo did not come to your door and take no for an answer. "I'll get my coat, hat and bag," she said. "Do you mind waiting there? I mopped the floor this morning."

***

"Just a simple dislocation," the doctor said and reset the bone and bandaged it. "Be careful and try not to fall again," he added, as he got up to leave. "Another fall like that and it will usually break."

Christian shook his head. "What are you talking about? I didn't fall."

"Of course you did," replied the doctor, "it's written here in Sturmbannführer Schmidt's notes." The doctor looked at Christian and then took a bottle out of his bag, poured a small amount and told him to drink it.

"What is it?"

"Laudanum," said the doctor, quietly. "Just in case you fall again."

There was something about waiting that made Christian anxious. He knew he would be interrogated further but it was the uncertainty of when and how. He did not know whether it was a fear of the unknown or just a fear of the known coming to an end. However, he had felt the same thing over twenty years ago in the Great War, as he sat with his men in the trenches on the Somme. He tried to think of something different, but when the cell door opened at one p.m., and Oberleutnant Maier led him out, he felt something like relief.

Christian's hands were again chained to the table and Schmidt came in and sat down, taking out a cigarette and lighting it.

"Feeling better now?" he asked. "I hear you were lucky, and your wrist was not broken. You have strong bones."

"Fuck off."

Schmidt took out his baton and placed it upon the table. "Now let's not be unpleasant, Herr Drewe. We have a long afternoon, and we must try to retain some civility. Let's do something different for a while," Schmidt said. "I'm going to tell you about Paul O'Montis."

"Paul?"

"He's currently serving a jail sentence in a prison in Bohemia. I know that because yesterday he was interrogated about the whereabouts of Tomas Skeres. It did not take long for him to tell us everything but unfortunately, just like Miss Kraus, he had never visited your villa and only knew it was somewhere on the Wolfgangsee."

"And how is he?"

"I believe he is in a considerable amount of pain, now," said Schmidt. "As a repeat offender and someone who insulted the Führer, Goebbels has requested that he be singled him out for special attention. Do you know what will happen to him when he has completed his prison sentence?"

"He'll be released," said Christian.

"No, Herr Drewe, he won't be released. When his jail sentence has been completed, he will be taken to a concentration camp and will be a protective prisoner under subsection 175, which means his treatment as both a homosexual and a Jew will not be pleasant. O'Montis, or to use his real name Paul Wendel, will be put in an isolation area in the concentration camp. You will appreciate that we need to keep those dirty pigs separate from contaminating the rest of the swine. We try, but most of the time you cannot change their perverse nature. It is likely that medical treatments will be carried out on Paul Wendel with the hope that we can stop his perversity. It may be that he will be sterilised, although probably castrated; and it is also likely that his treatment will be.... how can I put this... brutal. Our guards have little time for those types of degenerates. It is impossible to stop the attacks and beatings that are inflicted on them. It is likely he will be killed within a year, if the block elder does not like him, or he will commit suicide because he will see the hopelessness of his life. Almost no one with a pink triangle survives for long. That's the story of Paul Wendel, and no one will remember him. It will be as if he never existed."

"It is a story," said Christian. "The world will soon wake up to what Nazism is."

"Which is what, Herr Drewe?"

"Life without love or hope. I hear it in people's voices, wherever I go. People are scared, they are living in fear, however, it only needs a breath, a wind, a sound, a voice to stir them."

"People are like cattle. You tell them that their lives will be better if they stone a Jew and each one of them will pick up a rock and throw it. However, enough of this, I simply do not have time." Schmidt looked over to the door where Maier stood. "Bring her in."

"Christian!" Frau Huber screamed when she saw him without his glasses, with a cut on his cheek and his right wrist bandaged.

"I'm fine, Frau Huber," said Christian.

"Now," said Schmidt, "as we're all here together like old friends, let us have a chat." He looked over to Maier and said, "Bring Frau Huber a chair so that she can be comfortable for our little discussion about the whereabout of Herr Skeres."

"But I don't know where Herr Tomas is," said Frau Huber.

Schmidt breathed in, brought his baton down on Christian's bandaged wrist. Christian braced himself but could not stop himself screaming.

"Stop!" shouted Frau Huber.

"Now, Frau Huber, do not say another word until you have sat down, because I need to tell you the rules of our little game. I call it questions and forfeits. I ask one of you a question and if you refuse or fail to satisfy me that the answer is true, then a forfeit is paid, and, in this case, Herr Drewe suffers the forfeit. So, Frau Huber, if you lie to me, I will strike Herr Drewe on his wrist. It's as simple as that."

Maier brought in a chair and Frau Huber sat down, putting her coat on the back of the chair and her bag by her feet.

"Don't tell him anything," said Christian, as the pain shot through his arm.

"So, let's begin," said Schmidt, picking up his cigarette and drawing on it. "Frau Huber, do you know Herr Skeres?"

"Which one?" responded Frau Huber. Schmidt took a breath and then hit Christian lightly on the wrist.

"I should have said, Frau Huber, that at the end of each answer you have to say Sturmbannführer. It's just the rules of the game and if you don't, well, a forfeit is paid. I only gave Herr Drewe a little tap, as I hadn't told you that, but next time Herr Drewe will find it painful. Now let's try again. Do you know Herr Skeres?"

"Which one, Sturmbannführer?" Schmidt silently mouthed the word Sturmbannführer as Frau Huber said it.

"See, the game is very simple. Do you know Tomas Skeres, Frau Huber?... And don't forget to say Sturmbannführer."

"Yes, Sturmbannführer," said Frau Huber.

"And where is he?"

"I don't know, Sturmbannführer."

"Oh Frau Huber, you've got to do better than that if you don't want Herr Drewe to have a broken wrist." And Schmidt brought the baton down firmly on Christian's wrist. Christian screamed and tried to pull back his manacled hands. He clenched his teeth, breathing heavily as the pain started to subside.

"I had not expected Herr Drewe to be so stoic," said Schmidt, who placed his cigarette in the ashtray. "Normally, most people would have told me what I wanted to know by now, but Herr Drewe seems to have a stubborn streak."

"Why do you want to know where Herr Tomas is?" asked Frau Huber.

"Because we have evidence to suggest that he is a degenerate and because his lover Paul O'Montis openly mocked the Führer," said Schmidt. "There is no place for him or anyone like him in the German Reich."

Frau Huber kept silent. Schmidt smiled at her.

"Now would you please confirm, Frau Huber, that Tomas Skeres is a homosexual?"

Frau Huber glared at Schmidt, not saying a word. Schmidt quickly brought his baton down on Christian's wrist, and Christian tried not to scream. He felt himself blacking out and a feeling of nausea welled up.

"We'll wait for a few moments, Frau Huber, until Herr Drewe has composed himself, but you really must answer; you must. It's the rules of the game. Now, is Tomas Skeres a homosexual?"

"Yes, Sturmbannführer."

"And my next question, Fräu Huber, is, where is Herr Drewe's holiday villa?"

"I don't know, Sturmbannführer."

Schmidt slowly lifted the baton.

"I don't know, Sturmbannführer!" shouted Frau Huber. Schmidt held the baton over Christian's arm.

"Don't tell him!" cried Christian. "Don't say anything! Please."

"It's near St Gilgen," said Frau Huber, "on the Pilgrim's Trail to Fürberg."

Schmidt looked over to Maier. "Go and get a map of the area, Oberleutnant Maier. There's one in my office on the wall."

Maier left and closed the door behind him.

"All of this unnecessary pain could have been avoided," said Schmidt, "if you had decided to tell me the truth at the very start."

Frau Huber started crying and leant down to her bag. She slowly opened it, put in her hand and took out Christian's service revolver. It took Schmidt a moment to understand what was happening.

"Don't be stupid, Frau Huber," Schmidt said. "Put down the gun. You're not going to be able to walk out of here with Herr Drewe."

"Take his handcuffs off," said Frau Huber.

"Don't do this, Agnes," Christian said.

"Take his handcuffs off," Frau Huber repeated.

Schmidt took a key from his pocket and unlocked the chain.

"Can you stand, Herr Christian?" asked Frau Huber.

"Don't do this. Just put the gun down," he replied.

"Come with me," she said, taking him by the elbow. "We'll lock him in and go up the stairs."

"Agnes! Someone's coming!" shouted Christian.

Frau Huber looked towards the door, as Maier came back through it. She levelled the revolver at him as he tried to take out his own pistol and then closed her eyes and fired. She fired again and then a bullet hit her, and she dropped to her knees.

"Agnes!" Christian shouted. "Agnes!"

"Stupid bitch!" shouted Schmidt. "Is she dead?" However, Maier did not answer, as he placed his hand on the blood-stained uniform over his stomach.

Christian put his hand on Agnes' face but could not feel any breath. "Agnes!" he shouted. He ran his hand down her arm to her wrist but there was no pulse and then he felt his service revolver. He could hear soldiers running down the stone steps and along the corridor.

"Get her out of here," shouted Schmidt.

From the sound of his voice, Christian knew that Schmidt was behind him, he took the pistol out of her hand, swivelled around and pulled the trigger until there were no more bullets.

69

—·—

23 MAY 1939

Claire gripped the railing at the ship's stern and looked back at the shimmering lights of Hamburg, a city she did not know or ever want to know. Scores of people must have stood upon the exact same spot on the same ship with the same view, each with different emotions. However, for Claire, it was a sense of emptiness she felt and, as the wind blew, she found that tears were welling in her eyes.

She turned to go inside and looked out into the blackness of the North Sea. Hanna, Frieda, Aaron and Rosa were somewhere playing with the other fifty Jewish children, and she did not have the heart to take them away. It had been the first time in nearly three months that they had been able to mix with children of their own age, and they had abandoned her like a broken doll. She knew she should feel happy; she had achieved what she had set out to do. The Krauses and Bob Schless were already celebrating in the ship's bar and although she had an invitation to join them for dinner and drinks, she did not feel like going. Christian was not with her, and it bit keenly.

She walked slowly back to the weathertight door and wondered where Christian was now. If everything had gone to plan, he would be in Salzburg and should have met Karl Vogel at the land registry, where he would transfer ownership of his villa to Tomas. Christian had said that he wanted to see Tomas one last time but would only do so if he wasn't being followed. His plan was then to Paris and take the train and night boat back to London before sailing to New York. She tried to picture him sitting in a hotel restaurant in Salzburg in his dove grey suit, dark glasses and fedora. He would choose a veal steak and a glass of red wine, almost certainly a Burgundy, and sit there with his fingers gentle brushing the pages of a book. She tried to remember what it was he was reading when she left two days ago and a small smile glided across her lips as she recalled it was one of those Sherlock Holmes stories he so enjoyed. She pulled hard on the ship's door to open it. It seemed to weigh a ton and, as the warm air from inside enveloped her, she shivered as it made goosebumps on her skin and for a moment she thought about her father and how he had killed himself. She pulled the door shut behind her and tried to imagine herself joining Christian for dinner. However, she could not shake from her mind the image of her dead father.

***

The following morning, after breakfast, the four Friedmann children joined the other children. Claire watched as they got to know each other. It was like the first day at school where those that shone were encircled by friends and those who were awkward stood alone, with hands in pockets watching the others. Games were played, the boys choosing tag or some other amusement, which would allow them to run around the deck. The girls enacted strange little dramas of their own invention. Already little groups were forming. The older children separated from the younger children. The beautiful and the plain stood far apart as did the bright and the dull.

"I'll come and get you at lunchtime," said Claire to the three girls. "Tell your brother." But the words went unheeded and she knew that it was only at those times when they were alone, and when the children thought of their parents, that she was required to give comfort and support. That morning Claire gravitated towards Eleanor. They had only met a few times before and were so different. Eleanor was organised and motivated, wanting to be the perfect wife to Gil. When they spoke, Eleanor talked about her own children who were being looked after by her sister, and life in Philadelphia with its country clubs, boutiques and society events which Claire would never have been invited to. However, when Claire spoke about the nightclubs and theatres where she had worked and singers like Richard Tauber, who she knew, and the fashions of Vienna and Paris, they both quietly envied the other's life.

"And what do you plan to do," said Eleanor, "when you arrive in New York?"

"I'll stay in a hotel for a few weeks," said Claire.

"And after that?"

"Christian will want to find an apartment for us and the children when he arrives."

"You said 'us'," said Eleanor. "I knew you were friends, but..." she hesitated, "is there anything more?"

"I think so," said Claire. "We spent so long as friends that I sort of didn't realise that we had become something more."

"I'm not sure what you mean?"

"I'm not sure either," said Claire, and shook her head. "I suppose I miss him and, if I'm being honest, I'm also a little worried."

"Worried," said Eleanor. "About what?"

"I don't know but I've just got this feeling."

***

Sergeant Brun held the telephone to his ear and tried to write down some notes as Eichmann spoke slowly, setting out the things that Sergeant Brun needed to do and emphasising those things which were important.

"Above all," said Eichmann, "you must ensure that there is no record of this in any of the files. Do you understand?"

Sergeant Brun licked the end of his pencil and continued to scribble.

"Yes, Obersturmführer."

"Not a trace. If there is any suggestion that the Gestapo has detained and…" Eichmann hesitated for a moment, thinking of the right word to use, "removed a British subject, who had friends in the British consulate, there will be hell to pay."

"Yes, Obersturmführer."

"You must ensure, Sergeant Brun, that if questions are asked no one says anything, or, you'll wish that you had been shot with them."

A drop of sweat fell onto the piece of paper which Sergeant Brun was scribbling on.

"And what should I say about the deaths of Sturmbannführer Schmidt and Oberleutnant Maier?"

"Nothing. I'll deal with it," said Eichmann. "I will speak with their families and the newspapers."

***

Two days later Schmidt and Maier were buried with military honours, and a newspaper printed an article saying Schmidt had been gunned down by a Bolshevik Jew, who had been arrested in Schmidt's relentless service to the German Reich. Eichmann attended the service and stood next to Gretchen Schmidt and her daughters, saying it was a tragic event and how well respected Sturmbannführer Schmidt was by everyone who knew him.

"And what happened to that Jewish Bolshevik who shot my husband?" asked Gretchen Schmidt at the end of the service.

"He was killed," said Eichmann.

"Was he acting alone?"

"We're rounding up some suspects... there's a lawyer we're looking for, Karl Vogel, a notorious Jew-lover."

"The name isn't familiar," said Gretchen.

Eichmann shrugged and then turned to go.

"Once again," he said, "I'm sorry for your loss."

"And do you know where Sergeant Brun is? I expected to see him here."

"Sergeant Brun is on an assignment," said Eichmann, who nodded his head and walked away.

Sergeant Brun was ten miles out of Linz on a dirt track just off the road to Mauthausen. He took a spade from his vehicle and started digging. Two hours later, when he had dug a grave five foot deep, he dragged out the bodies of Christian and Agnes Huber and buried them. Afterwards, he lit a cigarette and looked out over the forests of larch and birch. All record of Christian Drewe had been removed from the Gestapo files and anybody who would have seen him had been brought into the Gestapo headquarters and told to forget what they knew. Sergeant Brun threw the spade into the back of the truck and was about to get in the vehicle when he turned, feeling that he was being watched.

EPILOGUE

The SS *President Harding* arrived in New York on the 3rd of June with the 50 Jewish children. It was one of the last ships to leave Germany with refugees which was allowed to disembark passengers in the United States. The MS St. Louis, which arrived a few weeks later and carried nine hundred Jewish refugees, was turned away at New York and returned to Europe, where an estimated quarter of the people on board subsequently died in the Holocaust.

During the voyage, Bob Schless gave daily English lessons to the children and became known to many as Uncle Bob. Halfway through the ocean voyage, Bob confided to Eleanor that he had "made a very great mistake in leaving Hedy behind. I am in love with her and want to marry her." Hedy Neufeld had been a former medical student who could no longer practise medicine because she was Jewish and helped Bob in interviewing parents and children. Since they both spoke fluent German, Hedy and Bob asked most of the questions. Bob sent Hedy a ship-to-shore cable that included a marriage proposal. The next morning, he met the Krauses and reported that Hedy had said, "Yes." Within weeks of arriving in America, Bob had returned to Vienna, where he married Hedy in July 1939. The couple returned to the United States, and Bob resumed his paediatric practice. He lived with Hedy for the rest of his life and died in 1972 at the age of 77.

The children were initially cared for at the Brith Sholomville. However, they became a curiosity, and it was decided in their interests to send them into foster care. Some children lived with relatives, and some were fostered by members of the Brith Sholomville. Gil and Eleanor looked after Robert and Johanna Braun, a brother and a sister.

After the war was over, thirty-nine parents came to America and were reunited with their children, including the parents of Robert and Johanna Braun.

Gil Kraus died in 1975, and Eleanor Kraus died in 1989.

Heinrich Steinberger, the young boy who was too ill to go on the ship, died three years later at Sobibor, an extermination camp in Nazi-occupied Poland.

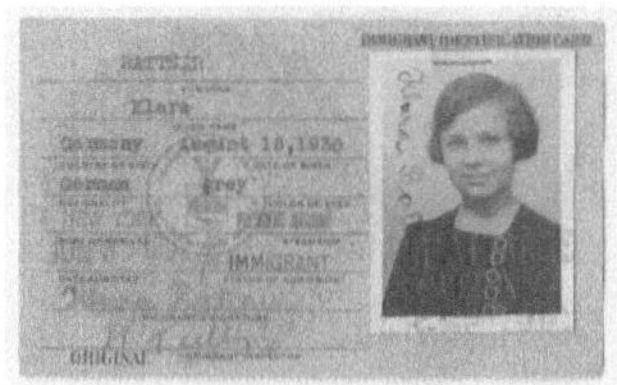

Klara Rattner subsequently stayed with an elderly great-uncle. In 1940, her parents escaped Austria and arrived in America via England. The family was reunited and went to live in San Francisco. Klara studied and received a teaching credential from UC Berkeley. She married a British engineer, Roy Lee, becoming known as Kay Lee. The couple lived in northern California, first in San Mateo and then in Atherton. They had three children.

***

For further information about the rescue of the 50 children see:

50   Children: One Ordinary American Couple's Extraordinary Rescue Mission into the Heart of Nazi Germany, Pressman S., (2015) Harper Perennial.

50   Children: The Rescue Mission of Mr. and Mrs. Kraus, A documentary film by Steven Pressman. www.perlepressproductions.com/50-children

The photographs above are reproduced with kind permission of Steve Pressman of PerlePress Productions.

***

Paul O'Montis was sent to the Sachsenhausen concentration camp on the 30th of May 1940, immediately after his release from prison. His camp number was 25131 and he was kept in Block 35. He was listed in the camp files as a "protective prisoner § 175". It is likely that Paul was subjected to torture by the SS and the block elders, according to first-hand accounts of prisoners within Block 35. In the death register of the Oranienburg registry office there is entry 3312 which states: "Paul Wendel, July 17, 1940, 2 a.m. Suicide by hanging." However, some people have suggested that he may have been killed by the block elder.

Recordings made by Paul O'Montis can be found on Spotify and YouTube.

Afterword

The title of the novel *Only Breath & Shadow* is taken from a quote by Sophocles: "A human being is only breath and shadow." 'Breath' refers to the very life force that humans possess, which is easily taken away. It is a fleeting, temporary thing that is a core part of human life. 'Shadow' represents the lack of substance and the temporary nature of human existence. When "breath and shadow" is combined it creates an image of something that is both insubstantial and short-lived. It highlights the vulnerability and insignificance of human life, reminding the reader that even the grandest human endeavours are ultimately temporary and inconsequential when viewed in the context of a larger, eternal world. However, the quote can be equally applied to the acts of a person. The measure of a person's life is what they do now (breath) and what they have done before (shadow). It is, ultimately, our acts that define us, despite our existence being transitory.

In the novel, the reader witnesses the escalating persecution faced by Christian's Jewish friends, the Friedmann family, and the immediate danger posed to figures like the prominent cabaret artist Paul O'Montis, a Jewish homosexual whose provocative satire leads directly to his arrest and transfer to a concentration camp. The inclusion of Paul's story, who will be tortured and ultimately die in solitary confinement, highlights the brutality aimed at individuals marginalized by Nazi ideology. The start of the persecution of minorities comes through the language of de-humanisation. It is a first step to actual brutality and it is of note that this type of de-humanising language is something that is prevalent today.

The protagonist, Christian Drewe, fought for his country and must come to terms with the unhealed wounds of his past and the moral pressures of the present. Christian initially struggles with emotional distance, feeling ineffective due to his blindness. However, when four Jewish children are placed in his care, Christian transforms. His final acts in orchestrating the children's escape, attempting to protect his friend Tomas Skeres, and confessing his long-held love for Claire Astor, reframe his life from a tragedy of war to a decisive sacrifice for love and principle.

The climax, which culminates in Christian's fatal confrontation with Gestapo Major Ernst Schmidt, echoes a moment from Christian's past when he led his men across no-man's land facing almost certain death. Christian chooses torment over betrayal, while his fiercely loyal housekeeper, Frau Agnes Huber, kills his interrogators to protect him, defining herself as a war casualty alongside him. This structure is intended to show that true sight resides in moral clarity, even as the world around the characters plunges into darkness. Christian has led a life feeling that his blindness has emasculated him but knows at the end that blind eyes see better than blind hearts. This recognition of an absolute truth is intended to echo the Alexander Pope quote that frames the novel: "And all our knowledge is ourselves to know".

Only Breath & Shadow marks an end to the Castle Drogo series, and although I have thought about two other books, which would be based around the same characters as my previous novels, I feel that this journey has reached an end for the time being.

There are elements of the novel that I have had to simplify and, for those readers who like historical accuracy, I must apologise. For example, when the story begins Austria is a separate country where they have their own police force with its ranks and titles, A sergeant in the Austrian police force would have generally been called a *Wachtmeister*. When the *Anschluss* took place the police forces were nationalized and absorbed into the German police system, primarily the *Ordnungspolizei* (Orpo) and the *Sicherheitspolizei* (Sipo, which included the *Gestapo* and *Kriminalpolizei*), and the ranks were standardized to the German system. Therefore, after 1938 a police sergeant in the Gestapo in Austria would have been called *Polizeihauptmeister* within the police structure, while simultaneously holding a corresponding non-commissioned officer rank in the SS, such as *SS-Hauptscharführer* or *SS-Oberscharführer*. This all seemed too complicated and confusing and therefore I used the English word, Sergeant throughout the text. However, the use of German does give a chilling effect, and where I wanted to emphasise this, I would revert to the German rank, especially with Major Schmidt's interrogation of Christian.

The concentration camps were also a subject, which was difficult to address. It should be remembered that in 1938-1939 these were brutal work camps where the treatment of prisoners was appalling. However, the genocidal killing of Jews, a-socials, Roma, Sinti, political prisoners and homosexuals had not yet begun. In order to understand what life was like in these camps in the 1930s, and to reflect the experiences of Otto and Anna Friedmann, I read the testimonies and memoirs of Jewish and other prisoners. The books *A Handful of Dust,[1] Dachau and the Nazi Terror 1933-1945 Testimonies and Memoirs,[2] Dachau Sermons,[3] Faith and Victory in Dachau[4]* and *The Harrowing of Hell: Dachau[5]* all tell stories that are in many ways identical. The Nazis started off by de-humanising minorities and stripping them of all legal rights. Many Germans and Austrians closed their eyes because they knew that if they spoke out, what was being done to these minorities would be done to them. The Nazis were therefore left unchallenged, and their brutality worsened until the point where it knew no limits. I was particularly moved by one account I read about the horrors of Dachau, immediately after its liberation. Marcus J Smith, a doctor, wrote when he arrived at the camp, which still had 32,000 prisoners many almost dead or dying, that many Jews who were struggling to stay alive did so that they could tell their liberators, "Remember us".

In addition to the books identified above, there are many other books and manuscripts that I must acknowledge, which helped shape this novel. First, is Eleanor Kraus's Memoir donated to the "United States Holocaust Memorial Museum" @ Collections Search - United States Holocaust Memorial Museum (ushmm.org) catalog irn9574 7.*[6]* Having started writing and researching I soon came across the remarkable story of Eleanor Kraus, Gil Kraus and Dr Bob Schless. It seemed serendipitous to have another group of people in Austria at the exact same moment as my book, and I decided to weave their story into my narrative. Gil and Eleanor brought with them fifty-four affidavits of sponsorship that Eleanor had prepared. However, Eleanor's Memoir does not say what happened to these extra affidavits. I assumed that they would have used one of the extra affidavits when one of their fifty children became sick and had to be replaced at the last moment. I therefore took the liberty of borrowing the three spare ones to help rescue the Friedmann children. My absolute admiration goes out to the Krauses and Bob Schless for what they did; nor can I imagine what they must have felt, being Jewish and travelling to Germany and Austria in 1939 to save fifty children who would almost certainly have perished if they had not have been rescued.

Details regarding the life of Klara Rattner and her escape from Vienna were taken from a transcript of an interview by Steven Pressman, which was donated to the United States Holocaust Memorial Museum on January 19, 2014. Steven Pressman produced the interview for his documentary film "50 Children: The Rescue Mission of Mr. and Mrs. Kraus". Further details can be found at https://www.perlepressproductions.com

Other documents and books that deserve mention include:

The Ross Baker Collection from United States Holocaust Memorial Museum @ Collections Search - United States Holocaust Memorial Museum (ushmm.org) catalog irn518514 (accessed 1 to 5 September 2024).

Diplomatic Twilight 1930 – 1940, Sir Walford Selby, John Murray (Publishers) Ltd, London (1953).

Desperate Journey: Vienna-Paris-Auschwitz, Knoller F. with Landaw J., Metro Books, London (30 June 2012).

The Vienna Coffeehouse Wits, 1890-1938 by Segel H.B., Purdue University Press (1995).

All the Light We Cannot See, Doerr A., Fourth Estates (2015).

The Berlin Novels, Isherwood C., Vintage Classics (1993).

Footnotes:

[1] "A Handful of Dust" in *The Nazi Germany Sourcebook: An Anthology of Texts*, Lina Haag, ed. Roderick Stackelberg and Sally A. Winkle (London: Routledge, 2002).

[2]*Dachau and the Nazi Terror 1933-1945 Testimonies and Memoirs,* Barbara (editors) Benz, Wolfgang : Distel (Author), (Verlag Dachauer 2002).

[3] *Dachau Sermons,* by Niemöller M. (Harper and Brothers, 1947).

[4] *Faith and Victory in Dachau,* by Overduin J. (Paideia Press, Canada, 1979).

[5] *The Harrowing of Hell: Dachau,* Smith, Marcus J. (State University of New York Press, 1979).

[6] (Accessed 10 to 18 September 2024) copyright: The Estate of Ms. Elizabeth Perle.

About the Author

Andrew started writing his first novel *Of All Faiths & None* in 2004, however, it was not until 2022 that he completed and published it. The story is centred around the Drewe and Lutyens families and the construction of Castle Drogo in 1910, which was the last great castle to be built in England. The book won numerous indie awards. In December 2024 Andrew published his second novel *A Remembrance of Death* which continues the story of the Drewe and Lutyens families. This was shortlisted for the Yeovil Literary Prize and won the HFC Steinbeck Award. His third novel, *Only Breath & Shadow* completes the Castle Drogo series and is set in Vienna in the 1930s.

Further information about the characters in his books and links to purchase his novels may be found on his website: www.ofallfaiths.com